The Other Hamlet Brother

Fatima,

Thank you for your support!
Enjoy!

Luke Swanson

Luke
Swanson

Black Rose Writing | Texas

ISBN: 978-1-68433-634-0
PUBLISHED BY BLACK ROSE WRITING
www.blackrosewriting.com

Printed in the United States of America
Suggested Retail Price (SRP) $19.95

The Other Hamlet Brother is printed in Baskerville

*As a planet-friendly publisher, Black Rose Writing does its best to eliminate unnecessary waste to reduce paper usage and energy costs, while never compromising the reading experience. As a result, the final word count vs. page count may not meet common expectations.

Praise for
The Other Hamlet Brother

"Buckle up! In *The Other Hamlet Brother*, Luke Swanson introduces us to the Forrest Gump of the Shakespearean world. Lovers of Shakespeare will enjoy this romp through the life and times of his characters, which proves beyond a doubt that all the world's a stage."
-Ian Doescher, author of *William Shakespeare's Star Wars* and the *Pop Shakespeare* series

"In a style reminiscent of Christopher Moore's comic fantasies, Swanson guides the reader through a playfully audacious riff on Shakespeare's greatest hits, finding comedy in tragedy, with laugh-out-loud moments intertwined with scenes of genuine pathos and heart. It's a work of endless imagination, a must-read for fans of the Bard and anyone wanting to know more about Denmark's most famous dysfunctional royal family."
-David Davalos, award-winning playwright of *Wittenberg*

"*Hamlet* meets *A Knight's Tale* meets *Gulliver's Travels* in this serious—but not too serious—nod to Shakespeare. Swanson wrangles words into unique turns of phrase that give you the perfect imagery, make you contemplate life, or leave you laughing hysterically. It's several stories compiled into one big Shakespeare sandwich...extra Hamlet. Shakespeare lovers will eat it up!"
-Dusty Crabtree, author of *Shadow Eyes*

"After reading *The Other Hamlet Brother*, you'll want to go back and read Shakespeare's play to figure out why the Bard left this part out. With subtle jokes and witty banter on every page, this book is part fantasy, part mystery, and wholly entertaining."
-William Steele, author of *Going the Distance: The Life and Works of W.P. Kinsella* and Ph.D. of literature

"With *The Other Hamlet Brother*, Swanson has delivered a humorous fantasy in the style of Christopher Moore. Fast-paced and irreverent in the right places, this inventive take on the tale of the moody Dane still manages to explore the idea of fate vs free will—an impressive feat."
-Alastair Luft, author of *One Kingdom Under Heaven* and *Jihadi Bride*

The Other Hamlet Brother

Contents

Chapter 1

A cutting breeze sweeps through every room in the Castle of Elsinore.

The vast chamber feels colder than usual today.

Normally, one has to really concentrate in order to keep from shivering. The heavy, gray stone walls seem to emit a dreary and ominous chill, even in the summer months, and the six-foot tall portraits of the castle's past occupants aren't exactly warm and fuzzy.

But that's on a regular day. Now, the air in the king's private chamber is bitingly cold. Practically arctic.

Claudius, high ruler of Denmark, paces back and forth, back and forth, surrounded by the tapestries, candelabras, and priceless works of art that usually fill him with happiness.

Today isn't usual, though. He wrings his hands, strokes his beard, snaps a tune—anything to keep himself occupied. Anything to detract his mind from the problem that has surfaced.

Young Hamlet, his nephew and son, has gone mad.

Sincerely, entirely, storm-the-gates-of-Troy mad.

Or has he? That is the problem. There are plenty of reasons to call the doctor and throw Hamlet in a padded cell for the rest of his days, but there is just as much proof that he's faking the whole thing.

Although why would he do a thing like that?

Claudius lowers himself onto a sofa that once belonged to his brother. He rubs his temples as he settles into the cushions. It's tough being King of Denmark these days. The Queen's temper fits are increasing in frequency, Prince Fortinbras and his entire Norwegian army are trying to wage war, and stock in ear poison has gone down three points in the last week.

The door flies open and a uniformed man scurries into the private chamber, an eager smile plastered across his mug.

Claudius groans. He doesn't think he can take Osric's chipper attitude. Not today.

"Greetings, Your Majesty," the aide squeaks.

"What is it, Osric?"

"Her Majesty wanted me to report that more wedding gifts have arrived from Austria, as well as from the Earl of Gloucester."

"Oh?" This piques Claudius's interest. His recent marriage to his sister-in-law has borne many fruits in a short period of time: prestige, a lovely bride, the throne of Denmark, and—his favorite—a mountain of presents from leaders across the continent vying for the new king's good favor. "What did Gloucester send?"

"Sixty stallions and ten dozen bushels of English trout."

"Ah, trout. That's just what this state needs." Claudius rolls his eyes. "Remind me, Osric, to request more trout in the future."

"Yes, Your Majesty," the aide nods.

"That was a joke, Osric."

"Of course, Your Majesty."

"Anything else?"

"Polonius has more news of your nephew Hamlet."

"Son," Claudius corrects. "He's my son now."

"He wishes to tell you himself."

"So be it. Fare thee well, Osric."

"Aye, Your Majesty. Long live the King."

"Long live the…" Claudius bites his tongue. "Yes. Dismissed."

With that, Osric spins on his heel and leaves the chamber.

Claudius slumps on the sofa. He is still getting accustomed to being addressed as King of Denmark.

Images of Claudius's brother, the late king, flash through his mind. A tall, imposing man, with rich brown eyes and a beard as majestic as a lion's mane. Each word he said was simultaneously laced with authority and compassion. The Queen loved him, the people loved him, young Hamlet loved him…

"And now he's fertilizer for my petunias in the courtyard," Claudius says to himself.

The portraits of past Danish rulers stare at Claudius as he lounges on the sofa. He stands and strolls past each one, basking in his ancestry.

There is King Bartholomew, his great-great uncle, who famously defeated the invincible Normandy army in the Subsea Valley. He was a champion at fisticuffs with a glare that was rumored to have made William Wallace wet himself. Next to his portrait is one of his queen, Esmeralda II, whose beauty radiates from the painted canvas.

Next in line is Claudius's not-so-great great-grandfather King Shermink. The portrait speaks for itself: The man stands barefoot in the snow with a ferret on his shoulder, holding a pink Japanese parasol. That Dane had been mad. Completely, totally mad. Shermink lived his life under the delusion that he was a little teapot, short and stout. But no one had been brave enough to commit the King to an asylum, so the people did their best to tolerate his bizarre speeches and decrees. Very little is recorded about that time in history.

Jacob of Cobalt follows Shermink, along with his sister Dorothy. Their reign was unremarkable but trouble-free.

Now, Claudius stops in his tracks. He stares at the last three portraits on the wall, and they all stare straight back.

Abraham the Wise. His father.

King Johan Hamlet, the Great Dane. His brother.

And King Claudius. Himself.

Such a rich lineage of leaders, ending with himself. Claudius sighs in disbelief. He is the King of Denmark. Old Hamlet's time has passed. It's his turn to sit on the throne. A smirk crawls across his face.

And then, the smirk disappears. He shudders, and he doesn't know why. The portrait of his brother glares at him, as if the oil and canvas actually holds a sliver of Johan Hamlet's being. The walls of the chamber feel haunted by kings past.

But that's ridiculous. Claudius hasn't believed in such supernatural hogwash since he was in diapers. He shakes his head to banish his heebie-jeebies. Absolutely ridiculous.

"Sir?"

The voice shatters the tranquility of the empty chamber. Claudius turns from the wall of portraits to find Polonius, his chief advisor and political ally.

"Don't sneak around like that," the King mutters, moving away from the paintings. "You nearly stopped my heart."

"My apologies, sir. Osric informed me that you were in here."

"Yes, yes, isn't Osric just a peach?" He clenches his jaw. "You have news of Hamlet's latest antic escapade?"

"Aye, sir, I do. 'Tis like nothing I have ever seen before. He stands in the center of the courtyard for hours at a time. In one hand, he clutches a quill. In the other, his father's sword."

"My brother's sword?" Claudius says incredulously. "Where did he find that antique?"

"I know not, sir, but many trustworthy soldiers say it is the very weapon the late King used to combat the ambitious Norway and smite the sledded Polacks on the ice."

"The Battle of the Lavet? The conflict in which my brother struck down Norway's king?"

"Aye, one and the same. And all the while, young Hamlet whispers, seemingly to no one in particular. He says, 'To die, to sleep no more, and, by a sleep to say we end the heartache and the thousand natural shocks that flesh is heir to...'Tis a consummation devoutly to be wished.'"

"What words are those?"

"Your guess is as good as mine, sir."

Claudius arches an eyebrow. "Could it be that Shermink's lunacy has been passed to him, Polonius? Do you think young Hamlet is mad?"

"That..." The royal advisor pauses, carefully selecting his words. "That is a difficult question, sir. He could simply be traversing a mental phase of grief after his father's death. Or perhaps, this may be a period of adolescent rebellion. Or..."

"Or?" the King presses.

"Or he could be putting on an act, playing us like a veteran actor on a stage."

Claudius sighs and nods to himself. "I've been mulling this over for a few hours. We need someone to uncover the truth for us. Young Hamlet would never open up to me, his surrogate father, nor his mother, whom he views as an incestuous wretch. No, no, we need someone he trusts."

"What of Hamlet's childhood friends, his classmates Rosencrantz and Guildenstern?"

The King snorts. "Ugh, don't get me started on those two buffoons. They would sign their own death certificates without even realizing it. If you knew them during their university years, you would feel the same."

"Is that so?"

"Oh, yes. Wittenberg isn't exactly an Olive League school. It hasn't produced a rogue scholar in quite some time."

"But they have a heck of a jousting team," Polonius says. He often places Wittenberg toward the top of his bracket during February Fanaticism.

Claudius begins pacing again. "I remember one parade during a particularly sweltering summer. They replaced the oats in the feedbag of King Hamlet's horse with laxatives. Heavy laxatives. Before anyone knew what was happening, there was a kilometer-long trail of a foul stench that made one's eyes water. And the sun only made it ten times worse."

"I can't imagine."

"I can," Claudius snarls. "As you know, the King is at the head of parades. And I, his brother, was in the last carriage."

Polonius giggles under his breath but then quickly turns stoic again. The last thing he wants to do is anger a man with such a vast collection of ear poison.

The King doesn't notice, though, still scowling at his memories. "Then, the following season, they stole the alligators from the castle's moat, hid them in our Ambassadors' bed chambers, then filled the water with soap, bubbles, and scores of ducks. We were the laughingstock of the nation! No, no, only summon Rosencrantz and Guildenstern as a last resort."

"Very well, sir. If I may be blunt, then, whom will we send for?"

The chamber goes silent except for the King's heavy footfalls on the stone floor. They echo like nails being driven into a coffin, making Polonius flinch with each step.

Boom, clack, boom, clack…

Finally, Claudius mumbles, "I don't know, Polonius. I don't know."

A thought strikes Polonius: a person they could summon to truly get inside Hamlet's head. It seems risky to even bring it up, especially with the King in such a cross mood, but it's the only solution he sees. He gathers his courage and clears his throat. "If I may be so bold, sir…"

"That isn't my favorite way to start a sentence, Polonius."

"Yes, sir, but how about…You-Know-Who?"

Claudius stops pacing. "Who?"

"You know." Polonius bugs out his eyes. "*Him.*"

"I have absolutely no idea who you're talking about," the King snaps. "Just spit it out!"

Polonius sighs, breathes a prayer, and says the name. "Tim."

Silence. Neither man moves.

"Tim?" The muscles in Claudius's neck tighten. "I hope you're not talking about who I think you're talking about. That name has not been uttered in this land for five years. Or is your memory fading in your old age?"

"But sir, who better to find out the truth about young Hamlet—"

The King clamps his hands over his ears. "Don't say it!"

"—than his twin brother?"

A roar shakes the chamber. "Polonius!"

"Sir!" Polonius stands straighter and raises his voice. "This is the only option!"

For a few moments, nobody moves. The temperature plunges a few more degrees. Even the figures in the portraits seem to look surprised. Not a single person in Danish history has ever spoken to the King in such a manner.

Thoughts race through Polonius's head at a frantic pace: Why did he say that? Who does he think he is? What will his punishment be? Does it hurt to have one's head axed? Will they at least let him comb his hair before lopping it off?

Finally, after a good minute of intense staring, Claudius lets out a breath, like steam escaping from a teakettle. "Fine. You're probably right."

Relief floods through Polonius's body. The heavens have opened and are shining down on him. He begins to bounce up and down on his heels, the crisp air reinvigorating his lungs. Colors are more vibrant, smells more refreshing. After this brush with mortality, Polonius has a whole new lease on life.

"Understood, Polonius?"

Polonius freezes. The King has been speaking, and Polonius hasn't heard a word.

Claudius groans. "You weren't listening, were you?"

"Sir, I—"

"Just tell an Ambassador to travel to England and summon Tim. Now. Let's get this resolved swiftly and quietly."

"Right away, sir." Polonius turns for the door, but pauses before leaving. He peeks over his shoulder at the King and speaks tentatively. "Tim is Young Hamlet's spitting image, not to mention your new son. He could also be our only hope to unlocking the truth about Hamlet's sanity. For being so important, he is an immense mystery. Just why, sir, has he been absent from this castle?"

A vicious glint flickers through Claudius's gaze. "Don't push your luck, Polonius. Send the Ambassador."

Polonius hesitates.

"Go," Claudius hisses.

Polonius exits the chamber, leaving the King alone with the glaring portraits.

Claudius releases an anxious breath and wilts onto the sofa. He sets his face in his hands, hoping that he hasn't made a colossal mistake.

Chapter 2

"I believe in England. England has made my fortune…" A wiry Sicilian sits before a massive, elegantly designed desk, clutching a mud-stained handkerchief in his fists. He pauses and wipes his eyes even though he isn't crying.

The Danish Ambassador can hardly keep himself from gagging at the man's overacting.

Two days have passed since the Ambassador had been given the odd task of tracking down the estranged son of the royal family, Prince Tim of Denmark. In those two days, he trekked across Denmark's ruggedly rocky terrain—all the regal carriages and stallions had been retained by ambassadors traveling to Norway. Evidently, the assignment of speaking to Tim was lower on the priorities list. Thus, the Ambassador was forced to rely upon his own two feet and his hope of finding a ship that could take him across the water. After finally reaching the frigid North Sea, he had bribed his way aboard a small fishing vessel en route to the island-nation of England.

While every citizen in Western Europe adores young Hamlet—the passionate actor and wordsmith—few even know of Tim's existence. The royal family never speaks of him, and the Ambassador can't imagine why the King would want to speak with Tim now after five long years.

He'd had plenty of time to mull over these thoughts as he drifted across the Channel, surrounded only by piles of rank fish and the even ranker sailors. The Ambassador is a man of sophisticated taste, always dignified and orderly—he hopes the new king will recognize the lengths he went to during his search for young Tim.

As soon as the ship had reached the dock, he parted ways with the fishermen and began the lengthy walk to the last stop of his journey: the bustling metropolis that never sleeps, home to the world's richest heritage and greatest artists (according to a postcard he had once received from a cousin), London.

And bustling it is. Upwards of three million people live within the city's limits, and that's just the souls brave enough to face the census-takers. The Ambassador once counted thirty destitute men and women in a single alley. They may be homeless, but they were by no means unemployed. Rather, they zeroed in on tourists like himself and tried to sell anything they could: second-hand jewelry, ragged clothing that was "all the rage in the New World," completely random guesses regarding the future. You name it, they pawn it.

It had taken two days of searching and negotiating for him to set up an appointment with the one man in the city who could help him find Tim Hamlet. Don Martizoa, the most powerful man in the upper west corner of London.

Now, the Ambassador waits in the back of a dark, mysterious office that is lit by a single candle. As the minutes crawl by, he silently says a prayer that he hasn't wasted his time, that this man will help him accomplish the most peculiar task the King has assigned to him.

Sporting stately garments and a bristly moustache, Don Martizoa nods from behind his desk. "Continue, friend," he says with a heavy-handed Italian accent.

"Thank you, Don Martizoa," the small man squeaks. "You are most gracious. As you know, I relocated my entire family from Sicily to London when I was newly married. The Great Tomato Famine, and all that."

"*Si*, I remember. Times were tough." The Don adjusts the carnation in his breast pocket as he muses. "What is an Italian without his marinara sauce?"

"Truer words were never spoken, oh wise and merciful Don Martizoa!"

The Ambassador almost groans. This guy is really laying it on thick. He must be trying to grovel his way out of some heinous debt, or about to ask for an earth-shattering favor.

"Last week," the Sicilian continues, "my wife and I discovered that our eldest daughter has become entranced by a man. A *French* man," he snarls. "All my life, I've wanted a son-in-law who talks with his hands and has a strong affinity for the word *capiche,* like all good Italian boys! Is that too much to ask?" His lower lip begins to tremble and he wipes away a tear. But it's the worst acting the Ambassador has ever seen.

"I see your troubles, brother." The Don leans forward, actually believing the other man's display of emotion, and strokes his chin. "You never go against the family."

"I say to my wife, for justice, we must go to Don Martizoa."

The Ambassador has had enough. He confirms his uniform is creased perfectly and his hair is just-so. "Alright, *signor*. Drop the curtain, show's over," he says loudly as he walks out of the shadows.

A confused sputter escapes the Sicilian's lips. "Excuse me," he hisses. "My time with Don Martizoa is not over yet! Wait your turn!" He turns back to the Don, trying to reel in his outburst. "Now, as I was saying, Your Beautiful Excellency—"

"*Signor* Martizoa, are you done with this weasel so we can talk real business?" the Ambassador says without wavering from his natural, prim-and-proper demeanor.

That did it for the Sicilian. He leaps to his feet, trembling in his baby-whale-leather shoes. "I'll have you know," he scoffs, "I am among the foremost businessmen in Southern England!"

"Oh, really?" the Ambassador deadpans. "All I see is a shrill little brownnoser with an awful poker face."

"Gentlemen, calm yourselves." Don Martizoa raises a hand, expecting it to magically cause the men to settle down. It works for the Sicilian, who, in true brownnoser form, plops back in his chair and shuts his mouth. The Ambassador, though, isn't scared of the so-called Don.

"No, no, don't get up, *signor*," he says to the Don. "We can handle this like mature, logical adults." Then back to the Sicilian: "Isn't that right, Mr. Poopy-Head?"

In record time, the Sicilian is back on his feet. "Why, I never! You Dutch are all the same!"

"Oh, my friend, I'm a Dane. And don't you forget it."

Don Martizoa again attempts to seize control of the situation. "Sit down, my Italian brother. And to the crazed Dane in my chambers," he scowls at the Ambassador, "you compel me to call my enforcers."

The Ambassador isn't concerned. In fact, he smiles. "Oh, I'm sure we don't need to involve Luca and Sonny or whatever their names are. I just need to talk to you alone..." His smile widens. "Mr. Marcus."

All color drains from the Don's face as he shifts in his chair. "T-That will be all," he stutters to the Sicilian, eyes fixed on his desktop.

Crestfallen, the wiry man objects, "But *signor—*"

"That's enough!" Martizoa bellows. "Out! *Capiche?*"

The Sicilian opens his mouth to argue one last time, but the Ambassador clamps a hand upon his shoulder and answers for him. "*Capiche.*" The Dane directs the Sicilian toward the door and shoves him out.

Silence blankets the gloomy office. The Don sits taut in his lavish armchair, shooting a poisonous glare at the Ambassador.

"What're you doin' here, Dane?" Martizoa says, his Italian accent suddenly replaced by a deep drawl.

The Ambassador responds, "I wanted to speak with you personally, Tex."

Martizoa winces at the name. "Don't call me that," he says with a twang. "I worked for years to gain the reputation I have now, and you just 'bout destroyed it in a matter'a seconds."

Richard Tex Marcus: AKA Roberto Alexander Martizoa: AKA Don Martizoa. A penniless scoundrel from the New World colonies who had arrived in London by mysterious means three decades before. Adopting the facade of a suave, omnipotent, non-negotiating Italian boss, he had built an underground empire from scratch and now has a hand in everything that happens within the city, from banking to building.

"Just what do ya wanna talk 'bout, *seen-your?*" Marcus says, butchering the pronunciation of the Italian word.

"I'm looking for someone," the Ambassador clasps his hands behind his back. "Someone in the play business."

Marcus snorts. "Lots 'a people are in the play business in this town. Most have no right. They stumble into this city with nothing to their name 'cept three cents and a dream of making it big onstage. A sucker's born every minute," he snickers and adjusts his diamond cufflinks, "and boy, do they keep me entertained."

"The man I'm looking for is a writer. Tim Hamlet."

Recognition flickered on Marcus's face. "My, uh, my memory's a bit smutty right now…"

"Make it un-smutty, Tex, or the big, bad Don will be no more."

Marcus groans and seems to weigh his options in his head. Finally, he rips the adhesive mustache from his upper lip. He rubs the sore spot as his nose twitches. "Fine, Dane. But I want you outta my town as soon as your business is done."

"My pleasure."

"Ole Tim's writing a play for the Masterpiece Centre, which I think is owned by a stodgy old ox named Bushacannyman. You'll most likely find him hanging around there. 'Bout six blocks west."

The Ambassador nods. "Thank you for your cooperation, Don Martizoa." He turns and moves toward the door. "Until next time."

He doesn't see, but he imagines Tex Marcus's expression is one of loathing. And he loves it.

Rays of the noonday sun temporarily blind the Ambassador as he exits the inconspicuous edifice in the middle of a crowded street. It's a huge difference from the dreary, intimidating office he had been in for the last hour.

The noises of London hit him full force: shouts, bangs, scrapes, whines. Overwhelming sounds of life assault him from all directions. He quickly gets his bearings and tries to shimmy his way out of the crowd, in the direction of the Masterpiece Centre.

Every street corner houses a different attraction, be it amusing or appalling. Or both. The Ambassador has traveled to London many times over the course of his professional career, but the city is always experienced anew. Within the limits of any great city, one can always find a new wonder, different cultures, and sensations the likes of which have never been felt before.

A stout, wooden structure looms at the end of the street, revealing more and more of itself as the Ambassador walks. A handful of pedestrians loiter in front of a pair of heavily gnarled doors, as if waiting for someone to exit. The Ambassador stops in front of the building and cranes his head. A hand-painted plaque dangles from its overhanging roof: *Masterpiece Centre*. Strung underneath is another: "*Presenting three performances of* **A Tale of Marge and Tina**, *coming soon!*"

The Ambassador ponders what an odd title that is for a play, then pushes open the double doors and enters the theatre.

He strides forward, hearing a clamor coming from the center of the building. He makes his way toward the activity. Along the way, he passes closed booths that, on business nights, would vend grossly overpriced sweets and cooked corn to theatre-goers. He scrunches his nose, almost able to smell the sugary treats. Eventually, he leaves the lobby section behind and steps back into the sun.

Empty seats rise high into the air, staring at him from every angle, making him feel like a hapless gladiator that has wandered into an arena. There is no ceiling, allowing the natural light of midday to blaze down on the stage.

The sight of the stage is enough to give him pause. He breathes deeply as he soaks in the majesty of the venue. Standing six feet off the ground, it ensures that no word, action, or facial expression is missed by any audience member, whether they sit on the front row or up in the nosebleeds. Unlike the scuffed doors at the entrance, the wooden platform gleams as if it were polished and finished an hour earlier. It takes him away from his task, if only for a moment, and allows him to relax.

Men stand on the stage, clutching rolls of parchment in their fists. Many are dressed in cheap costumes—some in armor, others in tunics, one even in a horrifyingly scant loincloth. Each is speaking, gesturing wildly, attempting to make his opinion heard over the racket.

A voice booms from the heart of the crowd. "Gentlemen, close your traps and get on the same page!"

A young man breaks out of the pack. Quills and scraps of parchment protrude from his pockets. His hair is slicked back, held in place by sweat and sheer willpower. Judging by the dark circles under his eyes and the throbbing vein in his temple, this young man is both the director and writer of the play.

The Ambassador smirks.

It's Tim Hamlet.

Ink-black hair. Eyes that could pierce leather. A tall, lean physique. An inbred wisdom that suggests he is older than his actual twenty years. He is truly identical to the prince that currently resides in Denmark.

The young man continues to bark at the group of actors. "Alright, fellas, we open in less than a week and there's much to do. Turn your eyes to act eight, scene nineteen, and get to your marks…" He screeches to a stop, noticing the only member of the audience: the Ambassador. "Can I help you, Guvnor?"

"I believe so, sir," the Ambassador answers. "But my name is not—"

"A Dane?" Tim interrupts, recognizing the accent and uniform.

"Yes. And my name is not '*Guvnor.*' It is—"

"Oh, that's just something we say." Tim laughs. "I'm a Guv, you're a Guv, he's a Guv, she's a Guv. We're all Guvs here."

The Ambassador clears his throat. "I see. Now, I am an Ambassador from the royal castle of Elsinore, and I wish to have a moment of your time…*Guv.*" The English slang drips from his mouth like a line of drool he had wanted to be an impressive loogie.

Tim considers the visitor for a moment, his expression stony and unreadable. Without breaking his gaze from the stranger, he says to the crowd on the stage, "Take five, gentlemen." He bounds off the platform, landing right in front of the Ambassador.

The Ambassador flinches, but Tim sets a hand on his shoulder.

"Don't be skittish, Hermes. Lemme get us some seats." He turns his head and shouts, "Someone bring out a pair of chairs for the royal guest and myself!"

After a moment, an actor wearing a loincloth drags two chairs from behind the stage and sets them facing each other.

"Take a seat, Guv." Tim sits in one chair as he gestures to the other. He empties the quills and parchments from his trousers' pockets and sets them all in a pile on the ground. "By all means, please. What's mine is yours." A heavy coin purse slips from his pocket. "Except that," he mutters and snatches it.

The Ambassador nods and sits, positioning himself to crease his uniform as little as possible.

"The last time I heard from Elsinore," Tim says, "it was regarding my father's snakebite. God rest his soul, and all that. Who is it this time? Mother, mauled by a bear? Osric, flattened by a chariot during rush hour? Ophelia, struck by lightning and then bitten by a rabid badger? Freak accidents seem to be becoming less and less freakish."

"No, sir. Nothing of that sort."

"Well then, to what do I owe your unexpected patronage?"

Something has been nagging at the Ambassador about the way Tim speaks, and in that moment, he realizes what it is. The young prince uses an English accent, not a Danish one. Most interesting.

The Ambassador reorients his thoughts and continues. "I bring a message from the new King of Denmark."

"Ooh!" Tim squeals sarcastically. "The *King* has a message for *me*? Good ole Uncle Claudie has something to say?" He drops the act and rolls his eyes. "What does he want?"

"The King has a special request he must ask of you."

"My father's body isn't even stiff yet, and Claudius is already making demands? How very political of him." He clenches his jaw, not bothering to hide his animosity. "At least King Hamlet was wise enough to leave me alone for these few years."

"You can't blame the King for wishing to make contact with his new son."

"I'll send a Christmas card next year. Happy? Thank you for dropping by, and have a nice day." He stands, turning to storm off.

"Tim," the Ambassador hisses. "I'm not finished. Shut your jowls for once in your life and sit. Down. Now."

Tension bakes the air between the two Danes. A moment later, Tim returns to his seat.

"You wouldn't talk to Hamlet that way," he says under his breath.

"Hamlet wouldn't be a smart aleck like you."

"That's probably true. He would flat-out insult you to your face, and then bore you to death with one of his pretentious, longwinded, bleeding-heart soliloquies."

The Ambassador allows a half-hearted chuckle in an attempt to ease the friction of the situation. Then he prepares to lob the harpoon. "Speaking of Hamlet…" he begins.

Tim senses the shift in the Ambassador's tone. "Oh no. What did he do now? Is he hanging around Rosie and Guild again?"

"Well, Tim, the current state of affairs in Denmark is volatile on a good day."

"And it's cataclysmic on a bad one, I take it?"

"Exactly. The crown prince of Norway, young Fortinbras, increases his threat of invasion every day. What's worse, his uncle is feeble, elderly, and completely unaware of anything that happens beyond his bedchambers. King Claudius has sent two other Danish Ambassadors to Norway so that they may inform the old man of his nephew's aggressive advances."

Tim nods, tracking the situation so far. "And the plan is…that the bedridden old man will convince his militant nephew to back off?"

The Ambassador nods.

"Not very likely." Tim raises an eyebrow but keeps his face otherwise impassive.

"I agree with you."

"Not to mention the fact that Fortinbras's father was killed by Old King Hamlet in battle about three years ago. His thirst for Danish blood will be substantial."

The Ambassador gulps as sweat forms on his brow. "I hadn't thought of that."

"Well, they don't call me a genius for nothing. In fact, they don't call me a genius at all, because all I have is nothing." Tim waits for the Ambassador to laugh, but when he doesn't get the reaction he wants, he crosses his arms. "Sounds like you Danes are trapped between an ocean and a desert." A small grin tugs at his mouth.

The Ambassador is speechless for a moment. Just a moment. In his rage, he snaps, "You seem awfully *blasé* about this!"

"Why shouldn't I be *blasé, mon ami majestueux*? I'm not Danish anymore, remember? I made that perfectly clear when I packed a burlap sack of my belongings and walked out of Elsinore five years ago. I have no quarrel with Fortinbras, myself."

"You can't have a prince's face and remain inconspicuous forever."

"I've done well so far. I have steady work here at the Centre."

"Ah, yes. So did you write this latest play? I saw the placard hanging near the entrance. *A Tale of Marge and Tina?*"

Tim blinks as the Ambassador's words sink in, then he growls and tugs at his hair. "Ugh…The title is supposed to be *A Tale of Argentina*, but the half-wit who painted the advertisement must have misheard me." He raises his head and stares at the bright sky. "That'll lower attendance, no doubt," he mutters quietly, "but if we get a new sign out by mid-evening, we may be able to draw some customers back. Half, at best. There'll still be a vast net loss…" He slumps in his chair. "Bushacannyman is gonna kill me."

The Ambassador is at a loss for words. A mere thirty seconds ago, the most self-confident man he had ever met had been sitting in that chair. Now, he's a miserable husk, dejected and brittle, as if a stiff breeze would knock him over. The Ambassador feels a great deal of pity for the young prince. Here he is, just entering his twentieth year, and he has already faced his family's rejection, his father's death, and the cutthroat world of show business.

With the softest voice he can muster—which is quite a challenge, as he has never taken on the role of comforter in his life—the Ambassador says, "I'm sure it will be a great show, Tim. You are an excellent writer, and I'll wager your directing skills aren't too shabby either."

"Oh, stuff it," Tim moans. "The set's not finished. My lead actor has pink eye. Five of my conquistadors quit, and the rest are threatening to unionize unless they each get a buffet in their dressing rooms. Plus, I haven't had a hit since *Waiting For My Joe* two seasons back."

After clearing his throat, the Ambassador continues, "Now sounds like a good time to move on."

"What, jump ship? Abandon my craft just because it's getting hard? I'm not an actor!"

"You have much potential, young Tim. In a few days' time, you could be back in Elsinore, where you belong, instead of here, writing some farce or a soapy drama."

"No no no," Tim wags a finger. "I don't peddle tragedy. Death isn't in my wheelhouse."

"What I'm saying, sir, is that King Johan Hamlet may have deserted you, but King Claudius Hamlet is reaching out."

"Just so that he can use me."

"Even so…" The Ambassador gestures to the group of disgruntled thespians, and then the empty audience seats. "It's better than being trapped between an ocean and a desert."

Tim shoots him a glance.

The Ambassador smiles. "I'll be at the eastern carriage station until nightfall. If you're interested in assisting the King—in 'jumping ship'—you can find me there." With that, he stands and marches toward the exit.

"Wait, hold on, Guv!" Tim jumps to his feet.

The Ambassador looks back, as calm and composed as ever.

Tim asks, "What does Claudius want me to do?"

"The King is having…problems with your brother. I'll give you more pertinent details if you show up at the station. Good day." The Danish Ambassador adjusts his uniform, nods to the prince, and leaves the theatre. Each step echoes in Tim's ears until they disappear into the distance.

.   ■   ■

The sun passes over the open-air stage, casting shadows in the opposite direction. It's been a long morning, and Tim feels it's just getting started.

He wipes a hand across his face, replaying the conversation in his mind.

Tim thinks, *King Claudius is reaching out? That's a first. I barely knew him when I was young.*

Memories flood his mind. Obscure, long-forgotten memories that he had tried to bury after leaving his identity behind. Learning to spar with Osric, alongside his twin brother. Cackling at a funny tale from the castle jester Yorick, alongside his twin brother. Flirting with the beautiful Ophelia during grammar school…competing with his twin brother.

Hamlet wins that contest, Tim scoffs. He had once asked the breathtaking Ophelia to go to the Fall Formal ball with him, to which she had responded with an enthusiastic *YES!*, but only because she had thought he was Hamlet. Now, Hamlet and Ophelia are inseparable. Tim wonders if the family will send him a wedding announcement when the time comes. Probably not.

He realizes he's still standing by the two empty chairs in the heart of the theatre. A loud ruckus draws his attention back to the stage. His motley crew of performers stands in a circle, jabbing their fingers at their scripts and having a brash, belligerent argument. Over what, only God knows. What Tim knows is that the cast gets into squabbles like this about ten times a day, so he lets them have at each other. It'll likely die down in a few minutes.

"Shape up, Tim!"

The thunderous voice of King Hamlet breaks free from its mental prison, where it has been dormant for five long years. That one command fills Tim with heavy emotions he can't identify. Now he remembers why he's avoided Danes for so long—these memories are like a pickaxe to the gonads.

"Get your head out of those plays, boy. The real world has enough worries."

Yeah, yeah, Dad. Hear ya loud and clear, he sighs.

That stiff-necked ambassador was the second Dane he's seen in five years. About a month earlier, another ambassador had shown up, handed him a notice, and darted away as if he'd left the stove on. Not a word was exchanged.

At first Tim, had been confused. He had almost forgotten that the Danish uniforms were that odd green color. Then he opened the notice— that was how he had learned of his father's death.

It's been a rough month.

Has it really only been that long? Time flies when you're miserable.

No one in London knows his true heritage. His royal identity. His bosses Bushacannyman and Martizoa would pop like balloons if they found out he's been holding back his "influence" and "riches"…both of which are nonexistent, of course. Elsinore has erased him from all records and family portraits—there's no way they would ever send him cash to help fund a flopping theatre.

And since no one knows he's a Hamlet, he has had no one to talk to about his dad.

But that's the thing. He has no idea what he feels. Usually, he's fairly emotionally self-aware. He's happy—he's sad—he's hungry. Easy. But the news of his father's death…He can't put his finger on it. His father was a gruff man, without a doubt. But he was his father. He'll never have another.

Tim will likely never be able to fully comprehend his feelings. He simply has no one to talk to, no verbal jousting partner with which he can sift through his emotions.

His twin brother is off in Elsinore, dealing with his new stepdad. Their relationship has always been awkward, and it's been nonexistent since the day Tim left Denmark for good.

His mother Gertrude clearly knows where Tim is—two ambassadors have showed up on his doorstep within a little more than a month—yet she hasn't said a word to him. That thought makes his stomach clench, but he quickly moves on.

The ambassador who had delivered the news of Old Hamlet's death had barely looked him in the eye.

Why didn't I talk to this second ambassador just now? He seemed like a nice guy. He would've listened. Instead, Tim had spent the whole time being sarcastic and stubborn. Now, the Ambassador is gone, and Tim is alone again.

He'll be at the carriage station tonight. I can talk to him then.

Whoa! Easy there, Guv, Tim says to himself. *You aren't going to that carriage station, because you aren't going back to Denmark.*

I can go just to talk to the Ambassador. He's the only Dane I've spoken to in years. The only one who might understand what I'm feeling.

Enough of this. *If I'm going to go full Dane, I should probably do it in private.*

He slinks toward his personal office, which is cleverly disguised as a disorganized broom closet. The actors don't notice him as he passes, still bickering over costumes or celebrity marriages or something else entirely pointless.

"Your public persona leaves much to be desired, Tim. Why can't you be more like your brother?"

Ha, ha! There's the kicker! The slogan for the Disappointed Fathers Alliance. Y'know, Dad, you don't need to roll out of bed just to remind me of all this. Especially since you sleep six feet under now.

Tim reaches the door to his office, which is easy to miss among the clutter that not even Magellan could navigate. He muscles it open, then drops himself into a rickety chair behind a small desk.

"You could be something great, Tim."

I have a lot to think about, and the last thing I need is my dead dad's disappointment pestering me.

Posters adorn the walls: advertisements for his previous plays. All his biggest failures.

Sicily in the Spring—Garbage.

Les Affamés—A box office disaster.

Sicily in the Summer—Worse than the original.

Henry XXX—Even the drunks booed.

The Comedy of Horrors—Started the tradition of throwing rotten fruit during a curtain call.

Add *A Tale of Marge and Tina* to the list. No one will even remember the real name of the show, anyway.

As a boy in Denmark, he had burned with passion for playwriting. He would read everything he could get his hands on, burn candles down to nubs writing at night, and he and his brother would even produce a few of his scripts.

He used to be good too. His words were compelling, his stories memorable. But now…Now he's a bargain-bin hack, and he's only twenty years old. Whatever spark he possessed in Denmark had been snuffed out the moment he set up shop in London.

Stacks upon stacks of parchment cover the desk, but Tim does his best to ignore them. Bills, mostly, but also drafts of scripts. Rewrites too dreadful to see the light of day, condemned to his cluttered desktop. There are plenty of those—most of his ideas are utter rubbish.

Two notes stare at him from the top of the piles of paper. They must have been placed there for him to find. Tim recognizes the handwriting of his bosses: Edgar Bushacannyman, the owner of the Masterpiece Centre, and Don Martizoa, the owner of Edgar Bushacannyman.

Undoubtedly, Bushacannyman and Martizoa both are harping at him about his plays not bringing in enough money. Tim crumples the notes into a tight ball and throws them across the room.

"Make something of yourself, boy!"

"And now, on top of everything, Dad's greatest hits are playing through my head." He groans and wonders if show business has finally made his sanity snap.

"*You're not crazy, Tim.*"

Hold on.

He doesn't remember his father ever saying that.

Only a truly insane bloke would conjure up a disembodied lecture from his deceased father.

I need to get out of this claustrophobic office. As quickly as possible.

The temperature has dropped a dozen degrees in as many seconds. A sharp pain stabs the center of his back, like a mouse warrior attacking with a small lance. Tim jerks out of his chair, collapses to the floor, then scrambles to his feet. His fingers tremble as he reaches for the door. An audible voice breathes, "*Tim…*"

"What the blazes is going on?"

"*I've been talking to you for a while now, son. Have you not been listening?*"

Tim freezes, his hand still outstretched for the doorknob. He wonders if the memories of his father's words are not memories at all, but an actual voice. Then he shakes his head, calling himself crazy to even suggest that notion. He grasps the knob, but it won't turn. He grits his teeth and twists with all his might. Then the metal instantly becomes colder than frost. He jolts back, panic rising from his core, about to consume him. Frantically, he spins around, but there is no way out. He is locked inside his tiny office.

"*Timothy Hamlet, look at me when I'm talking to you!*"

It feels like someone very large is watching him. With knocking knees, he looks back at his desk.

A broad-shouldered man sporting a suit of gleaming armor stands tall behind the stacks of paperwork. Eyes rich like the bark of a cherry-wood tree stare forward, never wavering, never blinking. The beaver of the cast-iron helmet is flipped up, revealing the man's drawn face and majestic beard. Tendrils of supernatural fog drift from his being as if he has arrived directly from the Unknown.

Then, a wide smile spreads across the man's face. He lifts his powerful arms, creaking the armor. "Mark me," he says like a glacial breeze. "My boy. My son…Tim."

Dad...

Tim's mouth drops open, but he has no words to speak. The figure standing before him looks like his father, sounds like his father, and speaks like his father. But how can it be? King Hamlet has been buried for more than a month. How can it possibly be?

Suddenly, Tim finds the one word to express his emotions: "AAAHHHHGGHH!"

The figure of the Great Dane rolls his eyes. "Calm down, Tim. I just—"

Tim cuts him off with another scream, and he turns back and starts clawing at the door.

"Tim, listen—"

He isn't listening. Just clawing like a helpless dog. And screaming. "AAAAAHHHHH!" Lots of screaming.

King Hamlet growls, sending a roll of thunder across the cramped office, which knocks Tim off his feet like a tangible push. Tim snaps into a fetal position. He looks back at the imposing figure, eyes wide.

"Tim!" the late King booms. "Quit acting like a toddler and man up!"

Beat by beat, Tim forces his heart to slow back to a normal pace. Or at least something resembling normal. There is very little that is normal about conversing with a dead parent.

"Okay..." he breathes. "Okay." He slaps on a twitching smile that even the worst actor would find unconvincing. "Can I help you...Father?"

Speaking that last word sends his heart into arrhythmia again. He staggers to his feet, sputtering incoherently. "What are you? How are you here? You're dead. I know you're dead. An ambassador told me so. A month ago, he told me. You're long dead...Stiff, cold, buried, caterpillar-feed..."

"Calm down, son."

"I am calm!" Tim screams, his face turning a shade of purple. "Why don't you calm down, daddy dearest?"

"Tim, son, you're in shock. Just give yourself a minute." He sighs, which sounds like a ghostly avalanche, and grumbles, "Hamlet took it much better."

"Wait, wait. Hamlet?" Tim cocks an eyebrow. "You've already talked to Hamlet? The melodramatic, gloomy over-reactor named Hamlet? You come back from the grave and the first person you visit is *Hamlet*? And I'm second?"

"No, of course not." The King fidgets and looks at the floor. "I…I appeared to some random guards first. You're actually third."

"Oh great! I'm third!" Tim throws his hands in the air and scoffs in disbelief. "I'm overflowing with warmth and affection right now! I was always the responsible son, the humble one, but you never looked upon me with the same pride you reserved for Hamlet. He was the outgoing one, the theatrical one."

"Tim, I've heard this over and over—"

"Hold on," Tim interjects again, then moans. "No, no, no, I'm not talking to you anymore. You're not real. The deceased don't walk and talk." He squeezes his temples as if forcing the apparition out of his mind. "I truly am crazy…"

"You're not crazy, son. Your mother and I looked into it."

"You should look again." Tim lowers his hands, suddenly exhausted. He leans against his office door and stares at the figure. "What do you want?" he sighs.

The ghost of the King takes an imposing step forward. There, before Tim's very eyes, the specter passes though the wooden desk as if it is made of mist. Or as if the specter is made of mist.

The King now stands in front of the desk, a smug grin contorting his beard. "You don't see tricks like that in Summer Stock." He laughs, making the air tremble.

Tim squeaks. "How are you doing this?"

"It's…complicated."

"I'm bound to hear."

"I am the spirit of your father, Johan Hamlet, the Great Dane—"

"Yeah, I picked up on that part."

"Tim, if you're going to listen, you're going to hear the whole tale." The ghost realigns his thoughts and speaks again. "King Hamlet, the Great Dane. Doomed to be bound to this corporeal earth, damned to walk the night and fast in fires."

"Your spirit is trapped on earth? Like some sort of purgatory punishment?"

"Indeed! Until the foul crimes done against my mortal soul are rectified and purged."

Tim's ears perk. "Foul crimes? As in, foul play?"

The ghost nods, impressed. "I should've come to you first. I had to go through this big, wordy speech with your brother before he got the picture."

"So someone killed you? Who?" Tim's apathy has melted away, and he has, for the moment at least, forgotten that he is speaking with a man who has personally ridden the Pale Horse.

"Like I said, you must hear the entire story. And, hark, what a story!" The King cracks his knuckles as if preparing for a boxing match. "Even whispering this tale will freeze your young blood. Make your jaw strike the floorboards. Force each hair to stand up like the quills of a frightened porcupine!"

"Just tell the bloody story!"

"Ah, yes. Of course." The King takes a breath, his eyes glistening in anticipation. "Now, Tim, hear. 'Tis given out that—" The King stops abruptly and straightens up. "On second thought…"

"Aw, c'mon!" Tim yells. "You're building up this story, but you keep interrupting yourself! Are you gonna tell me or not?"

"No." The King pauses, then raises a misty hand. "I'll show you."

Before Tim can form a word, the ghost floats forward, hand outstretched. His thick fingers extend like hungry serpents. Before Tim even has time to flinch, the fingers pass through his flesh and bones, and they grasp his mind. All of Tim's thoughts are replaced by a dull roar.

He wants to scream, to thrash, to wet his trousers, but every muscle in his body is frozen solid. He senses a ghostly hand physically prodding his brain from the inside—like he's an unwilling puppet being manipulated by Old Man Winter.

Blinding light explodes from every direction. Tim's office evaporates, like dust particles blown by a breeze. His body feels like it is being simultaneously stretched and compacted, over and over again. His feet leave the ground, and suddenly, he soars through a bright tunnel that could be miles long or mere meters.

So this is what it's like to be born.

A destination becomes visible at the end of the tunnel: a lush, beautiful garden, filled with fruit trees and blooming flowers.

Or to die.

Tim's journey ends. He stands in the middle of the garden, trembling, struggling to fill his lungs. He feels like he's about to lose his lunch, and he falls to his knees.

Only then does it strike him that he's no longer in the Centre. He staggers back to his feet. The noonday sun gives the garden a heavenly aura, making every leaf, petal, and blade of grass glow as if they had sprouted directly from God's paintbrush.

A breeze sweeps over the north wall, making the whole garden shimmer. Goosepimples rise on his arms. He smells the foliage, hears the singing birds, and squints against the bright sunlight. Either this is the most vivid daydream he has ever had, or the specter of his father has transported him somewhere.

Somewhere he recognizes.

The pieces of the puzzle slowly come together in his mind. How could he not have recalled this place as soon as he laid eyes on it? It is the garden located in the north courtyard of Elsinore Castle, the very place he had played and laughed during his childhood.

Why has Father brought me here?

He then notices a large, luxurious recliner positioned beneath the breadth of an apple tree, and a large, luxurious man is sprawled out on it. The signet rings and thick beard are unmistakable: It's King Hamlet, the Great Dane.

Tim's breath catches in his throat. He takes a few weak steps forward as he eyes the former king, in the flesh. He leans in to grasp his father's shoulder. He looks exactly as Tim had remembered, until his hand passes right through the sleeping figure.

Is this some sort of ghostly reenactment?

He thinks back to the last words the King's phantom had said before plunging his hand into his forehead: *"I'll show you."* This must be the story the ghost wishes to impart.

A story of foul play.

The King's chest rises and deflates in the manner indicative of deep sleep. Tim moves away from the recliner, habitually giving his father space, even though he is only a shadow. He remembers the custom the King held to nap in the orchard each afternoon.

A dark sparrow swoops in from beyond the castle's perimeter and settles onto one of the apple tree's limbs, eyeing the King with primal curiosity. Suddenly, the small bird turns its gaze onto Tim with equal wonder. Tim gulps as a rock forms in his throat.

I don't exist in this realm, so how can this creature observe me?

Tim dismisses the feeling as groundless paranoia. That sparrow is not really looking at him—it can't be. He fixes his attention back on the slumbering Dane.

But he notices out of the corner of his eye that the bird continues to stare.

Rustling emits from the far side of the garden. Tim looks toward the sound. Two large thistle bushes part as a man shoves himself through them in a poor attempt to sneak into the garden undetected. The man wears the standard green uniform of Elsinore, his light hair cropped efficiently, with a leather satchel around his torso. It is none but Claudius, brother to the King.

The sparrow still hasn't averted its gaze.

With the gait of a prowling lion, Claudius moves toward the docile King, reaching into his satchel. A dark gleam is present in the man's eyes.

Tim gasps. He wants to run, to scream, to tackle his uncle to the ground, but he knows that any action is useless in this world of shadows past.

But he does it all anyway.

"Claudius, no!" he bellows, sprinting and leaping at the sneaking man. As predicted, he passes right through his uncle and tumbles onto the mossy ground.

Claudius isn't fazed by his nephew's silent plea. From his satchel, he withdraws a heavy flask affixed with a moldy cork. He opens the bottle and towers over the King.

Tim stands. "Uncle…" He wants to say more, but he's at a loss for words.

Of course, Claudius doesn't hear.

But the sparrow cranes its head. It heard Tim's whimper.

The King's brother stands still for several moments. Then he lowers the bottle toward Old Hamlet's head.

Tim recognizes the large bottle. He saw it many times as a child in Elsinore Castle. It had sat upon his uncle's shelf for many years, part of a vast collection of ancient apothecary appliances. The vial is sickly green, and if Tim recalls correctly, it contains the nectar of the hebona plant.

Claudius tips the bottle.

What's he doing with an old flask of plant juice?

In the silence, the sparrow caws.

A stream of juice pours into the King's exposed ear.

Now Tim remembers. He remembers just what the juice of the hebona plant can do.

And he now sees it unfold before his eyes.

The King jerks awake and rolls off the recliner, clutching the sides of his head, hissing as a ravaged wolverine would. The inner canals of his body begin to blacken, turning his skin into a crisscrossing map.

Poison of the most potent caliber flows through the King of Denmark's body, destroying every organ, every muscle, and every thought.

Tim shakes his head in utter disbelief. How can this be so? How on this mortal coil could this be happening? He grasps his hands together to keep them from trembling, but that does little to still his emotions.

Fear, rage, confusion, curiosity, sorrow...

The King convulses on the ground, grinding his teeth together, unaware that his breaths have suddenly become a limited commodity. His gaze lands on his brother, who is still standing by the recliner, heavy bottle in hand. The King's rich brown eyes stare at Claudius, and a range of emotions cross them.

Fear, rage, confusion, curiosity, sorrow...

Then, still looking upon his brother's face, the King rests his head on the grass.

White light floods the garden, again blinding Tim and sending him flying through the extraterrestrial tunnel. This time, he is too emotionally ravaged to notice the journey. When he finds the strength to raise his head, he is back in his cramped office. The ghost of King Hamlet stands on the far side of the room. He offers his son a small, comforting smile.

Why does he look at me with such concern? Tim wonders for a second, and then senses that his cheeks are wet. He clears his throat and dons a sardonic exterior: "Cripes, my uncle's a jerk."

The ghost harrumphs. "So do you now understand the manner of my death and earthly imprisonment?"

"I get the gist. Uncle Claudie offs you, blames an unsuspecting snake, snags your crown, gets the Danish people to weep and mourn and buy wedding gifts, and now sits pretty on one of the dominant kingdoms of modern civilization."

"That's the gist, yes."

Tim begins to pace, inconspicuously wiping away his stray tears. "But why me? Why did you appear to Hamlet and me? Why don't you show this vision to someone with authority? The Ambassador? Or my mother, your wife, the Queen?"

The ghost opens his mouth to speak, then thinks better of it.

"What?" Tim can't resist goading his dear old dad a little. He smirks, "You don't want to talk to your new sister-in-law? You know that she married your brother, right?"

"Aye, don't remind me!"

"On the bright side, she saved quite a bit of money by serving the leftover wine and potato salad from your funeral to the wedding guests."

"They had potato salad at my funeral? Gertrude knows that I *love* her potato salad! That's an eternal insult!" He growls, but, again, thinks better of it and reins in his anger. "No, no, Gertrude isn't to blame. She's innocent. I love her. She's the light of my life…" he says under his breath. He then shoves a finger into his son's face. "And you are to cause her no more grief, understand me, Tim? Do her no harm, emotional or otherwise."

"Yeah, of course!" Tim nods. "Wait, what do you mean? She's in Denmark, and I'm here."

The ghost doesn't respond.

"No, no, no, no! Hold on, Melinoe. You're drifting down the wrong river! I am not going back!"

"Yes, you are."

"I…" Tim stammers. "Did you not hear me?"

"Yes, I did. And yes, you are."

"Stop saying that. Stop contradicting me. Stop messing with my brain. Stop being a ghost inside my office!"

"Tim, you need to calm down."

"Stop!" Tim grits his teeth. "Just…*stop.*"

"Son," the ghost breathes. "I need your help."

The young prince tries to quickly formulate a smart response, but his phantom father beats him to the punch:

"Why can't you return home to avenge my death?"

"Why should I?" Tim crosses his arms, as he had when arguing with the Ambassador minutes earlier. "I just had this conversation with the little butler that your brother sent. Why does everyone want me to go back to Elsinore and do them favors? I have a good life here. I have London eating out of the palm of my hand."

"Oh, you're feeding them *something*, alright."

"What's that supposed to mean? You never read the plays I wrote back when I was in Elsinore. Back when you were *alive*. You don't know a thing about my art, my works, my magnum opuses."

"Really? *Queen Arthur in Hamalot* is your magnum opus? *Troy Story* is art? *Henry XXX, Sicily in the Spring*? *A Tale of Marge and Tina*?"

Tim shakes his fists. "*A Tale of Argentina*! It's a riveting story of a native people's sovereignty and courage!"

"But it will be remembered as a flop that everyone thought was about two middle-aged women playing bridge." The ghost reaches out a hand to his mortal son, fog rising from his chalky skin. "Tim, return to Denmark. Don't let the throne be occupied by a traitorous fiend. Restore yourself in the Hamlet legacy."

"As I recall, you kicked me out," Tim boldly lies.

"Don't you dare rewrite history, boy!" the King refutes. "As I recall, you packed a bag, abandoned your family, and snuck out while the entire castle was asleep! We heard from you *once* after that. I heard from you only *once* before Claudius gave my ear a drink."

Tim snarls, "I'm not prince material! You knew that, Mother knew that, and Hamlet most of all knew that! He never let me forget it. Well, look at me now! I've found my own life. Found it without a crown on my head!"

"Tim…" The shimmering aura dims as the ghost sighs. Suddenly, the King looks centuries old. Tired, defeated. "Having one's life stolen puts things in perspective. A perspective I didn't know existed. One minute, I'm the ruler of a powerful empire. I have every luxury I could dream of, a rich legacy, a promising lineage. And then, everything changes."

The ghost's sadness wafts through the air like a palpable haze. Tim looks at his father with sympathy—it's an odd feeling.

The King continues. "I didn't have the chance to say the things I needed to say. I thought I had time for all of that. I didn't thank Osric for shining my boots every other day. I didn't have a hearty meal of venison and wine. I didn't smell my favorite lilies one last time. I didn't brush the mane of my old stallion Gilgamesh. I didn't apologize to the guard Marcellus for insulting him, calling him an inept man. I didn't take communion one last time, didn't talk to a priest, didn't pray. I didn't embrace my wife, tell her of my love, say good-bye. I didn't get to talk to you."

Tim stares downward, avoiding his father's eyes.

The ghost continues, "I hadn't spoken to you in years. If I had, I would've said that I was sorry. That I was a fool for praising your twin but turning my face from you. I shouldn't have let you walk out of Elsinore's gate. And you're right. You are a greater man than anyone would have ever foretold. You showed us."

Silence smothers the office. Tim shuffles his feet. He feels deep conviction in his bosom. Words form on his tongue, but he swallows them. He looks up.

And the ghost is gone.

Tim gulps. Was it all a mirage? A twisted fantasy? He strides across the room to where the figure had stood a moment before. As soon as he passes through the air, an icy chill makes his flesh crawl. He knows.

It was real. It *is* real.

He shakes his head, not believing the thoughts that are bouncing about inside:

Leave the actors.

Leave my bosses.

Leave London.

What madness has possessed him?

Tim pulls a suitcase from under his desk and begins to fill it with the few materials he needs. Never before has he ever considered setting his sights back on Denmark, but, for some reason that eludes him, he's packing his bag.

Why?

Does he want to see his home again?

Does he miss his family?

He honestly isn't sure. He packs in a frenzy, scared of changing his mind. Or is he scared his mind is made up?

Too late. He latches the case shut and strolls out of his office, past the bickering actors, and out of the Centre. An unseen force beckons him to Denmark—a gut instinct that has awakened for the first time in five years.

He's going home.

Chapter 3

The sun is dark, dusk consuming all remnants of its illumination and warmth. Even the stars are black and cold. Batten down the hatches, all bets are off, say your prayers. Night has taken charge of London's streets.

Slipping through the alleys and side-streets, Tim makes his way downtown, suitcase clutched to his chest. His destination: the carriage station, where he will meet the Danish Ambassador and receive more instructions.

Every shadow looms heinously, hiding some unthinkable nightmare. Tim shakes off his imagination and keeps walking. A rifle booms in the distance, followed by inebriated cackles. As Tim moves further and further east, out of the metropolis and toward the rushing River Thames, civilization seems to move progressively down the evolutionary ladder. In a few blocks, he should see a group of apes playing fiddles on the side of the road.

He hears a ruckus coming from the road, and he decides to join the crowd instead of being alone in the blackness. Oil lanterns illume the cobblestone world and all of its crooked inhabitants.

It is a melting pot of madness. People fill the streets, laughing, shoving, and babbling, many having already traded their wits for a pint of bourbon. Those lucid enough to see straight have pulled out hand-held instruments and formed a crude symphony— flutes and fiddles, ukuleles and euphoniums, bongos, bagpipes, and bugles. This scene is what many cities would call insanity, but London calls it Tuesday night.

Tim relaxes and holds his suitcase to his side. He strolls down the middle of the street, feeling in his element. He has been surrounded by eccentric blokes for the past five years and, if push comes to sucker punch, he is more than confident in his ability to talk himself out of a shady situation.

Now, where is that carriage station? Tim scans the buildings that line the street: laundromat, musket shop, Buckstars Brewery, inn, pet salon, another Buckstars Brewery…but no carriage station that he can see.

He sighs and runs a hand through his hair. If he doesn't get to the station soon, it's likely that the Ambassador will be gone, and then Tim will know nothing about his task except that his brother is having "problems."

At a crossroads, a squat tavern glows warmly like the Pearly Gates, and the crowd of soused patrons gathered by the entrance looks like a group of sinners about to be told by Peter that they're in the wrong place. A sign dangling over the door advertises the tavern's name: *The Bombastic Baron*.

Deciding he needs to ask for directions, Tim tucks his case in the crook of his arm, as he would a swaddled babe, and enters the tavern. His nostrils instantly regret that decision.

He has stepped into a different world. Light is scarce, but there is an overabundance of customers, whiskey, and reckless laughter. Dozens upon dozens of men are packed into the tavern, each gripping a frothing goblet. They sit around rickety tables, swapping words that sound more like slurs. A huge bar faces the thirsty from the far side of the room, a hairy-jowled bartender stationed behind it.

Tim gulps.

Which gentleman would be best to ask for directions? The husky Hungarian with a lopsided glass eye and a neck tattoo of a spider? Or perhaps the chap currently involved in an intense bout of mead-chugging?

The bartender is probably the safest bet. Tim begins to squeeze his way between the packed tables, heading for the bar.

Snippets of conversation drift through the air, quotes completely without context, stories that Tim will never know the endings to.

"More mead! Wench, more ale!"

"I ran into some loony Spaniard the other day. Gave him a piece of my mind, I did."

"And that's how to get blood out of velvet."

"Forget what Elizabeth says. I didn't vote for her."

"Aye, the doctor said that no one should be within five feet of me."

Just keep moving, ole Tim. No eye contact, no sudden movements…

He bumps into a gargantuan brute holding a bottle in each hand. The man glares down at Tim and rumbles, "Can I help you, Sparkle-Soles?"

Tim's gut drops into his feet. "N-No, I-I-I mean…I'm sorry, Mister—"

The brute drops his bottles and draws a long, slender knife from a sheath on his belt. He waves the blade back and forth, making Tim stiffen in fright. "I don't like your face, Skippy."

This is why I don't come to these sorts of places. I'm way more "drama workshop" than "gym class."

"Now, I don't want trouble," Tim says, frantically backpedaling. "I'm just in here to ask for—"

He backs straight into what feels like the Great Wall. He stumbles and falls onto his gluteus, feeling liquid trickle over his head. He holds his suitcase in front of his body to protect himself from the blade, but nothing happens.

In fact, the knife-wielding brute has turned from a mountain lion to a kitten. Face pale, he quietly retreats into the crowd.

What spooked that thug so much?

"You made me spill my rum," a voice growls from above.

Tim looks up and sees that he has backed into a new breed of trouble. He quickly jumps to his feet and sizes up his new opponents.

He nearly wets his trousers.

A horde of beefy, grimy, sneering men sit around a table, tattered clothing hanging from their bodies. Many sport wiry beards and metallic teeth. One has a patch covering his right eye. A rank stench wafts from the group, like a dead fish that's been sunbathing for a week. Each man glowers at Tim with a mixture of amusement and loathing. Then Tim sees the arsenal that each thug carries. Pistols, daggers, iron grenades, and cleavers dangle from their belts, silently begging some poor fool to challenge them.

But they are nothing compared to the beast that stands at the head of the table. The beast that seems to lead the pack. The beast that Tim has inadvertently angered.

"I said…" the monstrous leader grumbles in an incredibly thick Russian accent, showing off yellow teeth, "…you spilled my rum." After taking a heavy step forward, he tosses his mug across the bar, not looking to see where it lands. "I would like another."

He wears a long, frayed coat that was once a regal scarlet. His beard holds an art gallery of items, everything from leaves to bread crumbs. An old spyglass hangs from his belt, which seems to be the color of human flesh. A huge tricorne hat contains his wild locks. Rings adorn each skeletal, hairy finger on his right hand, but his left hand has been replaced with a curved hook that could gut an overweight elephant.

"S-Sorry, Guv—" Tim eyes the tricorne and tries to get on the man's good side. "Captain. I'm terribly sorry, Captain."

"I don't want apologies," the Russian snarls. "I want more rum."

The Captain's crew stands from the table, snickering as they draw their weapons. Tim backs away from the group of aggressors, even though that's what got him into hot water with these Russians in the first place. If the knife-wielding brute, who seemed threatening enough, is scared of these guys, then Tim definitely doesn't want to get mixed up with them.

"I'll get you and your boys a round, how about that? Will that make up for it?"

The Captain hacks, which Tim supposes is a laugh. "You sure are spineless, aren'cha, Tory? But sure, a round of drinks on you." He adjusts his hat with his hook, and the crew cheers violently. As they return to the table, Tim releases a breath of relief.

"You need to grow some grapes, Englishman." The Captain slaps Tim's back, pushing him toward their table. "Sit. Drink with us humble privateers." The crew laughs.

Tim gives them a shaky smile as he eases into a chair. He clutches his suitcase even closer to his chest.

The Captain lands next to him. "So, what do the locals call you?"

"M-My name?" Tim's mind races. For some reason, he doesn't think that giving these men his real name is a swell idea. "I am named…Tom." He has never been particularly proud of his improv skills.

"Well, Tom, this here," the Captain swings his hook over his men, a prideful gleam in his gaze, "is the crew of the *Crimean Cavalier*, the most feared vessel from the Baltic to the Mediterranean and back again!"

Tim's jaw hangs open. "The *Crimean Cavalier*? You mean Satan's Schooner, the Iron Fist of Rurik, the Russian Craft of Terror? That *Crimean Cavalier*?"

"You've heard of us?"

"More than heard of you. Your ship is dreaded by every able-minded man around these ports. In fact, there's a common saying: Fear the *Cavalier*."

A cackle jumps out of the Captain's throat. "Hear that, boys? Fear the *Cavalier*!"

His men repeat the cadence and take swigs of their drinks.

Whew. Looks like I found their one weakness: intense flattery.

Tim feels his nerves start to relax. Ironic, because he just found out that he's sharing a table with some of the most bloodthirsty pirates on the globe.

Leaning in his chair, he offhandedly asks, "So what's your moniker, Captain?"

"Me?" The seaman smirks and uses his hook to scratch a stained tooth. "Some call me the Seven Seas Caesar. To others, I am the Red Wraith, or perhaps the Plunderer from Down Underer. My real name, though, the one my comrades and crew use, is...*Captain Lidiya Travkin!*" He raises his hook triumphantly, which streaks in the lantern light. His men shout and applaud.

"Lydia?" Tim asks.

"No, no, no, not Lydia," the Captain says. He then thunders, "*Lydiya!*"

Tim nods. "Right...Just didn't know that Lydia was a man's name."

One of the crewmen calls out, "It ain't!"

Travkin whips out a pistol and fires. The crewman catches the bullet with his chest, and then flops over. His body is snagged and quickly carted outside—Tim never even sees the corpse. The process is extremely efficient, as if Travkin has done this sort of thing countless times.

Everyone in the bar looks over at the scene, beginning to protest the hostility, but one look at the Captain and his pistol makes them think twice. After a moment, they all turn back to their own business.

Tim freezes in his seat. All relaxation immediately vaporizes. He doesn't budge an inch, as if sudden movement will attract more violence. The acidic stench of gunpowder singes the inside of his nose.

The night has taken quite a turn.

The Captain puts away his gun, smiling again, as if he has just smelled a delightful bouquet instead of committing homicide against one of his own men. "So, where ya from, Tom?"

No words come to Tim's mind. Except for, *Leave, run, flee, vamoose, get outta here, you dunce!*

"Uh…I-I…maybe…" *Say something! Or else Vlad the Insaner will get suspicious!* "I really should be going…" He begins to stand, keeping his suitcase between his torso and Captain Travkin.

"Hey, now, where ya off to in such a hurry? Slow down!"

"Why?" Tim's wit kicks in despite his better judgment. "Everyone else is Russian around here."

"Ha! I like you, Tom."

"Thanks…I'd offer you my hand, but I don't think I'd get it back."

The Captain shrugs. "Eh, that's probably true."

Tim forces a chuckle and tries to walk away from the table of pirates. "Well, it's been fun talking with you…"

A smile plays across Travkin's lips. "You seem nervous. Is it the hook? The teeth? The horde of hairy, smelly, heavily-armed pirates?" He cackles.

"It's definitely two of those things." Tim turns to sprint, but he finds a couple of burly Russians blocking his way. They grasp his arms and shove him back into the chair.

Travkin says, "Have a drink, Tom," as if nothing is out of the ordinary.

Tim gulps, feeling ice creep through his veins. "Okay…Captain…"

"You see," the pirate locks eyes with him, "I've seen you around London. Running in and outta the Centre. I never knew your name, but I could tell that you work at the theatre. You're a man about town. You know all sorts of people. Rich, important, famous people."

"Now, that's not entirely accurate—"

"Never interrupt me. Like I said, I like you. You're not the uptight petunia I thought you would be, so please don't make me gut you." He nonchalantly sets his left "hand" on the table as a visual aide. "Now…Hard times have befallen the boys of the *Cavalier*. Pockets are empty. Worse, our reputation is diminishing. Despite your 'fear the *Cavalier*' drivel, we are quickly losing the fame that we once had."

"What about the Red Wraith, the Seven Seas Caesar?" Tim desperately asks, cold sweat forming on his brow.

"Relics," Travkin snarls. "Names of a myth rather than a current threat. No one has knocked their knees at the sight of us in years. We need to get back on top. We *must* strike horror into the hearts of men once more. And you're going to help us do that."

"H-How…?"

"Your connections. The one thing that will get us back in the headlines is a high-profile kidnapping. Not only will we get a glorious ransom, but also my name will be known again. All you have to do is choose the target and lead us to him. Think you can handle that, Tom?"

Tim has no words. All he had wanted to do was ask for directions to the carriage station. Now he has been roped into a kidnapping plot led by a washed-up Russian pirate with a lady's name.

Talk. Talk about everything. Talk about nothing. Get them talking. Talk your way out. Just talk.

Tim talks. "Well, I suppose it all depends on what sort of person you want to take hold of. There are actors, businessmen, bankers, fashionistas, royalty, architects—"

Travkin's eyes widen. "Royalty…" he breathes. "That's sure to get our name back out there. What royalty do you know?"

Certainly not the twin of the Prince of Denmark, that's for sure.

Tim clears his throat, mind racing. "Uh…Well, I'm sure you've heard of our Queen Elizabeth. Nice lady, I bet she'd help you out. Er, and then there's good ole Boris the First, your man in Russia. There's Fortinbras in Norway, he's one tough croissant. Ponhea of Cambodia, he's a personal friend. Charles in Sweden, Prince Bourbon in France, Philip in Portugal…Do any of them float your boat?"

A pirate across the table slurs, "I like bourbon!"

The Captain growls to the man, "That's a name, you currish barnacle, not a drink." He returns his scrutiny to Tim. "What about Denmark?"

Phlegm lodges in Tim's throat, and he nearly coughs. "Um, what about it?" His heart beats faster.

Does Travkin know who I really am?

"Their king, Hammond, died about a month ago. To swipe one of his heirs would be deliciously diabolical." He chuckles at the thought. "They'd pay anything to get their precious prince back."

The pirate who has an affinity for bourbon speaks up again: "Precious princes…They think they're better than us, those airy, half-faced boars."

Another crewman responds, "Shut yer trap, Pavlo. You'd chew a turtle's teat for the chance to be a prince."

"Would not! That's sick!" Pavlo says. He puffs out his chest. "I'd take on Denmark's whole army wearing nothing but chaps and ice skates. You, Lukas, you'd run home like a baby!"

Lukas' face turns purple. "There's no need for name-calling, you mewling maggot-pie."

Pavlo laughs, "Yer just a coward! A craven! A chicken! Buck, buck, buck!"

"Hey! No one poorly imitates my favorite farm animal! I'll knock you to the moon someday, I swear…"

"Don't swear, that's a sin!"

"Yer mother's a sin!"

The table erupts in drunken hoots and hollers. The pirates rib one another, the alcohol in their bellies turning them into the very farm animals Pavlo had mimicked.

Travkin raises his voice. "Simmer down, men."

No one listens. They keep laughing and shoving each other.

"Pigs!" the Captain bellows. "Shut up, you beetle-brained idiots!"

Still, the pirates don't pay their leader any mind.

Tim gets an idea. It's suicidal, but so is staying with Travkin and his boys. It's worth a try.

The Captain screams at his crew, "Close your bleedin' stew-holes, or I'll use my hook to give you a few extra nostrils!"

"Allow me," Tim hisses. Then he jumps out of his chair, swinging his suitcase like an Olympic hammer thrower. It smashes right into a pirate's face. The thug tumbles backward and rolls across the wooden floor.

Travkin glares at Tim with pure venom. "Tom, you British chum…" He raises his hook and swipes it straight for Tim's heart…

…but the young prince is too swift. Tim thrusts his suitcase into the curved blade. Travkin withdraws his left hand, finding that his hook is embedded in the luggage.

Pavlo gapes at the pirate sprawled on the floor. He screams, "What's happenin'?"

"Hey!" Lukas jumps up and glares at Pavlo. "Why'd you knock over Mikhail?!"

"I didn't!"

"Yer goin' to the moon!" Lukas lunges at Pavlo, and they collapse in a pile of fists and cursing.

The table explodes, the pirates cawing at one another like provoked mongooses. Vicious brawls break out, the crew of the *Cavalier* spiraling downward into a good old-fashioned Russian гражданская война.

The Captain shakes his left arm, trying to fling the suitcase off of his hook, but it stays lodged. He roars, "Tom, you're a dead man!"

Tim turns and runs toward the back of the bar, deeper into the crowd. By now, the patrons of the *Bombastic Baron* are ruffled, trying to catch glimpses of the massive horde of wrestling pirates. He quickly blends into the living camouflage.

The roars of Travkin fade as the throngs of people begin to react to the violence in their beloved pub.

"Oy, what's goin' on?"

"Fight, you Ruski! Fight, fight!"

"Rip his ears off and use 'em as puppets!"

"Don't spill the ale!"

A band of minstrels in a corner spots the fight. One of them grins, "Lookie, boys! And a-one, a-two…" They pick up their instruments and begin playing upbeat, twanged music.

The music is like oil poured over a flame. The brawlers get more energetic, throwing more punches, rolling around, growling, biting, shouting, all to the rhythm of the minstrels' melodies.

All except Travkin. He shoves through the crowd, paying no attention to the chaos. His eyes scan the tavern, searching for the man he thinks is named Tom—the man who could lead him to fame once again, the man who has made a fool of him.

"Come out and face me, you British lily!"

Tim has no intention of coming out and facing the big hairy Russian. He crouches behind the bar, among hundreds of bottles of frothy alcohol. Hopefully the Captain won't get thirsty and find his hiding spot.

A gunshot rattles the pub. Looks like the scuffle has graduated to an all-out battle.

Suddenly, a man flies over the bar with a squeamish scream. He lands facedown on the wooden floorboards, unconscious, tongue hanging out. Tim recognizes him as the huge brute who had drawn a knife on him earlier. With the war raging on, Tim thinks arming himself might be a good idea. He takes the slender blade from the man's sheath, steadies it in front of himself, and jumps out from behind the bar.

Time to leave.

He bounds across the tavern, weaving between bodies like a sewing needle. Heavy smoke floats through the air, stinging his eyes, but he ignores it and looks for the exit.

There. The oaken door that leads outside. The Gates of Paradise. About ten meters away.

"Там!" A monstrous Russian voice explodes through the bar. "Стой, британский слабак!"

Tim doesn't understand a word of that, but he recognizes Captain Travkin's bark and guesses it isn't too kind.

Sure enough, the tricorne hat appears, standing between Tim and the door. Travkin has dislodged the suitcase from his hook, making him look once again like the nightmarish Red Wraith that haunts the European seas.

"I'm gonna slice out your liver and use it as a canteen, Tom. You and me." He upholds his hook. "C'mon!"

Tim gulps, sheets of terror nearly drowning him where he stands. The snarling captain takes a step forward, and Tim nearly collapses.

He firmly grips the knife in his right hand.

He glances at it curiously. He hadn't consciously done that. Some sort of primeval instinct had taken over.

And suddenly, he remembers—he's back in Elsinore, dressed in white, a mesh mask covering his face. He holds a thin sabre, slices it through the air. His feet dance across the stone floor, too swift for any man to catch. He challenges Osric and wins. He challenges his father, the aides, the guards, and he defeats them all.

He challenges Hamlet. And he wins.

Tim was the fencing champion of Elsinore, able to cut down any opponent faster than a clock chime. He had forgotten. How could he forget something like that?

But he hasn't truly forgotten. He still has the skills—they're just buried under layers and layers of flopped stage productions. He's still the undisputed swordsman of Denmark.

"Aw," the captain says, bringing Tim's mind back into the tavern, "gonna dye yer trousers, Tom, you dandelion? C'mon and fight me!"

Tim cracks the joints in his neck, washing away the doubts in his mind. Sparks settle in his gut and quickly grow into a glowing fire. His long-prodigal confidence returns. A smile crawls across his face. He grips the knife and spreads his feet apart, equally distributing his weight.

"*En garde, mauviette.*"

The Captain lunges, hook flying through the air. Instead of reeling backward, Tim charges straight at his opponent, doing the opposite of what the pirate expects. Travkin screeches to a stop to avoid a head-on collision, throwing him off balance. Just as Tim expects.

Tim swipes his long knife upward, trapping it in the curve of Travkin's hook. Subsequently, Travkin's left arm is pulled up too, leaving his torso unprotected.

Tim then does something he didn't learn in fencing lessons.

He rams his knee into the Captain's billiards.

"Aw, *Bolshevik,*" Travkin curses, doubling over in agony and carefully grasping his jewels.

Tim begins to sprint for the exit, but Travkin quickly straightens up and holds out his hook again.

"Not so fast, Tom," he squawks.

"I'm out of Russian jokes, Captain. I can't do this all day." Tim thrusts with his knife and goes on the offensive.

Cut, advance, appel, feint, advance again, flank from the right, parry, strike…

A giddy laugh blooms from Tim's throat. How could he have forgotten the thrill of facing an opponent from behind a foil?

Travkin grinds his golden gnashers. "You laugh at me?" His rage comes not only from Tim's cackle, but also from the fact that a so-called British lily is beating the so-called pirate legend in a bout of swashbuckling. Any self-respecting pirate must be good at three things: getting blind drunk, bedding vaguely attractive women (the first two things are connected), and sword fighting. He cannot allow some sniveling, round-kneed writer to out-swash him.

With renewed vigor and anger, Travkin roars and hacks at his foe with his lefty limb. He discards all tact and strategy, allowing his rabid rage to take over.

Tim jumps to the side and rolls over an abandoned table. He stares at the Captain, the table separating them for a brief respite. Tim brandishes his knife. "Captain, we can talk calmly, or I can keep outmaneuvering you until the sun rises. Your choice."

Travkin hocks a phlegmy lump from his throat and launches it across the no-man's-land of the table. So much for talking calmly. He raises his hook and charges around the table. Tim runs the opposite direction. Like Achilles chasing Hector, they loop around and around and around and around the table.

After their fifth circuit, the Russian barks, places his hands under the wooden surface, and flips the table across the pub. It lands on a handful of brawling patrons, flattening them like tipsy rag dolls.

The Captain smirks.

Tim gulps. He strikes with his long knife, but Travkin traps it in the curve of his hook just as Tim did earlier. The Russian flicks his arm, ripping the weapon from Tim's grip and sending it flying. It soars across the bar and stabs into the far wall, quivering in fear for a few moments.

The fear is infectious. Tim's mind nearly freezes in arrhythmia. Here he is, unarmed, opposing a blood-guzzling pirate.

My odds are not favorable. Tim silently awards himself the title Understater of the Century.

"I'll rip ya limb from limb…" Travkin stalks forward, relishing the fact that he can now make good on his grisly threats. He runs forward with his hook ready to gouge. His arm is a waving windmill, all previous tact and skill gone. Now, he attacks with the veracity of a wild animal.

Tim yelps and flattens himself on the wooden floor, like one of a thousand bootprints. He starts to crawl between the brawlers' legs.

"Stop running across the floor like a cockroach!" Travkin swipes his hook, but Tim rolls out of the way.

"Cockroaches are immortal!" he responds.

"I eat measly cockroaches like you for breakfast!"

Tim opens his mouth for a witty retort, but then he looks closer and sees an insect leg tangled in the pirate's beard. Apparently he's being literal.

The Captain springs forward and wraps his bony digits around Tim's ankle. He drags the young prince to his feet and pushes his hook against the fleshy apple of his throat. "Finally…"

Tim Hamlet shuts his eyes and prepares to pass into the next life. Maybe he'll be chained to this mortal world as a misty specter until his uncompleted task is righted, just like his late father. Maybe he'll meet the angels and apostles at the Shining Gates. Or maybe—unless he speeds up his last-minute confessions—he'll spend eternity bathing in magma and searching for a flashlight.

No matter the outcome, Travkin's hook will ensure that his time on Earth is over.

A *crunch* fills the pub. A splintery, cracking, wooden *crunch*.

"Nobody move!"

The voice of an authority figure grinds the drunken violence to a screeching halt. All heads, including those of Tim and Travkin, swivel to the front door that Tim had been trying to reach so desperately. Now, the oaken door hangs on its hinges, kicked in by a gleaming leather boot.

Entering the scene is a flock of English patrolmen, led by a scruffy-looking Constable. He motions to his men, who begin to fan out among the crowd, some wielding rifles, others holding batons. The badges affixed to their jackets clash with the grimy, lawless tavern like a bust of Athena above the altar of a Lutheran church.

Travkin stares at the Constable as if he is an interesting piece of art, nothing more. He doesn't release Tim, nor does he lower his hook. To say the least, this is not the effect Tim had hoped a police officer would have on the Captain.

The Constable sizes up the *Bombastic Baron* with beady eyes, then straightens his cufflinks. "This ruckus shall end at once, lest any blood be splint. I will tolerate no democracy on my night watch, understand?"

Confusion grips Tim's mind despite the blade to his throat. He is fairly certain that the policeman meant *spilt* and *debauchery*, but the Constable had spoken with such confidence that no one else in the bar seemed to catch his misspeaks.

"Finally. A little respect," the Constable mutters. He begins to pace through the pub, adjusting his cufflinks, his collar, the badges on his breast.

The presence of the law does nothing to deter the bloodlust in Travkin's eyes. In fact, his hook presses a little harder against Tim's neck, as if the arrival of the policemen makes him feel the need to reassert his reputation as the Red Wraith.

A trickle of blood seeps from Tim's throat. He winces, "Uh, copper, a little help, please?"

Travkin growls to the Constable, "Stay out of this, Dogberry, if you ever want to walk in a straight line again."

The Constable named Dogberry seems to be accustomed to threats from the Russian pirate. He merely hoists the belt of his trousers. "Sure thing, Captain…" He reaches for his buttons, continuing his quest to adjust his every article of clothing he has, but he suddenly freezes. A mixture of surprise and vague recognition plays across his face.

Tim gulps, sharing a stare with Dogberry. He plants his feet on the ground, preparing to make a break for it.

The Constable squints, as if that will improve his vision. "No, it can't be…Prince Hamlet, is that you?"

Travkin turns his attention back to Tim. "Prince?" His brows furrow deeply. Bit by bit, he realizes that the man he's holding a blade to could be his ticket to international fame and a king-sized ransom.

And he also realizes that Tim has been playing him for a fool. "*Prince?!*"

Tim chuckles innocently. "Yeah, how 'bout that?"

The next few moments are a maelstrom of movement and noise.

Tim shoves his heels against the floorboards, flinging himself backwards, away from Travkin and his hook. Dogberry yells something, and the pregnant silence bursts. The tavern plunges back into chaos, police presence be damned.

All air rushes from his lungs as Tim lands hard on his back. He rolls across the floorboards, not looking where he's headed. All he knows is that he needs to get away from Travkin. Not even the entire Royal Guard would be able to quell the Russian's newfound fury, all of which is directed at him.

Why did I have to ask for bloody directions?

Another war has broken out in the *Bombastic Baron*. Knives, punches, and insults fly back and forth between the Russian pirates, the drunken patrons, and the English patrolmen. Even with the introduction of the police's rifles and batons, the pirates seem to hold the upper hand with their fists and pure savagery.

The pirate called Lukas jumps onto a table, clutching a medieval flail. Where he got a flail, no one will ever know. He scans the fight, venom in his eyes. He bellows, "Yer goin' to the moon, Pavlo!" Swinging the flail, he snarls and dives back into the crowd.

Tim sprints to the exit. He jumps over a toppled chair, ducks under an arcing sword, sidesteps a grappling twosome, and shoves another angry brawler aside. His escape is so close, he can smell the lantern oil from the streetlamps.

And just like that, he's there. He finally reaches the exit, then stops in the empty doorframe to survey the chaos of the *Baron*.

On the far side of the pub, Captain Travkin snarls and swings his hook at three patrolmen. His tricorn hat has an arrow stabbed through it. "Do you frilly Brits know who I am?! I am Lidiya Travkin of the *Crimean Cavalier*!"

The patrolmen pause for a moment.

"Who?" one says.

Travkin sighs, looking truly crestfallen. "Travkin, the Red Wraith? Captain of Satan's Schooner?" He lowers his hook. "Just forget it…"

"Is Lydia a man's name?" another patrolman asks, confused.

The Captain's lip curls. Then he spots Tim loitering in the door, outlined against the darkness. His anger resurfaces with a roar.

"Hamlet!" he yells, locking eyes with Tim over the crowds and across the pub. The air shimmers with his rage. "I'll find you, hear me? I will find you, and you will be my prisoner! Watch yer step! You will never be rid of me! I'll pull out yer spleen and use it as a jump rope! I'll cream you, you cream-filled Danish! Not even a chameleon can hide from me! I'll kick a puppy and make you watch! I'll beat you senseless with a baguette and then make myself a sandwich! You better run…!"

Tim rolls his eyes and leaves.

He hurries away from the tavern he had entered about twenty minutes earlier. So much had happened in that short amount of time…and yet very little had been accomplished. He has lost his suitcase, and all he has gained is a racing heart and a few new derogative nicknames. And the local police now know that the Danish prince is in London. *And* he still has no idea where the carriage station and the Ambassador are.

Achy muscles. A pounding head. A sense of total hopelessness.

So this is what family reunions are like. No wonder I've stayed away from Elsinore all these years.

He keeps his pace at a steady trot, moving through downtown as quickly as possible. The lively vagabonds have left the streets, leaving behind an empty, ethereal eeriness. Very little light bleeds from surrounding buildings, and even the moon is shy.

All he wants to see is the Danish Ambassador's face. Even his bile-colored uniform would be a sight for sore eyes.

A breeze licks his face. Salt.

He has arrived at a port on the River Thames. Docks rest in the shallow shore of the gushing river, and a large crowd mingles nearby. Maybe they're waiting to depart, maybe they just arrived from another nation.

Tim approaches the throng of people, searching for the Ambassador. Perhaps the Dane has wandered here, looking for Tim? He sure hopes so. He's tired of this night and its misadventures.

"Hello?" he yells into the crowd. "*Monsieur* Ambassador? Now would be a great time to show up out of nowhere!"

A few curious bystanders glance his direction, but otherwise, he may as well be invisible in such a huge crowd.

He groans and dives deeper into the crowd on the dock. His shoes thud on the wooden floor and echo off the water underneath. He stands on the caps of his toes to scan the bustling throng. Stretched out before him are dozens of faces he has never beheld and never will again.

Then, his night takes another turn. Two voices yell his name at the same time—one from the city behind him, the other from the crowd on the docks.

"Tim? Tim!" the voice from the docks says—bright, sunny, buoyant.

"Hamlet!" the voice from the city screams—enraged, raspy, grisly, and Russian. Very Russian.

Tim instinctively spins around in the direction of the murderous yeller. He has a few guesses as to who it is, and the sight of the tricorne hat bobbing up and down toward him confirms his suspicions.

Captain Travkin sprints out of the urban growth, brandishing his hook like an Olympic torch. His eyes are those of a starved jaguar. He doesn't care about the horde of witnesses on the docks—he fully intends to swipe his blade across Tim's gut and see what color his innards are.

Next, Tim looks into the crowd, searching for the other person who recognizes him. There, amidst the mass—a beaming smirk he knows and tolerates.

A lanky Athenian chap in a mismatched suit waves at him. "Tim, you highfalutin son of a gypsum! How've you been?" Nick Bottom shoulders his way through the crowd, trying to get closer to Tim.

Tim sizes up his options in a blink. He moves to intercept Nick.

"Why, Nick!" he forces joviality into his voice, acting as though a livid pirate isn't hunting him at this very moment. "How long has it been?"

"Three seasons, at least! Why, I haven't corresponded with you since I saw your magnum opus, *Queen Arthur in Hamalot*!" Nick reaches out to embrace his old friend.

But Tim wraps an arm around Nick's shoulders and spins him about-face, walking away from the city, away from the charging Russian.

Nick Bottom: six feet tall, one-hundred-forty pounds with rocks in his pockets, past the prime of his life. Quite past it—he's closer to seventy than sixty. He's an actor, or as he puts it, a *"thespian artist."* It would not be unusual to see Nick strutting around wearing a thick scarf in the middle of summer, or a strange pelt he claims is "wildly popular in Florence…but I'm sure no one here has caught on yet." Indeed, Nick Bottom is the sort of man who fancies himself above the mainstream blockbusters that other actors dream of headlining. He and Tim met a while back in a marketplace, and Nick latched onto the young playwright immediately. He has performed in a number of Tim's plays at the Masterpiece Centre, including *Sicily in the Spring* and *Henry XXX*.

Nick fancies himself the greatest actor in Athens, if not the known world. The problem is, he is the only person who thinks this. His skills on stage do not line up with his inflated self-image. One famed reviewer once penned a scathing editorial, saying "Nick Bottom has done to theatre what Brutus did to Caesar, except Brutus at least knew he was murdering something great. Bottom is utterly lost in his own world of *amour-propre,* and he never fails to make an ass of himself."

But Nick had paid that review no mind—just one of the critics, and haters shall hate. On the other hand, Tim, the director and writer of these shows, had paid the review a great deal of mind and never asked Nick to audition for another one of his productions.

And now here they are, side-by-side in the dead of night, with an upset pirate chasing one of them.

"Now, Tim," Nick says, letting the young prince guide him deeper into the crowd, toward the Thames, "when are the auditions for your next show? I believe I've seen signs for it around town. Something or other about Marge and Tina?"

"I, uh…" Tim shoots a glance over his shoulder. Travkin is gaining. "I'm not sure, Guv. Say, are you headed somewhere?"

"Why, yes!" Nick exclaims, overjoyed to tell of his exploits. "I was just in London for a few hours today to conduct some business with our mutual comrade Don Martizoa. Now I'm boarding a ship for Sweden, where I shall star in a wonderful little production. It's an independent play, very underground, you've probably never heard of it…"

Sweden…Just a hopscotch away from Denmark. From home.

"That's fascinating, Nick," Tim smiles, letting the actor lead him to a waiting rowboat. "Y'know, I'm ashamed that I haven't kept in touch with you—" The two step into the boat. "—because you truly are an amazing actor. One of the greats!—" They sit down, and the cabbie pushes off from the dock. "—Your work at the Centre was an inspiration. A miracle! Sophocles himself would beg you to star in his shows—"

The port fades into the distance as the rowboat bobs down the river. Tim has successfully hitched a ride with Nick. Behind a veil of fog, the tricorn hat stands on the edge of the dock, watching the prince of Denmark float away.

Tim pats Nick's knobby knee. "Why, I think we were destined to meet on that dock tonight, Bottom ole boy."

Nick replies with a warm smile. "I think so too, my Danish delight. Now, what were you saying about me being one of the greats…?"

Chapter 4

Their small rowboat floats through the thick ink of the Thames. Tim cranes his head to see their destination a few hundred yards yonder: a large commercial schooner, its two towering masts flapping in the cool breeze. He smiles, picturing himself sailing far, far away from London. Toward Elsinore.

"…and then I took a role in a play by *Monsieur* Franz Kaka, *Où Ai-je Reçois Tous Ces Citrons*. It's a very deep story, most existential. One audience member said that my performance changed her life. I was honored to be a part of it…"

Nick is still yammering.

Tim nods, politely humoring his friend. It's the least he can do, since Nick quite possibly saved his life by letting him tag along.

"Anyhoo, how've you been, my crème de la crème? Any new plots simmering up in that eggshell of yours?"

"Not currently, Nick," Tim smiles, remembering why he had become friends with Nick in the first place. "Right now, I'm heading home."

"Home?" the actor says, gaping his mouth to a comedic length. "Your cradle? Your natural habitat? The resting place of your ancestors, and the inheritance of your progeny? *Maison*? *Haus*? *Su casa*? Dare I say it…Denmark?"

Tim sighs and nods. "Elsinore, the one and only."

Nick rocks to and fro, exaggerating his shock—for dramatic effect, Tim supposes. "I don't believe it! Say it isn't so." A dollop of seawater splashes the cabbie's feet—he glares at Nick, and the rocking ceases.

The actor readjusts his mismatched suit, clearly annoyed at being silenced by a non-thespian. "But honestly, Tim," he continues, "why are you going back? The way you told it, they may as well have stolen your lunch and spat upon your shoes. They hated you, for Hecuba's sake!"

"Well, I didn't exactly live up to their expectations..."

"So?" Nick gesticulates wildly. "Who gives a flying frippery what anyone thinks? Look at me! The *Athens Gazette* called me one of the worst actors ever to be onstage. What did I do? I continued performing anyway! And when no one came to see my shows, what then? I jumped on a schooner and took my talent to the masses! Expectations, bah! Why, if I cowered before the expectations of the authorities, I would not be where I am today!"

Tim doesn't think that's the best example, but he keeps his mouth shut.

"I'm a primary artist, a thespian of the theatre! I have touched the depths of Truth—with a capital T, by the way—and performed in the most beautiful locales across the known world. I may not be John Hemmings or Richard Burbage, but I'm doing well for myself. I never dream of food, nor do I get wet when it rains."

Their small rowboat reaches the huge commercial schooner, otherwise Tim is sure that Nick would just keep going.

But he has a point, Tim thinks. *Nick cares so little about expectations, he wears mismatching suits. And he's as happy as a clam.*

A gruff voice bellows from the ship—"Ahoy!"—as a thin ladder made of crusty rope rolls down the side.

"I suppose this is where we get off," Nick says. He stands and tips his head toward the cabbie. "Evening." He sizes up the ladder, which is bobbing and weaving like a piñata, thanks to the Thames's current. The small rowboat and the large schooner jerk about at different rates, haphazardly moving up, down, and sideways without warning. Even for an athlete, getting from the rowboat to the ladder would be difficult—and Nick Bottom isn't exactly an Olympian.

With the agility of a newborn foal wearing ice skates, the actor manages to hop out of the boat and snag the ropes.

Once Nick is midway up the ladder, the cabbie tells Tim it's his turn.

Goodie gumdrops. This is like playing darts after downing a whole round of scotch.

He stands and wipes his sweaty palms on his trousers. The unsteady rowboat nearly makes him drop to his knees. Despite his better judgment, he leans over the side of the boat, and a swirling stew of dark water stares back. It might as well be the River Styx as the Thames. Never before has the young prince felt so—

"Just jump, you wuss," the cabbie growls.

Tim snorts. This sort of heady philosophizing is something his twin brother would do, not him. He claps his hands once and springs out of the rowboat.

Sure enough, he is far more agile than his friend Nick, and he snags the rope ladder with relative ease. The cords are coarse from years of manhandling in the salty Northern air. Tim makes sure he has a firm grip with both hands and both feet, and he begins to ascend.

The strong sea breeze prickles the hairs on his neck, the Thames's current literally rocks his world, and the gritty ropes scuff his palms. His head and legs still ache from the barroom brawl with the Russian pirates where he very nearly lost his life. His suitcase is lost somewhere in that very bar, and his pockets are completely empty. All of this began because of some mysterious mission involving his royal brother.

He hasn't felt this alive in years. A smile grows on his face.

The vessel he scales is truly massive. He reaches the top of the rope ladder and scans the ship. It is robust, tall and powerful, but narrow and efficient, like a buoyant rhinoceros. The two masts stretch to the starless sky, and the tallest bears the Prince's Flag of the Dutch Republic. Judging by the schooner's nationality and its destination of Sweden, Tim guesses it's a Bilander, a particularly lithe ship designed to navigate Holland's hairpin canals. He supposes this sort of ship was needed to pick up its thespian passenger in the Thames, and the open sea is its next call.

Nick Bottom stands next to the ship's handrails, grooming his ruffled hair. "Ah, I'm glad you made it, young squire." He sighs. "I hope you didn't see me climbing that infernal ladder."

Tim laughs softly. "No, Nick. I was a little busy myself."

"Good. You may not believe this, but I am no longer the physical specimen I once was. Squirming my way up the side of this boat, I looked like quite the *burro*, as a Frenchman might say, if he also spoke Spanish."

"No worries, Nick. We're here now. Trouble is behind us, right?"

There is a brief period of silence—save for the gurgling water sliced apart by the advancing schooner—as Tim's words sink in.

But then a voice calls out from below.

"Uh…Excuse me, fellas…Would it be too much trouble to pull me abroad?"

Tim and Nick stare at each other for a moment.

"Are my eyes failing me," Tim says slowly, "or were there only you, me, and the cabbie in that rowboat?"

"If you're crazy, then we're having the same aural mirage," Nick says. "Who the blazes could that be?"

The voice speaks again, "Anytime soon would be swell." It sounds out of breath and strained, like a bodybuilder holding a boulder above his head…or maybe like a man who swam all the way down the Thames, climbed up the side of a schooner, and is now dangling from the side.

The latter simile is more likely.

He and Nick lean over the ship's splintered handrail and see a man clinging to the side like a gigantic barnacle. A policeman, completely soaked, his scraggly hair and scragglier clothing stuck to his body. His long coat droops, practically a second flag for the ship to sail under. Tim squints to see better in the darkness, but the long coat sure looks familiar…

The man looks up at Tim and Nick. "Evening, Your Majesty. Constable Eustace Dogberry, at your service."

Tim gapes, at a complete loss. He and Nick reach out and pull him onto the Bilander.

"Constable…Why did you follow us?"

"Well, Highness," the dripping stick figure says as he stands on the deck, "you are quite a ways from your palace. As an officer above the law, I considered it my duty to escort you and your companion to safety and out of Travkin's pointy clutches."

Tim glances around—he clearly escaped Travkin without Dogberry's direct assistance. But the constable stares at him with wide eyes and a wider smile, like a puppy that brought its master a pair of slippers.

"Why, thank you very much, sir, for delivering me from that wicked pirate."

Nick raises a finger. "I'm sorry. What pirate?"

"Ahoy, gents!" A throaty voice erupts from across the ship's deck. "Quit standing like a couple of dreadnoughts and come say hi!" A burly sailor arcs his arms in a big, welcoming wave, and his ivory smile beckons the three men to approach.

Tim feels his pulse slow. At last, a kindly stranger to help him along.

The broad-shouldered sailor greets them with another wave as they walk across the oaken, rain-stained deck. He sports a royal blue jacket with golden patches on the shoulders, as well as a crimson collar, and rugged but durable leather boots.

The covert prince extends a hand. "Greetings, friend—"

The sailor lurches forward and wraps his arms around Tim in a sudden embrace. "One thing you'll have to learn about me, chap, I'm a hugger!" He lets loose a cavernous laugh and releases.

Tim staggers back, breathless and achy around the rib cage. "Whatever you say, seadog. A friendly face is always preferable to the alternative."

"I figure the same thing!" It seems a giant smile is the sailor's resting expression. "The name's Rogelio, and welcome to my ship, Mr. Bottom. I'm happy to take you and your guests to Sweden."

"Oh, excuse me," Nick shoulders his way into the conversation. "This Dane, however talented with a quill and turn of phrase he may be, is not Nick Bottom. *I*…" he pauses for dramatic flair, "am the international artiste Nicholas Bottom."

He holds a pose for a few moments—just long enough to be uncomfortable. The ship creaks as it slices through the water, desperately trying to break the awkward silence.

"Well then," Rogelio clears his throat, still smiling. "It's a pleasure to meet you, Mr. Bottom. And your compatriots?"

"Dogberry. At your service." The Constable dips his head in a deep bow, looking more like a flamingo than royalty.

Tim silently weighs his options. An alias seems like the smart move. But the last time he used a false name, he ended up attacked by a band of pirates, and his real name came out eventually regardless. Plus, Dogberry and Nick already know his true identity. And Rogelio's sunny grin seals the deal.

He nods. "Tim. It's a pleasure."

"Alrighty, Messrs. Bottom, Dogberry, and Tim, I'll show you to the passengers' quarters. And you can meet the two others already on board!" Rogelio beckons and bounces toward a staircase leading below deck. He rubs his hands together as if escorting them truly is the highlight of his day.

"We're sharing this schooner with other people?" Nick tips an eyebrow.

"This is a Bilander, actually, Mr. Bottom, not a schooner, and yessiree! Don't worry, they're salt of the earth, very friendly chaps."

Nick clicks his tongue, and Tim gets the feeling he is only containing an ego outburst because of his company.

Rogelio leads the three of them down the damp wooden stairs, which are warped by years of exposure to the sea and burly sailors' boots. The air moistens as Tim descends, and he can practically feel the mold already growing in his lungs. A line of lanterns steers them into a small living quarters with cots lining the floorboards and hammocks strung from the ceiling.

Two men sit on a bench. One is young and dressed in a fine velvet tunic, hair mussed in a manner that appears purposeful, and sporting a rapier with a decorative handle. He glances at the new passengers with lavender eyes and a wry smile.

If I could cast this guy in my show's leading role, teenage London would make me rich every night.

The other man is a boulder, with his arms crossed, bald scalp, and pockmarked face. The gray whiskers around his mouth are twisted into an aggressive frown.

Rogelio booms in the small space, "Hello again, my friends! I hope your accommodations are treating you well so far. I'd love to introduce you to Nick Bottom, Mr. Dogberry, and Mr. Tim."

The three newcomers wave. Tim feels like he's back in the first day of kindergarten.

The sailor resumes the introductions. "Now, here we have *Signor* Romeo Montague," he gestures to the dashing young man, and then to the fleshy statue, "and Sir Kent Earl. Or is it Earl Kent?"

The bald old man just glares.

Rogelio chuckles, rocking the ship. "Very good, then! I'll let you three get to know your new bunkmates. If you need anything—anything at all— simply give a shout." With that, the sailor bounds back up the moaning stairs.

Awkward silence follows as the three sit down. Romeo shifts in his seat. Kent grumbles and then swallows. Tim clacks his thumbs together, recalling his old doctor's waiting room. All this place needs to complete the picture is some cheesy music and outdated reading material.

Of course, it's Nick who breaks the silence. "So, *Señor* Montague, are you a fencing man?"

The handsome young squire looks confused. "Pardon?"

"Your foil," Nick gestures to the weapon on Romeo's hip. "You know, I used to swashbuckle with the best of them back in my university days. Best in my class. Best in the region, even. Or was it the nation? I get it all fuddled. Anyhow, my sensei said I could have been the greatest athlete he's ever seen, but I chose a different mistress: the—"

"No, sir," Romeo interjects as politely as possible. Tim detects an urban Italian accent, one that speaks of crowded streets rather than rolling hills. "This is not a foil, it's a rapier. Used for combat, not sport. Efficiently deadly, when employed correctly—"

"The stage." Nick finishes his sentence, reclaiming the center of attention. "I became an actor, a player of roles instead of mere games." Now that his metaphor and, more importantly, his braggadocious anecdote are finished, he leans back.

"Deadly, you say?" Dogberry speaks up.

Romeo's eyes cloud over. "Yes. Quite." He looks haunted.

Dogberry's eyes, on the other hand, light up like a kid watching a fireworks display. "By all means, please precede. You've seen combat? Real battles? The itty-bitty?"

Nitty-gritty, Tim silently corrects Dogberry's slip of the tongue. He smiles, though—the constable's constant misspeech is quirky but endearing.

Romeo nods to Dogberry. "A few." He chuckles at an invisible memory, then cuts it off. "It's a long story." Pause. "A *long* story. My situation back home is…complicated." His gaze lowers to the grimy floorboards.

Tim guides the conversation away from the unpleasant subject. "Where's home, Romeo?"

A dashing smile illuminates the young man's face, crinkling his eyes' corners and revealing a mouthful of pearls. "Fair Verona. God's template for Paradise. Ah, such beauty, wonder, and mystery, all at once."

"Verona?" Dogberry leans forward, scratching his bristly chin. "Isn't that near Messina?"

"Umm, perhaps a few days' journey north," Romeo responds, again trying his best to be polite.

"Well I'll be a Dutchman's cousin!" Dogberry grins ear to ear. "I used to work in Verona!"

"Is that right?" Romeo's face brightens.

"Sure! Verona's Prince and me, we're good compatriarchs. I was Constable in Verona for a while after I was transferred from Messina." He puffs out his chest in pride. "I was such an infectious leader in Messina, they asked me to take my talents to a more crime-addled city. So to Verona I went."

"Crime?" Tim says. "Doesn't exactly sound like God's template…"

Romeo shrugs. "Every rose has its thorns. No city is a true utopia, but Verona comes close."

Tim responds, "I'll have to swing by some day, check out the vistas and the villas."

Romeo smirks, widening the dimples in his cheeks. He turns back to Dogberry. "It does my soul well to meet another who hails from Verona."

"Absolutely, m'boy! Where are my manners?" The Constable sticks out his hand to the young Italian. "Eustace Dogberry."

Romeo clasps Dogberry's hand with his own. Both men appear to be wearing gloves—Dogberry's skin is leathery and crusted, while Romeo's is fair and pliant like silk.

"By Merlin's beard," Dogberry cackles, "that's a vice grip you've got. I would *not* want to tick you off."

"Why thank you, sir," Romeo settles back onto the creaky bench, waggling his eyebrows. Among new friends, this dashing libertine is almost an entirely different man from the bashful young pup who had filled his shoes a mere minute ago.

Nick clears his throat and tries to reinsert himself into the conversation. "So why are you on this course to Sweden, young Romeo?"

"Again," the Italian winks conspiratorially, "long story."

Tim shrugs. "We've got time."

"That we do," Dogberry says. "C'mon, Montague. A rouge like you, with a sword on your hip and a peculiar, vague backstory…You're pretty much the most interesting person I've ever met, for all intensive purposes."

Nick shifts, trying and failing to appear unoffended by not achieving that title.

"As a matter of fact…" Romeo speaks hesitantly, prying each word from his own mind and shoving them out his mouth. "I am…on the run."

Tim's eyes widen. "Really now? A fugitive from Verona?"

Nick throws his hands in the air. "And now he's an outlaw. I can't compete with that…"

"Is this true, Montague?" Dogberry asks, literally on the edge of his seat.

A beat of silence fills the room. Then, Romeo grins like a shark and spreads his hands. "What can I say?"

Dogberry hoots and slaps his knee.

"What happened?" Tim presses. The storyteller in him yearns to know the whole tale behind this charming lothario.

"Well…" Romeo beams and begins to weave his tale.

Even Nick is curious, and he can't help but tilt closer.

"Behold two households, akin in influence and power. Fair Verona itself is a testament to these families. Meet the Capulets, a dynasty of prudence and ire. They come from a tradition of strong morals and fierce loyalty, governed by a patriarch shrewd as Marc Antony and gallant as Galahad. He is a businessman and public servant, true, but above all, he is a father. He would die for the one he loves more than the stars: his daughter Juliet."

The universe takes a breath when Romeo says the name. The ship rocks as it crests a wave, angling the lanterns and hammocks, casting long shadows across the wooden floor and walls. Romeo's vibrant words compel him to stand, and he slowly steps into his spotlight.

"Then, I present the Montagues." He adjusts his tunic and rests a hand on his rapier's decorative handle, as if posing for a heroic marble statue. "My clan. My brothers and fathers. Descendants of medieval conquerors, we are true men of chivalry. Effective diplomats, master orators, tender lovers, ferocious warriors!" He roars and clenches his fists above his head. "Indeed, the Montagues are known in every corner of the globe. We are feared, loved, and everything in between."

Nick and Dogberry are utterly transfixed by the performance. They look upon the Italian with eyes like full moons, practically falling off their seats. Tim has seen these exact expressions on teenage girls lined up outside the stage door, waiting for one heartthrob or another.

But Tim is taken by Romeo's bravado too.

This tale has the makings of a Greek drama, he thinks. *Or a soap opera.* Despite the melodrama, he can't help but be riveted. Perhaps he can make a play of it once he gets back to London, with Romeo in the starring role. Nick could be the comic relief side character, and Dogberry would do well as the Masterpiece Centre's head of security. Sold-out crowds, standing room only, rave reviews in all the periodicals. Tim would be back on top in no time. And the Hamlets in Denmark would rue the day they turned their backs on him.

He gulps, banishing the daydream as quickly as he can. Best to focus on the tangible present, not an imaginary future.

"Thus, the stage is set," Romeo continues in a bold whisper, forcing his audience to lean in and listen. "Dual families, dueling households, locked in a grudge match for generations. But the two youngest defy these domestic quarrels for a chance at true love. She..." he reaches out, as if holding her hand from several thousand miles away, "is Juliet Capulet. And *he*," he grasps his own heart, "is Romeo Montague."

Tim hears a sad sniff from across the room. He looks and sees Dogberry covertly wiping away a tear.

Then a gravelly voice rumbles, "Oh, for the love of the Almighty, are you crying?" Kent shakes his head and scowls. "Suck it up and act like you've got something between your legs."

Nick guffaws. "It speaks!"

Romeo, having been interrupted, withdraws from center stage. "Welcome to the land of the living, sir."

The bald old man scoffs, arms still firmly crossed over his broad chest. Dogberry straightens his jacket, letting the insult roll off his back.

But Nick is still cackling, rocking back and forth like a lunatic. "That'll teach you, *Frog-Fairy!*" He beams with pride at the lame schoolyard taunt he came up with and looks to Kent for approval.

The old man levels his beady eyes at Nick. "If I were to smack you, I'd be arrested for animal abuse, so do us all a favor and shut your bunghole."

Nick's rowdy laughter stops immediately. He sits still, head lowered.

"So," Tim verbally steps between the old man and his actor friend, "Rogelio called you Kent. Is that accurate?"

The man sizes up Tim like a dominant gorilla evaluating a stranger. He eventually grunts in the affirmative. "Mhmm. Let's go with that."

Romeo looks confused. "I'm not sure I follow your meaning. Is that your given name or not?"

"Hold on a second..." Tim scratches his head in attempt to get his mental gears in motion. "Your accent is distinctly English. Born and raised." *Unlike me,* he silently gulps. "Strong and silent. Rogelio thought your name was Kent Earl...But I'd wager you're actually the Earl *of* Kent, a nobleman of England."

Kent's gray whiskers curl. "Think you're pretty smart, hot shot? Yeah, you're right about me."

"Brilliant deduction, my friend!" Nick calls.

"But," Kent leans forward, on the attack, "we English noblemen are sharp too. Your accent might sound like it's been bathed in British tea, but it's downright Danish, no mistaking it. I get the feeling your name starts with an 'H' and ends with an 'amlet,' but you're far more clever than that melancholy punk over in Elsinore, so I'd take it you're the long-abandoned twin, Prince Tim of Denmark?"

Again, the room is silent, but for the crackling flames in the lanterns and the creaking of the ship. Romeo gapes at Tim, suddenly very aware of his royal company.

Tim cracks a grin. "Pleased to meet ya, Kent."

The old man inclines his eggy head in a short, powerful nod. "Likewise." He, too, gives a rugged smile.

"Ah," Nick sighs, "I'm glad we're friends now—"

Kent snaps his glare over to the thespian, all traces of camaraderie and respect instantly gone. "Your family tree must be a straight line, son. Keep your comments to yourself."

"How…" Nick sputters, "*dare* you, my good sir!" He stands in his outrage. "I am Nicholas Bottom, winner of *three*—not one, not two, not four…But *three* Marlowe Awards! One for my leading role in *Richard II: Alchemic Boogaloo*, and then…"

Kent begins knocking the back of his head against the wall. "Lord above, kill me now."

"You scoundrel! You are most fortunate we aren't in the theatre district of Athens right now. If my fans heard you speaking to me this way, they would give you a firm talking-to!"

"Son, you don't have a posse. It's just a pose."

"Let me tell you something, sir." Nick sits right next to Kent. "My monologue in act ten, scene fourteen of *Apocalypse Soon* brought the audience to its feet."

They were leaving early, but I guess he's technically right, Tim thinks.

"Here," Nick massages his throat, "let me show you."

"I swear," Kent rumbles, "if you start to do your twerpy play, I'll ram my fist down your throat and find out what you ate a month ago."

Facing the prospect of performing, Nick pays the threat no mind. "Sweet moon," he croons, wearing his cheesy mask of theatricality, "I thank thee for your sunny beams…"

Kent groans and stares ahead, resigned to his torture. Arms crossed, jaw set, he turns back into the statue he had been when Tim first entered the quarters.

Romeo snaps his eyes to Tim. "So you have princely blood?"

Tim shrugs. "Yes, I am *a* prince, but I'm not *the* prince. I have no role in Elsinore. My name is Tim Hamlet. Prince Hamlet and I were once wombmates."

"I can see the resemblance. Uncanny. So, *Prince*," Romeo trills, "what brings you to these choppy tides?"

Tim laughs. "Now that, pal, *is* a long story. Speaking of which, we were hearing yours. Dual families, dueling households?"

"Ah yes," Romeo pushes his hair out of his lavender eyes. "Civil blood making civil hands unclean. It truly is a twisting, multifaceted tale. To sum it all up, my rage usurped my better judgment and took control of the situation. A man called Tybalt struck down a dear friend of mine with his blade." Romeo's words caught in his throat for a moment. "Tybalt Capulet. And I took my revenge." His hand unconsciously clutched his sword's hilt. "Some may say I was justified in acting. But my hands merely became as bloody as his."

Dogberry pats Romeo's shoulder. A companion offering his support. "I'm sorry, Montague."

Romeo exhales. "And now I run. I am banished from what I love—my Verona, my friends, my Juliet…It is all behind me."

The Constable spreads his arms. "Hey, you have us now."

"Yeah," Tim adds. "We're all moving forward. What could go wrong?"

Now midway through his soliloquy, Nick coughs and massages his fleshy neck. "Oh bugger. I've been wheezing since I arrived in England. This is no good, a downright tragedy. My voice is my livelihood. I think it's the Black Death."

"It's not the Black Death," Kent says.

"Oh, it's the Black Death. My nose is leaky, and I have these swollen bumps in my throat."

"The Black Death died out two hundred years ago, numb nuts."

"Come on," Nick leans into Kent, offering his neck. "Feel right here, do you feel little bumps?"

Kent doesn't budge. "No."

Tim cuts in. "Nick, I'm sure you're not ill."

"I want to believe you, Tim, but I can't take a chance. I've heard from very reliable sources that the Black Death is positively deadly, and dying isn't in my plan yet."

"Yet?" Romeo says.

"That's right. I haven't given my legacy performance yet. Every actor has a single role that will carry him through history, long after he is buried. But they tend to happen halfway through his career, meaning he has years of mediocre roles afterward. Once I peak with my most masterful performance, it'd be convenient for a carriage to strike me as soon as I leave the theatre. That way, fans and critics will yearn for more, my legacy will be cemented in glory, and I won't have to endure half-a-career's worth of going downhill."

"That's…" Tim gapes. *Insane.*

But Nick continues. "I have yet to peak, though. I can't die yet. Certainly not from the sniffles on a boat to Sweden."

"Well, you know what they say," Kent mutters. "What doesn't kill you…really disappoints me."

Dogberry examines Kent like an alienist—he even strokes the hairs on his chin. "That's quite a defense magnesium you've got there."

"I was the personal servant of one of the mightiest kings in all of history," Kent responds as if relaying the weather. "Thick skin and a sharp tongue come with the territory."

"Was?" Tim asks.

Kent snorts. "Long story."

"That seems to be a theme tonight."

"True." The old man's face spasms, which might be his way of looking amused.

Dogberry slaps his knees and pushes himself to his feet. "Well, Gentile-men, I need to visit the laboratory."

It takes Tim a couple seconds to translate that one. *Lavatory…*He chuckles as the Constable ascends the whining stairs.

Then, the room pitches violently to the side. Dogberry tumbles back down the stairs, and the other men slide off their benches.

"What was *that?*" Nick rubs his head.

Not good. Tim feels a pit in his stomach. *Definitely not good.*

Kent is already on his feet, shoulders squared, as if ready for a fight. "That's a storm, no doubt. An avalanche of water and lightning."

Nick yells from the floor, "How could you possibly know that?"

The ship pitches again, and now Tim hears the howling winds.

"Uh-oh."

A volley of footsteps pounds down the stairs. Rogelio sticks his head in the room. "Wind's blowing up a whopper, boys! Hang on tight!"

Dogberry's voice drifts from the floor, "I still have to pee…" He stands and hitches up his knickers.

"Do you need our help, Guv?" Tim asks, already moving.

Nick wags his head back and forth. "No! No, he doesn't! We aren't sailors! This is madness!"

Tim ignores his actor friend. "Romeo, Kent, Constable, let's go. This ship won't right itself."

Kent's beard curls into a warrior's grin. "That's more like it."

Romeo and Dogberry nod, both with shaky knees but anxious to assist.

Rogelio beams like a proud father. "Very well, my friends. To the deck!"

The five men dash up the stairs like a squadron of knights entering battle.

Just before moving out of sight, Tim looks back at Nick Bottom, who is huddled beneath a swinging hammock. "You'll know where to find us, Nick." He turns and bounds above deck.

Rain slices his face, and in an instant, he's soaked to the bone. He holds up an arm to shield his eyes from the watery bullets. The ocean is an overflowing cauldron, and Poseidon stirs it with his trident.

Rogelio begins snapping orders. "Dogberry, take in the topsail and keep it untangled. Earl Kent, tend to the longboats. Make sure they aren't dashed to pieces in case we need to make an escape. Mr. Tim, you and I will move cargo to the stern—that's the ship's rear. We need as much weight back there as we can get. Mr. Montague, you will man the wheel, steer the ship diagonally through the waves."

Romeo looks at the sailor, suddenly terrified. "I've never captained a ship before!"

"Well, you're gonna learn!"

Dogberry says, "We're all scared, Rogelio. Calm down!"

"Only when the sea does, sir!" Rogelio woofs. "Now move!"

They scatter across the deck, each man moving toward his assigned task.

Tim tries to stay directly behind Rogelio, but the rollicking waves knock him side to side. Water streams down his face like a blindfold, but the burly sailor is accustomed to the fickle sea, and he's a solid guide amidst the chaos.

"I hope you've made your peace with God, Mr. Tim!" Rogelio shouts over the storm's chorus.

"I hope I won't have to for a long, long time."

Rogelio chortles. "A seasoned sailor knows to never leave port without settling his spiritual debts. The sea is a different world, unpredictable and unforgiving! Just look around."

"Yeah." Tim staggers through the thick pool of foaming water already accumulated on the deck. "Strange weather we're having," he deadpans.

Rogelio throws his head back and laughs at the inky sky. "I should say so, Mr. Tim! A bit blustery?"

"Just a smidge." He laughs with the sailor, but the sound is instantly swept away.

Tim cranes his neck to make sure his new friends are still onboard. Romeo has reached the captain's wheel, which is spinning haphazardly like a crazed windmill. Dogberry and Kent are still en route to their duties, leaning against the rain.

A wave launches onto the deck like the hand of a submerged creature trying to drag the ship to the ocean floor.

Dogberry yells, "I don't have to pee anymore!"

"Alright, Mr. Tim!" Rogelio slaps a wooden crate fastened to the deck. "We need to get these to the stern, putting more weight on the rudder and helping Mr. Montague steer."

Tim nods. *Good plan. He's obviously been here many times before.*

"Get ready to heave. The wind will fight you!"

The two men undo the crate's binding and push it to the ship's rear. Tim's muscles cry out, achy from the cold water, but he pushes all the same. Adrenaline spurs his limbs in a way only the wrath of Mother Earth can.

The rain doesn't simply fall—it is driven, hard and brutal. A jagged spear of lightning rips the sky in two, and Tim feels the static jolt through his bones. He can barely push his feet through the water, which is denser than molasses. Even on this ship, above water, Tim can imagine drowning in the rain.

"Longboats secure, Rogelio!" Kent's robust voice pierces the howl, but Tim can't see him anymore. The torrential rain is a solid curtain. He and Rogelio may as well be alone in the sea.

"Good, Mr. Kent. Go help Mr. Montague with the wheel!"

"Sir, yes sir!" Kent surges across the deck.

Tim throws his shoulder against the crate and finally reaches the ship's rear. He turns and runs back for another box, but his feet are swept away by the rain and he collapses in a heap. His head bounces against the oaken floor, and sparks explode behind his eyes.

"Up and at 'em, Tim!"

He can hear Rogelio's voice, but it's bleary and stretched, warped as if in a dream. The whole ship tilts and pitches like a mad carnival ride, adding to the surreal sensation. He lays sprawled on the deck, the celestial flood burying him drop by drop.

Then, hope.

"Land! Land ho!"

Is that Nick?

Tim lifts his head, blurring his vision, but he can make out Nick Bottom clinging to the handrails along the ship's perimeter. His arm is stretched out to the sea, a tiny waterfall pouring from his pointer finger.

"There's an island! Romeo, steer us to the land!"

Romeo calls out, "I can't see it through the rain!"

"I can!" Nick insists. "Trust me!"

"Trust you?" Kent snarls. "You dunderheaded coward, you didn't even want to come out here and help."

"I saw an island! Why would I lie?"

Thunder barks from beyond the clouds, drumming through Tim's skull. He grabs the side of his head and tries to stand, but his weak legs can't hold him up, and he crashes back into the deck's pool.

"It's the emptiest head that makes the greatest noise, Bottom," Kent growls. "This isn't your moronic *legacy performance*. This is life or death!"

The sky detonates with lightning like jagged daggers, emphasizing Kent's point and mocking the feeble mortals trying to survive Poseidon's fury.

"The storm's getting worse!" Dogberry yells from under the soaked topsail.

"We'll be dashed to bits if we stay out here much longer," Rogelio asserts. "That island is our only chance. Mr. Bottom, give Mr. Montague a heading."

Nick points again. "Just to the left!"

"You'd better be right, Bottom." Kent staggers as the ship rocks, but his malice is unwavering.

"What's your problem with me, Kent?" Nick wipes rain from his eyes and straightens to his full height. "What did I do to you?"

"Um, guys…" Dogberry waves his arms.

Romeo slams his hands against the wheel. "Both of you shut your mouths so I can think!"

"Well, well, the pretty boy bares his teeth." Kent shoves a finger at the Italian. "Why don't you draw your little sword and we'll go a few rounds?"

"Guys?" Dogberry tries again.

Kent doesn't let Romeo respond. "Because you're a putz, that's why! Just a figurine accustomed to winking and getting everything he wants. I could twist that twig you call a sword into a pretzel!"

"I've killed stronger men than you," Romeo snarls.

Nick nods. "Yeah, Kent. Your grizzly, war-vet act isn't as scary as you think it is."

"Both of you versus me, right here, right now!" Kent balls his fists and spreads his arms. "C'mon!"

"Guys!" Dogberry shouts just as a massive wave gushes onto the deck. "Look out!"

That gets their attention.

"Huh?"

Tim gulps and decides it's time to have a chat with the big guy upstairs. *CRACK.*

The ship screeches to a halt, pitching violently to the side. A gigantic crevice bisects the deck, tearing the entire vessel in half. Splinters shoot every which way like shards of glass, mixing in the air with the fat raindrops. The floor drops, suddenly becoming vertical, like a massive cliff face. Romeo, Dogberry, Kent, and Nick scream as they're thrown into the broiling, salty cauldron.

Crap.

Tim tumbles into the cold water, flailing in a feeble attempt to swim against the angry sea. His limbs quickly tire, and the undercurrent spins him around until he forgets which way the water's surface is. His lungs quiver in his chest, and he begins to panic.

He opens his eyes to search for Rogelio or any of his fellow travelers, but the ocean is pitch black. Closing his eyes makes no difference. He kicks once again in some direction, any direction, but the water is like arctic lava, and it eventually forces him to surrender. His mind succumbs to the blackness, and his body floats at the waves' mercy.

Chapter 5

Sunlight.

For a moment, it's pleasant. Heavenly. Tim lies on his back, swaddled in golden warmth, eyes closed, the rhythmic ocean waves lapping against his legs.

Then, the sun scorches his skin. Sand is lodged in every cranny, and the salty air chafes his nostrils.

Tim snaps his eyes open, and the endless blue sky stares back.

Blue. A seagull caws nearby. The storm has passed.

The storm.

His joints ache at the memory of the wrathful sea. He tries to sit up, but his muscles scream in objection, and he remains on the damp sand. His head pounds like a war drum, his eyesight kaleidoscopic and nauseating.

Why is he on a beach? Typically, he wouldn't complain about finding himself in such an exotic location, but his last recollection is of the ship and the storm and Rogelio and—

CRACK.

The sound pierces his muddled memory.

The ship has crashed. They're stranded.

Panic grips his heart and his body reacts instinctively, leaping to his feet. He spins in a circle, searching for his companions and ignoring the feeling of gravel in his bones.

"Nick! Romeo, Dogberry, Kent! Rogelio!"

No answer.

Tim tries to run, but his feet sink into the sand, and he ends up flopping back onto the grainy ground. He spits out a mouthful of the sugar-white particles and staggers up again.

An expansive shore stretches to his left and right, farther than his eyes can grasp. A tropical jungle overtakes the sand a few dozen yards inland. Wooden shards of the Bilander litter the oceanfront.

At least they aren't shards of Rogelio.

Tim begins walking the beach. If he made it out alive, surely the others did too.

Or so he tells himself over and over.

As he walks, he sees an entire graveyard of the ship's remains. The beach is absolutely covered with debris, almost more wood than sand.

There's the ship's wheel. Tim steps over it, scanning the wreckage. Splintered planks. Spilled cargo. A huge fishing net. Another wheel…

Tim raises an eyebrow.

A soiled Welsh flag is wadded up in a small salty pool, a hermit crab picking at its treads.

Their ship had been flying the orange, white, and blue Dutch flag.

Tim looks back at the wooden graveyard. Different designs of cargo boxes, different types of wood, different architecture…Dozens of ships have wrecked on this beach.

What is this place?

Tim tries to swallow his paranoia, but he quickens his pace regardless. He steels his voice and calls out again: "Rogelio! Nick! K—"

He sees something move in the trees. He freezes and strains his eyes.

"Hello!"

Nothing.

It had been a figure, someone—or something—walking on two legs. Pale and thin. Drifting, as if made of air.

"Who's there?" he yells over the crashing waves. His shaky legs carry him away from the shore, toward the yawning tropical jungle.

A flicker. There, again. The pale figure dashes deeper into the brush.

"No, wait!" Tim wills his body to run. "Please!"

He chases after the pale figure, vaulting over gnarled, mossy roots and shielding his face from barbed branches. The aroma of the trees fills his nostrils—fresh and powerful, all-encompassing. Leaves bigger than his hands slap his shoulders, and mosquitos buzz past his ears like thrown daggers. Florae and brambles he's never even read about grab at his ankles, and one thing is perfectly evident.

He doesn't belong here.

But the figure ran this way. He can't be the only living being on this entire island. He can't. So he gives chase.

A primal screech explodes from overhead, and a small monkey soars from branch to branch, its amber eyes staring at the intruder. Tim instinctively cowers. He's never been on a lower plane than a mammal before.

"What are you doing down there?"

Tim spins and drops into a defensive fencing position. Then his jaw drops open.

A man sits among the trees' tallest branches.

No, he isn't sitting. He's floating, legs crossed as if sitting on an invisible flying carpet.

And no, he isn't a man. Not really. His features are soft like a child's, eyes glittering beads of obsidian. His smile is reckless yet gentle.

And…his skin is blue. Rich, royal blue. Silky veins cross his arms, neck, and bare chest. Baggy trousers are all he wears.

"Excuse me?" the specter says. "Mr. Man?" His voice jingles through the air like a flipping coin.

Tim clears his throat, still in a fencing position. "Y-Yes." He pauses, and the jungle breathes around them. "Are you…real?"

"What, you've never seen a spirit before?"

Two days ago, Tim would have answered with a hearty *no*. Now, he recalls his dead father reaching his fist into his skull, and he shivers in the balmy island heat. "I have, as a matter of fact." He drops his defenses and cocks his head. "Do you have a name, sprite?"

The blue figure chuckles, his chest muscles contracting. He drifts lower, lighter than a feather, until he is face to face with Tim.

"Why, I do. I am Ariel, spirit of the air."

"So is this your island, Ariel?" Tim takes a step back, realizing that the specter is as small as a doll. He could've sworn the blue figure had been a regular size when floating in the trees.

"Mine, it is not. I am the simple servant of the sire who sits on this sampling of sand." His words flit off his tongue like popping corn kernels, playfully musical.

"You have a master?" Tim asks, trying to sort through Ariel's lyrics. "Where is he? Does he know a way off this island?"

"But why oh why would one want to run? Such a paradise is surely a feast for the senses. In all my thousand years, I've never wished for elsewhere."

"You've never left this place? Ever in a millennium?" Tim tries to keep Ariel talking. While the spirit doesn't seem hostile or deceitful, he sure is uninterested in providing straight answers.

A breeze tickles the leaves, and Ariel begins to drift away, grinning in utter contentment. He reclines in the air and locks his hands behind his head. "I have plenty of friends, if that's your implication. There is my master, the magnificent maker of magical marvels, Prospero. As well as his daughter, the beautiful and benevolent Miranda."

Tim waits for Ariel to continue. "And?"

"That's it!" Ariel squeals in delight. "How lucky am I to have more than one close confidant?"

Twigs rustle behind Tim, and a raspy wind forms words: "Are you forgetting about me?"

Tim whips around and finds the most ghastly sight he has ever beheld. A stumpy gray creature emerges from the brush. It almost looks like a man—one that was formed out of clay, wilted by the sun, then abandoned in a polluted river, and dredged out decades later. One eye is yellow and slit like a crocodile's, large as an egg, and the other is the size of a button. Its steps are more like lunges, for it carries a hunchback, and its feet are like a bear's.

A shriek explodes from Tim's throat and he falls to the jungle floor. He scurries away from the monster, kicking dirt and leaves frantically. "What is that?!"

Ariel lazily turns his head. "Oh, yes. That's just Caliban."

Tim catches his breath, eyes shifting from the flighty fairy to the deformed creature. He settles on the gray form. "C-Caliban?"

"You rang?" The monster sighs and looks up at the buoyant Ariel. "Why do you never count me as one of your friends?"

"You hate us! Not a day has passed that you do not attempt to murder my master! Poison, falling boulders, sea urchins in his pillow…"

"So?" Caliban crosses its arms and plops on the ground. "You all have to be my friends. This is *my* island, after all. A 'thank you' every now and then would go a long way."

"This is hardly *your* island," Ariel scoffs. "My master is too quick and powerful for your tricks. You have no control here."

"I wash the dishes and scrub the johns. This is *my* island." The creature nods, thinking itself to have won the argument.

Tim, still cowering in the dirt, looks up at Ariel. "So you serve Prospero the wizard, and Caliban here tries to kill him?"

Ariel giggles again, making Caliban plug its cauliflower ears. "Hardly. Caliban is slow and stupid, like a silly slug. He's of the Devil."

"That's not very nice," Tim mutters.

Caliban shrugs, picking at its ragged pants. "No, he's right. Lucifer is my dad."

A bird chips from the trees, then shuts itself up. The awkward moment suffocates the three. Tim stares at the monster. "Huh?"

"Yeah," Caliban says self-consciously, "the witch Sycorax and Lucifer met at a party one night. Circe introduced them. A few Mai Tai's later, one thing led to another…" It gestures to itself. "They dropped me off here. Said this is my home. I know they were trying to get rid of me, but joke's on them! This place has great acoustics for my band. Down by the hot springs, the percussion sounds…" It attempts to make an "OK" sign with its forefinger and thumb. "…pretty sweet!"

"Your band?"

"Yeah!" A smile spreads across Caliban's stony face. "We're 'Caliban and the Cool Crew!' It's me, Ariel, Prospero, and Miranda. They haven't showed up to any practices yet, but I have all the songs and arrangements ready."

Ariel says, "Caliban, it's been thirteen years. We aren't joining your band. You'd try to kill us!"

"I wouldn't at band practice!" It snorts and fixes its reptile eye on Tim. "Well, maybe this sack of flesh would want to join. Or one of the other ignoramuses who just rolled in."

Tim perks up. "Others? Where?"

Caliban hooks a thumb over its shoulder. "That way."

Before the creature finishes speaking, Tim is already gone, sprinting through the trees. Away from the bickering spirits. He's had enough of the supernatural for a few days.

He keeps moving, making sure to always have himself oriented with the beach to his right. He wipes sweat from his forehead and glances up at the sun. It's about eight in the morning and already toasty.

The weather rarely tiptoes a degree over glacial at home in Denmark. The stone walls of Elsinore are adept at trapping the cold like it was a prisoner.

Tim hears voices coming through the trees and screeches to a halt to focus. Male voices, four of them.

"Oh bother, my *Louis Pourri* shoes are ruined…"

Sounds like Nick made it in one piece.

"Then why don't you slip into something more comfortable? Like a coma?"

Yep, Kent is alright too.

Romeo's voice comes next, and it sounds like he's cutting through the tropical brush with his rapier. "Face it, gents. We're lost in this godforsaken place."

"I can get us back to the beach," Dogberry pipes up, ever the soldier. "I remember the way. I have a photogenic memory."

Tim runs through the trees separating him from his friends. "Guvs!"

The four men whirl to look at the Danish prince, eyes wide. Romeo holds his rapier at the ready.

Nick smiles ear to ear. "Young squire! Tim, my good man, it's marvelous to see you!" He runs forward, throwing out his arms.

Tim smiles too and steps into the actor's embrace. He feels moisture on Nick's cheek.

"I thought I'd lost you, boy," Nick whispers, voice trembling.

"Oh, it'll take more than a raging tempest to get rid of me." Tim gives Nick a solid squeeze.

Romeo sheaths his sword and grins. "Welcome back into the fold, Prince Tim."

Dogberry follows Nick's lead, bounding over to Tim and slapping him on the back. "Glad to have you back, my sir."

"You too, Constable." He grips Dogberry's shoulder and turns his eyes to Kent.

Kent's stony face doesn't shift. But he nods slightly.

Tim gives his companions a once-over—Dogberry's uniform is tattered and missing a few of his brass badges. Nick's fashionable attire is, indeed, ruined by the water and sand, and a rather sizable gash is sliced across his forehead. Romeo and Kent look no worse for the wear, seemingly accustomed to such intense ordeals. Overall, they were all very lucky to make it to this island.

Wait.

Tim looks around. "Where's Rogelio?"

The smiles melt off the men's faces. They shift their feet and cast their gazes to the ground.

Kent says, "We haven't found him."

Tim wipes salt from his brow—seawater or sweat, he isn't sure—and swallows. "Well, we all made it, and he's infinitely more experienced on the water than we are."

"True," Kent says.

"Maybe we should head back to the shore," Romeo suggests. "We can walk the perimeter, find out how big this spit of sand is, look for passing ships, and find Rogelio."

Dogberry grunts his approval. "Good thinking, Monty. Quite the plaster man."

Master plan.

"Oh sure," Nick sighs, the wrinkles on his face accentuated by the sun and fatigue. "The strapping young pretty boy has an obvious idea. I hate to be the burr in your boot, but we're lost."

Tim eyes Nick, wanting to snap at him. A negative attitude is not what they need now. But he bites his tongue. The Athenian actor has his hands on his knees, breathing heavily, sweat forcing him to blink every few seconds. He's lightyears out of his territory, and scared to death.

With all the confidence he can muster, Tim says, "I think Romeo is right. I just came from the beach, and that's where we'll most likely find Rogelio."

Nick gasps for air a few more times and says, "But you found *us* here in the jungle."

Kent rumbles, "It's a crapshoot looking for someone in here. We may as well wander out in the open instead of wandering through the brush."

Nick's voice turns whiny. "But it's impossible—"

"Bottom, the last thing I want to do is hurt you. But it's still on the list."

"Guvs." Tim raises his hands to quell the bickering. "We're going to the beach. That's it."

Without waiting for any more deliberation, Tim whips around and stomps back the way he came from. He's probably overcompensating with the headstrong attitude and forceful steps, but he can't let the others know he's just as frightened as Nick.

What if Rogelio is dead? Not only has he been a jolly personality and good friend, but he's the most likely person to get them out of this situation alive.

How will they eat? Where will they find fresh water?

Will Kent eventually snap and wring everyone's necks?

And it doesn't help that Tim is leading them all right back to where he had encountered Ariel and the beastly Caliban.

Tim groans and pinches the bridge of his nose. Maybe *he'll* be the one to snap soon.

All at once, he regrets ever setting foot upon the road to Elsinore. His brother be damned. Claudius be damned. His father's ghost be damned…again.

Here, sweating on a merciless desert island, he rejects his Hamlet name even further. Not once has it done him an ounce of good—it nearly decapitated him in the Bombastic Baron, and it brought him to his present situation!

The Hamlets can solve their own problems. He snarls and trudges through the foliage.

"Tim!" It's Nick again. "Do you hear those voices?"

Romeo begins to object. "Nick, please—"

"Wait." Tim brings the party to a halt.

Buzzing. Rustling. Shimmering. The erratic breath of the jungle.

And then. A distant word. Definitely human, but too faint to understand.

"Yes!" Hope swells in Tim's chest, and he takes off toward the sound. Instinct spurs his feet, and it leads him in the direction of the beach.

The party of five bursts out of the trees, back into the thick sand. The splintered remains of the ship dot the shore, just like when Tim left, but now two figures stand amid the wreckage, their backs to the jungle.

Tim wants to keep quiet so as to observe these unknown persons before making themselves known, but of course:

"Hey!" Nick shouts. "People! Thank the bearded man above. Yoo-hoo, behind you!"

The duo turns and appraises Tim and company. Tim holds up a hand to shield his eyes from the sun and studies their faces.

The first is a young woman. Her gaze is blue as the sea, and the bright island rays have tanned her skin. Untamed hair frames her face, and Tim wonders if she has ever seen a comb before. She wears a dress made of many different colors of canvas, with jagged stitch lines running horizontally down its length, as if it was made piece by piece over the course of many years. She stares at the men as if reading a fascinating book, mouth slightly open in a crooked smile.

The second figure is a mountain of a patriarch, robed in seaweed, bearded like Merlin, and clutching a massive walking staff. His hands are gnarled and eyebrows cocked in suspicion. He raises his staff and calls, "Hail, castaways!"

A beat of silence follows, save for the waves. Tim sees no one else in their group is going to be the spokesman, so he goes for it. "H-Hello...sir...?" He's never addressed a beach-dweller wearing seaweed before and isn't sure of the proper title.

The man begins to walk toward them with slow, powerful steps. The girl stays amid the wreckage, watching.

"Welcome to our island!" He spreads his arms, gesturing to the beach, the jungle, the sea, even the sky.

"Well, thank you, Guvnor. Honestly, though, I wish we could have visited under kinder circumstances."

"Understood. There wasn't much left of your vessel to even wash ashore."

As he walks toward them, Tim realizes the distance had downplayed the man's incredible bulk. He is at least seven feet tall, with wide shoulders and robust muscles rippling beneath the seaweed, but is clearly quite elderly. It's a dichotomy Tim has never encountered.

He sees the shock on Tim's face and smirks, clearly pleased with his effect. "Allow me to introduce myself. I am Prospero, the wizard presiding over this isle. This," he cocks his head, "is my daughter Miranda."

Kent grumbles, "Wizard?"

Romeo: "Daughter?"

Dogberry: "Aisle?"

"Shut it, you two." Kent shoves his way to Tim's side. "You called yourself a wizard? What hippie-dippie cow chips are you smoking out here?"

Prospero's condescending grin deepens. "Oh, this earthly paradise has secrets only the most unbridled imagination could fathom, and I am its conductor, its gardener and shepherd."

"Bollocks." Kent crosses his arms to flex his biceps. That very movement had been impressive earlier on the ship, but appears a bit desperate next to the towering wizard.

Tim, however, silently nods. Memories of Ariel and Caliban echo in his mind.

"Miranda!" Prospero yells over his shoulder. "Stop hovering back there, it's uncomfortable. Come greet our guests."

The young woman picks her way across the beach with effortless agility—her bare feet expertly avoid the ship's shrapnel.

"You must excuse my daughter. She and I arrived on this island when she was but four years of age. Societal norms are alien to her. So if she seems empty-headed," the old man shrugs, "it's because she is."

Tim frowns. That's hardly a comment a dad should make about his daughter. *It sounds like the sort of cutting remark Father would have come up with in his prime.*

"S-S-Sh..." Romeo tries to speak, but is too flustered to get out a word. Tim is shocked to see the smooth, suave Italian heartbreaker red as a tomato, breathing heavily, staring longingly at the approaching girl. "She grew up...here? On this island? W-Without other men?"

Prospero's eyes sharpen. "Y-Y-Yes, Don Juan," he mocks sharply. "Don't get any ideas, or I'll conjure up a thunderstorm to wash all the product out of your hair."

Miranda takes her last few steps through the sand and hides behind her tree-like father. Her eyes probe each and every face, cautious and surprised by the sudden appearance of so many males. But Tim sees a great deal of kindness beneath.

The wizard harrumphs and forces her into view. "Miranda, don't cower. These are the gentlemen from the shipwreck. Meet..." He stalls and looks Tim up and down. "Who are you people?"

"Well, my name is Tim, from London. This is Nick Bottom of Athens, Kent of Kent, Romeo Montague of Verona, and Constable Eustace Dogberry of Messina."

Romeo glides forward, all charm and pearly teeth. "*Enchanté, mademoiselle.*" He dips his head and holds out an open hand to the lovely young woman.

And the lovely young woman looks at the hand like it's a strange insect in a museum. "Um...hi." Her voice is light and mellifluous, but confused by the Italian's advance.

Tim can't stomach the awkwardness and tries to subtly pull Romeo back. "Hello, Miss Miranda. As I mentioned to your father, your home is quite charming, for a deserted wilderness."

"Why thank you," she beams at the perceived compliment.

"Pleased to meetcha, madam," Dogberry salutes. "Yes sir, what Tim said is right. Your island is as beautiful as something painted in the Sixteenth Chapel."

The wizard's daughter smiles. "You really like it?"

"Well," Kent mutters, "we were *shipwrecked* here..."

"Pretty as a coast guard!" Dogberry cackles, likely meaning *postcard.*

Miranda ruffles her never-once-shampooed hair as she surveys the beach. "Well, I'm a fan, and it's nice to hear that others see its value. Even if you're clearly just trying to get on my father's good side."

"Very acute, my dear," Dogberry's weathered face curls into a laugh.

"I-I-I honestly like this place," Romeo interjects, eager to please. "Blood oath! Besides, there are so many good sides of your father, I wouldn't even know where to start."

Prospero and Kent sigh in unison, "Good Lord…"

Tim retakes control of the conversation. "Mr. Prospero, we really need—"

"Food." And Nick takes the lead. "We need food and water and dry clothing and some moisturizer, if you can spare it."

"Mr. Bottom is right, we'll need sustenance," Tim nods, "but we also need to get off this island as soon as possible."

"Now, that's what I like to hear!" Prospero gestures his staff down the beach. "Follow me to our quarters. We can provide you with food and drink, and I'll attempt to hail a transport for you."

Miranda says, "You're leaving already?"

"Hush, girl," he barks. The words echo through the air, pushing the tide away from the shore. He purses his crusty lips and whistles.

"Yes, Master?" Ariel the blue spirit appears at Prospero's side, hovering a foot above the sand, just because he can. This time, he is about the size of a teenager, not a grown man or a small doll.

Romeo and Nick scream bloody murder:

"*What the Gehenna?*"

"Oh my *cripes!*"

They clutch one another in fear, whimpering, sniveling, shrieking obscenities.

Ariel waves at the visitors, and his obsidian eyes dance in the sunlight.

Kent unleashes a warrior's cry and charges at the spirit, fists raised. "Die, demon! The devil—"

Time stops.

Tim can't explain it, but he feels the earth stop rotating. Waves freeze mid-crash, water droplets like opals in the air. All noise is cut off, from the screams to the wind. Everyone stands like wax figurines—Nick and Romeo in a fearful embrace, Prospero towering above them all, Kent leaning into his powerful attack…All frozen except Ariel. The spirit swims through the air toward the motionless Kent, humming to himself.

Tim gulps. *Why am I outside of this temporal trap?*

Ariel claps as if about to play with his favorite toy, then rearranges Kent's feet. The old Englishman remains frozen, face twisted in brutish rage, but now his legs resemble a soft pretzel Tim would buy at the Masterpiece Centre's snack bar.

The spirit returns to his place at Prospero's side, beaming with mischievous pride. He locks eyes with Tim, winks, and time resumes.

Just like that.

The Danish prince shudders.

"—will know who sent you!" Kent's roar shatters the silence, but he immediately trips over himself and gets a mouthful of sand.

Prospero and Ariel laugh together—a hurricane and a breeze. The wizard mocks, "Mortals! *Psh.* You think you can punch a spirit?"

Kent sits up from the sand and shoots a glare that would change the course of a charging rhinoceros. But it only makes the seven-foot wizard laugh harder.

Dogberry glances at the interlocked Romeo and Nick. "What, you've never seen a fairy before?" He waves enthusiastically at Ariel, who returns with a genuine grin.

Miranda crosses her arms and gives the Constable a wry smile. "You've had experience with spirits?"

"Oh, tons! Vodka, gin, tequila..."

Romeo suddenly realizes his position and shoves Nick away. He flattens his hair and rests a hand on his rapier, scraping together his scattered dignity.

Prospero wipes a tear. "Ariel, escort these dingleberries to our compound and get them something to eat. I'll head into the brush and get to higher ground." His cloak of seaweed sways with his powerful steps as he stomps up the beach and into the jungle.

Ariel drifts like a palm leaf in a breeze. "Use your feet to follow my lead, gentle sirs."

Kent wipes more sand from his beard. "If it'll get me off of this suntrap."

And so the party of mortals begins to stroll along the shoreline: the secret prince, the washed-up actor, the frowning Earl, the fugitive lover, the fearless constable, and the wizard's daughter, all behind the blue fairy.

"So Miranda," Romeo slows to match her pace, "you've truly never been off this island? Never seen a man-made structure or experienced the pleasures of society?"

The young woman smirks to herself. "Well, I guess it's true I can't remember a day spent any place else, but you couldn't convince me to leave if you tried. My home is equipped with pulleys, running water, and reclining sofas, all built by yours truly. We produce our own food and clothing from the sweat of our brows and the dexterity of our fingers. A few years ago, I fashioned a flute and a lyre from bark and leaves, and I mastered them within a few weeks. Over the course of my life, I've also become quite the astronomer and writer." She turns her smirk on the dumbstruck Romeo. "Homeschooled, of course."

Dogberry laughs and claps, "Your brains are unparalyzed."

She gives a small bow. "Thank you, Eustace."

Romeo gulps. "She's perfect…"

Kent scoffs. "Wipe your lip and take a cold shower, boy."

Tim shuffles through the sand, smiling at the company he never would have dreamt he'd be keeping.

Stranded on a magical island with such a zany lot—it's something out of a C-list script he'd toss in the trash receptacle.

The trees rustle, practically alive and whispering their secrets.

He looks up at the hovering Ariel, who is also ogling the group. "Something interesting, spirit?"

"Everything is amusing, dear one. At the moment: the manner of bickering between you humans." He reclines in the air, idly keeping pace with the group. "This corporeal creation fascinates me. The way clouds change their mood based on the sun's. Are there celestial warehouses filled with sleet and snow, and to where do they disappear in June and July? What happens when a giraffe gets strep throat?"

Tim laughs. "So many questions."

The foliage shimmers again, although no breeze prompts it. Ariel somersaults through the air and reclaims Tim's attention.

"And humans! An active anomaly of nature! So intelligent yet empty-headed, imaginative yet destructive. I shall never understand the textile shells you insist on donning."

"Clothes?"

"You were created with hair—if any more covering was necessary, it would have been included. I only conjured these trousers to keep Miranda from fainting when she and the mighty wizard arrived."

"When was that?"

"Nigh a baker's dozen years ago—what feels like this morning, for a sprite like myself. She was a wee child, and this isle is all she has ever truly known. Still, her humanity seeps to the surface. She bathes and gargles and wears the textile. And she fabricates tales of fiction!"

Tim smiles. "Ah, she's a storyteller? A woman after my own heart."

Ariel shrugs. "I shall never understand humans' preoccupation with false narrative."

"Now, hold on, little boy blue, I will defend narrative to my last dying breath."

"And I shall be floating here for a millennium after that." Ariel trills, "Your lives are full of toil, strife, and sweat. Enough to occupy every ounce of your concentration. What good is investing in the woes of unreal peoples?"

"Fiction holds a mirror up to nature, my friend."

"That may be so." Ariel's sparkling eyes survey his beautiful island, then return to the castaway scuffling through the sand. "But what happens when you care more about the reflection than the original?"

Tim begins to rebut. But he has no comeback.

"Still, this is no concern of mine. When I was born, I bathed in stardust and watched as the oceans were filled. Humans are a speck on the map of my existence."

For only the third time in his life, Tim Hamlet is speechless. He lets out a hollow laugh.

The past five years suddenly settle on his mind. Days filled with writing plays, holding auditions, repairing the theatre, building sets, making advertisements, hustling for funds to pay his boss Bushacannyman in order to keep doing all of the above…A life devoted to fiction, the mirror that Ariel had brushed aside like a bit of lint.

And all the while, his very real, flesh-and-blood family was on the other side of the sea, the emotional chasm between them just as icy and roiling as the waters.

But Father paid me no mind. He didn't respect me, didn't want me in his shadow.

But they're my family. He's my dad, not some character in a book you can close.

But no one reached out in five years. Ophelia, Osric, my parents. None of them. They should be the ones to apologize to me!

But maybe it takes greater courage and humility to bridge that gap.

Ariel drifts into Tim's line of sight, studying the mortal's face. "Pontificating much?"

Tim snaps back into the present. "Yes! Yes…" He pinches the bridge of his nose. His mind has been bouncing back and forth like a racquetball ever since the Danish Ambassador waltzed into his theatre.

"So why," Ariel asks, "is a mortal like yourself here in the center of the salty sea?"

Tim shakes his head. "I'm…"

When I get off this island, which direction am I going? Back to London? Or on to Elsinore? My home…or my blood?

He doesn't have an answer to that question.

At the back of the pack, Romeo is still trying to romance Miranda: "I am now a castaway, you must understand, my dear…a castaway of love."

Kent sighs. "Whoever told you to be yourself gives awful advice."

Again. A rustling in the corner of Tim's eyesight. He turns and gazes into the jungle.

And his knees buckle.

It can't be. It was just a flash, there and gone quicker than a bolt of lightning.

But he was there. The late King Hamlet, the Great Dane. Clad in his suit of armor, beard like a lion's mane, eyes brown and piercing.

Here? In the jungle on this cast-off island?

"I…" he begins to step out of the caravan, toward the trees. But how could he possibly explain it? *Oh, I just saw the apparition of my dead dad—who was wearing his suit of armor instead of his swimming trunks, silly old bean—and I need to have a quick chat with him, if you don't mind.*

"Tim?" Nick says. "You look like you've just seen a ghost."

Tim is so flustered he can't even think of an ironic response. "Give me a minute, Guvs. I…I need to see something." He begins to move up the beach. The waves crash against the sand, as if grabbing his ankles and trying to drag him back.

Ariel swoops into Tim's path. "Might I suggest we continue to Prospero's compound? Nutritional delights await!"

"Honestly, Tim," Romeo adds, "we're famished."

"I'll catch up." Tim tries to sidestep the sprite, but Ariel's aerial movements mirror his exactly.

Ariel's eyes sparkle. "I'm afraid, Tim-from-London, this is something I cannot allow."

Tim stops and tenses his muscles. "Why?" In the past day, he's developed a good sense for when a dead sprint is in order, and in this moment, his internal alarm bells are ringing.

"My mighty master says so."

Kent cracks his knuckles. "I don't like the sound of that."

Miranda steps next to Tim and looks up at the fairy. "Ariel, what are you talking about?"

For the first time, Ariel looks like he's made a mistake. He squints and bonks himself upside the head. "Silly, silly me. My master made it clear you are never to know. La dee da, memory charms aren't too taxing, I suppose."

Miranda recoils, her tanned face turning ashen. "Memory charms?"

Tim digs his heels in the sand, ready to run. "She's never to know what?"

Ariel shrugs. "You all will see soon enough!" He waggles his fingers, and Miranda's eyes turn into opaque orbs. Her legs fold and she tumbles like an unmanned marionette.

"Miss!" Dogberry dives and catches Miranda before her head strikes the ground.

Ariel trills, his smile nearly splitting his cheeks. "There! Squeaky clean!" He addresses the men, slowly floating high above them. "Now, if you all will pretty please follow me by the sea."

The sand beneath Tim's shoes begins to rumble.

"What if we say no?" Kent growls.

"Oh, my master would certainly like you lot to remain breathing, but I do not believe it is a hard necessity."

Okay. Time to go.

The ground shifts beneath the castaways' feet, as if a massive gopher is tunneling below. Tim is nearly knocked off balance.

A ball of sand swells from the ground like a bubble, quickly inflating to the size of a carriage. The men gaze in wonder, and even Ariel is drawn in, eyebrows arched in curiosity.

"We should have stayed in London, m'boy," Nick exhales.

The sand bubble bursts. Particles shoot through the air like tiny daggers, and everyone cowers and covers their eyes. Tim winces against the shrapnel, but he inches his eyelids open enough to see a familiar, horrifying form.

The hunchbacked demon with clawed feet and a reptilian eye bursts from the ground, waving its arms and gnashing what teeth it has left. Romeo squeals and reaches for his rapier, but his hands are too shaky to grab hold.

Ariel sighs. "Caliban…"

Finally, an emotion other than saccharine sunshine from the fairy.

He dives toward the monster like an eagle on the hunt, but Caliban's brute strength swats the blue figure away with ease.

In the midst of its roars and rampage, Caliban briefly locks eyes with Tim. It breathes heavily and hisses, "Run, flesh-bag, run!" It looks over its enormous shoulder and then dives back into the hole from which it emerged. Its grotesque feet kick in the air, and it disappears beneath the sand.

Tim's legs twitch, begging to sprint into the jungle and hide from the ghastly horrors this island holds. The top of the tallest tree, under a craggy rock, among a thorny bush…Anyplace would be better than in Ariel's clutches.

But his friends.

Dogberry cowers in the sand next to Miranda's unconscious body, his warrior's instinct buried by panic. Ariel swoops past, and Dogberry's muscles shake. Sniffing out pickpockets in Messina hadn't prepared him for this.

Kent snags Romeo's rapier from its sheath and snorts like a bull. He lunges forward to drive the blade into Ariel's translucent chest, but the metal melts as soon as it touches the magical skin. Kent gapes at the useless hilt in his hand.

Romeo rolls his shoulders, the smirk of a dashing rogue crossing his face. He clenches his fists and, while Ariel is distracted with Kent, fires a haymaker at the back of the bald blue head. In less than a second, Ariel turns and wraps his thin fingers around Romeo's neck. The Italian screams as if scalded by a dozen branding irons.

Three fighters of great renown. Crushed like bugs.

Physical strength won't best this specter.

Nick catches Tim's attention. Sweat trickles down his face, and his eyes are utterly terrified. Yet, in spite of his fear, he winks and mouths, "Showtime."

With that, Nicholas Bottom brushes sand off his pantaloons, strikes a pose, and begins doing what he does best.

"Lo!" he projects to the proverbial back row, face contorted in what could be interpreted as an expression of either dramatic intensity or intense constipation. "Dost not thou feel from the depths of thine fundamental orifices? Beyond the breach of humanity, beneath the stretch of eternity..."

Tim nearly smirks at his friend. Even in the midst of chaos and danger, Nick knows how to butcher a soliloquy and make a *burro* of himself.

Ariel—fingers still locked around Romeo's throat—stares at Nick, utterly dumbfounded. His eyebrows are arched, mouth slightly agape. Even the spirit with the power to seize time and swat warriors like mosquitos is thunderstruck by the thespian no-how of Nicholas Bottom.

And that's exactly what Tim needs.

One man can easily slip between the trees, remain out of sight, and ultimately survive far easier than a group of five. He remembers just ten minutes earlier: the bickering and yelling and lack of cardinal directions that had resulted from the whole group wandering through the foliage. No, if they stick together, Ariel and Prospero will find them in a heartbeat.

He gives one last glance to Miranda unconscious in the sand, his heart pinging at the thought of leaving her captive.

But this is her best shot. Everyone's best shot.

With Ariel's attention on Nick and the three fighters, the young prince races into the greenery. He's gone in moments.

Low branches and vines strangle him as he runs. Twigs claw at his face. But he cannot slow, even for a split second.

This family reunion is turning out to be a real nightmare. And he hasn't even gotten home yet.

Chapter 6

So.

What fine mess am I in now?

Tim bounds through the jungle, sweat beading his forehead and stinging his eyes. The humidity is unbelievable—it's like he's wearing a coat made of bath water.

But he can't stop.

To recap:

Prospero—a seven-foot tall wizard with an admittedly incredible beard—is the master of this desert island, as well as the sapphire specter Ariel.

Ariel, under the orders of Prospero, tried to lead Tim and his friends to their "compound" for reasons unknown. And when they tried to resist, Ariel turned sinister. Still smiling, but sinister. So, probably not-good things are going down at that compound.

Caliban—the demon that looks like a donation bin of body parts—leapt from the sand and fought off Ariel for a fleeting moment. He'd warned Tim to flee…which, honestly, Tim had figured out at that point, but it's the thought that counts. The monster appears to be on their side.

Then, it fled back into the sand. Probably smart. Brute strength worked in the moment, but it likely wouldn't hold up against Ariel's flight, swiftness, or manipulation of time.

Romeo, Kent, and Dogberry were handily dispatched by Ariel.

Nick is useless in a fight.

Miranda seems unaware of the peril, but even if she were aware, Ariel could do a little finger dance and wipe her slate clean again.

It's likely that the spirit took all the humans to Prospero's compound, which was their destination in the first place.

Rogelio is still MIA.

Likely dead.

Tim's heart throbs. It's the first time he's thought that in such blunt terms. He only knew the sailor for a very brief time, but he had been a warm presence on this strange, confusing journey.

He can't run anymore—the heat is wrapped around his chest in a hideous hug, and he can't catch his breath. He spies a fallen tree propped up against a mossy boulder, and he slides into the hidey-hole.

In the shade, he takes several deep, long, cool breaths. Flies buzz around his ears like sirens and try to drink the sweat on his skin, but any place hidden from Ariel's eyes is a godsend.

So.

He closes his eyes.

What next?

Memories of last night—

Good Lord, was that just last night?

—echo through his mind. Knife in hand, parrying and maneuvering his way past Travkin and his Ruski dogs. It had felt glorious to be in control of such a volatile situation. His old fencing skills and overall agility had come in handy.

But now, no sword can defeat Ariel and his magical master.

No, he needs a ringer. An ace-in-the-hole that knows the ins and outs of the turf. A weapon that had already shown it was willing to defy Ariel.

Caliban: offspring of Sycorax and Lucifer, self-described proprietor of this island. If anything has the potential of knowing how and where to upend Prospero, it's the gray beast.

Tim shakes away the files and emerges from his hiding spot. He squints against the sun and flexes his ears. Wings flapping, leaves rustling, hissing, screeching, cracking, thwacking…No voices. No sound of anything that walks on two legs.

Caliban had said earlier it was in a band—Caliban and the Cool Crew—of which it was the only participant. It also said the hot springs had the best acoustics for practice.

As good a place to look as any.

Back when Tim had first been exploring the jungle, looking for his lost friends, Ariel had found and him quite easily.

Is the blue spirit omniscient, knowing every nook and crack of the entire island? Can he sense all forms of life? It sounds impossible, but then again, ghost dads and seven-foot-tall wizards had sounded impossible just two days earlier.

Tim scans the jungle floor. Withered foliage, gnarly vines, black and brown earth, animal scat. There. That's what he wants. His eyes follow the trail of scat, and he sees a small path worn down by the paws of the island's primal occupants. It is invisible to the distracted eye, but when he focuses, he can find a crisscross maze of footpaths—the highway system for felines, reptiles, and whatever other surprises this island wants to hurl at him.

He cautiously walks along the scat path, making as little noise as possible while staying close to the trees. If Ariel's ears are supernatural, the endless screeching of the jungle will hopefully camouflage Tim's steps among the millions of feet. And if the spirit can, in fact, detect life-forms anywhere within his domain, hopefully Tim will blend in with the traffic of creatures.

Either that, or Ariel will simply find Tim with animal dung all over his shoes.

Fingers crossed. And toes, for good measure.

Every nook and crack of the island…

Tim moves through the jungle, alternating his attention between the treetops—looking for a sneaky blue face—and the earth beneath his feet. A colorful bird screams through the air, and his hand leaps to his hip where a sword would be. If he had a sword. Which he does not.

The tip of his shoe catches, and he stumbles to regain his footing. He kneels and sees the ground has a scar. A small crack has formed, and a colony of ants has taken up residence between the two sections of earth. The crack zigzags across the scat-path, and Tim looks in either direction for another.

A memory bubbles up the surface: young Tim and his twin brother attending school within the stone walls of Elsinore. Both of them nine or ten years old—well, Hamlet is nine or ten years old, plus thirty seconds more than Tim. They sit at faux wood desks, dressed in their royal regalia, and Osric directs their attention to a large globe in his hands. The New World is noticeably missing.

It was a different time.

Anyway, Osric takes red paint and draws lines all across the surface of the globe, bisecting oceans and nations alike. The earth, he explains, is comprised of many, many pieces of flat rock called plates. Some are gigantic, some are very small. These plates fit together like a three-dimensional puzzle.

Hamlet moans, already bored. Tim shoves him. Hamlet shoves back. Osric continues, undeterred by the boys—or merely ignoring them and barreling through to the end of his court-mandated school lesson for the day.

Where these plates rub against one another are called fault lines. Beneath these fault lines is lava. And sometimes, this lava can heat nearby groundwater that makes its way to the surface. And this heated water can create hot springs.

Osric sighs, exhausted from all those words spilling out, and dismisses the restless boys.

Tim spots another crack in the earth about ten paces to his left. He straightens to his full height, wipes his brow, and follows the small fault lines, hopefully in the direction of Caliban's acoustical hot springs.

Following animal crap and dirt clefts. What a crack detective. If only Father could see me now…

Tim shakes his head and keeps moving.

Hamlet had always been wishy-washy, as long as Tim had known him. Of course, Tim had technically known his twin brother for his entire life and even before then, but, as with all siblings, Tim began to see the formation of Hamlet's true personality about when they entered their teenaged years—just as Hamlet began to see Tim's. Sure, when they were five, they both enjoyed story time, rugby, and model dragons, but none of those qualify as genuine character traits.

No, Tim may have known his brother since birth, but he learned who Hamlet really *is* the eve of their fifteenth birthday.

For years, the weight of their royal duty had rested upon their minds. Every decision and every word was formed through the lens of "How will this come back to bite me when I'm king?" Only when they were nine years old and sweeping up the fragments of a shattered chandelier did they mutter that question at the same time and realize they could not both rule. Only one Hamlet son could become king.

Their father—Old Johan Hamlet, the Great Dane—sat them both down and explained the decree regarding the line of succession. Since both Hamlets were born within thirty seconds of one other, the two sons would, on the night before their fifteenth birthday, decide which would eventually don the crown.

From that moment on, their relationship was different. Everything became a competition. Game nights, romantic relationships, academics…Any activity became a chance for Hamlet to display his dominance over his brother. When Hamlet would finish his chores faster or knock Tim out of bounds on the rugby field, Tim would chalk it up to "brothers will be brothers" in his mind.

But he always longed for a friendship with his womb-mate.

Time passed, and for a young boy, the years between nine and fifteen may as well be decades. Both boys grew in wisdom and stature—Tim became more confident in his strengths, and Hamlet began to outgrow his petty rivalry with his brother.

Hamlet would spend his days reading poetry and courting Ophelia, the most popular girl in the known world. He mainly kept to himself and said very little—except when he craved the attention of others. At that point, he would talk up a storm like nobody's business. Hamlet was a boy of extremes with a fickle mind, which made Tim nervous anytime he would try to befriend him.

Tim would practice his fencing, read all the historical manuscripts he could get his hands on, and sometimes join his father on diplomatic journeys.

It was also around this time Hamlet became what he referred to as a "Lutheran." The brothers didn't discuss this much, and all Tim really knew was that it royally ticked off their father.

Oftentimes, however, the brothers came together out of a mutual love of the theatre. As they grew, they both loved nothing more than when a traveling group of players came to Elsinore to tell a new tale. Tim and his brother would sit side-by-side, as close to the stage as possible, necks craned up and swiveling to catch every movement. Eventually, the boys convinced their parents to construct a permanent stage within Elsinore's grounds so any troupe could come at any time.

The stories, the costumes and sets, the presentation of ideas as only narrative could manage…They filled the princes' minds and burst out of their souls.

It wasn't long before the brothers Hamlet embarked on their own theatric endeavors. Hamlet was a consummate director. He would pace back and forth across Elsinore's stage, considering every possible angle for each spotlight, where an actor was to stand, what hand gesture should accompany which word. The typically melancholy and standoffish prince would come to life in this role, and Tim was his favorite audience member/critic. No decision would be made without his brother's input.

And Tim was a natural writer. He'd spend countless hours, parchment in hand, scribbling away until his hand was a blur. In those years, a quill was practically fused to the skin behind his ear, and his fingers were splotched with ink like black stars in a pale sky. He loved drawing from history, science, politics, everyday interactions…Anything and everything he heard, he used to craft stories. And his brother Hamlet was his favorite reader/critic. No tales were finalized without his brother's input.

They would laugh and collaborate and stay awake on countless nights talking. But all the same, their fifteenth birthday approached like a chariot drawn by wild horses. They couldn't stop it, nor could they banish the knowledge of it.

Their mother Gertrude pulled out all the stops for their joint birthday party: desserts from across the continent, invitations to all in Denmark (all who could read the invitations, at least), and decorations that almost blinded passersby. It was all to take place the night before the big day—

one last hurrah before one of them was officially bestowed the burden of royal duty.

The brothers Hamlet decided to present a play for the party guests— written by one, directed by the other. At the end, the princes would announce which of them shall be the king's successor.

It was the night before the performance—the night before the twins would make their choice—two nights before they turned fifteen. Their play was largely complete, but both felt the need to iron out their respective wrinkles. Thus, the late night grew later as they both threw themselves into their craft, the tense decision looming ever darker and making them focus all the more on the theatrical fiction.

They were in Elsinore's grand ballroom, where monarchs of Denmark had been crowned for centuries. Generations. The very air had a weight about it, as if all the momentous occasions had left pieces of themselves behind. Gertrude had ordered the royal groundsmen to erect a temporary stage in the ballroom, so the twins' play could be performed there rather than on the smaller thrust stage in the palace's southern wing.

Outside the stone walls, a low breeze tickled the grass and flowers, prompting crickets to crescendo their symphony. Stars and galaxies swirled in a dance from horizon to horizon, the moon lighting the way for nocturnal travelers. In other words, it was about three in the morning.

BOOM. Hamlet bounded onto the stage, and his boots thudded against the wooden boards. "And as soon as the soliloquy starts, the other actors need to get offstage. Quietly and inconspicuously, of course, but..." The young prince beams at his twin, beckoning him to finish the inside joke.

"But..." Tim looked up from his scroll. "Of course they must go, all the same! Because for a soliloquy to be a soliloquy..."

The brothers finished in unison: "He's gotta be alone onstage."

"I know, I know," Tim smiled and looked back down at the script. He sat on a cushioned pew toward the back of the empty audience, yet he'd heard every word—the acoustics of the ballroom were solid, and his brother's vocal projection was second-to-none. "I may not know all the terminology and technicalities, but there literally wouldn't be a soliloquy without this." He tapped the quill behind his ear.

"Yes, we all bow before the delicate genius." Hamlet rubbed his hands, elated to be on "holy ground," as he called it. He treasured every moment onstage. "So, the other actors move off…" He followed his own direction, every footfall rumbling under his heavy boots.

"Good thing you're not the head of costuming too."

"And *voila*," Hamlet continued, ignoring the sarcasm that had boomeranged back on him, "I wrap up the soliloquy, lights dim, end of show. Ladies wipe their tears, everyone leaps to their feet in a thunderous ovation—"

"The heavens open, cats and dogs sign a peace treaty, scholars declare a new renaissance of theatre…"

Hamlet hopped off the stage and began sauntering down the aisle toward his brother. "Renaissances are overrated. Who needs a rebirth when there are perfectly good births all over the place?"

Tim tried to keep up with his brother's thoughts. "Are…are 'births' plays in this metaphor?"

"Same thing." Hamlet waved his hand.

Tim laughed and watched his brother cruise between the pews. Slow, nonchalant steps—the gait of a teenager confident that the world would match his pace. Each word he said sounded simultaneously spontaneous and intentional. Dark hair, eyes that could pierce leather, a lean frame.

They may look identical, but Tim would give anything to be just like his brother.

"But you better believe," Hamlet's stage-ready voice boomed through the ballroom, "the applause will be *thunderous.*"

"Eh, maybe not from Laertes," Tim said. "He's still ticked you stood up his sister last year."

Laertes: a few years older than the Hamlet brothers. Ophelia's big brother. Strong. Hot-headed. Liked to show off his facial hair. Protective of his little sister. Very protective. Too protective, if you asked Tim.

Hamlet ruffled his own hair as he thought. "Ah, big bad Laertes. He's one tough croissant."

"Speaking of which…" Tim took the quill from behind his ear and pretended to write something on the parchment. He ignored the butterflies in his gut and mustered up the courage to say, "I was wondering if you wouldn't mind if I gave my front-row ticket to Ophelia, and after the show and ceremony and everything, we took a walk around the palace, and I got her a cola or something?" It all tumbled out in one hot stream.

Hamlet's swinging steps stumbled for a moment. He clenched his teeth and avoided his brother's eyes. "Actually…We kinda have plans together the night after next."

Two nights from now. Our birthday.

Tim stammered, "Oh! I'm sorry. I didn't know you two were back together."

"It's new." Hamlet grimaced and sighed, "Hey, I'm sorry, buddy. I-I know you have a thing for—"

"No, no!" Tim's quill scribbled across the page, his pretend-writing growing a bit frantic. He looked up from the script and returned the quill behind his ear. "No worries at all. Promise."

They both knew there were, in fact, worries, but Hamlet didn't push it.

Silence echoed through the extravagant ballroom. The entire palace was long-asleep, and the only sound to be heard was the icy wind scraping against the stone exterior.

"So…" Hamlet shoved his hands in his pockets and paced down the aisle. At that moment, he looked stiff, awkward. Most people would think it unusual—Prince Hamlet could charm the socks off anyone—but this was the tone the brothers always used when talking to each other about matters of actual substance. "I overheard Osric talking with Dad about tomorrow night."

Tim's stomach dropped a bit. If the eavesdropped conversation had been about the birthday party, Father would have been speaking with Gertrude, their mother. But he was talking with Osric, which meant they were discussing the ceremony in which Denmark's next head honcho would be chosen.

History had no answer to the twins' dilemma. There was no precedent for two identical heirs, and the King had cooked up a choosing-ceremony himself. Tim and Hamlet had no idea what was in store, and any nibble of information was welcome.

Tim set the script on his lap. "Yeah?"

"Oh yeah. I heard how we're gonna pick."

"No way…" Tim rubbed the pathetic patch of fuzz on his chin. "What is it? Gladiator fight to the death? Spelling bee? Ten-page essay on 'Why I Want to Rule This Icicle of a Kingdom'?"

"Nah, nothing that dramatic, unfortunately." Hamlet flopped onto the padded pew in front of Tim's. He propped up his feet and peeked over. "Ballot."

"Ballot?" Tim thought he'd misheard.

"Mhmm." Hamlet laid his head down so Tim could only see his boots sticking up. "We each write the name of the dashing young lad who we think should be king. Dad'll read them and announce to the world." He twiddled his fingers to mimic confetti and fanfare.

"Are you kidding? They've been building this up since we were nine. After all these years of speculation and 'Oh, there's no precedent for this sort of thing…The fate of the kingdom rests on this decision…' La-dee-da, drivel-drivel-drivel. It's a secret ballot where there are only two voters and two options?"

"Yeah, it sounded weird to me too."

Now it was Tim's turn to stand and pace in the aisle. "I mean, what happens if we tie?"

Hamlet, still lying on the pew, shrugged his feet. "We discuss amongst ourselves for a few minutes and vote again, I guess."

Tim rubbed his eyes—the three a.m. fairies had arrived to stuff steel-wool in his mind. "But if we stay deadlocked long enough, they have to break the tie eventually. They can't keep serving punch to the audience forever."

Hamlet laughed. "Imagine the lines at the bathroom."

"They'll have to start taking orders for breakfast!" Tim noticed some ink splotches on the back of his hand and tried to buff them off as he thought. "But honestly, knowing Father, if we kept tying up the vote, he'd just snort like a bull and make the choice himself."

"Yeah, I can definitely see that." Hamlet rolled off the pew and stood. It looked like the fairies had gotten to him too. He stretched his arms over his head and let out a grunt. "I can see him now, decked out in his formal military garb, twenty-dozen medals on his chest. He'll be itching to get on with the royal stuff after sitting in the back row for our whole play."

Tim looked at the stage. From his vantage point near the back of the audience, it looked gorgeous: a cloth backdrop of the Danish landscape, framed by a thick red curtain. And that was it. Sparse and stripped down, purposefully drawing attention to the falseness of the stage, and leaving room for the spectator to fill in the blanks with the actors' help.

He loved the image of rural Denmark. It was just like the stage: sparse and stripped down. Rolling hills, an azure sky, colors that had a cold bite to them. Over the years, he had trekked across the kingdom on diplomatic missions with his father, exploring the plains and forests and villages and farmland. It was a good nation to call home.

The question popped out before he could snag it: "So who are you gonna vote for?"

The words echoed in the vast ballroom. Hamlet made a crooked smile. "I know this'll sound dumb, since this has been hanging over us for years…But I haven't really thought about it. I figured I'd go with my gut when the time came. My gut's never let me down."

"Well, do you want to be king?"

"Believe it or not," Hamlet sarcastically dragged out the words, "I've gone back and forth on the subject."

"What?" Tim widened his eyes. Sarcastically. "*You*, uncertain about something?"

"Shut it." Hands back in pockets.

"You go back and forth like a rower's oar, brother."

"Look, I know." And in less than a moment, the dark circles under Hamlet's eyes turned into bags of sand. His entire body sagged under some invisible burden. "I know. I'm erratic, neurotic, fitful." He sighed one last word: "Crazy…" He wiped a hand across his face. "You hear enough of that for long enough, it starts to seep into your bones."

Tim winced, regretting the timing of his sarcasm. Hamlet's mood swings were common, but their severity was always striking. He felt sympathy for his brother, but it also kept Tim from trying to get too close.

Hamlet shot a sad smirk. "I'm not crazy, despite public opinion."

"I-I don't think that—"

"Yes you do, and that's fine. It's my fault, I suppose." With great visible effort, Hamlet swallowed his sorrow and went on. "But, back on-script, if *I* were king, I think I could relate well to the masses. Public speaking comes naturally to me. And, y'know, I'm screwed up, like a lot of people are."

"True." Tim said. "You also know how to avoid of a fight."

"And like a true gentleman, I'll let that roll off my back."

"Honestly, that's a good thing. You could negotiate and talk your way out of a scrape."

"Don't sell yourself short." Hamlet lightly punched Tim's arm. "You're smart and silver-tongued, sure, but if the gloves came off..." He made a whipping sound and mimed drawing a sword. "I wouldn't want to be in their shoes."

"I'm no soldier."

"Even better. A man with a sword on his belt is far more fearsome than one who waves it around constantly. I can see your portrait in the king's chambers: Tim Hamlet the Hippo."

"The Hippo?" Tim feigned anger through his laughter.

"The most dangerous creature in the animal kingdom, but you wouldn't know it just by sight."

"And I suppose you're Hamlet the Eagle...or the Lion?"

"Nah." He leaned against a pew. "I'm Hamlet the Fox. Sly, charming, independent but loved by all." His words were positive, but he said them all so sadly. He shuffled back toward the stage.

Tim paused. "So you *have* given it some thought."

Hamlet chuckled once. "I'm almost fifteen years old and I might be given a crown tomorrow. Yeah, I've given it a bit of noodle-time." The boots had nothing to do with the heaviness of each step. He reached the stage and sat on its edge.

Tim followed his brother and popped a squat on the front row. Right next to where he had hoped Ophelia would sit the following night. He shook his head to evict the thought.

"I don't want to choose," Tim said, vocalizing an idea that had been percolating for years. "Let's make Father do it. Don't let him pit us against each other."

Hamlet cocked a brow. "You think?"

"Yeah!" Tim smiled, getting more excited as he spoke. "If we keep tying up the vote and force his hand, we'd get a concrete answer without one of us begrudging the other for the rest of our lives."

"If it's out of our control," Hamlet nodded, "there's not much we can get mad about."

"And we'd both be good at the job." Tim scooted forward on the padded pew. "I mean, it's not like when one of us is chosen, the other disappears. We'll have to live under the other's rule, still a prince. We'll be around each other—might as well not be miffed forever."

"Yeah…" Gears turned inside Hamlet's skull. He stared at the floor, but his mind was lightyears away, piecing thoughts together into a certain shape. "What if…" He locked eyes with Tim, practically vibrating with excitement. "What if we team-kinged this whole thing?"

"What do you mean?" Tim would be lying if he said Hamlet's mounting enthusiasm wasn't contagious.

"We lock up the vote, Dad picks one of us, right? That's inevitable. But then we just act as co-monarchs regardless. We're king together. Two Hamlets for the price of one!"

"Can we do that?"

"We'll be king—they can't stop us! Look, Tim…" Hamlet sat next to his brother, eyes shining brighter than Tim had ever seen them. "…let's make a pact right now. Twinkie promise…" He froze for a second. "I immediately regret saying that, but the sentiment stands. Let's rule together! No matter who Dad picks tomorrow night, when the time comes for one of us to sit in the big chair, we rule as a duo. Side by side, making history!"

"Really?"

"Yeah, man. We're brothers! Apart, we're pretty great, but together, we're unstoppable. I think quickly, you think ahead, I'm wide, you're deep, yin, yang, up, down, spaghetti, meatballs, the whole bit! Plus, for our royal portrait, they'll only have to paint the same guy twice."

Tim's heart almost beat out of his chest. His brother had never opened up to him like this—it was like a dream.

The Hamlet twins. Side by side.

"We're a team, man," Hamlet said.

A smile exploded across Tim's face. "Alright." He held out his little finger. "Twinkie promise."

Hamlet slumped down in the pew. "I'm never gonna live that down, am I?"

"Never." Tim elbowed his brother's ribs as they cackled.

They both let out a sigh as the laughter settled over them. Tim giggled under his breath one more time.

"What?" Hamlet asked.

"The Fox and the Hippo," Tim answered. "Sounds like a good children's book."

Night bled into dawn. It was the eve of their birthday…The day of the ceremony.

Guests trickled in from across the nation—men, women, children, fishers, doctors, builders, and beggars were all welcome in the halls of Elsinore. Food lined tables as far as the eye could see—shrimps and salmon, pastries, breads, ground beef and sausages. Oh, and wine. Lots of wine.

Among the throng were the twins' good friends Frederick Rosencrantz and Christian Guildenstern. The two boys were practically attached at the hip, never seen apart, except for when they used separate toilet stalls. They arrived with a satchel full of firecrackers from the East and a couple of devilish grins—Tim begged them not to set the crackers off, and Hamlet begged them not to set the crackers off until after the play had concluded successfully.

The Hamlet twins were dressed in formal black attire, with gold buttons and thread highlighting their every move. They stood by the front gate, greeting guests and schmoozing with their parents' regal friends. Ancient women in jewel-encrusted gowns fawned over them for hours, pinching cheeks and saying how they knew the boys when they were "this" tall, while the equally-ancient men sniffed around and grumbled about how "soft" princes were "these days." It was torturous, and the brothers were restless, wishing to get on with their play. Hamlet had worn his heavy boots from the late night before, and every now and then, he clomped his feet like a horse to make Tim laugh.

Finally, the time came.

Hamlet ushered the actors backstage and gave them one last dictatorial pep talk as Tim took his seat on the front row. Spectators filled the grand ballroom like water rushing into a wrecked ship, chatting amongst themselves and rustling the playbills distributed at the entrance. His mother Gertrude sat beside Tim, her garish crown likely obstructing the view of any audience members behind her—but no one would dare call her on it in a million years.

The lights dimmed and a few people shushed their neighbors, which prompted more shushes, which prompted more, and so on. Hamlet strode out from behind the simple set, wearing his black attire from the party. He locked eyes with his brother on the front row and waggled his eyebrows.

"Friends, Danes, compatriots, allow the brothers Hamlet to transport you. We shall tell a tale the likes of which you have never seen before, nor shall you likely see again!"

It all went off without a hitch. Hamlet's direction served the other actors well, but it was perfectly clear the boy in black was the star of the production. As he should be. His charm could bring together the worst of enemies, and his twin's writing played perfectly to his strengths.

The audience loved it. Tim smiled ear to ear as the spectators laughed, gasped, and hissed at the exact moments they were meant to. He wrung his hands to keep from leaping for joy—it's every writer's dream for an audience to react just as intended.

The last scene of the play arrived. The other actors exited stage-left—quietly and inconspicuously, of course—and Hamlet surveyed the crowd, eyes steely, jaw set. He took a breath and began the show's closing soliloquy.

"What is a man, if his chief good and the market of his time be but to sleep and feed?" He clenched his fists. "A beast! Nothing more!" A took a few enthused steps toward the audience, his boots thudding like a heartbeat. It was perfect. "Sure...He that made us with such large discourse, looking before and after, gave us not that capability and god-like reason to fester in us unused."

Chills raced across Tim's flesh. He could feel the collective breath of the audience being held as they sat in rapt attention. His words, being delivered flawlessly by his brother, had captivated them. These words that he had labored over and scribbled on a scroll, born in his mind and birthed through the quill...These words made him something special.

The soliloquy went on and reached its climax. Hamlet's eyes were on fire, his voice blasting throughout the ballroom with the power of a sledgehammer. "What a piece of work is man! How noble in reason...How infinite in faculty! How admirable in action! How like an angel in apprehension! How like a god..." He punched the air and scoffed, "The beauty of the world! The paragon of animals!" He paused, his sudden silence wrapping the every spectator in a blanket of tension. "And yet to me..." he whispered, and everyone leaned in. "...man is but the quintessence of dust."

Hamlet's head dropped as if his neck muscles suddenly gave up. He stood center stage amid the deafening quiet. Tim was pinned to his seat. No one dared move...or breath.

Then it came. Thunderous applause. Gertrude was the first to her feet, tears in her eyes and beaming with pride. Tim was right behind her, just about leaping into the air. He looked around at the rippling crowd—Osric, Rosencrantz and Guildenstern, several ambassadors, kings and queens...Every single person in the room clapped and cheered and hailed their praise. Tim even caught a glimpse of the beautiful Ophelia throwing a flower onto the stage for Hamlet.

Is Father here? I don't see him—

No matter.

Hamlet raised his head, all smiles and charm once again. He clasped his hands together and graced the audience with a bow. The applause spiked again. Hamlet beckoned Tim onto the stage and said something with a smile, but the cheering drowned out the words.

Tim smiled back, pure joy and satisfaction swelling in his chest. He held out his hands, silently saying he was content on the first row. Hamlet could own the stage.

Hamlet nodded once, and the following moment between the brothers was one Tim keeps in his heart to this day. They simply held each other's gaze. As the grand ballroom of Elsinore erupted in cheers, the brothers may as well have been alone.

The audience wouldn't have reacted to my words without Hamlet's performance. Nor would there be cheers and flowers for Hamlet without my writing.

Kinship. Partnership. Friendship. All in that fleeting, noisy second.

As excited as Tim was the night before, when they discussed their joint-kingship, he could barely contain himself at that moment. Finally. He and his brother were a united front.

Hefty footfalls boomed from backstage, and then Johan Hamlet—the Great Dane of Denmark—shouldered his way around the red curtain. He wore his formal, emerald-green military uniform, complete with a dozen medals pinned to his left breast (and a few overflowing onto his right). His deep-brown eyes surveyed the crowd with quick efficiency.

"Yes, yes," he waved the crowd down like it was a bucking horse. "Well done, boy. Very good, very fun." He'd clearly just walked in—the preceding show was in no way very fun.

One by one, the audience members retook their seats, and the air became much thinner as they all realized what was coming next.

"Go ahead and take a seat," the King said to Hamlet, and the teenaged prince slouched offstage, suddenly and pugnaciously eclipsed during his moment of glory. He plopped on the front-row pew mirroring Tim's across the aisle. Tim tried to make eye contact with him across the chasm of the ballroom, but Hamlet's gaze was stormy and directed at the floor.

"Now," Old Hamlet clapped his hands like Zeus creating a thunderbolt, "ladies, lords, and attendants, on to the main event! As you all are likely to know, my name is Johan Odysseus Hamlet…King of Denmark. And believe it or not, I am not immortal. Although…" he wound up for a punchline, "Norway and the Polacks may think so."

The Danes in the audience laughed as he overdramatically dusted off his shoulder. The cackles died down, and the King quickly polished one of his medals with his sleeve—Tim couldn't tell if it was part of the joke or mere instinct.

"Regarding my corporeal body, as well as the line of monarchs, it is clear that I need an heir, so that my passing is not the end of Denmark's leadership. But many of you also know this has hit an unforeseen snag. I have two sons who entered this world within moments of one another. Twins!"

A few foreigners in the audience murmured in surprise, and all were enraptured at the live melodrama playing out before them. The fiction the brothers had produced moments ago was forgotten.

"Only one son will become my successor, of course, and continue the Hamlet legacy of strength and honor. And we shall find out which it will be this very night! How, you may ask?" He paused for a reaction.

For skipping out on the play, Father sure is trying his hand at being dramatic.

"They each will secretly vote for which brother they believe would be the finest, noblest king of this land."

The crowd ate that up. They turned to their neighbors and hubbubbed and hullabalooed. Gertrude shot an impish smile sideways at Tim, who remembered he wasn't supposed to know about the secret ballot, and then covered his mouth in "shock."

Hamlet's the actor, for sure.

Tim stood slightly to look at his brother across the aisle, but Hamlet hadn't moved. Hadn't reacted. He sat motionless, with his eyes downcast, making his whole posture look like a question mark.

"A side-note of importance," the King added as if he just remembered. Which he likely did. "Although tonight we will find out who my successor will be, he will not bear the crown until his twentieth year. If I should fall before that time, my brother Claudius will become king."

Tim craned his neck toward the back of the ballroom. He'd known about this caveat, but Father rarely talked about his own brother. Uncle Claudius sat in the middle of the crowd, arms crossed, his light hair cropped close to his scalp. His assistant Polonius was next to him, head back, mouth agape, snoring like a banshee.

The King stroked his lion's-mane of a beard. "But how likely is that to happen, eh? Onward with the voting!"

Hamlet was to go first. The King beckoned him backstage.

Minutes ticked by with agonizing lethargy, and Tim's knee bounced the entire time. If the brothers' plan was to tie up the ceremony by voting for each other, why was Hamlet taking so long?

The King, still on center stage, barked, "Tim, be waiting for him when he comes out."

So Tim stood, his legs stiff and shaky at the same time, and made his way behind the rural backdrop he loved so much. A man in the Danish green uniform directed him toward a small door that led to the water closet. Such royal treatment, voting for who would take the Danish throne while sitting on a porcelain one.

He clasped his hands and rocked back and forth. Nothing to do but wait. Wait and think. Think and sway and sweat. Sweat and—

The door eased open before Tim had done too much sweating and too much thinking. Hamlet emerged, paler and more gaunt than he had been onstage. Or was Tim just projecting his own nerves?

"Hey." Tim forced a stammer to remain dormant. "Make the old man choose, right?"

Hamlet looked at Tim, but his eyes were distant. He flexed his brow and gave a smile that would disappoint an actor of his caliber.

The brother slid past his twin, leaving the lavatory door open. Tim's heart was gripped in a steel vice, and he also had a coppery taste in his mouth, and his shoes were heavy like iron. He shook his head to dispel the metallic metaphors and stepped into the closet.

It's good. We're good. Everything's good.

He wrote his brother's name on the waiting ballot, rolled it up, and returned to the stage. It took less than thirty seconds.

He handed the slip of paper to the King and took his seat. The cushion on the pew was still warm.

Johan Hamlet held two secret ballots in his mighty hands—he unrolled both, and their secrets were now known only to him.

His thick beard spread with a smile.

And in that fleeting, hushed second, Tim knew whom his brother had voted for.

Tim looked across the aisle at Hamlet, who, this time, looked right back. His eyes were heavy, face drawn, seemingly as confused as Tim.

The King pocketed the ballots and cleared his throat. "My friends…"

Tim felt like he was falling. His thoughts got tangled up a big pile. Kinship. Partnership. Friendship. The Hamlet twins, side by side…

He mouthed, *"Why?"*

Hamlet stared back. As hollow as Tim felt, his brother looked just as bewildered, as if there was a literal war occurring within his mind.

Suddenly, the crowd roared to life with cheers and screams, but Tim didn't hear a thing. Flower petals fell from the ceiling, musicians began to play triumphant chords. People swarmed Hamlet from all sides, slapping his back and screeching their congratulations. Gertrude sprang up to run to her son, and Ophelia weaved her way through the crowd and threw her arms around his shoulders.

The brothers kept their gazes locked the entire time. Tim held out empty hands, hoping Hamlet would offer an answer.

Instead, the future king shook his head and mouthed back, "*I don't know.*"

Hamlet is a boy of extremes with a fickle mind. He isn't a bad person. He was as dumbfounded that night as Tim was. But he isn't a brother to be counted on. And what kind of brother is that?

Chapter 7

There. The hot springs.

Tim is no private investigator, but he's pretty sure he's found Caliban's hidey-hole, given the mist flowing over the ground, the sudden uptick in the already-sweltering temperature, and the fact that the air smells of armpit.

He hops over one last elephantine root and enters a wide clearing. Without the shade of the tall tree trunks and umbrella-like leaves, the sun beats down directly on Tim's skin.

At this point, I'm already rouge—let's go for scarlet...and maybe vermillion, by the end of this nightmare of a beach vacation.

The clearing Tim has found himself in is more of a crater—the cracked earth angles downward toward a large pool in the center of the circle. The ground is barren here, except for a few brave blades of grass peeking out between the dusty fissures. Several spots are charred—large ovals of ash, spaced out evenly, leading down to the steaming pool.

Caliban's footprints. It has definitely been here recently.

Tim begins to walk toward the pool at the crater's center. "Caliban?" he hisses into the air. He's still uncertain how omniscient Ariel and Prospero are, and it would be tragic to be caught when he was so close to finding help. "Caliban, please be here."

Ting ting ting…

Tiny, tinny sounds itch the insides of Tim's ear. Faint and distant, like a mosquito coughing inside a suit of armor.

Is that…?

The steam from the pool licks his ankles as he gets closer to the center of the crater, and he wipes a sweat/condensation concoction from his forehead. He can hardly breathe through the humidity.

Around the pool, several rocky crags jut up from the ground, where tectonic plates have rammed into each other for thousands of years. Tim peeks behind a few of the rocks, searching for the twangy reverbs in the shadows.

Not here. But he's closer.

Ting ting…

He moves to the next crag, and there, crouching in the shade, is Caliban, clutching a guitar made of sticks, vines, tree bark, and dried mud. Its monstrous fingers pick at the strings, making the *ting* sound Tim had followed. The demon's alligator eye fixes on the Danish prince.

"Hey, flesh-bag."

Tim leans against the crag, gulping for air. He stills his beating heart and replies, "Afternoon, Caliban. I'm here for band practice."

The creature perks up immediately. "Really?" It scrambles to its feet and waddles out from behind the crag. "Alright, I've managed to piece together a drum kit, a xylophone, and a tambourine. I've always pictured Miranda on the *tamb*, so you pick from the others…" It sets its fetid fingers around the guitar's neck, ready to play. "Our first song is called 'Beelzebub Me the Wrong Way,' and then we'll transition directly into 'Wrong Side of the Tempest.' And a-one, a-two…"

"Caliban!" Tim hisses again and holds out his hands. "Ariel might hear you! Keep it down."

The stocky creature freezes in mid-strum and narrows its eyes—both the tiny one and the reptilian one. "You think I'm scared of Ariel? Hardly!" It drops the guitar and sits on the rock, arms crossed in a hellish pout. "On my island?" It scoffs. "Besides, they won't hear us. The acoustics here echo all the sound back at us." It gestures at the perimeter of the crater they're currently in. "No one ever hears my music."

Tim nods to himself. *Smart demon.*

He forces himself to sit next to the hideous creature. The stench is something he'd never imagined: a deadly combo of sulfur, BO, and a sickly-sweet body spray that tries to cover up the first two.

"Caliban, I need your help to find my friends and get out of here."

"No can do." It shrugs. "Prospero's got 'em by now. I did what I could on the beach."

"Why did you do that? Why help us?"

"Wait…" It turns its moldy gaze on Tim. "You're not here for band practice, are you?"

"Caliban…" Tim sets his hand on the creature's forearm in an attempt to make a connection. It feels like picking up dog-doo with a paper bag. He dismisses the thought and tries a new question—that's all he can do until Caliban actually answers one. "What's going on? Why did Prospero tell Ariel to take us to his compound?"

"That wizard and the girl have been squatting on my island for thirteen years. Rent-free, I'll add. And every now and then, the big hairy man will raise his stick into the sky, and the wind'll blow, and clouds'll get black, and rain shoots sideways. And, four times outta five, a busted ole boat will wash ashore, along with the few flesh-bags that can swim."

"Prospero caused the hurricane that sank Rogelio's ship?" Two days ago, Tim would have buckled at that news, but here he is—on a quest given to him by his dad's ghost, sitting next to Lucifer's illegitimate son.

Caliban lets out a sigh. "Haven't you been listening, or is all that hair clogging your thinking space? Yeah, then after a boat gets smashed, Ariel swoops in and leads the survivors to the wizard's fancy house, just like he did with you six. People go in, no one comes out. I hear he's got a hot tub and a foosball table."

Tim backtracks. "Six?"

"Mhmm. Ariel grabbed one before you and the others showed up. A loud, happy guy. Tried to hug Ariel when he saw him."

Rogelio. He made it!

"Wh-What does…" Tim is reeling from all information Caliban has been expositing. "What does Prospero do with all the castaways?"

"I dunno, I'm not invited." The creature sits up as straight as its hunchback allows, trying to mask its loneliness and melancholy. "That's okay—once my band makes it big, we'll definitely be invited into the house."

Tim feels a moment of solemn solidarity, and he pats Caliban's shoulder.

I know all about endlessly seeking someone's approval, only for the finish line to move at the last second.

His mind is close to galloping out of control. Too much has happened in the past twenty minutes.

People go in the compound…no one comes out.

"Caliban, help me save my friends. Please."

"Uh-uh, no way." Caliban bends forward, retrieves the "guitar," and proceeds to "tune" it. All the musical notes sound like rusty joints on a suit of armor.

"Why did you distract Ariel so that I could run away?"

"Psh…" Caliban shifts uncomfortably next to him. "I did that to screw with Ariel, that floaty little snot. You got away, so the wizard has gotta be mad at him. My mission is accomplished."

"Well," Tim ruffles his hair as he thinks. "Regardless of your intention, you wound up helping me. It's all the same to Prospero, I bet…And I also bet they're on their way right here, right now, to ask you some questions."

Despite Caliban's earlier assertions to the contrary, a flicker of fear passes across its craggy face.

"I'll tell you what, though, Caliban." While fear is still on the creature's mind, Tim stands and places his fists on his hips, hoping he looks brave, strong, and heroic. "I bet that together, we can bust into that compound. Without their invitation. I leave with my friends. You stay, and make it your new castle. The domain from which you rule this island!"

Breathless wonder beams from Caliban's face. "I would get the foosball table?"

Tim claps his hands with every word: "You would get the foosball table."

Without a moment's hesitation, Caliban lurches to its feet and flings the guitar into the the hot spring. The steam swallows it whole with a wet *plop*.

"Let's do it, flesh-bag." A rascally smile splits Caliban's festering mug.

Tim rubs his hands together and bounces on his heels. "Alright. I imagine it won't be easy to break into the home of a seven-foot wizard and his floating, blue manservant. So, Caliban, what can you do?"

"What do you mean?" The creature is quivering with adrenaline, ready to act.

"Well, Ariel can fly. He's fairly strong, and he can bloody-well stop time. You're the progeny of the Prince of Darkness—what can you do?"

Caliban's face lights up in realization. "Ooh!" It tumbles to the ground in a sitting position, grabs its left ankle, and pulls its beastly foot behind its head. The hunchback gets in the way a bit, but with a lot of grunting and great effort, it manages to hold the position. It looks up at Tim with a winded smile, like a schoolboy in a talent show showing off for his dad.

"What's happening?" Tim says.

"Look what I can do!"

"Caliban, I meant what supernatural abilities do you have?"

"I don't see you doing this."

"Okay…" Tim rubs his temples. "What was with the whole sand-bubble situation you did earlier on the beach? You can travel underground?"

The creature grasps its right ankle and tries to hoist it behind its head as well. "Only through dirt, sand, mud, and feces. I haven't figured out rock yet." It pulls too hard and strains a muscle. "AGH, MY BRIMSTONES!" A shriek of agony fills the crater as Caliban rolls around and holds its injured groin—all with both feet stuck behind its head.

Tim can only stare. This'll be much harder than he'd imagined…and he'd imagined it being nigh impossible.

He paces away from the demon caught in a pretzel shape, trying to approach the dilemma three-dimensionally. "The castaways are being held in Prospero's compound, so that's where we need to go. Neither of us has ever been in there, but that'll be the battlefront of this whole enchilada. We need reconnaissance."

Caliban finally frees its legs and stands. "Check out the flesh-bag and his big, fancy vocabulary."

"Reconnaissance, Caliban." Tim wipes sweat out of his eyes for the thousandth time. "We need to know the layout of the place, entrances, exits…what the blazes even goes on in there!" He throws his hands up and hangs his head in exhaustion.

"I don't see the big deal," Caliban says. "The wizard takes all the humans to his compound. Right this second, he's trying to give you a lift to where you're trying to sneak in."

Tim meets Caliban's lopsided gaze. "Caliban…" He feels the juices finally start to flow. "How good are you at improv?"

The creature puffs out its chest. "What self-respecting musician can't riff and scat?"

"Well, you can travel through scat—along with sand and dirt—but that's another conversation."

The joke whizzes right over Caliban's head, which isn't hard, considering the demon is only a few feet tall. "I can improvise with the best of 'em!"

"Good, because I'm terrible at it. Here's what we're gonna do…"

▪   ▪   ▪

"Unhand me, you fiend!"

Tim trudges through the jungle, Caliban hobbling a few steps behind him. A thick vine holds Tim's wrists together behind his back, making it look like the island-dwelling demon has taken the castaway prisoner.

Of course, this is all a show. A community-theatre-level show.

When putting this charade together, Tim had learned Caliban doesn't know how to tie a knot, so the vine was wrapped around his wrists a few times.

In order to appear haggard and battle-worn, Tim has slathered some mud across his clothes and face. It's tacky and looks far too deliberate to be realistic.

And then there's the acting.

Caliban hasn't said a single word so far. It stares straight ahead and walks with stiff, mechanical steps, like a rusty toy soldier. Nothing like a demon who has just taken a man captive.

And Tim…He's trying his best. His track record as a director is abysmal, to say the least, so he doesn't know how to coax the right moves out of Caliban, and he certainly doesn't know how to coax them out of himself.

When improvising like this, Tim falls back on the melodramatic. Some would call this "playing to the back row"—Hamlet would call it "playing to the bargain bin."

"This injustice shall not stand! Good will prevail!" Tim projects from his gut so that the entire jungle can hear him. "I say, you foul creature, a reckoning is coming!"

Caliban accidentally brushes against Tim's arm, and Tim flops to the ground as if he's made of feathers. He cries, "What savagery!"

The two pause for a moment, listening to the jungle breathe around them. Birds twittering, leaves rustling, insects buzzing. No sign of Prospero or Ariel.

Tim sighs and stands back up. "C'mon, Caliban. Let's keep moving." He moves on, the demon marching behind.

Did I seriously say "Unhand me, you fiend"? No wonder vendors sell rotten fruit outside the Masterpiece Centre on my shows' opening nights.

Hour three of their one-star, two-bit production is fast approaching. They've been at this for most of the afternoon—Tim's face has sunburned and peeled, and the layer of skin under that is now burning as well. Not a peep from the wizard. Daylight will start fading soon enough.

Tim clears his throat and starts again: "My stars, what a wretched predicament I find myself in!"

Good Lord, am I really that bad? I sound like an alien mimicking sounds I've heard a flesh-bag make.

He groans at his internal use of Caliban's phrase.

I need to get off this island ASAP.

The atmosphere shifts slightly, and the air in Tim's ears pops. He gulps.

Prospero appears a few steps in front of them—not with a *boom*, or out of a portal or anything ostentatious. He just strolls out from behind the air, his giant form immediately casting a shadow upon the young prince and the devil's offspring.

"Hello again, squirt." Prospero narrows his sharp eyes at Tim, his wooly beard twisted into a scowl.

"Prospero!" Tim buckles his knees as if relieved. "Thank the heavens above you arrived when you did! This ravenous gremlin has captured me and is taking me to the hot springs to cook me alive and eat my flesh!"

"The hot springs are that way." Prospero points his gnarled staff over Tim's shoulder.

"Well," Tim backpedals. "I mean, I'm no navigator. I'm not in charge here. And look, I-I'm captured." He shows off his bound wrists.

The wizard scoffs. "Okay, you're embarrassing me. You're done." He turns his venom to Caliban. "You...*slave*," he hisses. "Explain yourself in the next ten seconds, or your every nerve will catch on fire." He clutches his staff with both fists, flexing his mighty arms.

Caliban starts sputtering. "The...I-I-I just, y'see...he's, he's man...like..."

Tim cringes, feeling Caliban's pain. *Oh no. Textbook stage fright.*

He's never seen performance anxiety this bad. It's a chariot-wreck he can't look away from.

Caliban wipes its palms on its tattered trousers, then stares up and to the right. The demon has graduated from stammering to making guttural noises. "See, i-it's *grrr* and I *vooo* like *huuu*..."

Prospero tightens his grip on the staff, and Caliban's ramblings morph into screams of agony. A gray square shoots out of the demon's mouth, directly into Prospero's hand. Caliban falls to its knees, hunchback heaving, all attempts at theatre forgotten.

Tim tenses up, his sweat turning ice-cold.

The wizard examines the tooth in his giant hand, repulsed. He tosses it into the brush like a piece of garbage and rumbles, "Enough." He saws his staff through the air with one powerful thrust, and an instant later, Ariel cannonballs from the sky.

"Tim! I wondered where you wormed off to!" the specter says in his singsong manner.

"Ariel, take the man to the cavern," Prospero thunders, glaring at Caliban as he speaks. "I need to have a word with this vermin."

Caliban shudders and whimpers, looking like it wants nothing more than to curl into a ball and disappear into the dirt. It shoots its mismatched eyes at Tim for no more than a second, but in that second, Tim recognizes more human emotion than he thought was possible in a demon.

Fear. Uncertainty. And yet, trust.

Tim covertly winks. *Stay the course, my grimy, slimy friend.*

Before Tim can see Caliban's response, Ariel swoops between them. "Very well, Tim." He clasps his blue hands around Tim's forearms. "Relax and stay as stiff as you can."

Tim hesitates. "I'm not sure I—"

ZIP.

"—follow."

A second ago, he and Ariel were in the heart of a jungle.

Now, they're standing in front of the mouth of a cave at the base of a mountain.

His body feels like it's been compressed by a giant rolling pin. He doubles over, suddenly grateful for his empty stomach.

"Forgive my impatience," Ariel chirps. "Human transportation limbs have always been far too cumbersome for my taste."

"How did…?" Tim gawks at the monstrous mountain. Trees and bluffs sprout from its side like insect antennae. It's so tall and so sharp, it practically rips a hole in the blue sky. It's impossible to miss, and yet, he hasn't seen it all day—he and Ariel must be on the other side of the island, miles and miles away from where they were eight seconds ago. "Actually, I don't need to know."

"Enter, if you please!" Ariel flourishes an arm toward the yawning mouth of the cave. "Welcome to your new home."

Don't like the sound of that. But there's no place to run or hide where Ariel won't catch him. Tim sees no option other than to walk into the compound he had sprinted through the jungle to avoid.

His shoes click against the stone floor, and the noise bounces eternally from wall to wall, on and on and on. Moss and fungi dangle from the ceiling, and the walls are slick with condensation, as if the cave is sweating. With each step deeper into the cave, Tim feels the weight of the gigantic mountain pushing down on him. It feels like one loud noise will bring the whole thing crashing down.

They keep walking—well, Tim walks and Ariel glides—for what feels like miles, until the tunnel widens out into a gigantic cavern. Tim gasps at the immense size. The mountain is practically hollowed out to house Prospero's compound.

And it truly is a stronghold fit for a sorcerer. Crystals are imbedded in the walls and ceiling, filling the cavern with a low luminescence and casting a dreamlike aura over everything. Massive stalactites have sprouted from the granite floor, like monuments to Prospero's might. In fact, one stone column has been carved into a likeness of the wizard, complete with a long beard and condescending expression. The statue is truly a sight to behold, at least three times bigger than its fleshy counterpart.

"Rejoice, Tim, and behold!" Ariel's voice echoes all the way to the top of the hollow mountain…and then all the way back down.

Tim gives the spirit a side-glance. "A bit dramatic, eh?"

If Ariel heard him, he doesn't let on. "Follow me, my bipedal fellow." He floats forward into the cavern. Here in the darkness, his skin glows like a blue moon on a clear night. "There is a matter of major magnitude we must mitigate posthaste!"

The air is cool within this stone citadel. Tim takes a deep breath and observes his new surroundings. The floors, walls, ceilings…Everything is dark rock.

No wonder Caliban has never been able to sneak in. Very smart of Prospero to set up shop in a cave.

Against the far wall is an elevated platform, upon which looms a granite throne. A lion's pelt is draped over the seat, to cushion Prospero's mighty buns. From this throne, Prospero would have a view of the entire cavern. There's a racquetball court, a bar fully stocked with coconuts and pineapples, a set of barbells…And there: the much-sought-after foosball table of Caliban's dreams. It's all carved out of rock.

And there's more—a shadowy corner that Tim can't quite see. He squints against the darkness and makes out a faint shape…Several faint shapes, in fact. Tall, slender posts are lined up side by side, spanning wall to wall, creating a sort of enclosure. A cage. But what's kept in there?

"By Neptune's chariot, is that who I think it is?!" The voice booms from the cage. A voice Tim never thought he'd hear again.

"Rogelio?" Tim rushes toward the enclosure. As he gets closer, the shadows take shape. There they all are: Rogelio, Nick, Dogberry, Romeo, and Kent, disheveled and captive, but seemingly unharmed. They stick their arms between the posts, waving and yelling.

"Tim! Get us out of here!"

"Good to see you, ya princely culver!"

"Looks like you're finally good for something."

As Tim gets closer, he hears more voices. More shadowy figures in the cage. Dozens of men, of all shapes and sizes.

What the devil…?

"Listen, Tim!" Rogelio's voice rises above the chaos. "Don't—"

"Tut-tut." Ariel flicks his wrist, and an invisible blanket of silence smothers the hostages' cries. "No more of that." They still wave their arms and move their mouths, but Tim's frantic footfalls are the only sounds in the cavern.

He stops running and stares into the shadows. A crowd of at least twenty men has gathered at the posts that divide the cage and the rest of Prospero's bachelor pad. With ice in his joints, he turns his back on the hostages and returns to Ariel.

The blue fairy smiles earnestly. "I don't want you distracted."

"Distracted? From what?"

Prospero marches into sight, his voice filling the entire cavern. "From the reason I brought you here. The reason I've brought twenty-six men to my island over the past year." He lets out a low groan. "And I regret it more every day."

"You always have the option of abracadabra-ing up a nice yacht to send us all home."

Prospero leans down to glare directly into Tim's eyes. "I'm not a quitter."

Tim tries to ignore the queasy feeling in his gut that always arises when a buff, seven-foot wizard gets in his face.

The young prince returns Prospero's stare. "How's Caliban?"

The wizard straightens up. "Breathing." He scrapes his staff against the granite floor as if striking a gigantic match.

At that magical signal, three large chests careen down from the dark ceiling—Tim barely gets out of the way. They land with resounding *THUD*s, as if weighing twenty tons apiece.

"Guess what, Tim? I don't like you," the wizard says. "You're a measly sack of potato skins I wouldn't think twice about launching into the atmosphere. If I had to choose a roommate, and the options were you or a boar with the flu, I'd get a lot of hand sanitizer and go with the boar. But…"

He sighs and gives Ariel a look. The spirit nods encouragingly, and Prospero continues, "…you're here, and this is what we're going to do." He gestures with his staff at the three chests.

Tim takes a slow step closer to the boxes—each is about the size of a funeral casket. As he approaches, he feels a glacial breeze. Cold mist rises from the chests' surfaces, as if they had been stored in the Arctic until a moment ago.

An image appears in his mind: his ghostly father, popping out of one of the chests, dressed in armor, grinning like the devil, hissing "Mark me…"

He expels the thought and focuses.

In the cavern's surreal lighting, it takes a moment for him to realize the three chests are made of three different materials: gold, silver, and bronze.

Each chest also has an inscription on its lid.

Prospero harrumphs before Tim can read them. "Pick one."

Tim looks up from the chests. "What do you mean?"

"It's not complicated. There are three caskets here. I'm sure you can count, can't you? Pick one and open it."

This whole thing is one big melodrama.

Tim flexes his fingers. "I need to know what I'm picking. What I stand to win."

"Everything, you skunk. Everything in your miserable, cretin little life has been leading to this." Prospero's lip curls as if he's looking at a pile of roadkill. "From the moment you slid out of your mother and started stealing oxygen from this world, you've been on a path to these damning caskets. Every sunrise, every mouthful of slop, every solitary step has led you to this point. Now…" He hisses, "pick."

Well then.

Tim leans forward to read the chests' inscriptions. The words are carved into the lids in an elaborate script, as if with a razor-sharp quill.

The gold chest reads, "*Who chooseth me shall gain what many men desire.*"

Silver: "*Who chooseth me shall get as much as he deserves.*"

And bronze: "*Who chooseth me must give and hazard all he hath.*"

Despite the coolness of the cave, a drop of sweat tickles Tim's brow. But he refuses to wipe it away. He feels the silent eyes of all the male captives boring into his back—likely, they were each forced to make this decision as well. And, given their lodging behind bars, they chose poorly.

There are twenty-six men in that cage. Prospero said so himself.

How is it possible every one of them picked incorrectly?

Tim takes a deep breath to calm his nerves, says a quick prayer to any god that might be listening, and snorts. Loud enough to make it echo. "I'm not putting my fate in the hands of some cockamamie shell-game, old man."

Steam just about comes out of Prospero's ears. He snarls, "Who do you think you are?"

Fear racks Tim's bones more than it ever has in his life, but he keeps a mask of apathy. "What, you think I'm gonna pick a treasure chest with some fortune cookie nonsense written on top, without knowing anything about the stakes behind it? You're out of your wrinkly mind."

Prospero's fists tighten around his gnarled staff, and Tim just about falls to his knees in terror. The memory of Caliban's impromptu dental surgery just a few minutes before flashes through his mind—that was just a taste of the pain the wizard can inflict on someone. It takes every ounce of willpower in his body to not run and cower. And it takes even more to pretend like he's completely undaunted.

Tim has followed his gut. Now he has to live with it.

Or maybe die with it.

Those are definitely the two options.

Prospero glares at Tim. His forearms tremble from clutching his staff so tightly.

Still furious, still clenched, still looking ready to commit first-degree murder, Prospero mutters, "Curses," and evaporates the three chests. With all the enthusiasm of a snake at a shoe store, he says, "Congratulations, Tim. You passed."

The prince exhales and practically deflates from relief.

He'd been confident that Prospero values common sense over empty intellectualism. The old wizard is a straight shooter, or at least he thinks he is—his patronizing attitude toward Miranda and Romeo and pretty much everyone is evidence of that. The idea that such an old-fashioned patriarch would leave anything up to a game show was ridiculous. Unless the whole thing was a charade to weed out those who Prospero sees as undesirable. Which, it turns out, it was.

But Tim still doesn't wipe away the bead of sweat—not yet. There's still much to be done.

"I passed what?" he asks.

The wizard walks away briskly. "Don't. I hate you. Don't talk to me. Ariel," he addresses the glowing fairy, "catch him up on what's going on. I'll…" He sighs and glowers at Tim again. "…I'll go get her."

With that, Prospero steps behind the air and disappears.

All at once, the cavern is silent, but for the echoes of Prospero's parting words. It's a welcome respite.

"Congratulations, Tim!" Ariel swoops in, smiling like a crescent moon. "*Prost, huzzah,* and *kudos*! Truly, in hundreds of sun-cycles, no mere man has accomplished what you have."

"Thanks, Ariel," Tim says, "but where did he go?"

"Our master went to Miranda's boarding. She presides in a lumber hut in the center of the island. He shall bring here her with us, and the festivities may begin!" He claps and cheeps, barely containing his glee.

"No, I-I mean…" *I feel like my cheese is sliding off my cracker.* "Ariel, just…what in Frigg's name is going on?"

"Oh, what a tale! As I told you, the mighty wizard arrived on these shores thirteen years ago, as if birthed by the waves, carrying nothing but his sorcerous scepter in one hand and toddler Miranda in the other."

Quite the image.

Ariel continues, "I have resided here since the sun was in its adolescence, and never have I seen such paranormal prowess. With a flick of his little finger, Prospero carved this citadel for himself. I vowed my servitude to him, but Caliban…did not. The dozen-plus-one years have passed largely unremarkable, aside from the occasional attempted homicide courtesy of Caliban."

Tim's eyes flick to the stalactite cut in Prospero's likeness. Even though the wizard himself is gone, the statue's granite eyes have a grave power of their own.

Ariel leans in, smiling recklessly. "As the years turned to dust, my master realized he needed an heir, so that his magic will live on even after his flesh has turned foul."

"Hold on." Tim calls time-out. "What about Miranda?"

"I'm glad you asked! At the point of Prospero's realization, she had entered her sixteenth year. The perfect time for her father to seek out a male mate for her. The inheritor of the sorcerer's legacy."

Tim sees where this is going. And it's weird.

"So," the fairy said, "five-hundred-fifty-eight-thousand-twenty-three minutes ago, Prospero began his matchmaking mission. Every month, with Miranda safe inside her private quarters that are locked from the outside, Prospero journeys to the peak of this mountain. He holds his scepter aloft, speaks the ancient language of the mystics, and the mortal world obeys his voice. Cosmic fountains weep their wages, the winds of the Anemoi come to do battle, and the waters churn as they did before the world took form. When all is done, and the sun smiles once more, castaways crawl upon our shore."

Tim looks over at the captive men, huddled in the shadowy cage. He'd been thankful for the coolness when he first entered the cave, but looking at them now, he sees they're damp and shivering.

"We bring them here, to the almighty Prospero's almighty bastion, and he presents them with the three caskets, just as he did with you, and he refuses any explanation, just as he did with you. No matter which casket they choose, they are dismissed as feeble, feckless fools, for Prospero wants an heir who does not bow to the wind. And..." Ariel squeaks again in excitement, "After a year of searching, he has shipwrecked her soulmate!"

Tim is floored by the idiocy of the entire situation. "Wait...I'm Prospero's heir?"

"I've been drafting my speech for the past few months." Ariel conjures a single tulip and sticks it to his left pectoral. "Prospero said I would be what's known as the 'best man,' but that term leaves a tart taste on my tongue. I prefer 'superior spirit.'"

Tim feels his stomach hit the soles of his feet.

"I'm going to marry Miranda?" Pause. "Now?"

Ariel is glowing, literally and figuratively. "That's why our master went to fetch the girl presently." He twirls in the air like a figurine on a music box. "Oh, I am truly fortunate to be part of such a joyous day!"

Tim's mouth becomes drier than a desert while his hands drip like a sponge.

I've never even successfully asked someone out.

Growing up inside Elsinore's gates, his interactions with females had been mostly limited to nurses, maids, and the daughters of those nurses and maids. But as soon as he met Ophelia, he'd been smitten. She was the daughter of Polonius, his uncle Claudius's aide—she was brilliant and witty, bold and personable, warm and kind.

That is to say, he never stood a chance. She took up a long-lasting on-again-off-again relationship with his brother Hamlet.

I doubt I'd get an invitation to their wedding. Even if I wasn't prisoner on a bloody magic island.

He refocuses on the weird situation at hand.

"Well, then, Ariel." He smears a smile across his face. "Since today suddenly became so momentous, I'm gonna go have a chat with my friends." He nods toward the cage. "Would you mind turning up their volume?"

The spirit purses his lips. His beady eyes zip to the statue of Prospero—he feels its glare too. Then his fingers fiddle with the petals of the tulip, and he smirks again. "Very well, fair Tim!" He waves his hand, and Tim can instantly hear the captives muttering amongst themselves.

Tim runs across the stone floor to the cage's bars. As he gets closer, he sees that they, too, are stalactites, grown tall and slender, side-by-side.

The men gather around the prince, babbling over one another, trying to get their piece said to the newcomer who has passed Prospero's test.

The prisoner closest to Tim is about his age, with caramel skin and midnight hair. His clothes would be bright and colorful in the sunshine, but the shadows of the cavern mute them. The man reaches a hand between the bars—his fingers are pruny from the constant moisture—and grabs Tim's arm. The man gasps: "You're still warm."

A familiar voice rises from the throng. "Stop jostling, you denizens! I know this man. Let me speak. Do you know who I am?! Really…? You don't? Well, that stings. But still, I must speak with…" Nick Bottom breaks through the crowd and comes face to face with— "Tim! Welcome to the lair of the loons."

The lanky Athenian looks every minute of his many years. Down here in the surreal light, he looks almost skeletal. His mismatched suit is soaked, and it hangs from his slim frame like a sail on a windless day. The slice on his forehead that he sustained during the shipwreck is dark red and swollen. Even an afternoon in captivity has taken a pricey toll on the old actor, but his devil-may-care smile is as toothy as ever.

Tim grabs the nape of Nick's neck. "Good to see you, Guvnor."

"And the same to you, my Danish delight. It looks like you bested the wizard at his admittedly stupid game. Atta boy."

"How's everyone holding up in there?"

"Just as you'd expect. Kent wants to punch his way through this igneous captivity, but his age is catching up to him. Romeo and the Constable are doing well…Oh, and you'll be delighted to know that Rogelio is alive and with us, as well!"

"I heard. Does Prospero feed all these men? Give you water?"

Nick shrugs. "Honestly, from what I've seen today and heard from the others, we eat well. The island is bountiful when it comes to fruits and fishes, and the floating blue boy brings three-square a day. Just an hour ago, in fact, we had a meal of lobster and crab—not as good as what I've eaten at the Grand Royale Inn and Suites in Amsterdam, but quite delicious after what we've been through today."

"Crab and lobster? Wow." *Ariel brings them food. Good food, too. Maybe the spirit does have a heart.*

"Indeed." Nick chuckles. "Dogberry called the crustaceans 'crushed Asians,' which a few of the men in here weren't amused by."

"Prospero says he has twenty-six captives. Does that sound about right?"

"By my estimate." Nick nods, his thin hair bouncing like raw spaghetti. "I tell you, I've traveled all over the world, and I've never seen a collection of such diversity. East and West, city and farm, first-class and coach…Prospero's tempests sure cast a wide net."

Tim presses, trying to keep his friend on-topic. "Nick, have you seen anything in this place that isn't made of stone? Is there a pool or a stream? A small patch of grass or dirt?"

"Sorry, chum, I haven't seen anything like that. What do you have in mind?"

"Spread the word: Be ready. I'm not sure how, but we need to get that staff out of Prospero's hands, and to do that, we'll need to make as much confusion as we can. Run around, scream, fight, do a monologue, anything."

"Excellent. But how will we get out of this cage?"

Tim clicks his tongue. "Working on it." He backs off from the bars. "Keep on your toes."

As Tim strides away from the stone paddock, Prospero reappears, Miranda at his side.

"What's going on, Father? Why did you bring me to your—" Her wide eyes land on Tim and she stops cold. Her feet shuffle as if debating fight-or-flight. "Who's that?"

The wizard groans. "You forgot the castaways from this morning? Idiot girl!"

Tim catches a shifty grimace on Ariel's face.

Ariel didn't tell Prospero that he accidentally spilled the beans and erased Miranda's memory.

"Daughter," Prospero continues, trying to bury his pompous tone under layers of syrupy warmth, "the time has come. You and I both know that I will not be the gardener of this island forever. Days go by, and the bill comes due. I know you have been wondering about my activities in this cavern. Well…" He puffs out his broad chest. "I have found my heir."

Miranda looks confused. "What do you mean? I've been right here for thirteen years."

"No, no, I mean one who is strong enough to know how to wield the scepter and wise enough to know when." He clears his throat. "Miranda, meet Tim." He sweeps his arm toward the young prince.

Miranda's eyes move to Tim, but not for long. She stifles a gasp. "Who are those men? What are you doing to them?"

"Now, honeycomb," Prospero says through gritted teeth—his fatherly exterior is already slipping. "Finding a proper groom for you took a great deal of…" He thinks and settles on, "…trial and error."

Miranda is barely listening. Her blazing eyes are still on the men in the cage. "Ferdinand! Gonzalo! Ahmed! Nolan!" She turns her wrathful gaze upward to her father. "You said you built new ships for all of them. Sent them home with supplies, goodie baskets, and 'one heck of a story.' You've been lying for the past year?!" Her fists clench. "They were my friends." She scoffs and gestures at the captives. "*Are* my friends!"

"Darling," the wizard growls, all pretense dropped, "I did what I did to find a proper heir. Only the perfect specimen can have my approval!"

Tim jumps in: "I thought you hated me."

Ariel, who is floating off in the middle-distance, nods. "I believe the male man is right, master. You do hate him."

"And again," Miranda throws her hands up in frustration, "I'm right here! Just give *me* the stupid stick!"

"Can we go back to why you chose me?" Tim says. "Because I'm honestly curious. You hate my guts, but because I didn't want to choose a magic box—"

The wizard smashes his staff against the cavern floor, creating a roll of seismic thunder. "I don't care! Shut up, and stuff the questions up your arse, both of you!" A glacial breeze slices through the cavern. "Now, we're all gonna get together and have a nice ceremony and make precious memories that'll last a lifetime and do whatever other wedding garbage I have to deal with so that I can have a successor!"

This time, Miranda keeps her mouth closed, but it looks like her jaw is going to shatter from the force. Her glare could boil water, but she doesn't say anything.

Prospero lets out a deep breath. "Now…" He waves the staff, and out from the ground comes a decorative pergola, complete with vines and flowers and a few ornate cherubs, all made of dark stone. "Tim, if you'll join us under this froufrou thing, we can get this show on the road."

Tim gulps. "Wait." His brain reels as he tries to think of a way out. "Can't we have a small reception or something, share a few drinks? We need to get to know each other…Dad…"

The wizard squares his shoulders. "What'd you call me?"

Tim's life flashes before his eyes. "Nothing, nothing." He feels an invisible clock ticking on and on. "But can't we slow down the show just a tad? Share a drink? And Ariel can give the speech he's been working on!"

Ariel squeals in delight.

Prospero's mask of contempt softens ever so slightly at the mention of drinks. "Fine." The pergola sinks back into the floor. "But don't ever use the D-word again, you krill."

The blue spirit flutters down from his airborne perch. "Oh, rapture!"

"Miranda," Prospero grunts, "join us for drinks. Get to know your new bugaboo." He strides across the cavern toward the full bar, which is located next to the foosball table, and slams a palm on the granite surface. "Pick your poison, Tim."

Tim locks eyes with Miranda for a brief moment. He feels her anger and confusion and betrayal. He also feels the brilliant gears turning within that uncombed head of hair.

She stares back. Sizing him up too.

At seventeen years of age, Miranda has thrived amid insane adversity, and now she's been godsmacked with the reality that her dear old dad has been conjuring tempests, killing God-knows-how-many, and kidnapping the survivors, all in a twisted attempt to find her a husband—not for her sake, but so that he can have a male heir.

What a Tuesday.

The mere fact that she hasn't collapsed from mental fatigue is remarkable.

Tim holds out his hand to the wizard's daughter.

She stares a moment longer, then folds her hand into his. Her skin is rough from years of island-living, but it's strangely comforting. They walk to the bar, side by side.

As they move, Tim murmurs under his breath, spacing his words so that their footfalls cover them up: "Stay close to him. When the time comes, get that staff."

She squeezes his hand in response.

When they reach the bar, she slams her palm on the counter, just as her father did. "Pineapple daiquiri. Coconut shavings on top."

Prospero laughs deep in his chest. "Gotta love those girly little drinks, eh?" He reaches under the bar and pulls out a perfectly crafted fruit cocktail. Miranda takes it and sips while the wizard gulps brown beer from a massive stein. "And you?"

Tim clears his throat. "Coffee, please. No cream."

Prospero's smile falls off his face and practically splats on the floor. He groans and slams a mug on the bar, dark liquid sloshing out.

Tim grabs the mug, lifts it slightly—"Cheers"—and throws his head back, draining the coffee in one go. The hot drink sears his esophagus, but he does his best to ignore it.

"So, Tim…" Miranda plays with the condensation on her glass. "What are some of your hobbies?"

The prince takes the empty mug from his mouth and wheezes for air. "Keep it coming, Guv."

Prospero's lip twitches, but he scratches a fingernail against his staff, and fresh coffee fills Tim's mug.

"Much obliged." He takes another big gulp. "Well, I write plays here and there. I'm a bit of a household name in London."

"Really?" Prospero drones doubtingly.

"Oh, believe it." Tim finishes his cup, and it's refilled before he even sets it back on the bar. "All my shows are performed in a lovely venue called the Masterpiece Centre in the heart of the city. It seats…five thousand patrons. Plus, there's capacity for another thousand in standing-room-only."

He smiles, basking in the glory of his tall tale. He'd never been able to brag about his talent and career to a girl's father before—mainly because there was nothing to brag about, nor anyone to brag to. He chugs another cup of coffee and decides now's as good a time as any.

"My debut show, *Sicily in the Spring*, was a tremendous success. Sold out every performance. I followed that up with *Waiting For My Joe*—speaking of which, refill, please—and that show swept the Anthony Awards that year. Best Play, Best Writing, Best Direction, Best Use of the Word 'Prestidigitation' in a Play, and so on…"

Chug.

"I have a table reserved for me at all times at Sardine's…That's the hottest restaurant in the city. I have an appointment with a sculptor next week so he can study my face and make a statue of me—I still haven't decided whether I want it to be marble or bronze. I'm also quite the fencer. Just yesterday, I crossed blades with a murderous Russian pirate."

Another cup.

"But enough about me. Miranda, please, tell me about yourself while I enjoy some of this coffee." Mug to mouth. Tip back head.

"Well…" Miranda eyes her new fiancée with skepticism, and Tim eyes her from over the rim of the coffee mug with desperation. She clears her throat—Tim needs her to stall so he can drink, and she gets that message loud and clear. "There's not much to say about me. My father is the rezoned Duke of Milan, kicked out by his brother."

Wow. Royal sibling squabbles are way more common than I realized.

"So we rowed around for a bit and ended up on this island. I was too young to remember coming here, but…" She pauses and smiles at the memory. "I remember the sun. The warmth. The grainy sand all over me. I'm used to all those things now, of course, but the flickering memories I have of Milan are of cathedrals and carriages and cobblestoned streets. So as a small child, warm sand was…magical."

Tim has all but forgotten about the mug in his hand. And the wizard and the fairy and the demon and his whole sordid affair with Denmark. He is completely pulled in by Miranda's words and her easy smile.

"Umm," she says, "I never had any official schooling, but as years went on, I figured out enough to get us water, food, and shelter. We lived well. We were happy…" Her eyes dart to her scowling father, then back to Tim. "But I began to wonder about the world. Never wanted to leave, mind you. Honestly. But an imagination isn't easily tamed, and I began to make little stories."

"Ariel told me about that," Tim smirks.

"Oh Lord." She shakes her head, embarrassed. "How much did he say?"

"Not much, I promise," he laughs and suddenly remembers the mug. He takes another deep gulp, and as it refills, he continues. "I wrote my first play when I was…oh, probably about eight or nine. I'd grown up reading the classics from my father's library, and I would watch them anytime a troupe of players came through town. *Prometheus Bound, Antigone,* all the Chester Mysteries…I loved the craft and the storytelling, and I wanted to contribute, y'know? So my first one…" He snorts. "…was about a soldier who loses an arm and leads his army to victory anyway. Utter nonsense. Arm and army…I thought that was so clever."

"Most of my stories were about a young girl on an island." She shrugs. "Shocker, right? She crafts a longboat and takes to the open ocean, and she has all sorts of adventures. She helps a village on the brink of famine. She comes across gigantic creatures who patrols the edge of the world, to make sure no ships fall off. In one story, she passes through a fog and gets trapped in a world outside time."

"How'd she get out?"

"Her father's pocket watch. She used the ever-changing second-hand as a compass needle. It led her back through the fog and into the real world." She thinks for a second. "I look back on them now, and they're terrible," she chuckles and sighs. "So cringe-worthy."

"Believe me, I know the feeling. You always think you're brilliant when you first start. Only when you wise up do you realize your weaknesses."

"With wisdom comes humility." She raises her daiquiri in a playful toast.

"Alright, lovebirds." Prospero drops his empty stein onto the rock bar. "Sounds like you're fully acquainted. Let's light this candle. Ariel?"

The blue spirit—who, all this time, has been floating in a corner, sipping from a teacup—swoops in. "Hello!"

The wizard marches away from the bar and back to the stone pergola. "It's wedding time."

Tim takes one last swig of coffee. "Come on, come on…" he mutters to himself. A chill runs down his spine, and then, finally, a painful pressure in his lower gut. The sensation of a waterfall trying to fit through a drinking straw.

"One more minute, Guv." He sets down the mug and wobbles away from the bar. "Before we hitch the wagon, I really need to use the bathroom."

Prospero groans. "Are you serious?"

Tim nods at the much-used mug. "Quite."

Miranda catches his drift and goes along with it. "Classic Tim, huh, Father?" She forces an airy giggle.

The wizard's beard twitches as he sizes up the two, clearly knowing something's up. But he decides that Tim poses no threat—especially not with him bouncing from foot to foot. "Find a corner. Far from us. I don't want to be smelling your incontinence for the rest of the day."

As Miranda sets her drink behind the bar, she leans in and whispers to Tim, "I'll stall him as long as I can. You do what you gotta do."

Tim whispers back, "Who, me? I just have pre-wedding jitters."

The two lock eyes. He smiles. She winks. They part ways.

He waddles deeper into the cavern, thighs clenched together. The gallons of black coffee are playing their part, for sure. With each beleaguered step, the voices of Miranda and her father grow less solid and more waiflike, the colors drain, and the shadows grow. The surreal lighting doesn't extend this far back into the cave, and he's truly alone.

His eyes scan the ground for fissures, crevices, faults…and it strikes him that this is exactly how he had found Caliban just a few hours earlier.

Well, it worked before.

There. A crack running along the cave's floor and up the wall. Thin like a spider's web. Maybe too thin.

But he sees no other openings. In the distance, Prospero's tone is getting increasingly impatient. It'll have to do.

He plants a foot on either side of the fissure, unbuttons his fly, and peeks over his shoulder. No one's watching—good.

He relaxes and releases, hoping beyond hope that he isn't risking the wizard's wrath and embarrassing himself in front of Miranda for nothing.

"Find it, Caliban, find it…" he hisses to the empty air.

His bodily liquid flows into the fissure, through the endless underground channels and highways, until—

POP. The air isn't empty anymore.

Caliban the demon unfolds itself out of the liquid in the fissure, then immediately doubles over, breathless. "Whew!" it exhales, "that one wasn't easy."

Tim buttons his fly and hisses, "Quiet, man, hush-hush." He smiles, then sniffs. "Ah, sorry about the odor."

"Think nothing of it. I have a cologne that smells exactly the same."

"Alright," Tim takes a breath, "now things are gonna get tricky."

Caliban looks taken aback. "What, you tinkling on a crack, and me traveling from mud to sand to groundwater to your tinkle and into this cave was the *easy* part?"

"Believe it or not. Now, stick to the shadows until Armageddon breaks out. We have to get that staff away from Prospero, but none of us have a prayer as long as Ariel is in the fight."

Caliban nods and cracks its knuckles. "I catch your drift."

Tim thinks for a moment. "Don't hurt him. He's not evil, but he's definitely loyal to the bearded boss. Just…keep him occupied."

"Yeah, yeah, sure thing, but how's the foosball table doing? Is it okay? Is it awesome?"

Tim looks Caliban in the reptilian eye. "In all my travels, I've never seen a grander foose."

From across the cavern, Prospero barks, "Tim, hurry up!"

He answers, "Coming, coming!" then says to Caliban, "Good luck, friend."

The demon scoffs. "Luck's for humans."

Tim shrugs—"Fair."—then walks out of the shadows, feeling relieved for two major reasons. First: He has successfully smuggled some supernatural back-up into the cave. Second: All the coffee he'd chugged is now out of his system.

Miranda and Prospero are trading words under the decorative pergola. The wizard holds a lace veil, and his daughter is less than pleased about it. She spots Tim emerging from the corner and opens her mouth to call out to him.

Tim rolls his two index fingers over each other, mimicking the movement of a wheel. It's an old hand gesture leftover from his failed attempts at a stage director, basically meaning "keep going."

Miranda redirects her attention up at her father. "And another thing!"

Tim chuckles quietly. "Hey, Ariel?" he says.

A moment later, Ariel drops down, tulip still stuck to his pectoral. "Hello again! Did everything come out as it should?"

"Yes, yes it did." Tim proceeds carefully. "Ariel, I have a request for you, groom to superior spirit."

Ariel chirps, "Please! It's my duty to make this day as euphoric as possible. I'm afraid I am rather uneducated in the realm of bachelor parties, but I could do my best—"

"Nothing that elaborate, Ariel, but I appreciate it. You see…Marrying Miranda and joining this family is, of course, exciting and the highlight of my day. But I'll be bound to this island for the rest of my life. I'll be leaving my life and friends behind. So I was hoping for a bit of magic from you."

Ariel leans in, eager to please. Perfect.

Tim continues. "I was wondering if you could take away the sound from the men in the cage, like you did earlier, but not only that. I'd be eternally grateful if you could turn them invisible within the cage, as well."

The fairy opens his mouth to question, but Tim presses on: "I fear they'll distract from my future with Miranda, and honestly, they're painful reminders of the life I'm leaving."

Ariel's luminescent skin ripples as he mulls it over for a second, but only a second. A warm smile spreads across his face. "What's a best man for?"

I can't believe that worked. Adrenaline blossoms in Tim's gut, but he can't let it on. Instead, he gives Ariel a melancholic, bittersweet grin. "I appreciate it, friend."

"Oh, I was genuinely curious," Ariel says. "What is a best man for? I know not."

"But you said it's your duty to make today euphoric or whatever."

"Indeed! That's how I approach every day. But my master was sparse on details when it came this this 'best man' post. Anyhoo, I'd be happy to grant your request! And in the meantime, I'd welcome any advice on how to best perform my BM duties, if some were to materialize in your noggin." With that, Ariel flourishes his hands like a symphonic conductor.

Tim spins around to look at the cage, and just like that…It's empty. Or, at least, it looks and sounds empty.

Another puzzle piece in place. All that's left to do is lock them together.

Tim feels a wave of trepidation traveling from his gut to his brain, but he walks under the pergola before it takes hold.

"About time," Prospero says. "Ariel, get it going!"

"With vigor!" Ariel swoops in.

So there they are, under the stone framework—Tim and Miranda facing each other, Ariel hovering between them, Prospero looming behind his daughter, arms wrapped tightly around his magical staff.

Tim takes a breath. "'Til death and all that, right?" Despite his best efforts, his voice quivers.

Miranda reaches out and takes his hands in her own. "And all that—"

"Dearly beloved!" Ariel blurts out, silvery tears seeping out of his eyes. "We are gathered here today…" He chokes up and wipes the moonbeams away from his cheeks. "I'm so sorry, I promised myself I wouldn't do this…"

Prospero rolls his eyes. "Skip to the do's."

Tim says, "But Ariel's been writing his speech for months."

Ariel meekly shrugs. "I have."

"You've been stalling, Tim," Prospero rumbles, "and I don't like that. We're gonna get this over with, and I'll throw you into a cage until you're more agreeable."

Miranda asks, "Which cage? That one?" And she turns her head to gesture at the very large, very empty paddock.

"Well, yes, why not—?" Prospero follows his daughter's lead and looks at the cage. And his face goes ashen. "*What?!*" he cries. "Where are they?" In a panic, he forgets the wedding entirely and sprints toward the stone bars. He lumbers as quickly as his massive frame and seaweed robe allow, bellowing and huffing obscenities in languages Tim has never heard of.

"Master," Ariel speaks up, "don't fret! They…"

But the spirit's assurances are buried by Prospero's rage. "How did they get out?! When I find them, they'll wish I'd let them drown in the ocean!"

"Master—"

As Prospero nears the cage, he waves his staff, and the bars sink into the stone floor. "Where are these cretins…?"

Then, there's a roar, like the eruption of a long-dormant volcano. Twenty-six captives surge into existence, exploding out from behind their wall of invisibility and silence. They shake their fists, running for the first time in too-long, yelling like soldiers charging into battle.

Prospero screeches to a halt. "How dare…?" He brandishes his staff— or at least, he tries to. The stampede of hostages rushes over him, knocking him to the hard, unforgiving ground.

Ariel gasps and clutches the sides of his bald head. "Master! Oh me, oh my!" He zooms forward to assist the wizard—but he suddenly stops mid-air.

"Hey there, pal," a voice croaks.

The blue spirit twists around and sees the stumpy gray demon clutching his ankles. "Caliban? Our master didn't invite you in here!"

"I thought I'd bring band practice to you." Caliban barks a laugh and yanks Ariel close to its putrid body. Ariel tries to squirm his way out, but the demon's strength holds fast.

Tim and Miranda look at each other for a split moment—the calm before the storm—then dash out from under the pergola.

"Quick!" she yells to the rioting captives. "The staff, while he's down!"

"I got it!" A man wearing a once-bright-now-faded-red robe leaps onto the fallen Prospero's back. "I'll take that, you tyrant!"

The old wizard begins to stir, his shock quickly wearing off and being replaced with fury.

Tim grimaces and yells to the robed man, "Watch out!"

Too late.

Prospero springs to his feet in one terrifyingly fluid movement. His massive arms reach around and pluck the man from his back. "Unworthy," he hisses in the man's face and tosses him aside. The wizard glares at Tim. "Big mistake, boy!" He raises his staff like Moses, and lightning sprouts from the tip. The crystals embedded in the cave walls begin to glow brighter and belch sparks as well, flashing in Prospero's vengeful eyes.

Across the cavern, Caliban yelps at the Zeus-like display. It flips Ariel to hold him like a javelin and, with a mighty grunt, hurls the spirit. Ariel flies through the air like a blue harpoon and smashes into Prospero's gut. The wizard and his fairy tumble to the ground, and the lightning disappears.

"Nice shot, Cal!" Miranda calls.

Prospero props himself up on one elbow. "*Et tu*, daughter? You wish to depose me? Shame me?"

Miranda opens her mouth to answer, but another captive's voice snarls, "How's it feel, gramps?" A dozen men gather around the downed wizard and begin kicking and hitting him with all the muscle they can muster. One boot catches Prospero in his jaw, and red spittle runs down his gray beard.

"No!" Miranda yells as she and Tim reach the crowd. "Don't hurt him! Stop!" She shoves the violently frustrated men away from their captor.

"That's not what we're doing here!" Tim joins the fray and tries to separate the riot from the wizard. "The staff is what we're after—" He looks down and gulps.

Prospero and Ariel have disappeared.

Shoot. Where'd they go…?

Speaking of which, Tim realizes he hasn't seen his friends in the riot. Dogberry, Romeo, Kent, Nick, Rogelio… *Where are they?*

The voice of a vindictive god booms from the far side of the cavern: "You mortals thought you could outwit and overpower a sorcerer?"

Tim and Miranda turn around on shaky feet.

The wizard sits upon his granite throne, positioned above all the non-magical creatures he considers lesser beings. With his powerful physique, his lion-lined throne, and a devastating weapon in his fist, he looks every inch a god. He slowly stands, and his shadow hungrily envelops the cave.

"Such betrayal, Miranda. I expected better from you, after all the years we've spent together, just us."

"I could say the same," she calmly retorts. "Kidnapping, violence, coercion. I expected better from *you*."

Tim tenses, ready to throw himself between Miranda and whatever spell Prospero fires at her. Lightning? Ice? Literal fire?

For a moment, he's shocked. *I'm honestly willing to jump in front of a magical missile for her.*

But the situation at hand doesn't allow for much inner monologue.

Prospero tilts his staff—

And a huge pineapple arcs through the air and smashes against his head.

"Gah!" The wizard staggers, sweet juice dripping down his mane. "Who the...?"

"Ha! Bull's-eye!"

Tim smiles. There's that big, jolly voice.

Rogelio the sailor hoots and hollers from behind the bar, a coconut cocked and ready to be thrown. "You know what they say: Just fru-it! Get it? 'Do it,' fru-it?"

"A coconut's a seed, you dingus." Another familiar voice calls from the racquetball court. Kent the English warrior tosses a rubber ball into the air and whacks it with a stone bat. The ball sails across the cavern and bounces off Prospero's broad chest.

Kent sends another ball, and the wizard easily swats it away—only for the coconut to nail him in the ribs.

"Two for two!" Rogelio whoops.

"Stop it, you mice!" Prospero flexes his considerable biceps, and his staff crackles with lightning once more.

"Well, my friend," the roguish Romeo Montague pops up by the barbells, curling a weight with each arm—likely still showing off for Miranda. "You brought the mice into your home, and now you have an infestation." He drops one weight and heaves the other at Prospero.

A rallying cry bursts from the captives: "Yeah you do!"

All at once, a storm of projectiles rains down on the wizard—fruits, shoes, crystals ripped from the walls…anything the captives can get their hands on. Since Prospero is so tall and standing on an elevated platform, he's a perfect target. He instinctively holds out his arms to protect his face.

"C'mon, you scallywags!" Kent whips his soldiers into shape. "Let him have it!"

The men cheer and throw everything they have with everything they have. Cups from the bar, weights, racquetballs…

One man goes to pick up the entire foosball table, but Tim shoves it back to the ground. "That's promised to someone else," he warns.

Tim feels the atmosphere shift, and he knows that means Ariel is on the move. Sure enough, the blue fairy appears out of thin air and bullets toward the riot, glowing like a comet. "Halt, you human hurdlers! Or upon this hour, I shall—"

"Oh no you don't." Caliban leaps and snatches Ariel out of the air, like a bullfrog catching a fly.

"Unhand me, spawn of Sycorax and Satan!"

"Nah, you're coming with me." Caliban wrestles Ariel into a tight embrace and bounds to the cave wall. It clenches its eyes shut in concentration, and then hops into one of the crystals.

Tim can't believe it. The demon has dragged Ariel *into* one of the gemstones embedded in the wall. *I guess we can add crystal to the list of materials Caliban can travel through. And it can bring other supernatural beings along for the ride.*

Prospero teeters from the improvised onslaught of sundries. As the wizard struggles to stay upright, Tim spots two men crawling onto the throne's stage.

Nick Bottom and Constable Eustace Dogberry quietly position themselves behind each of Prospero's tree-like legs.

The Athenian actor gives Tim a big toothy smile that says, "*You told us to be ready, m'boy!*" He has wrapped a strip of cloth around the bloody gash on his forehead, and he looks like the oldest, scrawniest buccaneer Tim can imagine. And there's no one else Tim would rather see at this moment.

The two men wind up their legs and kick the backs of Prospero's knees. The wizard tumbles like Goliath, flailing his arms in a feeble attempt to regain balance.

Dogberry leaps up and pries the staff out of Prospero's hand. "I got it!" he calls out, simultaneously elated and surprised. "I got it!"

But Prospero is already standing back up, towering over the wiry policeman. "You don't know how much danger you just put yourself in."

"Constable!" Romeo yells from across the cave. "I'm open!"

Prospero shoves Nick off the platform, and the actor lands hard on his rear. "Agh, bruised my Bottom!" he exclaims, and he can't resist chortling at his own pun.

"Not the time, knucklehead," Kent snorts, waving him arms. "Dogberry, throw it! Get it out of his reach!"

The Constable pulls back his arm in preparation to fling the staff, but Prospero clamps his massive fists around the wood.

"Let go, cretin, and I'll let you live." Prospero nearly wrenches the staff out of Dogberry's grip.

"Not today, you lizard!" Dogberry clenches his jaw and focuses on his hands, as if trying to set them aflame with his eyes.

"Eustace!" Miranda gasps. "Don't!"

Purple sparks jump from the staff. Dogberry grins triumphantly up at Prospero. "Prepare to feel the wrath of—"

A ball of violent violet energy bursts from the staff, launching Dogberry and Prospero in opposite directions: The wizard lands on his feet and slides, absorbing the hit easily enough; Dogberry slams into the wall, dazed and covered in purple char.

The burst of magic sends the staff flying end-over-end through the air, and everyone in the cavern stares up at it, shuffling around with their hands up, yelling "I got it!", "It's mine!", "Come to papa!", and the like.

Prospero scuttles through the crowd, knocking the captives over like bowling pins while their attention is directed upward.

The staff completes its aerial arc and plummets…right into Tim's hand. Tim hangs from the side of the tall Prospero statue like a weather vane, arm outstretched and holding the magical walking stick.

Prospero stops in the center of the cavern and knocks over one more captive, seemingly just for kicks. He glares at Tim, but he also dons the faux-fatherly voice he had used earlier. "Tim, hand it over. Only I can wield this magic! You saw what happened when your rent-a-cop tried to use it a moment ago."

Tim smiles as he looks down on Prospero. From this angle, the wizard looks surprisingly aged, his wrinkles more pronounced and his muscles saggy. Nothing like the mighty stone figure Tim hangs from.

"Oh, I can't use it." He tosses the staff like a boomerang and Miranda catches it. "She can."

The paternal visage evaporates. "Miranda!" he bellows as he sprints toward his daughter. "Don't even think about it!"

She responds by pursing her lips and leveling the staff at her charging father. The rock floor cracks beneath her feet, and her wild locks are blown by an unfelt wind.

"NO!" Prospero leaps and grabs the staff. He pulls with all his might, but Miranda may as well be a marble statue—she doesn't budge an inch. The wizard snarls and leans back, father and daughter grappling for victory. "Not like this…" he hisses to himself, and then lets out the roar of a cornered beast. He twists his arms and, with every ounce of strength he has, drives his body downward.

The staff snaps in half with a deafening *CRACK*. Prospero lurches away from his daughter. He holds half of the gnarled wood in his shaky hands, and she has the other. He narrows his eyes at Miranda. "Look what you did. All this power, all this majesty…worthless now. If I can't have it…" He drops his splintered half and kicks it into a shadow as he walks toward the cavern's exit. "Have a good life, everyone."

All is quiet, expect for the wizard's heavy, sullen footsteps. The dozens of captives stand dumbfounded, moving out of Prospero's path like the Red Sea.

Tim slides down the stone statue, landing with a *thud*. He looks at his friends scattered around the cavern…and he realizes they're all looking at him for orders, a plan of action, something. All he can do is slump against the statue, defeated.

Then, a faint sound. Like gravel scraping together. The crowd of captives ripples as they look around the cave, searching for the source of the noise.

Tim's ears perk up too. Suddenly, the smooth rock wall behind him moves, and he scrambles out of its way.

The twenty-foot granite statue of Prospero frees itself from the stalagmite base it has been confined to for all these years. It rips its blocky feet out of the ground and takes a few practice steps.

Tim shrieks and scurries out from under the statue's massive stone feet. The dozens of captives cower at the cave's edges.

"Cripes!" Nick exclaims.

"Y'know," Kent grumbles, "this should shock me more than it does."

Prospero turns to face his granite likeness, his scowl turning into a mask of disbelief, then rage, then...fear. "My gods." His hands quiver, instinctively searching for a staff they no longer hold.

Light footsteps pad across the cave floor, and Miranda takes her place between her father and the self-glorifying monument he had created. She holds her half of the broken wand high above her head, sweat beading her forehead. "I'm a quick learner, Father, you know that."

Prospero's eyes flit from his daughter, to the animated statue, to Tim, to the broken staff, and back around. He tries to scoff and square his shoulders, scraping together the remains of his arrogant persona, but Tim knows a bad performance when he sees one. Prospero is beaten—everyone knows it, especially himself.

Still, he growls like a crippled lion and charges at Miranda. "That staff is mine!"

Miranda flicks the wand and steps aside. The granite statue reaches down, scoops its fleshy counterpart into a big bear-hug, then straightens up and freezes. Prospero is lifted off the ground, his legs still running and flailing, but the statue is lifeless once more and not budging.

"This is...Miranda, unhand me! I'm..." Prospero fights against the stone arms holding him hostage, writhing and yelling, a fish on a hook. "I rule this island! I am its conductor, gardener, and shepherd! How dare..."

"Father," Miranda quietly interrupts. With that one word, Prospero sighs and stops fighting, going limp in the statue's hold. He hangs his head, his mass of hair and beard obscuring his face. Miranda sighs too: "We have a lot to work through, Father."

Tim breathes and feels the cave breathe with him. Nick, Dogberry, and Rogelio rush to embrace him, laughing and slapping his back, and Romeo and Kent quickly join in—the back-slapping, not the embracing.

"You did it, chap!" Nick beams with tears in his eyes. "I never doubted you."

"Well played, Tim!" Romeo adds.

"Oh, boys!" Tim embraces his friends, "I'm so glad to see you all. But *you're* the ones who clinched it. None of this would have gotten off the ground without you. And then, *she* finished it." He looks over at Miranda, and when her eyes meet his, he quickly finds his shoes very interesting.

The other captives begin hooting and celebrating, many rushing out the cave's exit, ready to see and feel sunlight again.

Tim remembers something and runs to one of the crystals embedded in the cave wall. He squints and leans his forehead against the crystal. Two figures are bouncing around inside, one a radiant blue, the other a gray splotch. Tim taps the crystal: "Caliban, Ariel, you can come out now."

He backs up and, a moment later, the two creatures stumble out of the gleaming rock. Caliban collapses on the floor as if it just rode a merry-go-round eighty times, but Ariel zips through the air.

"Master?" He gawks at Prospero dangling from the statue's arms. But the wizard doesn't respond, doesn't even look up.

Ariel looks around as if searching for something he'd dropped. Suddenly, he smiles at Miranda and dives to her feet. "Master—"

The young sorceress shakes her head, and a few leaves fall from her tangled hair. "Prospero isn't your master. Nor am I, Ariel. That's not something I want. You can stay on this island if you wish, or you can go."

"I'm confused," Ariel thinks aloud. "Baffled, bewildered, bemused…"

"Ariel, you're free, a servant no more. Do as you wish." Miranda waves her wand, a kind smile making her eyes glisten.

The spirit rises into the air, his blue skin glowing like an alien moon. "But I am only a few thousand years old. I can't retire yet!" He laughs as he glides out the cavern's exit. "Thank you, dear one! The stars of eons thank you, worlds past and future thank you, and I, Ariel of the Deep, thank you!" With that, the spirit fades away.

Miranda turns to Tim and exhales. "What a day." She taps the wand against her leg, chuckling in disbelief.

"Tell me about it."

They share a smile as the captives rejoice and cheer. Nick leads a chorus of an Athenian victory hymn.

All is right.

Tim begins to speak: "Miranda, I—"

A horrible screeching sound cuts through the entire cavern. Tim whips around and sees Caliban pushing the foosball table across the floor.

"Yeah, this is better, closer to the middle," it mutters to itself. "Tomorrow, I'll carve out a big pool here, make a nice hot tub over there. Gonna have to make it way darker and danker in here…"

"What's he doing?" Miranda asks.

"Oh yeah! I kinda promised Caliban it could have this place as a castle."

"Nice," she nods. "The place isn't my style anyway."

.   .   .

"Tim! Come look quickly!" Rogelio's big voice calls from down the beach.

The young prince mutters, "Oh no, what now?" and sprints to the water's edge, where his five friends are waiting.

The caravan of former captives has trekked through the jungle, from Prospero's cavern back to the ocean side. While the trip had been daunting earlier today, it was a breeze with Miranda as a tour guide.

"You'll never believe what's happened!" Rogelio says.

"Try me." Tim trots to the shoreline, tensed up and ready for catastrophe.

"Look, look!" The sailor grins ear to ear and points out to the sea.

Tim uses a hand to shade his eyes against the setting sun. In the distance, he picks out three white sails against the rosy sky.

"Look at the flags, my friend!" Rogelio urges, bouncing up and down in the sand. "Three ships, flying the Lion of Saint Mark! We're saved!"

Dogberry cheers, "Hairspray!"

He means hooray, Tim thinks. *That one wasn't even close.* He vocalizes to Rogelio, "But why?"

"Those ships." Rogelio reaches out as if trying to pluck the ships from the water. "I would know them anywhere. They belong to my cousin Antonio. He's a merchant in Venice, and his fleet does business all over the map. All Venetian ships fly the flag of the Lion. Yes, yes, those are Antonio's three grandest vessels, searching for our shipwreck!" He flaps his arms over his head and yells, "Over here!"

"So…" Tim's rigid muscles slowly, slowly relax. "Something didn't go horribly wrong? A coincidence is actually working out in our favor?"

"It'll only work out," Kent snips, "if they see us and steer this way!" He too begins to wave like a windmill. "Hey! HEY!"

"Allow me, chaps. I'm quite adept at projecting to the back row." Nick clears his throat and bellows, "*HELP!*"

All six men jump up and down, signaling and screaming until their mouths are dry and raw. They clap and stomp their feet, but the three ships continue to bob across the horizon, painfully unaware of the castaways just out of view.

Tim sets his hands on his knees and pants, utterly exhausted from this chain-reaction nightmare of a day. From the bar in London, to the hurricane, to the shipwreck, to the duel with the wizard, it's been one disaster after another. And the rotten cherry on top is that it could all be fixed…if only the ships' captains would turn their heads ninety degrees.

But no amount of shouting will catch their attention at this distance.

"C'mon…" he wheezes.

BOOM.

Tim's eardrums vibrate, and he spins around. A kaleidoscope of colors explodes in the airspace over the island, flashing and crackling like gunpowder being cooked on a stovetop. As he watches, the colors shift and pop, a living organism made of smoke and sound.

He smiles. "Miranda…"

"They're coming!" Nick cries, and he falls to his knees in the sand. He stretches his arms out, as if asking the entire universe for a hug. "Oh Lord above, they're coming."

Sure enough. The three ships flying the Venetian Lion have set their sights on the small, magical island.

"Rogelio," Tim slaps the sailor's shoulder, "remind me to send your cousin a birthday card."

Within the hour, the three ships arrive and loiter a hundred yards out to sea. Each sends a courier rowboat to shore. Rogelio greets all of the skippers by name, gives them a huge hug, and asks how their families are.

By now, the colorful pyrotechnics and arriving ships have attracted the twenty-six freed castaways. Rogelio calls to the mass of men gathered on the beach. "Gentlemen! These fine rowers have informed me that my cousin Antonio is offering the use of these three ships! They're the *Emerald Dusk, Castiglione's Courtier,* and the *Breeze of Eden*—the finest crafts human hands can construct. There're going to take us all home!"

The men respond with a resounding "*Huzzah!*" They hop in the rowboats, chattering and cheering and singing like men walking out of prison. The boats pitch a bit too much, and one of the skippers gives Rogelio an apologetic shrug.

Rogelio sees that only Tim and company remain on the beach, and he laughs. "Not a worry, my friend. We have been on this island for only a day. Go on, take the men to the ships. Get them new clothes and a hot meal, and send one courier boat back to us. We'll still be here when you return."

The three small boats push off, the ex-captives waving to the eclectic group left on the beach. "Thank you!" "I'll never forget you men!" "May God bless you and yours!"

Eventually, the ovations and voices shrink into the distance and are overtaken by the rippling ocean. The six friends are left standing on the beach.

A gull caws. The water sighs as it washes ashore and then retreats back, leaving a line of froth as evidence.

"Thank you, boys." Tim's voice sounds small amid the magnitude of the ocean. "I'd be dead without each of you. Rogelio the Captain. Kent the General. Romeo the Warrior. Dogberry the Guardian. Nick the Legend. I'm honored to have stumbled into this misfit band of heroes."

"M'boy," Nick slaps the prince's arm, "we could all say the same of you."

Kent's beard curves into a smile. "Tim the King."

No one has ever used that word about him.

Tim tries to shake off his emotions, and when that doesn't work, he covers them up with sarcasm. He says to the actor, "You'll have one heck of a résumé now, Nick. 'Previous roles include Leon in *Sicily in the Spring,* and Rochester in *The Stoolpigeons*. Born in Athens. Attended Boudrillard Performance Academy. Was once shipwrecked on an island with demons and wizards. Can juggle…'"

"*A* demon," Nick corrects, "and *a* wizard. I never sensationalize."

"I've been running for too long," Romeo blurts out, surprising himself as much as the rest of the group. "Ever since Rogelio said the ships will take us home, that's all I've been thinking about. Verona. Juliet. To hell with the charges against me." He grins recklessly. "I'm going back. It's my *home*."

Nick says, "Good luck, my striking young friend. Remember to keep your head up and let your heart lead."

Kent jumps in, "But get another sword before you enter town. Just in case."

The courier boat has almost returned. Tim is shocked to realize he wants it to take longer.

"I guess we're all parting ways here." He looks each of his friends deeply in the eye. "I'll miss you all. I truly will. Those other men may forget our names and what happened on this island today, but I vow I never will."

"You're a good man, Tim." Dogberry clasps Tim's forearm, and Tim clasps Dogberry's. "Welfare, sweet prince…and farewell."

"Please, it's Tim. Don't remember me as a prince. Remember me as your friend."

"Oh, I can definitely do that." He lets go of Tim's forearm and wraps him in a big hug.

The skipper drags his rowboat onto the shore and beckons them in.

Rogelio says, "After you!" and dramatically gestures like a maître'd.

Tim hears a rustling in the jungle, and he hesitates. "I…I'll be just a minute."

Nick nods with a knowing glint in his eye. "Take your time. We'll be here when you're ready."

Tim walks up the beach to the foliage, thinking of when he sprinted along this very path earlier this morning. Sunrise to sunset. How time flies.

Dainty footfalls grow louder and louder until Miranda breaks through the tree line, the splintered wand held lightly in one hand. "See you at practice, Cal!" she calls over her shoulder.

Tim moves to stand next to her, and they survey the beach, ocean, and sky stretched out before them. "You joined Caliban's band?"

"Well, according to him, I've been a member for years. But yeah," she snickers. "He told me I'm on tambourine, and I told him I'm more into percussion."

"He?"

"Yeah," Miranda replies, confused by his confusion. "Caliban."

Tim is taken aback, realizing he'd been thinking of the demon as an "it" all day. A deep shame bubbles in his gut. He obfuscates: "How's your dad?"

"I built him a small hut next to mine." She thinks before continuing, gazing at her wand as if it's a pet snake—familiar, but forever potentially dangerous. "We have a long, rocky path ahead of us, but he's the only father I have. Right?"

Tim doesn't answer.

"So," Miranda bashfully says, "are you really a successful writer?"

"Writer, yes." Tim groans. "Successful...not so much."

"Hey, you're more successful than me. This island doesn't have much of a publishing scene, believe it or not."

"Nah, don't sell yourself short. Technically, you're as successful as they get. You write, so you're a writer. Storytellers are all things to all people. You're a philosopher, an architect, a teacher, an orator, a historian...all rolled into one. You create entire worlds out of nothing. Now that's real magic."

He takes a breath, the salty beach air exfoliating his lungs. Despite all the hardships this island has brought, and as much as he wants to leave, this place is undeniably beautiful. "Did you ever name it?"

"The island?" Miranda smiles lightly at a silent thought. "Never out loud. I figured Father would chastise me for being arrogant enough to think I could name his isle. But yeah, for as long as I can remember, I've called it *Focolare*."

Tim swishes the name around in his mind. "I like it. What does it mean?"

"It means 'hearth,' which in Milan symbolizes home and family." She pauses and looks at the swaying trees for a moment. "Where are you headed now, Tim?"

"My *focolare*. And I'm terrified. You?"

"I...I don't know for sure." Her eyes scan the red horizon. "For the first time in my entire life, the world is wide open to me, and yet, I have a strong compulsion to stay here and build something of my own." She glances at Tim, then down at her bare feet. She kicks at the sand. "I'm sure that sounds insane."

"Not in the least. After the couple days I've had, nothing will ever sound insane again." He laughs, and she joins. The sound gives him chills.

Their laughter fades, replaced by the rolling waves and rustling leaves.

"We're both at big crossroads." She places a hand on his shoulder. "I wish you the best of luck. Words seem so feeble, but please believe me."

"Words are the strongest material there is." He places a hand over Miranda's. They don't move, and he smiles wistfully. "It's not fair."

She smirks. "Oh?"

"The first girl I ever get along with lives on a magical desert island."

Miranda laughs and squeezes his shoulder. "We'll be in touch, Tim."

"How?"

"What are the astronomical chances that we would ever meet in the first place? Life has a way of working out."

They stand on the beach, the sun caressing the ocean, their hands overlapped. Tim truly never wants the moment to end.

But it must. Eventually, Miranda removes her hand, and as much as he wants to stay rooted next to her, he begins to walk toward the rowboat on the shore.

"Y'know, fun fact..." He looks over his shoulder at the brilliant girl in the piecemeal dress. "I'm the prince of Denmark. Crazy, huh? And you're the daughter of the Duke of Milan. If we'd gotten married back there, we'd have quite a bit of power to wield." He stammers, "Besides you being an all-powerful sorceress or whatever."

Miranda giggles. "Yeah, besides that."

"What am I talking about?" Tim playfully throws his hands in the air as he walks. "You don't need me at all." He says it jokingly, but it stings because he knows it's true. "Next time you want to chat, just conjure up a tornado to drop me here."

Her laugh follows him as the ocean laps against his ankles.

This is it.

He turns and looks at the sorceress of the island one last time. "Good-bye, Miranda."

Her sad smile glistens in the sunset's waning light. "Until next time, Tim."

He climbs into the courier boat and sits with his dear friends, and the skipper shoves off. They all lurch into the chaotic rhythm of the sea, and Tim fights every instinct he has to look back. Instead, he looks at Nick.

One bittersweet tear dots the actor's cheek.

Exactly.

Chapter 8

"Docking in ten minutes! Minutes ten in docking!" A sailor walks across the *Emerald Dusk*'s deck, hand cupped around his words. "Disembark to prepare! Prepare to…" He continues down the stairs, delivering his oddly-arranged announcement to all the ship's passengers.

Tim leans on the wooden railing, watching the inky water churn as the huge ship slices across its surface.

The ship had departed from the island five days prior, stopping at various ports, letting people off and taking people on, and Tim quickly became a party of one. It was curious; aside from the fact that he loved and appreciated his friends, he had grown accustomed to the idea of traveling in a group. He had tried to leave London solo, and he was almost shish kebobbed by a Russian pirate. He liked having people to watch his back, people he could count on when troubles arose. People he could talk to who were actually there.

But now, he's continuing his journey the same way it began: surrounded by strangers, yet alone.

He imagines what might have happened if his friends had been with him in that dingy London bar. Kent and Romeo would have pummeled Travkin, no doubt. He smiles wistfully at the thought.

Also, as the ship had sailed away from the island, the weather had instantly switched. The air became bitterly cold, and the water turned from bright blue to sludgy gray. As he stands on the deck, Tim flips through the old geography lessons Osric taught him in school. If his memory serves him (which it tends to do very well), there are no tropical islands off the coast of England, Milan, Denmark, or anywhere remotely close to them. Miranda's magical island seems to exist in a world all its own.

He chuckles to himself. Sounds about right.

The climate in Elsinore is always nippy, and that's putting it kindly. Tim and Hamlet used to celebrate summer vacation by building snowmen and chopping firewood. His blood is accustomed to lower temperatures…or so he thought. As the ship left the magical tropics and neared Denmark, his clothing became more and more layered—two shirts, a coat, sturdy boots, a couple pairs of socks, and doubled-up undies. He imagines he looks nothing like an urban playwright anymore.

Ever since leaving the Masterpiece Centre, he'd been caught up in a whirlwind of misadventure—literally, as it turned out. From the Russian pirates to the shipwreck …He hasn't had a moment to sit down and consider why he's doing what he's doing. But, for the past five days, as he traveled aboard the *Emerald Dusk*, he'd had time to do exactly that.

Why is he returning to Elsinore?

Is it because of what the Ambassador had said? There's a problem with Hamlet, and Tim, as his twin brother, needs to come help. Is it simple as that?

Or is it what the King's ghost had said? Claudius murdered Old Hamlet and stole the throne. Justice must be done, avenge the king, blah blah blah.

Could it be that he simply misses home? He's been gone five years. Is it possible that part of him wants to visit his old stomping grounds, to see Hamlet, Osric, his mother, and the others?

None of those feel completely right. All of those reasons hold sway, to be sure, but there's some bigger force at work. A deep, primal instinct—something he can't quite pinpoint—is drawing him home to Elsinore.

And there it is. He leans further over the edge of the ship, nearly toppling into the water. But he has to get a better view.

Denmark. About a hundred yards away. Fog rolls off the rocky shores, as if the very nation is exhaling.

His gut feels twisted up in knots.

Is this what the docs call "fight or flight"? Maybe I can choose C: all of the above.

The sailor peeks out from below-deck like a meerkat and announces their impending destination: "Denmark! Port of Verkwister!"

The passengers begin to gather on deck, and Tim smirks. *Tourists,* he thinks. Outsiders, mostly. He can tell from their wardrobe—the people wearing light jackets and house-shoes must know nothing of Denmark's climate and landscape. They'll be shivering and blister-stricken within an hour of disembarking.

And a few of them are holding gaudy brochures that read "*Top 10 Must-See Sights in the Great State of Denmark!*" Those are a pretty good giveaway too.

He also knows that Verkwister is a fairly secluded town on the northern tip of the country, and there aren't a ton of hotels or transports available. All the people on this ship would likely triple the town's population. If he wants to rent a good, solid horse that'll take him all the way to Elsinore, he needs to get off the *Dusk* fast and be the first in line at the rental shack. But he isn't worried. Most travelers are naturally slow-moving creatures—they'll take their time collecting their luggage, saying their good-byes, getting lost in the terminal, and so on. No, he'll have plenty of—

"Passengers, attention, attention, passengers," the sailor broadcasts. "The port authorities tell me there are only a few horses left to be rented. If I were you, I'd hurry to get one." He takes a breath and: "One get to hurry I'd, you were I if…"

Tim groans and stops listening. The passengers are already crowding around, getting ready to disembark, and men spill out from below-deck, like toothpaste being squeezed from its tube. So much for his home-turf advantage.

Sure enough, the second the ship docks and the gangplank hits solid ground, dozens of passengers flood the port. Tim meanders off the *Emerald Dusk*, suddenly in no hurry. There's no point even trying to get a horse anymore, and he doesn't feel like getting trampled as if he's in a shopping bazaar on *Jeudi Gris*.

His boots scrape against the gravelly earth, and it suddenly hits him. He knew he was coming home…but now he's here. His breath trembles once. Then he inhales as much of the crisp Danish air as he can. His lungs burn, and it feels great.

He turns and salutes the strong wooden vessel that brought him here. "Well done." He walks away from the ocean, away from the rest of the world, each step carrying him deeper into Denmark.

As quickly as the travelers descended upon the horse-rental shack, they're gone, leaving only footprints and peanut shells in their wake. The rental agent behind the counter looks crazed and exhausted, likely at the tail-end of his twelve-hour shift. Working at a port in such a tiny town usually means agonizingly long hours, since there aren't an abundance of extra employees lying around.

Tim sighs at the litter on the ground. "Tourists," he gestures to the ship.

The Dane behind the counter laughs and attempts to flatten his wild hair. "Now that's an accent I recognize." No luck. His hair stands straight up as if trying to surrender. "And where are you returning home from, my good man?"

"Is my English accent that bad?" Tim smirks bashfully.

"Eh, honestly, it's not bad. It'd fool most. But not a lifelong Dane. No, you can always hear that accent shining through. Like when you pick out a specific person singing in the middle of a choir. If you know what you're looking for, you can't help but hear it."

Tim chuckles. Kent too had picked up on his accent back on Rogelio's ship. He supposes he could drop his English accent, but he oddly doesn't want to. Just because he's back in Denmark doesn't mean the past five years are expunged.

"I'd like a horse, Guv," Tim says, "if there are any left."

The Dane checks the roster on the counter. "Looks like we've got one more."

"Really?" Tim is shocked. Maybe Lady Fortuna is finally on his side.

"Oy," the Dane yells to one of his co-workers, "go get Elmer! Someone's renting him!"

A few minutes later, Tim sees why Elmer hasn't been spoken for yet.

Elmer is a saggy, stumpy, U-shaped horse long past its retirement age. Patches of bald skin speckle its light gray fur, and its eyes are brown and foggy, like two dirty windows. And is that...? Tim looks closer. Yep—a smoldering cigarette dangles from its lips. On the whole, Elmer looks ready to punch its ticket to the big glue factory in the sky.

"I think I'll walk." Tim pats Elmer, and the horse snorts its gratitude. "Thanks anyway."

The long-lost Hamlet brother wraps his coat tighter around his body and sets off for the Castle of Elsinore.

For now, the scenery is craggy and gray. Even the sunshine is dull, despite there not being a cloud in the sky. But he knows, as he moves further south, the geography will level out into rolling fields of greenery, dotted with farms and livestock. Finally, when he nears Elsinore, towering foliage, thick forests, and twisty paths will be the name of the game.

Denmark is certainly a deck of cards with many suits. One must be able to play them all.

Paths in this region of the kingdom are more hypothetical than actual. Gravel and dirt clods are kicked to the side by hooves and boots, forming a sort of trail for later travelers to follow—the more people who walk the same pathway, the more defined it becomes. Unfortunately, it's the chilly time of year, and Verkwister is as far-flung as a town can get while still being legally called "Danish." So Tim needs to chart his own course, vaulting boulders and kicking earthy debris out of his way.

He's very thankful for his heavy-duty boots. He chuckles at the thought of the visitors on the *Dusk* trying to do the same thing with their fashionable centro-Euro footwear...then he feels bad for chuckling at their misery...then he shakes his head and chuckles again. *Nah, they deserve it. Tourists.*

The day reaches its peak just as Tim leaves the rocks behind and enters the grassy plains. The wind blows a bit harder, but the sun shines a bit brighter too, lifting Tim's spirits. Plus, the roads are paved here, and he takes a break at a rest-stop for a bit.

The barbecue-mutton sandwich on display in the window catches his hungry eye, and he sits down for lunch. And a few minutes later, as he dashes to an outhouse, he curses his gullible appetite. (*Never trust meat sold at a roadside convenience shoppe*, Tim scolds himself. *That was a tourist move.*) The journey continues.

In the distance, peeking over the green horizon, he sees long shadows waving at him. Curious, he picks up his pace. What sort of creatures have such gangly arms? They keep rotating up and down, up and down, again and again.

Finally, he walks enough so that the creature sits atop the horizon, and he lets out a deep belly-laugh.

It's a windmill, tall, wooden, and colorful. He hasn't seen one of these in ages. A memory flashes across the stage of his mind: him and his father touring the countryside, visiting each of the happy farmers who work this land.

He saunters past the windmill and returns its friendly wave. Since there's no one around to appreciate his joke, he supplies his own laugh-track. And he finds the act of him laughing at his own joke so funny, he ends up laughing at that too, trapped in a cycle of hysterics.

Once his laughter peters out, he lets out a long sigh that warms his entire body, despite the brisk air.

As he walks, he sees a squat, bohemian-looking building up ahead. Is that a Buckstars Brewery? All the way out here?

Man, those places are everywhere.

He grabs a black java to-go and takes a sip. *Whew!* He likes it dark, but not dark as tar. Six sugar packets later, he's back on the road.

The sun grows pale as it inches down, down, down, and Tim shoves his exposed fingers under his armpits. The evening chill has come to play.

Trees begin to dot the landscape, and soon enough, Tim has entered one of Denmark's untamed forests. Large birds soar from branch to branch, causing dry leaves to drift to the ground like brittle snowflakes. Foliage blocks the dwindling sunlight, but he can still see the dirt path beneath his boots well enough.

He hears a tussle up ahead. Two animals tumble onto the trail about fifteen yards in front of him, and he stops to give them space.

A mid-sized red fox and a young gray wolf nip at each other, clawing and braying and shuffling in circles. At first, Tim thinks they're fighting, but it quickly becomes clear that they're playing together. Both animals' tongues dangle from their jaws—it looks like they're smiling. The fox stands on its hind-legs and paws at the wolf, its fur shimmering like a flame as it wriggles and dances. The wolf rolls on its back so it can use all four legs.

Heavy footfalls echo from within the woods. Tim and the two animals stiffen, ears tuned to the new sound. No, not feet at all—hooves.

Enormous antlers make an appearance first, emerging from the trees like long trumpets announcing the arrival of a king. The deer is massive, one of the biggest animals Tim has ever seen. The small canines dash into the thick forest, gone in a flash.

Tim is frozen in place at the sight of the animal. But it doesn't even look at him. Without so much as a glance, the deer marches across the dirt path, from one side of the forest to the other. Surveying its kingdom, it seems.

He moves on, trying to not be bothered by the animals' indifference toward him. Really, really trying.

Night gets closer with every second. Just like that, seconds turn into minutes, which turn into an hour, and Tim feels the fatigue of the day overtaking his legs. Trekking across northern Denmark is taking its toll. He needs to rest soon.

The path forks—he takes the left, fairly confident in his internal map. Another fork—right this time. And so the path winds and weaves, deeper into the woods.

Until he reaches another crossroad. One he's certain he's seen before.

"Wait…" He spins and takes in his surroundings. Yep, he's definitely been here in the last hour. "Ugh, for crêpe's sakes, am I lost?"

Yes. Yes I am.

"Of all the bloody…" Tim kicks at a pile of dirt, sending a grimy cloud all over himself. He grimaces, dusts off his coat, and forces his heart to stop beating like a reverberating gong.

Calm down, Guv.

Don't call me that.

He sizes up the crossroad and does his best to visualize the forest from the perspective of a bird, where he is now versus where Elsinore is seated.

Hopeless. He's taken too many turns that may or may not be correct to know where exactly he is.

He rubs his hands to warm them. The sun is almost gone.

Clip clop. Creak. Chatter.

Something is coming along the path directly toward him. Something, and a whole lot of somebodies.

The something is an enormous wooden wagon, rickety and shaped like a box, pulled by two brawny reindeer. Several torches are mounted on the sides of the wagon, bringing light to wherever it rolls.

The identity of the someones, Tim can't tell. He sees a dozen people. One drives the reindeer, some nest on top of the wagon, many walk alongside it. But *all* are gabbing and jabbering with great energy. They sing random tunes, wave their hands as they talk, don silly voices, and burst into fits of laughter.

Tim pulls his coat closer around his body, sticks out his thumb, and moves toward the torches, like a moth drawn to the warmth.

The driver sees him on the path and pulls on the reindeers' reins. "Whoa, whoa!" The huge wagon sputters to a halt. "Well, howdy-doody, fellow wanderer!"

The entire group stops chatting amongst themselves and turns its collective attention on Tim. The torchlight bounces off their wide smiles.

Tim gives a reluctant wave. "H…Howdy-doody." He clears his throat— the odd greeting tastes like syrup. "Do you gents and ladies happen to know the way to Elsinore Castle?"

A delighted gasp ripples through the group. They chitter to each other as if sharing a delicious secret.

"Elsinore?" The driver slaps a knee. "Why, the universe sure is a funny governess, *innit*? We're headed to Elsinore right this very gosh-darn minute."

Tim smiles in relief. He opens his mouth to ask if he can hop on the wagon, but before he can form the words—

"Can we give you a lift?" the driver says with unmasked sincerity. "Please? It'd be our pleasure! Aw, c'mon now, you'd just about make our day if you joined our little parade. Pretty please with cherries on top? And some of those crushed peanuts too—oh, I just love those."

Tim can't get a word in edge wise. He blurts out, "Yes, yes, by all means. I'll let you take me to Elsinore."

The driver beams, utterly elated. "Hallelu! Troupe," he addresses the others on the wagon, "we have a guest!"

The eleven men and women let out a cheer.

"To be honest with ya, friend," the driver stands and stretches his legs, "we were looking to camp out and catch some shut-eye. If it's alright with you, I think we'll cook up some grub, seize some rehearsal time, and rest our souls for the evening." He climbs down from his perch behind the reindeer.

"I don't mind at all," Tim says, already warmed by the torches.

"Sounds like a ten-outta-ten evening, if I do say so myself. And I *did* say so myself! Ha!"

With that, the others begin to set up camp—unhitching the reindeer, pulling out cots and chairs, sparking a fire to cook over, and so on.

Tim has never been much of an outdoorsmen, so it isn't much of a compliment for him to think that it looks like a nice, cozy campsite, but he goes ahead and thinks it.

This looks like a nice, cozy campsite.

The driver walks up to him, his kind eyes sparkling. "Oh, you'll need a hefty sleeping bag tonight, friend. Remind me to give you my cot when we all turn in."

"Thank you, honestly," Tim says. "But don't go out of your way for me. There's no need for all of this, Mr…" He realizes he hasn't caught the driver's name.

As if reading his mind: "Horace Bastion. And please, it's our pleasure! We're all about laughter and memories here. Making your day better makes our day better! So following that karma-logic, would you really want to take away our joy by not letting us make you as happy as possible?"

Tim wants to respond, but he can't think of a worthy rebuttal. It simply doesn't make sense to refuse hospitality and a comfy bed, and making him happy does seem to make Horace happy. So…

He shrugs and smiles. "Very well, Horace. Accommodate away."

The man jitters like a kid about to open his Christmas presents. "What a night! Thank you for entering our story, brother." He offers his hand.

"The name's Tim." They shake. "I hope this is a good chapter for us both!"

"Right this way, Tim, and let's nourish our bodies, whaddya say?"

As soon as the words fall from his mouth, two of the travelers swoop in with chairs and steaming bowls of stew. They plant the seats within the torches' warmth, hand the bowls to Tim and Horace, and skip back to get their own dinners.

Tim settles into the chair and immediately exhales in bliss. The seat is padded with what feels like goose feathers, and there's an extension that allows him to recline and prop up his weary legs. The stew in his bowl is hearty and delicious too.

What a chapter this is turning out to be.

The group of men and women fan out across their newly-assembled campsite. Songs are sung. Jokes told. Laughs shared.

"Horace," Tim says, recalling a detail he had heard a minute before. "You said you lot were looking for some rehearsal time. Rehearsal for what?"

The driver sits in the chair next to Tim. "Yes, of course! Where are my manners?" He finishes his stew in two swallows and licks the remnants from his lips. "My troupe and I were invited to perform at tomorrow's noon, at the castle. Requested by Prince Hamlet himself!"

The others overhear the famous name and cheer excitedly.

Tim smiles. So Hamlet still invites theatre troupes to perform in the castle. He wonders if they will use the stage he and Hamlet had requested be built so many years ago, or if it's been flattened and reconstructed, bigger and better.

Horace continues, beaming with pride. "We are the Incredibly Magnificent Players Roving Over Viborg!"

Tim chortles. "Not short on self-esteem, I see. And I take it you're from Viborg?"

"Born and bred. We're very proud of our hometown, but we're ready to take a royal stage, to be honest. Imagine, making a *prince* laugh! Making his day better…now *that* would definitely make our day better."

Yeah, imagine that.

"So you're players?" Tim grins. *Splendid! Finally, someone I can talk shop with.* "What sorts of shows do you put on? Which writers do you subscribe to?"

Horace nods with a pensive smile on his face. "We humble folk use the greatest playwright ever to exist: our gut. The universe whispers its words very subtly, my friend. So subtly, you can't hear it if you're trying to. Thus, we allow the universe to use us as its puppets. Whatever stories pop into our minds, we spit them out as they come to us."

As Tim listens, he sinks lower and lower into his chair.

Oh no...

The grim realization dawns on him. He gulps. "So you're..."

Incredibly Magnificent Players Roving Over Viborg. IMPROV.

Horace beams ear to ear. "Impromptu performers. Spur-of-the-moment thespians. Every tale we tell is one-hundred-percent, pure-grade extemporization."

Tim gives a polite smile and quickly shoves a spoonful of stew in his mouth to hide his expression. His poker face has always been more of a go-fish facade—AKA, not very good.

"As a matter of fact, Brother Timothy, we'd be honored if you could act as witness to our little rehearsal. We're all a bit nervy about the performance for Hamlet tomorrow, and your feedback would give our auras a boost."

The entire troupe holds its breath, waiting for Tim's answer. The torches crackle in the cold night.

Improvisational theatre is a noble enough art form, Tim supposes. Back in his youth, Tim had read books on books about theatre, and he'd been particularly interested by improv. He read that it can elicit genuine emotion and laughter from an audience, when done properly.

As he'd grown up, however, he'd never seen it done properly. And he'd searched high and low for credible performers. Bearable improv, it seems, is like a flushable toilet, or God—he's heard good things, but has never actually seen it.

The players look at him so eagerly, so ready to please.

"Sssuuuurrreee..." The word slides out of him, like a baby bird being kicked out of a tree.

Horace wiggles his hands. "Jubilee!"

At once, they all scramble to and fro, twittering to each other, as if backstage on opening night. A few of them blubber their lips or pop their tongues, doing all sorts of weird vocal warm-ups.

A man swoops in and pops a frothing mug into Tim's empty hand.

"Oh...thanks." Tim takes a sip.

A frizzy-haired lady offers him a blanket.

"I'm good, thank you," he says.

"Okie dokie!" She holds up another. "Would you like this blanket instead? This one's orange."

Tim takes a silent breath. "No thank you."

"Are you sure?" she presses, smiling wide.

"Yes, I'm—"

Small hands clamp onto his shoulders from behind and begin massaging.

"What the…?" Tim waves the doting players away like they are gnats. "Get off! I'm fine! I'm fine."

They're practically hanging me with hospitality.

The eleven players line up in front of their box-shaped wagon, facing Tim, bouncing on their heels, ready to perform. They've left a large gap of dirt between them and Tim—he supposes this is where they'll be "playing."

Horace strides into the center of their makeshift stage. "Salutations and good greetings to all who have been led to this place today!" He gestures wildly and projects his voice as if addressing a stadium full of patrons, rather than one uncomfortable guy eating stew. "We are the Incredibly Magnificent Players, and we're roving into your hearts."

He pauses for applause.

The night sighs.

Tim jerks, realizing his role. He quickly sets his bowl and mug on the ground and claps a few times.

"Thank you, thank you!" Horace tips an invisible hat. "We don't have time for dillying or dallying, I'm afraid. The world spins on. So first off, I'll let you know that you are not mere spectators tonight, nosiree. We are *all* a part of the play called life."

Tim swallows a groan. *Audience participation. Hamlet's gonna hate this.*

"So, from the crowd…" Horace takes a few animated steps toward Tim and cups his ear. "Give me a place where you'd be surprised to run into an old friend."

A beat of quiet. Horace and the players are frozen in place, all eyes on the man in the front row.

I'm also in the back row, if you think about it.

Tim nods. "Umm, I want you guys to rehearse well, so maybe something out of the ordinary? A dragon's lair?"

Horace thinks for a moment. He half-turns to look at his troupe. "Do we have any material for dragon's lair?" They all grimace and look at each other helplessly.

Tim dejectedly changes his answer. "Restaurant."

Horace snaps his fingers, instantly peppy again. "Restaurant!" He strolls to the side of the performance space, filling time while the players prepare their improvised scenes. "A restaurant, what a good suggestion. A place where friends and strangers alike may meet and eat. Meet and eat…in a restaurant." He gestures to the "stage." "Take it away, brothers and sisters."

The frizzy-haired lady and a gawky guy hop out of line. She awkwardly squats, as if sitting at a table, and mimes using a fork and knife. The guy walks into the scene, swinging his arms way too much. He acts surprised to see her.

"Julie? What are you doing here? I haven't seen you since kindergarten."

The lady feigns stage-surprise too. She gapes, her chin just about touching her belly button. "Dan! Wow! How've you been?"

"Oh, you know me. I've just been…" He flexes his bony arms. "Working out."

Someone in the line yells, "Freeze!" The two performers obey.

A short woman jumps out of line and taps the guy on the shoulder. He slithers back, and she takes his spot, flexing. "Oh, holding up the planet is such hard work!"

The frizzy-haired lady adapts to the change in scenery. "Here, lemme help." The two players grunt and "comically" struggle to carry the imaginary Earth.

"Freeze." An overweight man takes Frizzy's place. Then he just stands there, looking at the short woman holding nothing.

Her eyes dart nervously to Horace, then to Tim, then back to Chubbers. "Uh…A-Are you gonna help me…carry this suitcase up the stairs?" She's reaching.

Chubbers shrugs. "Sure." He mimes helping the woman carry something, but he's like a limp puppet. At least she strains with the weight of the "suitcase" and walks up invisible stairs—he just holds his hands in a vague shape.

"Whew!" She sets down the suitcase. "We made it! To the top floor!"

He just stands there. "Sure did." He's giving her nothing.

Tim has never wished for the end of the world before. But he's close now.

"Alright!" Horace jumps in, clapping and sending the players back into their line. "Good job, good scene, everyone!"

So there is a God! Tim inwardly rejoices. Outwardly, he taps his palms together.

"Next game! Now, from the audience, I need a volunteer to join us…"

Why have You forsaken me?

An hour ticks by with agonizing patience. By the time the show finally wraps up, Tim feels like he's aged fifty years.

The players stand in their line, hands interlocked, and take a big, sweeping bow. Tim musters all the good will he has left and applauds.

"Thank you, thank you," Horace gleams, then turns to his cohorts. "Well done, all! Rest your bodies, minds, and souls. Tomorrow, we bring Elsinore to its feet!"

Tim grimaces. The show was far too long, awkward, and flat-out unfunny. He can't in good conscience let these poor players do anything like this for Hamlet. His brother will tear them to shreds.

And to be frank, Tim isn't sure he's a fan of improv as a whole. Clever jokes and rapport take a great deal of forethought. Tinkering. Laboring over every word to make sure it's perfect. Tim is a writer, after all. The idea that someone can create a good story out of thin air is, truthfully, quite silly to him. Silly, and a little threatening.

Horace jogs over to Tim, practically bursting with glee. "Wow, we were on a roll tonight, Brother Tim, lemme tell ya. You're one lucky son-of-a-scarab to have a private showing. Whew!" He whoops and sits next to Tim. "Now…notes. Go."

Tim clears his throat. "Horace, pal…" He selects each word carefully—takes it off a shelf, considers it, polishes it, and makes absolutely sure it's the right one before setting it on a conveyor belt and sending it out of his mouth. "You and your troupe are definitely performers. You have a knack for bringing the audience into the show. But I know Prince Hamlet fairly well. He's a traditional guy, and he might not be ready for interactive theatre."

Horace thinks and nods. "Is that right?" He seems to be receiving the words well enough.

Tim senses that Horace is open to advice and seizes the opportunity. "Oh yes, Hamlet has a severe case of tunnel-vision when it comes to theatre—his way is the only way. Perhaps your troupe could open with a bout of improvisation, yes, but then…" He gasps excitedly, as if the idea has just come to him. "Then you could perform one of the old standards. Something from the ancient Romans or Greeks?"

"Hmm." Horace considers this idea. "This may be a shock, but we are classically trained actors. A few moons ago, we all branched off from our dramatic company in Viborg and formed our own."

"I know this must be tough for you, Horace," Tim says. "Going back on-script probably feels like you're abandoning your thespian principles. But I promise, this is the right route for a venue as prominent as Elsinore."

"You think we can still do a bit of a riff at the start?" Horace's eyes are wide and a little desperate. It sounds like he's asking for permission.

Tim wants to tell him no. *Never speak again without a script glued to your hand.* But he can't. Horace might be bad at improv and terribly unfunny, but he's more sincere and eager about his craft than most of the actors in London.

"Sure," Tim says, then quickly amends: "But brevity is key. Under two minutes. That way, every line and every joke you tell *has* to be a good one."

"Interesting…" Horace marvels at the theatrical theory. "You're saying a shorter set is better. Just like life…It's so brief and fleeting, and that's what makes it meaningful."

"Whatever you say, Guv. You should probably go over this new game plan with your troupe. Do you have any classic scripts you can run through tonight?"

"But of course. We're impromptu players, but we don't burn scripts and dance on their ashes, like some other improv troupes."

"That's a thing?"

Horace continues, "There should be a cupboard full of 'em in the wagon. Would you mind picking out a good one while I tell the others?"

"You got it." Tim stands and walks toward the giant, boxy wagon, rubbing his eyes. Even here, in the middle on the Danish woods, he has ended up directing a bunch of actors.

Hamlet would whip them into shape, no sweat. This is his specialty, his passion. He would bark commands like a general marching into battle, and the actors wouldn't be able to help themselves but listen to and respect him.

And Tim would watch from the back row, tinkering and laboring over the script. Scratching out phrases, penciling in new thoughts, crumpling up useless scenes.

Ah, that sounds great.

There's a reason Tim's shows in London always flopped like dying fish. His brother is the director, not him. Plus, as a duo, they had always been able to rein in the other's more outlandish ideas. When Hamlet got too tyrannical and caught up in the minutia of actors' hand gestures, Tim would remind him of the bigger picture. And when Tim's scripts got too absorbed with their own cleverness, Hamlet would say something like, "Get your head out of the ink, brother."

Two halves of a whole.

Pretty great apart, but unstoppable together, in Hamlet's own words.

"Hello!" Chubbers steps in front of Tim, right in the middle of his pondering.

Tim stumbles to a stop, reorienting himself. "Um…Hey there."

"I'm glad you watched our rehearsal! How do you think I did?"

Tim remembers the portly fellow's performance—wooden, awkward, and unimaginative. And now he's standing right in Tim's path, gawking and scratching his belly. A mind reader would charge this guy half-price.

"I'll never forget it," Tim says with a thin smile. "I think Mr. Bastion is just about to make an announcement. Might wanna go hear what he has to say."

"You can see the future?"

Tim sidesteps the man and moves under the wagon's immense shadow. The troupe's transport is truly huge. "Do they smuggle elephants in this thing?" he murmurs.

One of the tethered reindeer looks at him and snorts.

"Oh! Sorry," Tim stammers. "Didn't know I said that one out loud."

Great, now my internal asides are slipping out. That's just what I need.

Tim smiles at the beautiful creature. "I don't suppose you know a horse named Elmer? Well, if you do, he could use a nice card or something." He hoists himself into the wagon before the reindeer can respond.

It's dark and chilly inside the wooden hull. Tim sees the outline of a lantern dangling from the ceiling, and he fumbles with the switch for a while. Eventually, an orange light bathes everything in sight.

What a mess. What an ungodly clutter. Dirty laundry, threadbare costumes, crusty dishes…Everything is strewn everywhere, and Tim can't tell where the floor stops and the piles begin.

He trapezes his way through the chaos, searching for the cupboard Horace had mentioned. "If I were an improv actor, where would I keep my scripts?" Following this line of thought, Tim goes to the very back corner and digs through mounds of rubber chickens, deflated whoopee cushions, other lame props.

And here it is. A small cabinet with loose hinges, sitting on the floor.

He gets on his knees and opens the cupboard. An avalanche of papers tumbles out. "Oh, my darlings, what have they done to you?" Tim laments, scoops the loose-leaf pages together, and begins to thumb through them.

There are hundreds of stray papers, and it looks like they're several different plays, all jumbled together. Tim peeks in the cupboard and is slightly relieved—at least a few plays are neatly stacked and separated with twine.

But these poor scripts are hopelessly entangled. Each paper has a page number in its bottom right corner, but there's no way to know which pages go together to form a whole.

"Aha!" He finds one of the title pages and sets it aside. After a few minutes of sifting through the carnage, he finds six title pages total. *Perhaps*, he thinks, *some of these would be worth checking out later at a library*. He reads the plays' names.

A Midsummer Night's Dream. Sounds pleasant. Maybe too pleasant.

The Tempest. He chuckles softly, remembering the horrendous hurricane he survived nearly a week ago. He thinks of Caliban and Ariel. Mainly, he thinks of Miranda.

King Lear. Likely an old medieval tale. Could be exciting.

Much Ado About Nothing. A light, frothy comedy. Meh.

The Merchant of Venice. His heartbeat thuds in the quiet wagon. Odd. Rogelio had mentioned his cousin is a merchant in Venice.

No. Just a bizarre coincidence.

The last title lands in his gut like a rock.

The Tragedy of Romeo and Juliet.

How...?

Tim shoves the pages away from him as if they may bite.

The runaway from Verona had said that his love was named Juliet. Coincidences don't get this big.

Slowly, anxiously, nervous of what he might find, Tim scans his eyes over the heap of pages, the plays that are shuffled together. Familiar names jump out at him: Kent...Dogberry...Nick Bottom...Prospero and Caliban and Ariel and...Miranda.

He picks up a random page and reads:

"*KENT: Trouble him not. His wits are gone.*"

Another page:

"*DOGBERRY: Our watch, sir, have indeed comprehended two auspicious persons, and we would have them this morning examined before your worship.*"

And another:

"*MIRANDA: I have suffered with those I saw suffer—a brave vessel, who had, no doubt, some noble creatures in her, dashed all to pieces.*"

That sounds just like them. Those are things they would say.

These are the names of his friends, but here, they're mere characters. Scribbles. Indications of which actor should say which lines.

His head spins, but he doesn't know why.

So his friends' names are all included in these scripts. What could this mean?

I have no idea.

And that makes his vertigo even worse.

He needs air. Yes, getting out of the wagon, away from these inexplicable scripts...That will help.

Leave the pages behind. Ignore them. Soon enough, time will make him forget he ever saw them.

Yeah right. Like I'm gonna forget those ink-black names staring at me from a sea of parchment.

Tim reaches back into the cupboard. He needs to bring a play out to Horace so the troupe can begin rehearsal. Surely, there's something here by Sophocles or Aeschylus…Something that doesn't feature one of his friends as a fictional character, preferably.

He rifles through the stack, his fingers trembling. He tells himself it's because of the cold.

Ah, here. *Hecuba's Anguish.* That's a good one. And it's right on top, so he doesn't have to keep digging.

He picks up the script, in a hurry to escape. As he withdraws his arms from the cupboard, he knocks the stack of plays to the floor. He grits his teeth, wanting nothing more than to leave—no one would even notice these spilled papers among the rest of the clutter.

But he drops to his knees and begins to pick them up.

Thankfully, twine kept the plays separated, and he restacks them one by one in the cabinet.

Medea.

Lysistrata.

The Trojan Women.

He freezes. Script in his hands. Title page whispering to him.

The Tragedy of Hamlet, Prince of Denmark.

It's a thick script. Many pages. A lengthy character list.

Good thing he's on his knees. He isn't sure his legs would be steady right now.

"Oh, Tim?" Horace's voice comes from behind Tim. "Found one for us?"

"Y-Yeah." His mouth is dry. "*Hecuba's Anguish.* You, um…" He reorders his thoughts, eyes fixed on the play in his hands. The one named after him. "It has a female lead. You should hold some quick auditions."

"Right on," Horace affirms. "Can I see the pages, when you have a moment?"

Tim swallows the cotton lodged in his throat and stands. He quickly rolls the *Hamlet* play like a scroll and hides it inside his coat. Then he turns to face Horace, brandishing *Hecuba's Anguish.*

The two exit the wagon and breathe in the cold night air. Cold, clear, undeniably Danish air.

Tim returns to his plush chair as the players discuss their new production. The script in his coat's inner pocket is like a boulder dragging him to the bottom of a frozen lake.

But he doesn't dare take it out. Doesn't dare look at it.

Not now.

Not yet.

Chapter 9

The morning sun bleeds white light across Denmark. Tim walks alongside the players and their wooly mammoth of a wagon. He squints against the sunlight and realizes the forest has broken up—behind him is a thick swath of trees, and ahead, there's nothing but a dirt path and crunchy grass.

"The natural world has no administrator," Horace pontificates to no one in particular. He sits at the head of the wagon, driving the reindeer. "One moment we're in the woods, and the next, we're forging across the plains! Untouched land, as far as the human eye can reach!"

Untouched. Except for the path we're walking on, the water wells every couple of miles, and the crumpled sandwich wrappers left behind by other caravans.

The players are spread around the wagon, just as they were when Tim first encountered them last night. Some jig on the roof, some dangle from the sides, some have their boots on the earth. They run their lines for the upcoming production, practicing choreography, inserting ad-libs in an attempt to make each other laugh. They frequently succeed. The air is filled with merriment and songs.

As desperately as he tries, Tim can't stop thinking about the play rolled up in his coat pocket.

One of the players shouts, "There it is!"

A spire peers over the horizon, followed by a tower, then a slanted roof, stone walls, and massive gates…The Castle of Elsinore is in sight.

From this distance, it still looks like a child's toy, but Tim knows its majesty, its immense weight. He can already feel the grit of the old mortar as he runs his hand across the outside walls. He smells the azaleas and orchids blooming in the north courtyard. All at once, the layout of the entire compound comes rushing back—every hallway, broom closet, dungeon cell, and creaky floorboard. The tapestries and portraits, the grand ballroom and drafty basement. He remembers everything.

"Alright, everyone," Horace calls to his troupe from the driver's seat, "respect and dignity. This might be our big break. If you needs to shear your fingernails or give your feet a good scrub, now's the time." He takes a breath. "But, y'know, have fun with it too!"

As the group of players nears the gates, the sound of sloshing water reaches Tim's ears. The moat surrounding the castle is dark and deep, not exactly a welcome-mat. Tim looks closer—the alligators have been swapped out for eels. Money must be tight with Claudius as king.

An enormous drawbridge drops like a gavel, creating a path across the moat. Horace cheers, and his troupe follows suit.

The reindeer pull the players' wagon across the bridge and onto the grounds of Elsinore. Tim's boots rap against the wooden bridge, and then stomp on dead grass. And just like that, he's home.

Before Tim has the chance to soak in his return, he spots a green uniform making a beeline for the wagon. His gut tells him to conceal his visage. Any member of the castle's court is sure to recognize his face, which is identical to that of the sitting prince. Tim finagles his way deep into the crowd of players and pops the collar of his coat.

Why am I hiding? According to the Ambassador, King Claudius sent for me.

He doesn't have an answer. Perhaps he wants to scope out the situation first, get a lay of this land. See what his brother, mother, and uncle/stepfather are up to before revealing himself.

Yeah, let's go with that.

No matter the nebulous reasoning, Tim hunches his shoulders to hide the lower half of his face.

The guard strides up and addresses Horace. "Greetings, player."

"Howdy-doody, chum! How are you on this fine morning the universe has gifted us?"

The guard isn't sure how to respond. "Very...well, sir. Messrs. Rosencrantz and Guildenstern are inside and wish to address the entire company. You may leave your wagon with the attendants, and they shall escort your beasts to the stables as well."

"That sounds peachy, my companion," Horace says as he climbs down from the driver's seat. "Lemme just grab some reindeer feed. They only eat cage-free oats, y'see."

Tim calls out with a raspy voice, "I'll get it, Mr. Bastion!" Before anyone can turn to see who spoke, he jumps inside the wagon.

He hastily rummages through the piles of frayed costumes. Frederick Rosencrantz and Christian Guildenstern were good friends of the Hamlet twins growing up, and they would be sure to recognize him sooner or later. He needs to separate himself from the players.

He finds an old flat cap and sticks it over his dark hair. There's a musty scarf and a horrendously plaid jacket, both of which he throws on. He thinks back to being inside this wagon last night—*Quickly, so no one gets impatient and comes looking. Also so I don't have to remember those scripts with the names—*

Yes, there's the bag of feed Horace requested. Tim grabs it and leaves before the memory of the scripts can rise too close to the surface.

With his hair and lower-face covered, Tim swerves through the crowd of players to Horace's side. "Here ya go, Mr. Bastion," he says, still using a false raspy voice.

"Well, thank you, Brother Timothy." Horace takes the bag and hands it to one of the Danish attendants. "Sounds like you're getting a ferocious cold. Y'know what helps with that? Some cage-free oats boiled in vinegar. Clears the sinuses right up!"

The uniformed guard leads the gaggle of players across the front lawn, toward the castle entrance. Tim hangs around the back of the pack.

"Ooh"s and "Ahh"s emanate from the players as they take in the splendor of the castle grounds. Even Tim is caught up a little bit. Soldiers ride by on tall stallions, brandishing lances and shields. Their boxy wagon is dwarfed by the King's official stagecoach—it's decked out in gold and opals, only used for occasions when Denmark needs to make visitors feel inadequate, like parades or peace talks. Topiaries dot the lawn, shaped like elephants and dragons. Most of these actors have never seen an elephant or a dragon, and they're mystified by the leafy figures.

Iron double-doors swing open, and the troupe scuttles into the castle. Tim is grateful he grabbed the extra layers of clothing—it's even colder in here than it is outside. But the players don't seem to notice. The high ceilings and countless candelabras are truly breathtaking.

A man greets them. "Morning, chodes. About time you made it. Hamlet loves this artsy-fartsy bollocks, so you better cheer him up."

From his position in the back of the group, Tim can only see part of the speaker's face, but he immediately recognizes him. That's Guildenstern. Or…is it Rosencrantz?

Another voice joins. "No kidding. Hamlet's moping like a bloodhound, so do whatever he says." A second man stands beside the first. "Put on any dumbo play he wants, got it?"

Okay, now *that's* Guildenstern…maybe. It's a weird feeling, but for the life of him, Tim can't remember which face belongs to which man. The years have blurred Rosencrantz and Guildenstern into one.

Doesn't matter. They're always together, and their personalities are practically interchangeable.

There's a hallway to Tim's left, one that'll lead him into the residential section of the castle. He pulls his plaid jacket tighter around him and slips away from the troupe.

"Godspeed, players," he whispers. "May Hamlet have mercy on your souls."

Off he goes, deep into Elsinore's heart, the scarf fluttering behind him like a limp wing. The walls and floor are both made of gray stone, so his footfalls explode and echo all the way down the hall, then all the way back. It sounds like he's being followed, but a quick glance confirms that he's alone.

"Halt! Who are you?"

Well, not quite alone. As Tim passes an intersection, he spots a telltale puke-green uniform in the corner of his vision. The guard cocks his head, clearly not recognizing the figure wandering through the castle.

Tim begins to consider his options. But the guard draws a baton, and Tim's mind immediately jumps into overdrive. Instinct takes over, and he runs.

"Wh-Who? What? Cease!" The guard is positively baffled. Very little excitement happens in Elsinore's day-to-day, and he isn't prepared for a foot-chase. He hitches his britches and follows Tim.

Doors whiz past the prodigal prince as he maneuvers the castle's corridors. The guard's lumbering footsteps fall further and further into the distance behind him. The current head of security needs a firm talking-to about the guards' physical capabilities.

But then.

More footsteps, echoing all around him.

Perhaps he spoke too soon.

He screeches to a stop and strains his ears. Several voices, at least three. They speak in a clipped tone—more guards, it sounds like. Reinforcements, looking for the mysterious intruder. It's difficult to catch everything they're saying, but he hears the words "man," "trespassing," and "plaid."

Tim groans. He knew his travesty of fashion would do him in.

He rips off his scarf and plaid coat, as well as the heavier coat he wears underneath, leaving him in only in a wool shirt and the old flat cap. He shivers, but he'd rather be cold up here than down in the dungeon. He throws the excess clothing into an expensive-looking vase and keeps moving.

The footsteps are closing in from every direction. Guards will swarm him in a matter of seconds.

There's a door ajar right next to him. He sighs, hopes his luck hasn't run out, and jumps into the room. He slowly shuts the door behind him, careful to make the latch's *click* as quiet as possible.

"Hamlet?"

He knows that voice. His palms get very sweaty, and the tips of his ears feel like they're on fire.

She sits at a bedside table, a sewing needle in one hand, but she sets it down and stands. A silk gown drapes down her body and kisses the floor. "Hamlet, darling, are you alright?" A look of concern rumples her smooth face. "You're white as a sheet."

Ophelia. Daughter of Polonius.

A long, slender neck. Eyes like topaz. Each word she speaks can silence a raging storm.

She and Hamlet are embroiled in an intense on-again-off-again bond that seems to be on at the moment.

And she thinks Tim is he.

Tim takes off the flat cap and holds it to his side. He tries to speak, but something's lodged in his throat. It feels like years of pent-up emotion, embarrassment, social anxiety…but it's likely just phlegm.

"My love," she says, approaching him, "you're starting to frighten me. Can you not speak?" She extends a hand to caress his face.

Wow, those eyes. She looks at him with such devotion and apprehension—she's truly worried about him. She wants to help him.

No, not me. She thinks I'm Hamlet. She has never looked at me like this. She never would.

Tim remembers a time back in grammar school. He had worked up the nerve to ask Ophelia to the Fall Formal ball—she'd enthusiastically accepted, but only because she had mistook Tim for his cunning and aloof twin brother. Tim was aloof as well, but while Hamlet was mysterious in his standoffishness, Tim was merely self-conscious and lonely.

And now here they are, Ophelia once again mistaking Tim for his brother. He can't really blame her—he's been gone for half a decade, and he looks exactly like Hamlet.

As he stands in Ophelia's bedroom, thinking and remembering and inner-monologuing, she is still walking toward him, her dainty hand outstretched.

"You look like you've been chased out of hell," she says.

Tim doesn't doubt it. He's pale from shock, blushing from embarrassment, shivering from the cold, and sweating from the capture he just barely evaded.

Speaking of which…He tunes his ears. The guard's boots are clamoring about just on the other side of the door. Tim can't leave now, or he'll walk right into them.

But he can't speak to Ophelia either. He may look identical to Hamlet, but as soon as he opens his mouth, she'll know.

Her hand is inches from his face. He panics and grabs her wrist.

She gasps. "Darling, what is it?"

Tim holds her away at an arm's length, listening, waiting for the guards to leave the hallway behind him.

He looks at Ophelia, his heart hammering for multiple reasons. She has only gotten more beautiful over the past five years. He didn't think that was possible.

"Hun," she presses, her jaw settling, "*talk* to me."

Tim wants nothing more than to do just that. Instead, he sighs and lowers his eyes in the melodramatic way he has seen Hamlet do dozens of times.

He only hears a single set of footsteps outside the door now. The heavy boots begin to walk away. Finally, they fade into the distance.

Aaaaaaaannnnnddddd... Wait a few seconds for good measure, to make sure the coast is clear.

He releases Ophelia's wrist and lets out the most exaggerated sigh he can manage. (It's a pretty good performance, if he says so himself.)

She gapes at him, utterly confused and more than a little scared. Her face whimpers *Why is my dear Hamlet acting this way?* Tim's heart pangs— he has never wanted to make Ophelia do anything but smile. But he has to go now.

Keeping his gaze locked on Ophelia, he reaches behind himself, grabs the doorknob, and slides out into the hallway. He only looks away when the door eases shut between them.

He releases an anxious breath and replaces the flat cap on his head. It'll take a few minutes for his heart to slow down and his face to return to its natural hue.

His timing is perfect—the hallway is empty, the guards gone.

The way she looked at him. Such longing, such compassion...

He can't dwell on it. Off he goes, deeper into Elsinore.

The hallway begins to widen, the doors disappear. He's exiting the residential wing and headed toward the castle's center. The grandeur is upped a notch, since this is the part of the castle guests would most likely see. The tapestries are threaded with gold. Staircases lead nowhere, just for show. Suits of armor line the walls, clutching lances or swords. Houseplants that would normally die in this cold are propped up with wiring.

A voice booms nearby. It sounds like it's coming from within a vast empty space.

I'm near the ballroom. Tim nods and moves in that direction.

Sure enough, Tim turns a corner and sees a magnificent archway, encircled by gilded vines. Tim hides behind the archway and peeks inside the ballroom.

Just as he remembered it. Chandeliers hang from the ceiling, threatening to crush you with their opulence. Organ pipes cover the back wall, just in case someone wants to play music that sounds like a dying calf. The entire space has an air of vastness about it, as if it's somehow larger than a physical room—it has a radiance, a mood of its own.

Wait, there's something different. On the eve of their fifteenth birthday, the Hamlet brothers had performed their original play on a temporary stage Queen Gertrude had ordered to be set up. Now, there's a permanent stage, bolted to the floor, never to be moved.

The booming voice that had drawn him to the ballroom is coming from that stage. It's a familiar voice, speaking in an unfamiliar tone.

Horace Bastion, leader of the improv players, stands on the stage, thundering with the dramatic authority of a seasoned thespian.

Two men stand on the tiled floor in front of the stage, watching Horace. Even though he can only see their backs from his vantage point, Tim can tell one of the men is on the upper-side of middle-aged, short and jangly. The other man is younger, just entering his peak years, with a lean frame and dark hair. His clothes are all black, from his collar to the soles of his shoes.

"Out, out, thou strumpet Fortune!" Horace proclaims, ringing throughout the ballroom.

It's one of the key speeches from *Hecuba's Anguish*, the play Tim had chosen for the players to perform. And boy, is Horace performing it. Every syllable gushes with emotion, his face like a mirror reflecting the scene he's describing.

"All you gods in general unite to take away her power, break all the spokes and fellies from her wheel,"—Horace flings his arm like an enraged fisherman casting a line—"and bowl the round nave down the hill of heaven, as low as to the fiends!"

Tim is in absolute awe. All traces of the unfunny improv games are gone, replaced by one of the most commanding orators Tim has ever seen.

The older of the two men in the audience sighs. "This is too long." He scratches his thin beard, and Tim instantly recognizes him. It's Polonius, right-hand-man to King Claudius.

The black-clad spectator looks aghast at Polonius. "Well then," he snaps, "since you're such an expert in the art of drama, I'll make it a priority to take the script to the barber for a trim." He turns back to Horace. "Please, Mr. Bastion, pay no attention to this old coot. He only likes musical numbers or erotic scenes, and he sleeps through anything else. You, my friend, stand on the stage, the holy ground. That makes you the most important person in this room. Continue, I beg."

"Right-o, my brother." Horace winks and then furrows his brow, back in the speech's mindset. He continues.

But Tim isn't listening anymore. His eyes are locked on the back of the younger man's head, the one who yipped at Polonius.

No mistaking it. That's Prince Hamlet.

He's gotten taller since Tim had seen him last...*But so have I. We're identical, after all.*

When was the last time I saw him?

Tim clenches his eyes shut.

And just like that, he's a teenager again. Fifteen years old, plus a few days. He creeps out of his bedroom in the early morning, while the sun is asleep and the crickets sing. He has a bag slung over his shoulder, carrying all his worldly possessions. People assume that because he's a prince, he has his own stallion and a huge boat and piles of jewels and stuff like that. But no—that's his mom and dad. All he truly owns are a few articles of clothing, his books, and his quills.

He tiptoes down the hallway, but he hears another door squeak open.

It's Hamlet. The future king.

In the dark, Tim can't make out his brother's expression. Is he sad? Confused? Angry? All of the above?

Hamlet doesn't say a word. He sees the bag. He sees his brother leaving under the cover of night. He closes the door and goes back to sleep.

Tim walks out of Elsinore. And that's that.

He shudders and opens his eyes. He doesn't like that memory very much. Back to the present. The ballroom.

Hamlet intently watches Horace, studying the player's gestures and inflections. Ever the director.

Despite them being almost the exact same age, Hamlet seems so adult, so fully grown. His movements are smooth and intentional, like a trained dancer. He's grown into his body, with wide shoulders and strong legs. And his intellect…Even from across the ballroom, hiding behind the archway, Tim can see the clockwork of Hamlet's mind, always moving and piecing things together.

Do I look like that? Have I grown?

Looking at his brother after all these years, Tim feels so small.

He's still the puny child who got rejected by Ophelia. The sorry little sap who poured everything he had into creating fictional stories where he could dictate the ending. The kid who wasn't chosen to be king because both his dad and his brother thought he wasn't good enough.

The Hamlet brothers haven't seen each other since they were fifteen years old. Now they're twenty. That may only be five years, but those ages are a world apart. They transitioned from boys to men without ever speaking to one another.

They're both completely different people now.

Crouching outside the ballroom, Tim rocks back on his heels. He had never realized it until now…but he doesn't know his brother anymore.

Horace finishes his monologue and strikes a powerful pose.

Polonius sniffs. "Dear me, that was good." He wipes a tear from his eye. "The ending got me."

Hamlet nods pensively, then says to Horace, "Well done, Mr. Bastion. I'll speak with you and your players about tonight's performance." Then to Polonius: "Make sure the troupe is comfortable and well-fed. Hospitality is a currency all kingdoms accept."

"Aye, sir." Polonius smiles, still misty-eyed from the emotional monologue. "I will give them everything they deserve!"

Hamlet snorts again. "Everything they deserve? This actor just brought you, an airy old fishmonger, to tears. I think they deserve *more* than what they deserve."

The king's aide is clearly confused by Hamlet's words, but he nods and says, "Um…yes, sir." To Horace: "Right this way, Mr. Bastion. I'll take you to the chamber where your company is waiting."

"Please and thank you greatly." Horace hops off the stage and follows Polonius out a side-door. "By the way, if your eyes got a bit sweaty from that there speech, I gotta balance the equation by making you cry from laughter as well. We players are actually more adept at impromptu pleasantry than scripted calamity…" His voice fades as they walk away.

The ballroom hums in silence. So much hollow space, filled with dust and air. Hamlet stands in the center of the massive room, a black speck amid the white and gold grandeur. He slides his hands in his pockets, and he thinks. He doesn't pace or mumble to himself, like Tim would do.

Before he knows he's doing it, Tim stands and walks into the ballroom. He's drawn to the stranger who shares his face, the prince he recognizes but doesn't quite know. He approaches his brother's back.

His boots echo in the huge room, just like Hamlet's did the night before their big performance. The night they decided to be co-kings. The Fox and the Hippo.

Hamlet turns. He flickers when he sees Tim. A candle caught in a breeze. But he quickly rights himself. "Now there's a face I recognize." He screws up his expression, as if digging through his memory. "Craig from aerobics, right?"

Tim lets out a dry chuckle. He's about ten paces from his brother, and that's where he stops. He keeps his distance. "Hi, Hamlet."

The prince looks at Tim for a while. A long while.

Finally, as if he silently made up his mind about something, Hamlet wanders forward. A leisurely gait, one that's in no hurry. He stops in front of Tim. Yep—they're still the same height.

"Hey, Tim." Hamlet picks a bit of lint off his brother's shirt. "You look good."

"I look like you," Tim replies.

"You're welcome." He looks Tim up and down. "What, are you a hat guy now?"

Tim has forgotten about the cap he's using to conceal his dark hair. "Oh, right. Yeah, I kinda like it." He pauses. "So, what fine mess have you gotten yourself into, Guv?" He hadn't meant for the English slang to slip out

Hamlet doesn't answer. He just cocks an eyebrow. "What do you mean, *chap*?" He bathes that last word with sarcasm. "Who says I'm in a mess?"

"A Danish ambassador found me in London. He said King Claudius wants me here to help. You're in some sort of pickle, apparently."

"That's not possible." Hamlet looks confused. "All of our ambassadors are in Norway right now, trying to defuse that powder keg."

Tim recalls the encounter in the Masterpiece Centre that had started this big misadventure. "No, he was definitely Danish. Prim and proper, with a uniform the color of nausea."

"What was his name?"

"I…I never caught his name." Tim gulps, but he doesn't let Hamlet see. He begins to pace around the ballroom.

"Doesn't ultimately matter, I suppose." Hamlet stands with his feet planted solid, following Tim with his head. "If you've come for Father's funeral, you're about a month late. Same with the wedding."

Ah yes, our mother Gertrude's union with our uncle Claudius. Tim still hasn't fully grasped that whole situation. He's been in London, so he hasn't had to face the reality of having a stepfather to whom he's already related. Hamlet, on the other hand, has had to stare this new reality in the face every day for the past month. "I heard."

Hamlet shrugs, pretending to not be ruffled. "Have you seen Gertrude or Claudius yet?"

"No, just you." Tim doesn't feel the need to tell Hamlet about his awkward encounter with Ophelia.

He laughs without humor. "Well, you can imagine. They're newlyweds. Inseparable. Claudius spends every second he can either in Father's old chambers, or sitting on his throne. It's pathetic."

Tim thinks back to the encounter in his London office. His chat with the ghostly King. Even the recollection is chilling. The ghost had said that he'd told Hamlet about his murder.

"Hamlet…" He proceeds with caution, stops his pacing, takes a breath. "Have you…Do you know Father's cause of death?"

Hamlet barks another sore laugh. "Your small talk is as marvelous as ever, brother. Next we can gab about the bubonic plague and the impending war with Norway. Real parlor room conversation."

His words swirl about, filling the room. Tim lets them hang in the empty air. He knows how to deal with Hamlet's moodiness—let him vent, give him space, be patient but persistent.

Tick tick tick. Moments pass. Hamlet breathes, arms crossed. Tim tries again.

"Do you?"

Hamlet doesn't answer straight away. He stares at the stage. "Snakebite. You know that, everyone knows that. He was in the garden taking his daily nap, that lazy old codger."

"Well..." Tim's voice is shaky. This is it—the moment that Hamlet either opens up to him, or sends him packing out of Elsinore again. "I heard something different."

The black-clad prince keeps looking at the stage. But his arms come uncrossed.

"I heard," Tim says, "Uncle Claudius gave Dad quite the earful."

Hamlet's head snaps so he can glare at his brother, his eyes practically glowing red. "You make a *pun* about my father's homicide?" He balls his fists. "How dare you?!"

"So you do know."

Hamlet clamps his mouth shut, realizing his emotions have betrayed him. He looks his brother in the eye for the first time.

Tim continues. "When I was in London, I had two visitors. One was the Ambassador. The second was Johan Hamlet. Dad. He told me something terrible. Uncle Claudius—"

"Killed him," Hamlet finishes the sentence. He speaks softly, almost in a daze. "Claudius. Ear poison. In the garden. Checkmate." He runs his hands through his hair and sputters, "I thought I was crazy, Tim." Tears dot the corners of his eyes. "I always have, a little. But when Father showed up like a phantom, I truly thought I'd lost it. He told me he was killed in such a horrific way. By his own brother, no less. And...And I thought I'd cracked. It was a delusion from my fevered brain. All the grief and anxiety finally won. But..." He grins and banishes the tears, his tone growing more and more animated each second. "No, no, no. Not today, old noodle. I'm not crazy yet! Father's ghost spoke to you too!"

Tim begins to smile as well. Hamlet's energy is always infectious, be it positive or pessimistic. And right now, at this moment, Hamlet's confident liveliness fills the ballroom. "Oh, I saw him," Tim says. "He walked through my desk and stuck his icy claw in my head."

Hamlet releases a laugh from deep within his chest. He swiftly closes the gap between them and throws his arms around Tim. "Christ, am I glad you showed up." Then he whispers, "You're not crazy, you're not crazy…"

It takes Tim a moment to realize Hamlet is whispering that to himself.

Tim also can't recall the last time his brother hugged him. Or was happy to see him.

They separate, and Hamlet sighs jubilantly. "So you ended up in London, eh? Explains that *cockamamie* accent you've got going on. Must've been one halibut of a journey getting from there to here."

"Sure was." Tim chuckles. He doesn't even know where to start. "I got in a bar fight."

Hamlet snorts. "No you didn't."

"Yes I did! It was at a pub called the *Bombastic*—"

"Don't lie, Tim. It's unbecoming." Hamlet waves away the discussion as if it's his prerogative to do so—which, in Elsinore, it technically is. "Back to Uncle Claudius."

"Right." Tim nods. "That's one of the reasons I came back. To…" It sounds silly, but he says it anyway. "To investigate. See if Claudius really did kill Father."

"Yes, precisely. Precisely!" Hamlet rubs his hands together like a detective on the trail. "We can't take the word of this apparition at face value. I've had the same thought. It could be some supernatural trickster, like Loki or a leprechaun. Or it could be a demon, trying to convince me to kill a man for a crime he didn't commit."

Or we could both be bonkers. I haven't entirely ruled that out.

"Right, we need to make sure…" Tim speaks as his brain processes Hamlet's last few words. "Wait. Kill?"

"Oh yes," Hamlet says, his face grinning wryly, but his eyes seething. "If Claudius is indeed a Brutus, that's the only course of action. Get him offstage for good."

"Brother…" Tim can't find the words. "You can't."

"Sure I can. Poison in wine, knife in gullet, pillow over face…There are plenty of options."

"You've never killed before."

"What a time to start, eh?" He chortles. "Dispatching the treasonous king of Denmark, taking my rightful place, saving the state from a corrupt administration. Sounds like the makings of an illustrious legend, if you ask me."

"There's no coming back from that, Hamlet."

"Oh, please, what do you know? Don't tell me you've become a master assassin during your sabbatical."

Tim feels a hot surge of anger bubbling in his chest, but he desperately pushes it down. "No, but I've met two men who have killed. Both of them in the past week, as a matter of fact." *Captain Travkin and Romeo Montague.* "One of them is mad, a pirate, a scoundrel, unrepentant and dastardly. In short, he's a bad guy, and I know you love to play the hero in your stories. The other is a friend of mine and…He's haunted by that murder. He didn't talk about it much, and he put on an air of cockiness, but I could see it in his eyes. He's a prisoner in that moment."

"Stop." Hamlet's voice is low and glum again, his mood seesawing back below sea-level. "I've made up my mind, and you know that isn't an easy thing for me to do. I have a plan to weed out Claudius's guilt, and once I know he's my father's killer, I'm going to send him to hell."

Tim is taken aback. Just as he saw clouds in Romeo's eyes, he now sees bloodlust and resolve in his brother's. He decides to move on and circle back to the issue of murder at a different time. "So what's this plan of yours?"

Hamlet lights up. "You're gonna like this." He clears this throat, clearly very proud of what he's about to say. "Rosencrantz and Guildenstern invited a troupe of players to perform tonight, so I'm going to make a request of them. I will have them perform *The Murder of Gonzago* for the entire castle—everyone will be invited."

"*Gonzago*? Why does that sound familiar?"

"Osric had us read it one summer vacation. Remember, it's got the lemur—"

"—and the washing machine!" Tim finishes the sentence, remembering now. He scoffs. "Why would you have them put on that play? It's so stilted and old-fashioned. There's a reason it's been relegated to being taught in classrooms and not being performed on actual stages."

"It's a terrible show, to be sure. That's the point! The script is boring and conventional, but I'm planning to insert my own scene. That way, when the audience hears a shift in tone, they'll all sit up and listen. Gertrude, Polonius, everyone…but especially Claudius. However, this scene I'll write is no ordinary scene, not in the least. It will contain events that are eerily similar to Father's murder. In the scene, a man will kill his royal brother. With ear poison, no less! And when this scene occurs, I'll be watching Claudius. Oh, I'll be watching most intently. And in that moment, I'll see on his face whether or not he's guilty."

All is quiet. Hamlet finishes speaking his plan, practically patting himself on the back.

Tim just about slaps his own forehead. "Are you *serious*?! Hamlet, have you been drinking toilet water for the past five years?"

Hamlet looks confused. "What? Did I not explain it well?"

"You explained it just right. And now I'm convinced your potatoes are completely mashed. What kind of plan is that?"

"A good one!" Hamlet rears up like a cornered beast. "You said yourself that killers are haunted in their eyes and they never get over it, or whatever philosophical dung that was. It stands to reason that when Claudius is reminded of his crime, he'll show it. Will he look ashamed, or sneaky, or sad, or pleased with himself—who knows? But he'll give himself away all the same."

Tim tries to reply, but all he can do his shake his head.

Hamlet throws his hands up. "I'm preaching to the choir right now! You write stories, or at least you used to. Are you telling me you don't think they can have an impact on real life? Just minutes ago, Polonius heard a total stranger give a speech, and he was moved to tears. He didn't stub his toe—he wasn't at a funeral—he didn't have a cold. No, he felt emotion based entirely on fictional words spoken by an actor. That's downright sorcery!"

Tim shudders in his boots. He can't help but remember that he'd said practically the same thing to Miranda on the shore of her island. To disagree with Hamlet now would be hypocritical.

Screw it, Hamlet's talking about murder here. Time to be hypocritical.

He takes a breath, doing his best to keep his frustration in check. "Hamlet, we need actual evidence. There are steps we can take. Claudius is a meticulous man. He's bound to keep records of all his vials and extracts, what with how expensive they are and how much pride he has in them. We can do some digging, see how much hebona nectar he had before Father died and how much he has now. We can talk to the guards on duty that afternoon. If Claudius was snooping around the garden, he would've been seen. Also, Claudius said Father's official cause of death was a snakebite— we could scour the orchard, look for nests, see if any poisonous snakes even live there." He sighs. "I mean, cripes, Hamlet, take your pick! Any plan is better than one that hinges on our ability to read the supposed guilt on someone's face."

"It'll work, brother! Trust me. The play is the thing to capture the conscience of the king."

Tim's frustration is officially out of check. "Ending your argument with a rhyme doesn't make it more compelling!"

"So high and mighty." Hamlet grimaces, looking disgusted, disappointed. "Little Tim doesn't get his way, so he throws a tantrum. You were so sore that you weren't chosen to be king, you left in the middle of the night! God, what a child. You left without saying good-bye, without ever reaching out to us or visiting…"

"That's not why I left," Tim seethes.

"Yes it is, and you know it! And you're still so bitter about it. Guess what—not everyone gets to be king. Grow up!"

"That's *not* why I left."

"Then why, Tim? Why did you go?"

"Because we were finally together! For once, we were on the same page. The Hamlet brothers, acting as one. In this very room, we decided to be a team. And then you changed your bloody mind…just *because.* It's not the fact that you were going to be king and I wasn't. I couldn't care less about that. It's that we were friends—no competition, no animosity. And then you *changed your mind.*"

There it is. The reason Tim left—the real reason. He's never come right out and said it. Hamlet is a man of extremes with a fickle mind, one that can't be counted on. One day he's an ally, the next he's an opponent. And Tim couldn't live with that. Can't live with that.

So, five years ago, he'd set out in an attempt to sever all ties to his family name, and to go somewhere no one would recognize the face he shares with the Danish prince. He'd landed in London and started writing plays, unknown, forging his own path. Becoming his own man.

And have I done that? Am I really my own man?

Tim shoves the voice in his head aside. He growls, "And now you've got this cockamamie scheme, trying to send our uncle to the gallows based on a few lines in a play. What a load of crock."

Hamlet plants his feet—unmovable. "I'm not asking for your permission, Tim. Or your help, for that matter. I ate breakfast with Father the morning before he died. I sat in the front row of his funeral. Then the bands switched out, and I was in the front row for the new king's wedding too. You showed up ten minutes ago. I didn't invite you here. I have no use for you."

Tim staggers, like his brother's words are an arrow in his chest.

Everything is quiet. Hamlet's eyes are back on the empty stage, cold and sharp.

What did you expect? He hasn't spoken to you in years. He didn't stop you from leaving. When you didn't come back, he didn't look for you.

"Shut up," Tim hisses to his inner thoughts.

"Excuse me?" Hamlet twitches. More shocked than anything.

Tim is shocked too. He hadn't meant to say that out loud.

But his anger makes him keep talking. "I'm so sick of your mood swings." Words he's been holding onto for years come exploding out. "You're all buddy-buddy one second, and rabid the next. It's infuriating! I can't have a single normal conversation with you. You're happy, you're depressed, you're manic, you're angry. Just pick one! Being your brother is exhausting, you know that? You act like it's the greatest privilege in the world to share your name and your face, but it's a god-forsaken chore. No wonder we never really talked when we were kids. I never knew if you were gonna make me your co-king or bite my head off! I'm glad I left!"

A pause, like the moment a wave crests and hangs in the air…but it doesn't crash down yet.

Neither brother speaks. Tim pants, his tirade leaving him drained.

Hamlet keeps his eyes locked on the empty stage. "I wish I wasn't like me." Almost a whisper. "But I am. I've tried not to be. I'd change if I could."

Those small, quiet words nearly deafen Tim. He closes his mouth and looks at his brother. He doesn't see the future king of a nation, nor a gregarious actor, nor a charming socialite, nor a melancholy loner.

He sees a boy at war with himself every second of every day.

Tim's anger, frustration, and painful memories aren't gone. They never will be. There will never be a magical moment when his relationship with his brother is repaired, and they hug and walk into a bright new future. That simply won't happen.

But for the first time, Tim sees that Hamlet has anger, frustration, and painful memories of his own.

And in that moment, Tim's ill feelings go from a boil to a simmer.

He clears his throat. "Have you written the scene you're gonna add to *Gonzago?*"

Hamlet replies, "No, not yet."

"Would you want some help?"

Finally, Hamlet's eyes turn from the stage to his brother. "I still have some of your quills. We can grab one and get cracking."

The twins begin to walk out of the ballroom, their pace slow, wary. Side by side, though. Together.

"We should get out of here," Hamlet says. "The castle attendants will start hauling in the pews soon for tonight's performance."

Tim smiles cautiously. "It'll be cool to see a play in here again. I never thought I would. My theatre in London is nice, but there's a grandness to this place."

"Your theatre?"

Tim feels a jolt of pride. "I'm a playwright in London." He's wanted to tell his brother that for years.

And Hamlet's expression is worth every moment of anticipation. He's awestruck. "That's *incredible*. London: home to the world's richest heritage and greatest artists! Whoda thunk? Got the city bowing at your feet yet?"

Tim clicks his tongue. "Not quite. Turns out I don't have a directorial bone in my body. Nor do I have much control. I write and write and write—the first draft is pretty much what makes it onstage." He shoots Hamlet a glance. "I don't have someone to tell me to get my head out of the ink."

A soft smirk plays across Hamlet's face. Then he looks at Tim apologetically. "Oh, by the way. You won't be watching the play tonight. Sorry."

"What? Why not?"

"Your presence in Elsinore is still a secret. We want a clean reading of Claudius's emotions while he's watching the play, and having a long-lost prince show up would throw everything out of whack. And I doubt your sophisticated disguise of a flat cap would conceal you for long. Can you imagine? 'Ladies and gentlemen, give a warm Denmark welcome to Prince Hamlet. No, the other one.'"

Tim sighs, but he's still smiling. "It's not fair, you know. Hamlet is my last name too, but anytime someone says it, they're talking about you!"

"Hey, if you wanted to go by 'Hamlet,' you should've called dibs."

"You called dibs in third grade! I didn't even know that going by 'Hamlet' was up for grabs. I assumed we were just gonna use our first names, like normal people."

"Like idiots," Hamlet laughs.

"I'm gonna start using your first name again," Tim says slyly.

All the color drains from Hamlet's face. "Tim, don't you dare."

"Why?" Tim cackles. "It's such a strong, lovely name! Just rolls off the tongue."

"I will fight you right here and now. Don't think I won't."

"Dear brother, am I the type of person to just say your name out loud, in broad daylight? Why, if my name isn't Tim Hamlet...and your name isn't—"

"Tim Hamlet, I'm begging you." He's serious, Tim can tell. "Please."

Tim elbows his brother lightly. "Don't worry, Hamlet. I won't say it. I'll maintain your moody mystique."

Hamlet exhales. "Thanks."

The twins exit the ballroom together. Not holding hands and skipping into the sunset. But together.

Chapter 10

It's showtime in Elsinore.

Everyone who resides in the castle is filing into the ballroom. Attendants, servants, nurses, cooks, and all their families shuffle like lines of livestock, braying and mooing to one another. Some are excited to see a show, some are rolling their eyes, but most are here by pure obligation.

Tim watches from a shadowy hallway, cap pulled down as far as it can go without obstructing his vision. The two of them had convened in Hamlet's bedchambers and written the new scene involving two brothers and a vial of ear poison. It was just like old times—Tim scratching out lines of dialogue, Hamlet spouting ideas nonstop.

After the scene was finished and the ink dried, Hamlet had flown off to deliver the script to the players. "Stay hidden in here," he'd said.

Yes, brother. Whatever you say, brother.

As soon as Hamlet was out of sight, Tim had slunk out of the bedroom and taken his place here. It is remote and dim enough to watch the crowds enter the ballroom without being caught.

There's Osric! Tim has not seen him in years, and he looks exactly the same. Lively, jittery, and fidgety. Brimming with energy. His feet barely touch the ground as he scoots into the ballroom.

Oh, wow—there goes Ophelia. The torchlight throughout the castle seems to get brighter as she passes. She's put on an elegant dress for this night at the theatre. If Tim could put her face on a placard next to Romeo's, he would make enough money to buy the Masterpiece Centre and retire young. She is unaccompanied, he notices. She must be meeting Hamlet inside.

Tim wonders, *Where's Laertes*? He usually acts as his little sister's chaperone at these types of events. He must be traveling somewhere.

And *voila*. The main attraction. Here come the newlyweds.

The crowd parts like a bad haircut as the King and Queen of Denmark arrive.

Uncle Claudius. Mom.

Gertrude nods at the men and women, saying short pleasantries as she passes. She has not aged much in the past five years. Make-up cakes her face and fills in her wrinkles, and jewels dangle from every visible body part.

Right next to her, his arm linked around the Queen's, is the recently-crowned Claudius. Indeed, while the physical crown of Denmark is mostly symbolic and not meant to be worn for long periods of time, Claudius has it on top of his head right now. It is heavy and cumbersome, not properly balanced, what with all the gold and gems. But Claudius wears it all the same, walking stiffly to keep it from falling on the floor.

Tim stares at his uncle—they had rarely spent time together when Tim was growing up. Are those the eyes of a killer? The gait of a predator?

Truth be told, Tim has no idea. While the brothers were writing the scene, Tim kept vocalizing his opposition to the plan. But Hamlet couldn't be dissuaded, and he fully intended on proceeding with or without Tim's help.

Tim hopes that, when the time comes and the scene plays out in front of Claudius, Hamlet sees what he needs to see.

Once the King and Queen are in the ballroom, the stragglers pick up their pace, and the doors swing shut with a decisive *CRASH*.

Out here, in the halls of the castle, it is bare and frigid, but warm light seeps out from under the door. Tim hears Hamlet's resonant voice welcome everyone to the performance. Hamlet's words are muffled, but charm is made manifest in *how* things are said, not *what* is said. Tim can tell his twin brother is schmoozing the people like a pro. They explode in laughter. And then they hush as soon as the prince starts talking again.

Tim finds himself smiling wistfully. He wishes he could captivate people like that.

He also wishes he could be in that room so he can witness the side of his brother reserved for the stage. He wants to see the big, charismatic, flashy Hamlet everyone loves—not the flawed, complicated man he has to deal with.

He wants to be blissfully unaware of the Hamlet that exists offstage, captivated solely by the persona onstage.

But that's not how real life works.

Muffled applause bleeds out from the ballroom. *The Murder of Gonzago* must be starting. Undoubtedly, Hamlet has taken his seat, chosen strategically so he can have a perfect view of Claudius's face.

Tim takes a breath. He hopes Horace Bastion and the other players can live up to Hamlet's intense expectations. They might be obnoxiously accommodating, but they're nice, and no one deserves to be roasted by a disappointed Hamlet.

He strolls out of his hidey-hole and stretches his legs.

It felt good to write a scene again, especially with Hamlet as his partner. After finishing it, holding even that single sheet of parchment felt like he had climbed a mountain no one had ever laid eyes upon. Flipping through an entire script would give him a rush like nothing else—

Oh no.

A thought godsmacks him, and he almost falls to the ground.

The script. The one he had found in the players' wagon. *The Tragedy of Hamlet.* Where the devil is it?

He'd had it in his coat pocket.

The coat he'd thrown into a vase earlier today while running from the guards.

For some reason, the thought of anyone else having that script makes him feel faint. As if someone else were holding his beating heart in their hands.

Without thinking, his feet begin pounding down the hallway. He twists and turns through the veins of the castle, searching for where he had abandoned his disguise earlier today.

It was around Ophelia's bedchamber, he recalls. In the residential wing.

As he zips through the castle, his footfalls slowly become louder than the muffled performance. Eventually, he gets his bearings, and the halls begin to look a little familiar.

Then…

"Hey, you in the cap!" A guard shouts and draws his baton, the command echoing in the empty hall. "Identify yourself!"

Tim rolls his eyes so hard, he almost catches a glimpse of his own brain. *Not again.*

The guard runs after him, shouting and harrumphing.

Second verse, same as the first. Tim dashes in the opposite direction.

Whereas Tim has outrun Russian pirates and a vengeful wizard in the past week, this guard has likely filled his days pacing down corridors, eating pastries, and occasionally climbing a set of stairs.

"You won't get away this time!" the uniformed man calls, huffing and puffing a bit more than he wants to let on.

Wanna bet?

Tim needs a place to lay low until the play is over. He had assumed the guards would be in the audience, but he had clearly been wrong.

He spots a stone staircase that leads down, down, down. The stones are scuffed and grimy, incongruent with the rest of the castle's architecture. *Where does that go?* It's familiar, but he doesn't quite remember.

The sounds of more thudding boots join the chase. About five guards, Tim would guess—maybe more.

He peers at the bottom of the stairs and sees a bunch of cobwebs and shadows. Looks like a winner. Down he goes.

If he thought it was quiet in the empty hallways, it's like outer space down here. And—*cripes*—just as cold. He reaches the bottom of the staircase and bounds into the dark room.

Stone floor. Stone walls. A single flickering torch, hanging from an old chain. Dirt. Dust. Webs. Frozen roaches. Rat skeletons. Frozen roaches inside rat skeletons.

Not exactly a place Tim would book for a tea party.

As soon as he sees what's in the room, he realizes why he has never been down here.

Blocky stone caskets sit in single-file rows throughout the space. Simple, austere, unfussy coffins.

Tim hears the footsteps at the top of the stairs pass by. Soon, the sounds are gone, and he is left alone with his own frosty breath and generations of Hamlets past.

He wraps his arms around his torso, regretting the fact that he had not grabbed his coat before hiding down here. Plus, he could have used this time to read through the mysterious play.

Gooseflesh ripples across his body, trying and failing to warm him up. He rubs his arms and visualizes a roaring fireplace.

A focolare.

He can sneak back up the stairs and hide in a closet or behind a tapestry—it sounds like the coast is clear. He doesn't have to wander through the cluster of caskets. But that's exactly what he does. A morbid curiosity draws him closer.

There are rows and rows of stone sarcophaguses, each bearing the name of a person he's never heard of...but they all share his surname. Hamlet, Hamlet, Hamlet.

What a curious thing, family is. Complete loyalty and centuries of reverence, based on nothing but a name. A couple of syllables scrawled on a birth certificate. It all seems foolish, when Tim thinks of it that way.

Laurence Hamlet, Kenneth Hamlet, Benedict Hamlet, and so on and so on and so on. Tim doesn't recognize a single name. A brood of complete strangers, buried in the basement.

Hold on. Here's a name that rings a bell.

Bartholomew. And there, below the name, is an ornate engraving of a crown.

That's right—King Bartholomew. One of Tim's great-greats. Beneath the crown is a brief epitaph: "*A king to be feared. A Dane to be honored. A man to be followed.*"

Quite the obituary.

Next to Bart's casket is one belonging to his dearly-departed bride, Esmeralda. Her inscription is even more to the point: "*What he said.*"

Down the line, Tim finds another royal. Ah, King Shermink. He remembers the crazy stories he'd heard about this guy. According to the court records, Shermink would give his annual Christmas speech dressed as Old Saint Nick himself, and he allegedly had a tattoo of a sphinx on his lower back.

Beside Shermink's coffin is a small stone box. Tim bends down—it's a casket for Shermink's ferret, Ibsen. Tim reads the epitaph and learns that Ibsen was Shermink's adopted son. Interesting, but not surprising.

Next are the coffins for Jacob of Cobalt and his sister Dorothy, positioned side-by-side. They say that the siblings were never apart, and it's kind of sweet that their bodies will be entombed together as long as Elsinore stands.

Tim gasps. He definitely recognizes the next name—Abraham Hamlet. His grandfather.

Everyone used to call him Abraham the Wise, but Tim knew him as Papa. He died when Tim was very young, so the only memories he has of him are shrouded by a film of dust, much like his casket. If Tim closes his eyes and concentrates, he can vaguely picture himself sitting on Papa's lap in the ballroom, watching a jester perform.

Tim chuckles at the memory and moves on.

The last coffin is smooth and light gray, with barely any dust on it. Just as Tim reads the label on the lid, he realizes a second too late who it belongs to.

Johan Odysseus Hamlet.

"Hi, Dad."

He runs his fingers over the inscription, feeling his father's name. He holds his breath and waits to hear a voice, or feel a ghostly chill, or see a supernatural glow.

Instead, there's nothing but silence.

"What, *now* you shut up?"

He doesn't know what he had expected. For the ghost of his father to reappear and congratulate him? Hug him? Tell him the moral of this whole strange journey?

But no. The coffin doesn't move. No spirits rise. The dead man stays dead.

Tim shakes his head. *Father wasn't much of a mentor to me when he was alive. It's foolish to expect him to be one now.*

That's just how it works, though, isn't it? A drunkard could spend his entire life ranting and raving, making everyone around him miserable—

but when he's in a coffin, being lowered into the ground, there's not a dry eye in the house.

Death venerates everyone. It turns a man into a legend. A person's life is reduced to a handful of memories, and memories can be cherry-picked.

In life, Old Hamlet had been a stern, cold man. Not cruel, but far from loving.

"There are…" Tim begins to speak, not knowing where the words are going. But he doesn't stop himself. "There are a lot of things I never go to say to you, Father." He feels the inscription of the King's name again. "And for the life of me, I can't think of any of them right now."

He can't conjure any words, no matter how he tries. So he stops trying. Instead of speaking, he remembers.

He remembers all the international diplomatic trips he took with his father.

He remembers his father's sharp smile as he read the two ballots bearing Hamlet's name.

He remembers his father howling at him, telling him to be more confident, or to shape up, or that he could be something great if he tried.

He remembers his father clapping from the sidelines at his fencing matches.

Good memories. Bad ones.

They are all tangled together.

They all form a portrait of Johan Hamlet in Tim's mind.

They all work together to make Tim the person he is today.

If Johan Hamlet had been any different, Tim would be different too. And Tim likes who he is.

I've never thought that before.

I like who I am.

Tim leans down and kisses the lid of the coffin.

"Thanks, Dad. Thanks for me."

A minute passes. Five minutes. Ten. He stands in the silence by his father's casket. He feels he owes him that, if nothing else.

He leaves the crypt of the Hamlets and creeps back up the stairs. Every inch of altitude makes him a bit warmer—Elsinore's chilly hallways are a tropical paradise compared to the stone basement.

He scans the corridors, sees no green uniforms, and scampers through the halls. The castle is still quiet. If Tim has to guess, he'd say the play is likely reaching the midpoint of act one—still in its adolescence.

He makes it back to Hamlet's bedchamber without any issues or obstacles.

The bed is messy and unkempt, drawers thrown open, silky underpants all over the place. Most would look at this room and assume it has been ransacked—Tim knows this is merely his brother's natural habitat.

As he eases the door shut, he considers running back out and grabbing the mysterious script from the vase. But no. He has had enough close calls for one day. He can get it later. Maybe tonight, while the castle sleeps. There is no frantically ticking clock that he's aware of.

He settles in a large easy chair, and his eyelids instantly weigh a ton. Ever since he left London, his sleep has been fitful on a good night...nonexistent on most.

As he stretches out in the plush lap of luxury, he thinks back to his apartment in London. Cramped. Musty. Technically not an apartment at all, but a sliver of space between his building's top floor and the leaky roof. His roommates were inconsiderate too—they squeaked at all hours of the night and let their food rot without proper refrigeration.

This chair right here is the most comfortable he has been in the last five years. He might just take a little snooze while he waits for the play to end, don't mind if he does…

Suddenly, Tim hears a surge of voices murmuring throughout the castle. *The play can't be over already.*

The door flies open, and Hamlet tumbles in. His hair is wild, his black clothes rumpled, sweat dripping from his face. He looks frenetic, on the verge of exploding.

Tim stands from the chair and offers his brother a kerchief. "Did you have a nice swim?"

Hamlet ignores the sarcasm and wipes the sweat from his eyes with his own sleeve. "Tim," he fizzles, vibrating in his skin, "he did it. By God, he did it!"

"Wait, slow down." Tim tries to keep his brother from careening off the edge, but it looks like Hamlet is already gone.

The prince grinds his teeth and pulls Tim in close. He speaks in a low, panicky voice, as if telling a conspiratorial secret. "During the scene...The scene we wrote that mirrors Father's murder, remember? That scene played out, and Claudius stood up and left. He stormed right out of the room!"

Tim steps back to give him room to breathe. "Hamlet, calm down. Deep breaths, alright?"

"How can I be calm?" Hamlet yelps. "The judge and jury have spoken. Guilty!"

And what does that make you, Hamlet? Tim doesn't want to hear his brother's answer to that question.

Before Tim can respond, Hamlet reaches into a deep pocket and withdraws a large butcher's knife. Both brothers stare at the blade with wide eyes.

Tim nearly vomits. *Did he do it already? Did he kill the King and rush here? Is that why he's so hysterical?*

No. Tim kicks the logical gears of his brain into motion. The knife is clean—no blood, no smudges, not even on the hilt.

"Where'd you get that, Hamlet?"

"Oh, I've been carrying this around for a while. Never know when it might come in handy." He says it as if describing a pair of shoes he had just bought. "I followed Claudius out of the ballroom. Very sneakily. He retreated to Father's chambers, and..." He snickers incredulously. "That sap, he fell to his knees and he started *praying*. His lips moved silently, and he was alone. Just him and me." The knife smiles as Hamlet put it away. "So I had to leave. When I kill that man, he's going to hell. I can't risk him getting a halo just because my timing is off. No, when he's in a drunken stupor, or gambling away the kingdom's wealth...That's when I'll strike."

Tim can't believe what he's hearing. It is madness, no doubt, but it is calculated to a frightening degree. He almost wishes his brother were entirely insane—drooling, babbling, and weeping in a corner. Instead, he speaks lunacy with eloquence and wit.

If Tim didn't know better, he would think Hamlet was the villain of this story.

Hamlet then grabs Tim's arm. "Come on. We have somewhere to be." He dashes out the door, dragging Tim behind him.

The hallways are full of people again, the audience in the ballroom having scattered after the King and Prince left. They meander to and fro, still dressed to the nines, but looking lost and confused.

Hamlet barrels through the crowd, Tim along for the haphazard ride. Tim yanks his cap over his eyes so people can't get a good look at his face, but Hamlet doesn't seem to care about anonymity anymore.

"Brother," Tim hisses, "where the devil are we going?"

Hamlet yells in response, "To talk to Gertrude!"

"*What?*" Tim is as baffled as the crowd. "Why?"

"I dunno! I just feel it in my bones. We're gonna say some words to her, then she'll say some words back. That's probably how it'll go."

They move up a grand flight of stairs, Hamlet fluttering like a bat, Tim floundering like a fish on Hamlet's line. The stairs wind up and up and up…

Tim hadn't thought out how his first encounter with his mom was going to go, but this is not it.

The royal bedchambers. The crème de la crème, the height of luxury, the penthouse suites of the castle. The twins reach the top of the stairs, and they face two doors. One leads to the King's chambers, the other to the Queen's.

Hamlet wipes away a fresh layer of perspiration and barges through the second door. Tim has no choice but to follow.

"Gertrude!" Hamlet whinnies. "What's the meaning of all this?"

I was about to ask you the same thing, brother.

From under the cover of his flat cap, Tim sees a woman standing in the center of the room. But he avoids looking at her for as long as he can. He looks at the huge vanity mirror, surrounded by candles; the ermine-fur rugs, pillowcases, and bed sheets; the luscious tapestries that cover the back wall; the huge, life-sized portrait of the new King and Queen in their wedding attire. *I've never been in Mom's room, come to think of it. This place is five-star.*

He has run out of things to look at.

"Timothy?" Gertrude Hamlet covers her mouth in shock. In her bedroom, she has taken off all the gaudy jewelry and traded her grand ballgown for a nighttime dressing gown, though she still has make-up painted on her face.

"Hey, Mom," Tim responds. He pushes the cap back from his eyes.

"Oh, Timothy!" Gertrude rushes toward her son, arms open wide, tears ruining her mascara. "It's been so long!"

Well, this isn't the reaction I was expecting. Tim smiles and steps forward, opening his arms to her.

"Save your sentiments, wench!" Hamlet's coarse words shatter the air, and Gertrude stops in her tracks. "We don't accept your affection. Nor do we want it!"

Tim mutters, "I might accept it. I might want it."

Hamlet claps a hand on his brother's shoulder. "I know it's been years, Tim, but stay strong! She's sleeping with the enemy! And that's not even a figure of speech!"

Gertrude turns her teary gaze from Tim to Hamlet. She bites her lip to keep from frowning. "The enemy? What's that supposed to mean? Son, have you forgotten who I am?"

"For God's sake, no, I haven't," Hamlet responds with a sneer. "You're the queen, your husband's brother's wife. And you're my mother." He squares his shoulders, as if inviting an attack. "Though I wish you weren't, you rotten hag."

If Hamlet is asking for an aggressive response from Gertrude, she more than obliges. "I will *not* be spoken to like this, Glenn!"

Both brothers freeze.

Hamlet's rebellious, petulant stance instantly turns inward—he blushes, and his jaw locks into an ashamed grimace. The use of his real first name has turned him into an embarrassed statue. He squeaks, "Please don't call me that."

"It's your name, Glenn." Gertrude crosses her arms. "I, your mother, named you that, and don't forget it."

Tim gulps and gives his brother a nervous side-glance. "Hey, I didn't say it."

"Now," Gertrude continues, boring holes into Hamlet's red face, "if you don't mind, I'd like to hug the son I haven't seen since you and Johan teamed up against him."

Tim takes a few small steps toward his mother, away from Hamlet. The prince doesn't react, still immobile, rendered comatose by the single-syllable he has eschewed for decades.

Gertrude throws open her arms once again, and Tim rushes into the embrace. Right there, in the middle of the ice-cold Danish castle, a blossom of warmth covers his body. Only a mother's hug can do that.

She clutches him tightly, sobbing into his shoulder. "You left, Timothy. You left without a word. No destination, no letters, nothing…" She pulls away and heaves a shaky breath, giving Tim an even shakier smile. "I was so relieved when Johan found out you were living in London. We could at least send you correspondence. But you never responded."

Hamlet's small voice speaks up from behind Tim. "You knew where he was? You and Dad knew he was in London, and you didn't tell me?"

Going against every instinct in his body, Tim backs away from his mom's embrace. "Well…I got one correspondence from Denmark in the past five years. A little over a month ago, an ambassador told me Father was dead." He shrugs timidly. "And that's it. Once."

"Well, Timothy," she dabs at her running make-up, "as I mentioned, you left without telling us."

"He was fifteen, Gertrude." Hamlet steps forward to stand next to his brother. "He was hurt and young. You're his mother, and even when you knew where he was, you sent a uniform to tell him about Father's death. Why didn't you go to him yourself?"

The Queen's eye twitches just a fraction. Just enough. She responds to Hamlet, biting each word, "He. Left. Us. He didn't reach out, he showed no remorse."

Tim takes a breath and says what he has wanted to say for years. "I'm sorry I left, Mom. I am. I'm also sorry that none of you ever came after me."

She begins to respond, but her verbal arsenal is empty, and that upsets her. She moves away from her sons and sits on the edge of the bed. Tim desperately wants her to respond, to say that they did try to reach out to him, that they sent search parties all over Europe, called in favors to get him home, felt his absence every single day…But she doesn't say any of that. She just sits with her back perfectly straight and her legs crossed just so—a perfect image of poise.

Hamlet scoffs. "Treacherous woman. Marries a murderer, disregards her own son. Mother of the year, no doubt about it."

Gertrude throws her hands up. "What on Earth is all this talk about murder?"

Just then, across the room, one of the tapestries shifts, as if a strong breeze has blown in from nowhere. Tim and Hamlet both notice.

Someone is hiding behind it.

Hamlet's eyes glow wildly, and he draws his massive knife. "A rat! A fiend! It's Claudius!" He charges at the tapestry, waving the blade, fully intent on killing whoever is lurking there. "To hell with you!"

"No!" Tim leaps and grabs Hamlet's wrist. He twists his brother's arm so the knife drops, kicks it away, then shoves Hamlet to the ground. "Stay." He moves to the expensive tapestry and yanks it aside.

An older man in a Danish uniform cowers there, hiding behind his trembling hands. "Don't hurt me, don't! I have a goldfish to take care of!"

Tim is completely shocked. "Polonius?" *Why the devil is Claudius's right-hand-man here, hiding in Mother's room?* Tim looks back and sees Hamlet sprawled on the floor, just as confused. Good—his lethal anger is dormant, for the time being. Best to get Polonius out of here before the beast is roused again. "Get out of here!"

"Yes, Sir Tim, with great pleasure." Polonius straightens up and begins scurrying out of the room. "Oh, and good to see you again." He curtsies to Gertrude as he passes. "M'lady." And to Hamlet. "M'man." He exits.

A goldfish... Tim shakes his head and yells at the closed door, "You have two children, you nincompoop!"

No one talks for a minute. Hamlet waits until his breath is steady, then he stands back up and retrieves his knife.

Tim looks his brother squarely in the eye. "Hamlet, you just about killed your girlfriend's father. That doesn't rattle you at all?"

Hamlet tucks away the knife. "I'm fine," he says curtly.

"You two, together at last." Gertrude says it quietly, to herself. Then she furrows her brow. "Why did you want to kill Claudius?"

"Don't act so innocent," Hamlet spits. "What you've done makes heaven weep. Attila the Hun would find you distasteful."

Gertrude shudders and clutches her chest.

"Oh," Hamlet continues, "she feels! I'm honestly shocked. I figured your evil deeds would have hardened your heart into granite by now."

She stands from the bed, fists clenched. "I won't tolerate this! I don't even know what you're talking about!"

Tim rushes to Hamlet's side and hisses, "Brother, cool it. I know you're angry, and I'm right behind you, but she's our mother. There's no need to thrash her like this—"

"No need?" Hamlet shouts. "There's plenty of need. She uses her marriage vows like one uses a tissue while sick with the flu. And not only that, she throws her arms around a Judas!"

Gertrude has given up trying to talk to Hamlet. Instead, she quivers in her dressing gown, tears staining the silk.

"Hamlet, stop!" Tim presses. "These words are dagger that she doesn't need to feel!"

"Yes, you two lie in the sweaty stench of your dirty sheets, conspiring, colluding, corrupting! Claudius! What a lowly name. A murderer and a villain. A lowlife who's not worth a twentieth of a tenth of your first husband. A thief of the throne. He took the crown and shoved it in his grimy pocket!"

Tim feels something change. It's a sensation he thought he would never feel again—one he had *hoped* he would never have to feel again. He gulps.

Ethereal mist drifts across the floor. The air feels full of invisible rain. His spine turns into an icicle.

The ghost of Old Hamlet appears in the Queen's bedchamber. And he doesn't look happy.

The living Hamlet hasn't noticed yet. "He's a king of shreds and patches. And another thing!" His mouth screeches to a halt, jerks around a bit, then hangs wide open. "Oh no." That is all he can say.

Tim is shaken to his core as well. Just like before, the King's broad physique is accentuated by a suit of gleaming armor. The beaver of his battle helmet is flipped up to reveal his cherry-wood eyes, majestic beard, and earth-shattering scowl. Tendrils of fog drift from his being. It's enough to make a grown man weak at the knees.

Speaking of which, Hamlet crumples in front of the ghost, holding out shaky hands to protect himself. His stance looks remarkably like Polonius's just a minute before.

"Angels above, shield me," Hamlet sputters. "What can I do for you, my king?"

A mask of anguish covers Gertrude's face. She stares at Hamlet, completely ignoring the phantasm of her dead husband.

She can't see him. Of course she can't.

The ghost doesn't answer Hamlet's question. He just glares.

Hamlet grovels even lower. "Speak, spirit! Am I taking too long in avenging you? Have you more information of your death? Just tell me, Father! Speak!"

"I…" Gertrude starts to speak, but her voice falters. She swoons where she stands, and Tim rushes to her side. He steadies her, and she finishes her thought. "What Claudius said is true. My son is mad. Truly mad." She looks at Tim, eyes wide and fearful. "Your brother has lost his mind!"

"Mom…" Tim speaks slowly, bracing himself as he braces her. "I can see him too. The ghost of Father is standing right where Hamlet looks. I swear."

Hamlet glances away from the ghost and at the others. "See, Gertrude? Tim is in the madhouse along with me."

"I don't believe you." She shakes off Tim's helping hands. "Either of you."

"I get it," Tim says. "We sound screwier than a toolbox. But I've never lied to you, have I?"

She purses her lips.

Hamlet slowly gets to his feet. He gazes at the ghost with adoration and affection. "I see him standing here as surely as I breathe. His beard, his eyes, his drawn face…"

Tim nods. "And I see the same."

But Hamlet continues. "…I see his military uniform. I see each medal pinned to his breast, polished and gleaming. Just as they were in life!"

What? No. Tim shivers. He sees Old Hamlet's ghost too.

Except his sees his father wearing a suit of armor.

The deceased king gives Tim an eerie, knowing smirk. One that says, "*I'm still smarter than you, boy. Don't forget it.*" He turns and walks out of the room—right through the door. The spectral mist follows him and evaporates moments later.

Hamlet continues to stare at the spot where the ghost had stood. "Father, please. Tell me what you have come to tell me!" He pauses, listening to the silence. "Why do you say these things?"

He still sees the ghost. He hears it talking to him.

And he sees a different ghost than I do.

Maybe Hamlet had been right before—perhaps this ghost is actually a devious demon, preying on the family. Or it could be some sort of trickster god taking a vacation on Earth, screwing with mortals while it's in the neighborhood.

Or maybe…Maybe Tim's earlier instinct had been right.

Maybe they're both bonkers. They have both cracked in different ways.

"Timothy, you're feeding your brother's delusion." Gertrude sighs. "I expected better from you."

Tim barely hears her. He rips off his cap and ruffles his dark hair, feeling dizzy, submerged in confusion. "Yeah, well, you're acting like you couldn't care less about your sons. I expected better from you."

Hamlet mutters to the ghost he sees, "Good-bye, Father." Then he turns back to Tim and Gertrude. "Alright, what're we talking about? Catch me up."

Gertrude huffs. "You've infected your brother, Glenn. You madness is contagious!"

"Don't flatter yourself." Hamlet jabs a finger against his temple. "My noodle isn't the problem here—it's your crime. Your complicit corruption!"

The Queen doesn't answer right away. She strolls over to the vanity mirror and straightens her locks, examines her features. Finally, without looking away from her own face, she says, "You're being shipped off to England tonight, Glenn. For your safety. Your friends Frederick and Christian will travel with you."

"W-What?" Hamlet tugs at his ear, unsure he heard correctly. "England? Tonight? Why?"

"It's far away," Tim answers, knowing better than anyone, "but not too far away. They can keep their eye on you without ever having to speak to you…Without having to dirty their hands dealing with you."

"And for my *safety*?" Hamlet sneers. "My safety, my foot! Claudius is kicking me out of Elsinore because I'm *right*. I know his dirty little secret, and he's trying to gag me!"

Gertrude applies a fresh line of lipstick, despite it being nearly bedtime. "Claudius didn't make the decision." She licks her fingertips and begins snuffing the candles that surround the mirror. "I did. Just now, as you were speaking." Only once all the candles are extinguished, threads of smoke coiling from the wicks, does she look at her sons. "You're mad, Glenn, and as such, you're a danger to yourself. And yes, you're a danger to everyone in the castle too. You nearly killed Polonius, which is bad enough—but you nearly killed him thinking he was the King! Do you hear how alarming that is?"

"I won't go." Hamlet trembles and shakes, on the verge of another meltdown. "I won't!"

"The carriage that will take you to the port of Verkwister shall leave in an hour." She nods, settling the debate.

"No!" Hamlet bellows. The door nearly splinters as he storms out.

Tim stares at the open door, then turns to his mother. Even after this emotional night, her elegance is undeniable. The smeared make-up and stained gown do nothing to dampen her poise.

He looks closer.

No. She doesn't know.

Tim believes she honestly doesn't know about Claudius's alleged murder. But she has her sins, all the same. She let Tim leave when he was just a teenager, and she did nothing. She didn't reach out. And now, she treats her sons with such coldness.

What can I even say to her?

She says nothing to him. So he returns the favor.

Then: "*AGGHHH!*" A blood-curdling scream erupts from the staircase outside the bedroom.

Tim races out, leaving his mother behind. She doesn't follow.

The sight he finds makes him gasp.

Hamlet looms at the top of the winding stairs, knife in hand. Blood drips from the blade. A body has rolled down a few of the stairs, leaving a splotchy red trail.

Tim edges forward, trying to identify the body. Green uniform, thin beard, wrinkled hands.

It's Polonius. His face is trapped in an endless silent shriek. Dead.

Hamlet drops the knife and looks at his brother. Helpless. Terrified. His voice is distant: "I thought it was Claudius."

Dear God.

The world begins to pitch. Nothing is as it should be.

He has never seen a dead body. He had seen his father die in a vision, but that was just a ghostly reenactment. This is horrifically real.

It looks inhuman. An empty husk.

That's enough.

Tim's feet begin to descend the staircase, and he doesn't fight them. He gives the corpse a wide berth.

After a moment, Hamlet realizes Tim is walking away, and he snaps out of his stupor. "Hey, brother? Where are you going?" He scuttles after Tim. "I need a hand here." He coughs a dark laugh. "I'm in a bit of trouble."

"I have to go, Hamlet." Tim works hard to keep his tone level.

"Go where?"

"Elsewhere."

"But…" Hamlet grabs Tim's shoulder and spins him around so they're looking at each other, Hamlet a few stairs above his twin. "You can't walk out now. You can't do that to me!"

Tim says, "Do you realize what you've done?" The simmer in his gut slowly rises. "In a ludicrous attempt to avenge Father's death, you killed the father of Laertes and Ophelia—the woman you supposedly love. In a matter of seconds, you turned them into orphans."

The grim reality of the situation falls from a great height and lands right on Hamlet's shoulders. He looks ready to collapse.

But Tim isn't done. "Mom said that your madness is contagious, but she was only half-right. It isn't your insanity that's spreading—it's your sorrow. Everyone around you is miserable. And if they aren't, you drag them down to your level."

"Tim…" Hamlet says quietly. Desperate. Pleading.

"You killed him. There's no coming back from that. You can wash off the blood and drag away the body, but it'll never really leave you. You're stained. This whole place is stained. Even our name is damned." Tim turns and walks down the stairs. "Good-bye, Hamlet."

He doesn't hear any footsteps coming after him.

At the bottom of the grand staircase, he takes off the flat cap and drops it. He walks through the crowded castle, letting everyone see his face. *Take a good look, Elsinore. I'm not coming back.*

Ophelia falls in step beside him. Beautiful, fair, bereaved Ophelia. "Hamlet, love, what was that show even about? The murder scene came out of nowhere."

Tim can't bring himself to look at her. She has no idea her life has been inextricably changed forever. "I'm so sorry," he whispers.

She turns pale and stops. "Tim?"

He keeps moving. He cuts a path through the crowd, navigates the labyrinthine hallways, and finds the vase. He reaches in and grabs the heavy coat he had abandoned what feels like years ago. The script is still safe inside. He puts on the coat and makes his way toward the exit.

Osric passes him, as peppy as ever. "Oh, hello there, Tim!"

For the first time, Osric's bubbly personality rubs Tim the wrong way. *Does he not know he lives in a hellhole? How can he be so happy surrounded by death and madness?* He doesn't respond aloud.

Noises around him are muffled. Faces are hazy. Colors are muted. He doesn't even feel the cold anymore. A gray, throbbing numbness has consumed his whole body.

Tim Hamlet walks out of the gates of Elsinore and doesn't look back.

Chapter 11

By the time Tim realizes where he is, he's back in the middle of the Danish woods. And it's morning. White sunlight dribbles between the branches, providing no warmth whatsoever.

In his anger-fueled trance, he had simply walked forward. His legs moved, his heart pumped, and his mind went blank. Now, he feels the full extent of his passions, and he wants nothing more than to slip back into that emotional coma.

He doesn't know where he's going. He keeps going anyway. As long as he moves away from Elsinore, he should be good.

His family is cursed. There is no other explanation. Johan was a gruff, oaken man who never used a kind word when a threat would do just as nicely. Claudius is a throne-snatching weasel at best—a murderous snake at worst. Gertrude is a whole host of issues wrapped into one. And Hamlet. Good ole gloomy, charming, jovial, scornful, up-and-down Glenn Hamlet.

(Even way out here in the woods, after merely thinking about Hamlet's first name, Tim looks over his shoulder.)

Tim had started to trust Hamlet again, which is something he had thought to be impossible. They had laughed and planned and stood next to each other. And the minute—the exact godforsaken minute—Tim had felt a kinship with his brother, Hamlet tumbled off the deep-end and killed someone.

Isn't that just a pickaxe in the gonads? That's bound to ruin your weekend.

Shut up.

Not even his internal sarcasm can lift his spirits. It's like he's trapped in a boiling pot of anger...but his skin is so callused at this point, he can't feel it.

Should he scream? Break something? Let out all his fury and frustration? Probably. His innards feel twisted into knots, like he's a scarecrow about to burst at the seams.

But he just keeps walking in silence.

The forest breaks up, and he begins to move across the expansive plains of Denmark. At first, it looks like the sky is completely clear of clouds...but then he realizes the opposite is true—it's hidden by one big sheet of gray. Somewhere up there, the sky is blue and the sun is warm. Up there, not down here. Down here, it's cold and glum.

On the horizon, Tim sees a few distant shapes. That shape looks like a windmill, it's arms spinning lazily in the wind. And over there—probably a stray deer. Won't get far without its pack. And...Tim squints.

As he gets closer, a cluster of figures come into focus. Small, bright-blue tents—seven or eight of them, each only large enough to house a couple grown men. Wagons, horses, chairs, and cooking gear. It's a campsite.

And there are the campers, spread out across the field. Men. They're tall, strong, wearing clothing that would keep them warm in a blizzard. Smart. Prepared. They speak loudly to each other, laughing and trading casual pleasantries. They're friends. Or, at least, friendly.

One man hangs laundry from a post. Another is sparking a fire. A scruffy-faced man unloads a case from the back of a wagon as another unhitches the horse.

Tim approaches the camp, keeping a safe distance to the side. He marches past the wagon and gives the campers a fleeting glance. Under their scarves and coats, they all wear dark-blue uniforms.

The scruffy-faced man spots Tim and gives him a bright smile and a wave. "Morning, traveler!"

Tim responds with a nod and keeps walking.

What happens next is a flurry of movement, noise, and panic.

The horse whinnies like a possessed creature and rears up on its hind legs. The man with the reins holds his hands aloft in an attempt to calm the animal, but the horse has none of it. It pedals its strong hooves in the air, then drops to all fours and lets loose a powerful kick. The hoof smashes through the side of the wagon, rocking the entire structure.

The front axle snaps in two, and the heavy wooden wagon collapses— with the man's legs trapped underneath.

He cries out in agony, pushing against the wagon with one hand, pounding the cold ground with the other. "Help! God above, this is crushing me!"

The scruffy-faced man immediately drops the case he was carrying and rushes to his comrade's side. "I got you, I got you," he huffs. He plants his feet and rams his shoulder against the side of the wagon. The heavy structure begins to move, but only just. The trapped man can't pull his legs out.

Tim sprints to the wagon and mirrors the scruffy-faced man, using his whole body to push against the wooden wall.

They lock eyes, and the other man says through gritted teeth, "Go on three. One-two-three!"

Both roar and push...but Tim roars a little bit louder. His anger translates itself into physicality. He takes all his pent-up frustration and shoves it against this blasted wagon.

The wood creaks as it tilts, and the trapped man crawls out of harm's way. Tim and the scruffy-faced man let the wagon crash to the ground, and then they do the same, spent, weary, and panting. The whole ordeal only lasted about fifteen seconds.

Other campers trot over and tend to the man's legs. It looks like no permanent damage has been done—any longer, though, and it might have been a different story.

A camper who appears to be a doctor helps the injured man into a tent.

Tim takes it all in, slumped against the busted wagon, trying to catch his breath.

The scruffy man beside him says, "I appreciate your quick instincts." He, too, is winded, but his vivid smile lights up his face. "Franz's legs woulda been mush without you." The way he speaks is open and pleasant, like a next-door neighbor. "To whom does Franz owe a thank-you card?" He holds out a weathered hand.

Tim takes it and shakes. "Tim."

"Erik Fortinbras. Pleasure's mine." He shambles to his feet. "I'll check on my man and be right back. Don't rabbit on me!" He jogs into the tent.

Tim stays on the ground, panting, thinking. The handful of on-looking campers dissipates, leaving him in the quiet cold.

That name—Erik Fortinbras. Tim knows that name. *But it can't be.* This guy is young and disheveled, unshaven, wearing a tunic, and helping his men unload supplies. There's no way it's the same Erik Fortinbras that Tim is thinking of. *It can't be.*

Tim stands and dusts himself off. He considers continuing on his aimless way...but he stays. Erik's friendly demeanor is a factor, but, to be honest, it's mainly his gut. Some unseen instinct tells him to hang around.

As the man emerges from the tent, Tim looks closer and gauges him to be closer to twenty years old than thirty. "You wouldn't happen to be the prince of Norway, would you, Guv?"

Erik's smile doesn't flicker. "You sound surprised."

A small chill runs up Tim's spine. The prince of Norway...here, in Denmark. According to the Ambassador and Hamlet, tensions between the two countries are at an all-time high. And now, Fortinbras is here with a handful of men in blue uniforms. Scouting? Raiding? Plotting?

Tim tells himself he doesn't care. Let Fortinbras ride in, let him take over. The Hamlets deserve as much.

"I've just never seen royalty so..." Tim gestures to Erik's dirty, unkempt appearance. "So-pissed-icated."

Erik claps and howls at the joke. "Oh my..." He wipes a tear. "You are a hoot and a half, Tim. A good Samaritan and a comedian." He dusts off his clothes. "Yeah, I don't really care for robes and pelts and crowns and all that."

"I can relate." Tim sees Erik's confused expression and smiles. "My surname is Hamlet. Welcome to Denmark."

Understanding slowly dawns on Erik's bewhiskered face. "So you're the Tim Hamlet I've heard about?" He beams and shakes Tim's hand once more. "I do declare, rumors about you are rarer than a pink slab of steak. Lemme tell you," he leans in, as if about to confide a secret, "I think you were right to leave that brood of crazy behind. As hard as it is to walk away from family, you gotta separate yourself from toxic environments."

Buddy, you have no idea. Tim decides to feel out the situation a little. "So how's your uncle the king doing?"

"Oh, he hasn't been outside in a while. Got a bad case of the sniffles, I like to say, but I'm afraid it's much worse than that. Would you wanna take a stroll with me?" He gestures to the fields beyond his small campsite. "I do my best talkin' when I'm walkin', if that makes sense."

Tim can't help but smile and nod. "Sure thing, Erik." The two begin to pace between the tents, but Tim keeps a healthy distance between himself and the prince. The way the past few days have gone, he wouldn't be surprised if one of Norway's royals tried to kill one of Denmark's right here and now. Can't be too careful.

"My uncle's been under the weather ever since he became king," Erik says. "It's like the position's poison. Not far off from the truth, I imagine." He talks as if he's simply thinking aloud, casual, off-the-cuff. "It killed my pops, after all. That's why my uncle's king, you see. Ah, you probably already know that. Your dad killed my dad in battle, after all. I've heard you're the smart one in your clan."

His father was killed too. And then his uncle became king. What are the odds?

"I've never been to Norway." Tim tries to drive the conversation in a different direction.

But Erik doesn't bite. "Why'd ya leave Denmark all those years ago?" Before Tim can even open his mouth to obfuscate to question, Erik follows up: "Wanted to be your own man, I bet."

Tim's face gets very hot.

Erik shrugs innocently. "Makes sense. Believe me, I probably understand more than anyone else could. It's hard to chart your own course when people's eyes bug out at the mention of your last name. But you wanna build a fresh legacy, be your own person. I get it." His lopsided smile and folksy style of speech is immediately endearing. He looks at Tim as if they've been friends for years.

The two meander through the encampment. Their footfalls crunch the dry grass. Every now and then, Erik yells a word of encouragement to one of his men. The grin never leaves his face.

"My dad—Jakob was his name—made a wonky little wager with your dad Johan. They spoke together before the battle began, then went off to fight. This was about three years ago, and I was at school in Wittenberg, so I don't know exactly how things went down. What I do know is that…" He smiles sadly. "…my pops never made it back."

The Battle of the Lavet. The day my father killed Erik's father. He must be looking for revenge. And he has every right. Tim tenses up, prepared to defend himself.

That makes Erik laugh. "Oh, trust me, friend, I don't hold that against you personally." He slaps Tim's arm. "You weren't even in Denmark, for crying out loud! You didn't kill my dad. You hold no responsibility for what anyone else did, does, or will do. And can I be frank? Even if old Johan were standing right in front of me, I wouldn't try to kill him. I'd be mad as all get-out, you betcha. But I don't want anyone to die. There's enough of that as is."

Tim is shocked. His impression of Norway's prince has been all wrong. "You mean you aren't looking for war with Denmark?"

"War? Not a lick! I want nothing but peace. I get woozy just looking at blood, being honest."

"Sheesh!" Tim lets out a breath. "Word around Elsinore is that you're right on the brink of invading us."

"Well…" Erik considers something for a moment as they walk. *Crunch, crunch, crunch.* "That's true, I suppose. Cocoa?"

Tim nearly trips over his feet. "Come again, Guv?"

Erik grabs two mugs from a passing man. "It's a drink! We call it 'toasty cocoa.' Perfect for a nippy day like today. Take a sip and feel it warm your belly." He hands a steaming mug to Tim.

"No, I meant…" Tim drinks from the mug and stops in his tracks.

"Delicious, huh?" The Norwegian prince's smile just about touches the tips of his ears.

They start walking again.

Tim clears his throat. "It's pretty good." The truth is it's the most delightful drink he's ever tasted in his life, but he doesn't want to let that on. "You said something about invading Elsinore, if I heard correctly."

Erik nods and looks at the ground, as if he's a doctor about to deliver bad news. "Yeah, friend, I hate to say it. 'Invade' is a bit too strong of a word, if you're asking me, but that's about the gist of it."

Tim can't believe it. He puffs out his chest. "Erik, you seem like a nice chap, but I can't accept cocoa from an invading general, trying to curry warfare—"

"No, no, Tim!" He looks truly saddened by Tim's words. "I absolutely hate violence! If violence had a face, I would punch it. The usual royal games—deceit, murder, debauchery, all that—are unappealing to me. Notice, I'm here with only myself and a few close attendants. No shields, no flags, not a single sword or arrowhead."

True. This sure doesn't look like a military operation.

"I'm on an operation of peace, my friend." Erik downs his cocoa, then gestures to Tim's. "Gonna drink that?"

"By all means." Tim gives the prince his mug back, anxiously waiting for him to explain his words.

Erik holds the mug, takes a deep breath, and surveys the landscape as they stroll. "I love this crisp air. Brisk, eh? Charges you up, know what I mean?" He drinks, and the cocoa leaves a brown line on his upper lip. "Just beautiful." He wipes away the cocoa-stache and discards the mug. "Tim, my friend…Your family is dangerous. I think you know this better than anyone. My plan is to step in cordially and sit down with the new king, Claudius. We'll chat, drink some cocoa, and I'll tell him I would be a better ruler."

"You? The prince of Norway?"

"Well, I'm not a pitch-perfect candidate, by any means. But I'm whatcha got. Denmark is bleeding, and it needs surgery fast."

They have exited the small encampment, and now they are wandering across the vast Danish countryside. Fields stretch before them in all directions, as far as the eye can behold. The breeze whips past them, unobstructed and unfettered.

As they walk, Tim thinks of how Erik smiles and talks to his men. In the brief time they've known each other, Tim already agrees that the Norwegian would make a better ruler than Hamlet or Claudius. He asks, "And if Claudius reacts the way I know he'll react?"

Erik sighs. "Desperate times, and all that. It hope it doesn't come to it, but our army is waiting for my word to advance."

Tim feels lightheaded. "This is bloody mad, Erik."

Erik cackles. "Don't I know it! But I see no other course of action. The Hamlet line is more like an exclamation point, and that's not always a good thing. For generations, Danish monarchs have either been seriously unbalanced or—even worse—they're as lucid as can be, in full control of their devious little noggins."

They pass an old windmill, and Tim stops. He looks across the landscape, just as Erik had done a minute ago, and he tries to see with new eyes. He has always loved the Danish countryside—the fields, the rolling hills, the gray sky, colors that have a cold bite to them. Sparse and stripped down. This view…He wouldn't trade it for anything.

Erik seems to know exactly what Tim is thinking. He lets the moment breathe, then continues. "When Johan Hamlet killed my pops three years ago, I knew something had to be done."

Tim wraps his arms around himself. He is suddenly chilled to the bone, and he would love some cocoa.

"Something's gotta change," Erik says. "I don't want to speak ill of the dead, and I certainly don't celebrate anyone's passing, but as soon as I heard about Johan's funeral, I made plans to come here and speak with the new king. I know next to nothing about Claudius, but I think now, while he's still getting used to the throne, is the best time to step in and try to transfer power peacefully. You think Johan would've given up an inch of control? Call me a pessimist, but I'd wager no."

"You'd win that wager."

They stand in the Danish field. Erik has said his piece—he is waiting for Tim to respond. But Tim doesn't know what to say. So much life-changing information has been dumped on him over the course of their walk.

Erik breaks the silence with a pensive laugh. "I just thoughta something. My pops and I used to build stuff together. Woodworking. That was our thing. We started off small, when I was young. Birdhouses, jewelry boxes, figurines, all that good stuff. Then tables, cabinets, chairs. Finally, we started on carts and wheels and the like. That's when he died, so I didn't get all his instructions." He grimaces, but a smile still breaks through. "I built the wagon that broke today and nearly crippled Franz." He slaps a hand over his mouth to stifle his giggle. "Oops. Good thing you were there to help, or else this wouldn't be funny at all." He sighs as his laugh peters out.

Tim thinks. "My dad and I would travel sometimes. But I wouldn't call that our 'thing.' It was more like I would tag along sometimes."

Erik nods in understanding.

More silence.

Tim says, "You know I agree with everything you're saying. Those people don't deserve to be in power. The Hamlet name is damned in every sense." Pause. "But it's my name too."

Erik's eyes grow wide as racquetballs, and he grins excitedly. "I just had a slam-bam idea. Tim, my friend...Come with me. Lead with me! Be my number-two man in Denmark!"

Cripes, that sounds familiar. If there's such a thing as the "co-king zone," I'm definitely stuck in it.

Erik is over the moon. "With a Hamlet on our side, the Danish people probably won't even notice a change in power. The Good Hamlet! The Noble Hamlet...We'll workshop your moniker a bit, make it real snappy. I'll sit in Norway and rule over both states, but you'll be the Danish governor. Picture it: Denmark becomes the first addition to the Norwegian Empire!" He shimmies. "Whew, I just got chills."

"It's the weather, Erik. You're in Denmark—everyone has chills."

A shadow passes over them, and Tim looks up in time to see a huge brown eagle soar over them. Its wings are outstretched, not flapping, slicing majestically through the sky.

He almost tells Erik *"Thanks but no thanks"* right here and now...But what other option does he have? On one hand, there's his poisonous family in that arctic castle. On the other, he could return to London and continue failing at his lifelong dream.

And now here's Erik Fortinbras—a genuine fellow, one who seems honest, kind-hearted, and decent. And he likes Tim. He's a friend.

Why not? Tim searches for reasons not to join forces with Norway. Some part of him knows he shouldn't abandon his family and his nation. But they have made it impossible to stay loyal. The Hamlets have lied, killed, and connived. Wouldn't it be delightfully satisfying to see Gertrude and Hamlet escorted out of Elsinore...only for Tim to waltz in as their new governor?

Why on Earth not?

"That sounds like a good plan..." Tim hesitates. "And I'll have to let you know my answer later."

Erik, of course, smiles. "A man who doesn't make life-changing decisions at the drop of a hat? My kind of guy!"

"But Erik, I have to be honest." Tim can't believe what he's about to say. Neither logic nor emotion can explain it. "I have to go back and warn them."

That surprises Erik, and it shocks Tim too.

"At least give them a heads-up," Tim hastily adds. "Maybe Claudius will be more receptive to your offer if he's been told about it ahead of time." The breeze stops, and he can hear birds singing, even though none are in sight. "They're still my family—I owe them at least a word or two."

Erik nods. "I respect that. And I trust that you're a man of your word, Tim Hamlet." He grins and slaps Tim's arm again. "You're a stand-up guy."

When you stand up, you're an easier target.

Tim looks out at the empty landscape one more time, then says, "I don't want to mooch off your hospitality—"

"Why, Prince Hamlet," Erik throws an arm around Tim's shoulder, "it'd be my honor if you would be a guest in my camp today. And please, share a meal with us. And sleep in one of our tents!"

"I'm not one to turn down an invitation," Tim laughs. "Thank you." He pats his coat pocket. "I've got some light reading to do tonight."

.　　.　　.

The moon is a spotlight illuminating the small camp. The scene is set.

Tim sits at a small desk inside a one-person tent. A candle illuminates the interior. Apparently, this is where Erik sleeps, but he gave it to Tim for the night and bunked elsewhere. The wind whistles outside, making the blue walls of the tent ripple like the surface of a lake.

His stomach is still full from the best veal stew he's ever eaten. Part of him wants to curl up on the royally padded cot and drift off to sleep, forgetting all about Denmark and kings and murder and coups.

And this script. This baffling, chilling, mysterious script. He wants to erase that from his mind too.

The twine-bound stack of pages sits on the desk, right under his nose. Its title whispers to him...*The Tragedy of Hamlet, Prince of Denmark.* There is no author.

He reaches to open it. His fingers shake.

Why are you so scared? It's a script. You're a writer. You've cranked out dozens of these. Just flip the pages and read.

Still, Tim sits for a while longer. He listens to the howling wind. The candle stands resolute—it doesn't flicker.

He turns the first page before he can talk himself out of it.

As is usual, the second page of the script is a list of all the characters a director will need to cast. At the top is the lead protagonist: Hamlet. No first name.

Following are plenty of names Tim recognizes—Ophelia, Gertrude, Claudius, Osric, Fortinbras, and many more.

Further down the list are names Tim has never heard of—Reynaldo, Cornelius, and Francisco, among others. The list is quite lengthy.

The play opens with a harrowing scene: Elsinore sentries standing guard outside on a foggy night, discussing the sight of a ghost. The ghost of the former king.

Tim thinks back to his encounter with his father's ghost in London. The King had said he'd already appeared to Hamlet, to which Tim had objected to being the second choice. The King had then responded, "I appeared to some random guards first. You're actually third."

This scene he is now reading seems to be that very appearance. It's a surreal experience, reading a script about something that Tim believes to be fact.

The guards spot the ghost. They yell, "Over there!" "No, over there!" "He's flying!" Tim smirks—the author is subtly telling the director that they're going to have to invest in some special effects.

The next scene introduces King Claudius. He addresses the Danish court with his trademark grace—he really overdoes the "royal we," but it's effective. He explains his new marriage to his sister-in-law and how his mourning of Old Hamlet has been replaced by newlywed bliss.

So Tim deduces that this play takes place relatively recently. Johan Hamlet is only just put in the ground, and Claudius has married Gertrude.

Tim shakes his head. *It's silly how I'm thinking that this play has anything to do with what's actually going on in Denmark. These are merely striking coincidences so far, that's all. Names and places…Coincidences happen all the time. Art imitates life, and all that rot.*

Claudius concludes his speech by explaining he has sent ambassadors to Norway to defuse a conflict. That certainly lines up with what Tim was told in London, but still. Just a coincidence.

A character named Laertes shows up…the son of Polonius and brother of Ophelia. (Tim pales as he reads on.) Laertes requests that he return to France, where he had been before returning to Elsinore for Claudius's coronation.

So what? All these characters share names and relationships with people in my real life. Coincidence. Sheer coincidence. Tim is getting tired of hearing himself think that word.

And then the play introduces its title character…There's Prince Hamlet. Dressed in black, sulking in a corner. Claudius tries to act fatherly to his new son, but Hamlet has none of it.

Once everyone is gone, Hamlet dives headlong into a bleeding-heart monologue.

Not just a monologue. He's alone onstage, so it's a soliloquy.

Hamlet says he wishes he were dead. He prays for the day his flesh evaporates and his life is no more. He curses God for making suicide a sin. He laments his mother's hasty marriage, and he practically buckles under the weight of his father's death.

Wow.

Tim takes a breath. The way Hamlet talks, the "I'm-smarter-than-you" wordplay he sneaks into all his conversations. His melancholy, his charm, his wit…That's his brother, no doubt.

How on Earth did an author recreate all of this so accurately?

Maybe this script isn't a transcription of what really happened.

No. Tim tries to move on before he can finish his thought. But it's too late.

Maybe it's the other way around. This script is reality. What happens on the page happens in the flesh.

That's insane, even for Tim's inner thoughts. There's no way a splattering of ink on a piece of paper can dictate what happens in the real world.

Is this the real world?

"Shut up!" Tim yells at himself, then stiffens. He doesn't want to wake his hosts, especially not with this foolishness.

But he simply can't hide behind the word "coincidence" anymore. It's clear that there is more than mere happenstance at play here. An author must have written this script in Elsinore, hiding and taking notes as recent events unfurled.

But how did the writer get Hamlet's private thoughts—

Tim keeps reading.

What a whirlwind of a play. Even as Tim sits in his comfortable tent, the drama leaves him breathless as if he just ran a marathon. Just when you think things are as bad as they can possibly get, another tragedy rears its fearsome snout.

Hamlet encounters his father's ghost and learns of King Claudius's deceit. He decides to don an "antic disposition" in order to make people lower their guard around them. He's going to act crazy. And he's going to kill Claudius, no matter what.

Hamlet stomps into Ophelia's bedroom, sweaty and haggard. He doesn't say a word and backs out slowly.

Rosencrantz and Guildenstern show up with a troupe of players. They've been summoned by Claudius and Gertrude to learn the truth about Hamlet's antics.

The lead player performs a scene for Hamlet and Polonius. A scene about Hecuba.

Hamlet nurtures a plot to root out his uncle's guilt. He adds a scene to the players' performance. A scene designed to mirror Claudius's act of treason against Old Hamlet.

Hamlet encounters Claudius praying. He wants to kill the king, but doesn't, worried that Claudius will go to heaven. Turns out Claudius was merely trying to pray—his words didn't quite make it to God.

Hamlet storms into his mother's bedchamber, ranting and raving about her crimes. Gertrude denies knowing anything about Claudius's evil act, but Hamlet doesn't believe her. Then Old Hamlet's ghost shows up again. Gertrude doesn't see the ghost.

Hamlet hears a voice from behind a tapestry. He thinks it is Claudius, and he stabs through the cloth. Polonius's dead body falls to the ground. Hamlet is shipped off to England to get him far away from Elsinore.

Stop.

Tim forces himself to pause. To catch his breath. He's been reading this play like it is a fiction. He has to, otherwise he will go completely mad. But he has to face the facts.

This script is reflecting the story of prince Hamlet...the real one. Tim's brother. To the letter. Down to the finest detail.

It's impossible. And yet here it is.

For twenty years, Tim has lived a relatively normal life. Yes, he is a prince, a twin, and a playwright, but a sober-minded man can wrap his mind around all that. In the past week, though, he has encountered murder, ghosts, madness, and misadventure. He felt his father's spectral hand reach into his skull and implant a vision. He sword fought a greasy pirate in a greasier pub. He was shipwrecked and survived. He saw an elderly wizard with insanely good biceps appear out of thin air. He allied with the spawn of Lucifer against a blue fairy, and he peed in a cave in order to summon that demon. His life has gone from run-of-the-mill interesting to bonkers-bananas-ridiculous in a matter of days.

But even after all that—all the mischief and mayhem and supernatural malarkey—he cannot comprehend this.

How can there be a script that conveys what has happened in reality?

Tim looks at the open pages—there are still many he has yet to read.

Everything has been accurate so far. Can it be? Can this script tell Tim what's going to happen? Will the ending of this play be the ending of Hamlet's story?

Tim slumps back in his chair.

A thought strikes him:

He isn't anywhere to be found in the script. The "young Hamlet" is implied to be Glenn. Par for the course—whenever someone speaks of "Hamlet," they're inevitably talking about his brother. Glenn's ownership of the family name is stubborn and pervasive.

But he has influenced the story on the page. He truly has.

He was the one who barged into Ophelia's bedchamber and freaked her out. The script says Hamlet did that...which is technically true, since that's Tim's last name as well.

He told the players to perform the show about Hecuba. They were going to do an improvised comedy show, but Tim convinced Horace to learn the speech he would eventually give to Polonius and Hamlet—the very speech contained in these pages.

He helped his brother craft the scene that would supposedly confirm Claudius's guilt. The words he came up with just yesterday are penned in dried ink in this script. The ink is even cracked a little—these words were written long, long ago. Tim shudders.

And yet...

Though he has contributed to the story, he in no way feels in control. He is merely a pawn. A character in the play. This script is God, and he has no free will.

Indeed, he had saved Polonius from Hamlet's blade. He had stopped Hamlet from killing the old man. But as soon as Hamlet had left Gertrude's room, he had run Polonius through.

It makes no sense, now that Tim thinks about it. Why was Polonius still there? How had Hamlet confused Polonius for King Claudius out in the open?

The script says that Hamlet needs to stab Polonius, thinking the old man is Claudius...and that is what happened, despite Tim's intervention. The story had gotten off track...and it needed to be righted.

All the world's a stage, am I right?

He needs to read on. He is terrified to his core, and all his hairs stand straight up like little trees. He wants nothing more than to run out of the tent and forget this whole thing ever happened. At this point, he wouldn't even mind returning to London and opening *A Tale of Marge and Tina*—bring on the rotten fruit-flingers.

But he needs to know how the story ends. So he keeps reading.

The play reveals to the audience that Rosencrantz and Guildenstern have been tasked with escorting Hamlet on a ship to London, unknowingly carrying orders for Hamlet's execution. Cue dramatic music.

But Hamlet escapes thanks to a band of pillaging pirates, and he sets his sights on Elsinore. All of this occurs offstage, of course—an action set-piece like that would be a nightmare to execute well.

And the hits just keep coming. Laertes hears of the death of his father and flies into a rage. He storms from France back to Elsinore, amassing a group of protestors as he goes. Laertes means to kick Claudius to kingdom come, but the King convinces Laertes that everything is Hamlet's fault. Once they hear that Hamlet is returning to Elsinore, they concoct a plan to kill the pesky prince once and for all.

Cue *more* dramatic music.

Tim wants to roll his eyes at how soapy this whole plot is, but he can't lie…It's compelling stuff. He's sucked in.

During the conversation between Claudius and Laertes, they receive horrible news. In the wake of Polonius's murder, Ophelia goes mad with grief and drowns. Is it suicide or an accident? The play leaves that ambiguous.

Tim feels his heart pang. *Ophelia…* He knows his childhood friend isn't dead in the real world. This page merely says that she will die soon. This instinctive sorrow he feels in his soul further cements the terrifying belief that this script tells the future.

So much death. So much despair.

The murder plot will go like this: Laertes and Hamlet will compete in a bout of fencing. However, Laertes's blade will be laced with highly potent poison, so that all he has to do is nick the prince's bare skin. (*Looks like Claudius is getting to use his cache of poisons more in these later scenes.*) They also have a back-up plan, in case Hamlet is a better sword fighter than Laertes. If Laertes is unable to strike the prince and draw blood, Claudius will announce Hamlet the victor and offer him a goblet of poisoned wine. (*Geez, if Claudius has a problem, he just throws some poison at it, I guess.*) Either way, *voila*, one dead Hamlet.

Hamlet shows back up at a cemetery in one of Elsinore's darker courtyards. He encounters two very funny diggers, who trade jokes for a while and lighten the mood. Hamlet finds the grave of a jester he had known as a child.

Yorick…Good Lord, he's talking about Yorick. I remember that good-natured goofball. Wow.

Hamlet cradles Yorick's skull and launches into another self-indulgent monologue.

Thankfully, a group of people shows up and cuts him short. It is Ophelia's funeral, and Hamlet crashes the ceremony and behaves like an absolute boar. He raves, babbles, and even attacks the grieving Laertes.

Conditions are perfect for their duel the next day. The aide Osric prepares Hamlet for the match, just as scattered and sprightly as ever. Hamlet quips at him for a page or two.

And here it is. Tim feels the thinness of the unread pages. This is the last scene.

He practically holds his breath as his eyes fly across the words.

Hamlet apologizes to Laertes for Polonius's death. He says it was his own madness that killed Laertes's father, not his will.

Wow. It's very unlike Hamlet to apologize.

Hamlet and Laertes engage in an intense duel, but Laertes is clearly outmatched. Hamlet scores the first hit, and Claudius offers him the poisoned goblet. Hamlet turns it down and continues the match. After scoring the second hit, Gertrude decides it's time to toast her son's victory.

Oh no. Tim gasps.

She takes the goblet.

Claudius implores her not to drink. But not too hard…He can't let anyone know that he knows it's poisoned.

She drinks.

The King is distraught, but he must suffer silently and watch his wife die at his hand.

At this point, Laertes doubts the nobility of this plot, and he is hesitant to continue the fight. But they duel again, and it happens. Laertes cuts Hamlet with the poisoned blade.

All the air is sucked from Tim's lungs. *That's it.*

The two scuffle and somehow end up switching swords. Hamlet erupts in rage and wounds Laertes as well. Now they are both dying of poison, but only Laertes realizes it.

Queen Gertrude crumples to the ground, dead.

Laertes despairs that he has been slain by his own treachery. In his final moments, he tells Hamlet that King Claudius is to blame for the poisoned blade and goblet. He forgives Hamlet and, with that, dies.

Hamlet grows even angrier, surrounded by death. He stabs Claudius with the blade and forces the poisoned drink down his throat. The King dies crying for help.

Hamlet, the Prince of Denmark, collapses center stage. He says he wishes for his story to be told, and for the invading Fortinbras to become the new ruler. He rests his head on the ground and speaks no more.

Prince Fortinbras swoops in, along with an ambassador who says that Rosencrantz and Guildenstern are also deceased. Fortinbras takes in the gruesome scene and orders that Hamlet be carried away like a fallen soldier. He begins to clean up the carnage, and asks for his soldiers to show respect for the fallen prince.

Lights dim. Curtain drops. The end.

Tim sits for a while, shell-shocked. The whistling wind is the only sound to accompany his cold thoughts on this cold night.

He wants to think *"What a play. A bit melodramatic, and the piles of corpses at the end were a bit much, but it sure was effective! I might stage this bad boy in London one day. Now for a good night's sleep."*

But that is nowhere close to what is on his mind.

If he is right, and reality is a reflection of what is written on these pages, there is no happy ending on the horizon.

He ticks off the body count on his fingers. Old Hamlet, Polonius, Ophelia, Rosencrantz, Guildenstern, Queen Gertrude, Laertes, King Claudius, and Prince Hamlet.

Almost all of the principal characters.

Tim shakes his head. *No, not characters. People. Friends. Family.*

He rubs his eyes and rereads the last scene. Then he re-rereads it. The more he absorbs the words, the more they cease being ink on a page and morph into tangible images.

His mom's face turns a shade of green as she crumbles to the ground, ravaged by poison.

Uncle Claudius weeps as a sword pierces his heart. He cries, "Mercy! Please, mercy—" but his plea is cut off by the poisoned drink being dumped down his throat.

Death by death, minute by minute, the grand ballroom's tiled floor becomes slick with red blood. Onlookers scream and scatter. Some faint.

Others can only stare. No one ever thought the carnage of a battlefield would come to their court.

It's horrific.

But Tim can't stop reading.

As he dissects and examines this climactic scene for what feels like the twentieth time, he realizes something is off. Before the duel, Hamlet express regret to Laertes about Polonius's death. He even goes so far as to admit he was out of his mind when he attacked the old man.

How incredibly unlike Hamlet.

Not only that, he goes on to best Laertes at fencing. Hamlet is no slouch when it comes to swordsmanship, but he's hardly a champion. Back in the day, that title belonged to Tim.

But it's strange. Before this moment, Hamlet is arrogant and self-aggrandizing, interrupting Ophelia's funeral and poking fun at Osric. And after he apologizes, he flies into a rage—that's par for the course for him.

That apology and that admission of madness, though…Hamlet would never do something like that. Also, why would he advocate for Fortinbras's ascension to the Danish throne? The more Tim looks at it, the less the puzzle pieces fit together.

Unless.

But.

However.

There is no first name. The script doesn't say which Hamlet.

It could be me in this final scene.

Tim feels lightheaded. Not because he is surprised by this revelation…Quite the opposite. It's like everything fits together perfectly, and he is seeing the full picture for the first time.

He stands and paces around the tent.

So that's it. Throughout this whole journey, he has felt like there is a bigger force at work pulling him to Elsinore. A deep, primal instinct—something he couldn't quite pinpoint. He had thought it was the need for closure with his father. Or maybe he had wanted a closer relationship with his twin brother. Then he had been *sure* it was the fact that he wanted to be his own man, make his own decisions, be the author of his own fate.

But, it turns out, none of that is the case.

He was drawn home because that's where he is supposed to be. It was written in this script. He had to influence the players, and run into Ophelia, and write Hamlet's scene, and do all sorts of things that he didn't even realize had an impact on the story as a whole.

No improvisation is allowed on this stage—what the script says is what needs to happen.

And the script says one of the Hamlet twins is going to die.

So, ole Tim, which one is it going to be?

He wipes a bead of chilled sweat from his brow. Is he really thinking that question? "*Which one?*"

Yes, I am. That's the reality I've been dealt.

Only Tim knows what is going to happen, how this story is going to end. Everything else has happened to the letter, from the appearance of Old Hamlet's ghost in scene one all the way to Hamlet getting banished to London. The rest of the story will play out exactly how this script says—he can feel it in his bones.

He can try to tell the others, but they'll only laugh in his face. He can already hear Hamlet's taunts: "You read a play, and now you think we're all gonna die? And people say *I'm* the loon of the family."

This climax is going to play out, no matter what Tim does. Ophelia is going to drown, Laertes will show up, he and Hamlet will duel, and all these terrible things will happen just as they're described in these pages. It's tragic, but it's a fact Tim can't change.

And so…He can walk away. He can go with Erik, or he can return to the Masterpiece Centre, or he can swim the ocean until he finds Miranda. He can do whatever he wants. But he will do it with the knowledge that he knew his brother was going to die and did nothing.

Or…He can take his brother's place. Become "Prince Hamlet" for this final scene. He would die, but his brother would live.

He stops pacing, his shoes suddenly full of sand. It feels like an invisible snake has curled around his chest.

Would Hamlet do the same for me?

No. No way. He knows that answer before he even finishes thinking the question. If Glenn Hamlet were in this exact situation, he would get as far away from responsibility as he could. He would monologue and brood and go back and forth on the issue. He wouldn't put himself on the line for his mother, his twin, or even Ophelia. He is not a bad person...but he is far from a hero. He isn't a brother to be counted on.

Would Father do this for me?

Likely not. He would fabricate some important excuse, and he would sell it with vigor—"I'm the king of Denmark, boy. You're my son, yes, but I cannot simply trade my life for yours. Where would that leave my court, my citizens, my armies? Here, have a brandy from my personal cabinet. You deserve it. Enjoy your last night of life."

Would Claudius make this choice? Bartholomew? Shermink?

Not even close. The Hamlet men would leave each other high and dry, no doubt.

And that's exactly why I'm not going to.

His breath shudders. He has made a decision without even realizing it.

This demonic script has robbed him of his free will, it seems. Things are going to end badly, no matter what. But there is still one choice he can make.

He will die for his brother.

Not despite the fact that his brother wouldn't die for him.

Because of it.

Tim Hamlet feels exhausted. Normally, he would stay up all night, making some sort of plan, psyching himself up for what's to come.

Now, though, for the first time, he knows exactly what is going to happen tomorrow. There is no use worrying about it for another second. So he blows out the candle, curls up on the cot, and falls fast asleep.

Chapter 12

The gritty stone walls, the rippling moat, the towering gate sealed shut…

Tim is back at Elsinore, locked out, just as he has been for years.

It's early in the morning, the sun just now making its entrance. He had slept in Fortinbras's tent until his body naturally stirred, and he ate a hearty breakfast of sausage, biscuits, and gravy. Erik is quite the cook, it turns out (surprising Tim not at all). After completely filling his belly for the first time in recent memory, Tim set out, feeling like a wishy-washy boomerang, heading back to the very place he had sworn off.

But now, he knows he will never leave again. He is going home for the last time…He'll end up in the cellar next to all his rotted ancestors.

A thought strikes him as he stands outside Elsinore. The placard on his stone coffin will read "Prince Glenn Hamlet."

Oh, that would drive Hamlet absolutely nuts. Good thing he'll never have to see it.

Before leaving Erik's camp, Tim had given him some very important, very specific instructions. Erik had listened intently, nodding and asking the occasional question to clarify something. He will make an excellent king.

"Now," Erik had said, "you're positive all those things will happen just as you say?"

Tim responded, "If I do my job, yes."

With that, the two princes shook hands, and Tim departed.

Tim gazes up at the wall. He wants to climb over, but the moat presents an issue.

The script is rolled tight in his coat pocket, close to his heart. Every breath makes his chest burn and head feel light…It might be the cold, but it could also be the demonic pages pressed so close to his body.

How do I get back in? I want to sneak in undetected. After all, Gertrude thinks I stormed out after Polonius's death, never to return. If no one knows I'm back, when I take Hamlet's place, no one will think something's awry. He'll be able to leave this place and live his life without being pursued.

What will Hamlet do after this is all said and done? I'll be dead, and he can't ever come back to Elsinore.

That's a thought for another time. For now, he needs to get inside.

He pauses and thinks about the timeline of the play he read over and over last night.

Hamlet is sent to England. He escapes when pirates attack the transport. Laertes shows up at Elsinore. Hamlet crashes Ophelia's funeral. Duel to the death. Curtains.

Tim has no idea where he is in this chronology. Has Ophelia drowned yet? Is Laertes inside right now? *No clue. Just get inside, Guv. Think later.*

Maybe he can swim across? He inches to the edge of the moat and peeks over the edge. The eels aren't swimming around—they look frozen solid in the frigid water. So that threat is neutralized…but if the cold-blooded creatures are dead, there is no way he would survive the dip.

That's when he hears the horde of tromping footsteps behind him. He turns and sees a huge crowd of people seething out of the woods. They shout, chant, and move like one giant organism. And they don't look happy.

The crowd chants together: "Two, four, six, eight! Dethroning the king would be real great!"

One of the voices sighs. "Mmm, no. Next."

"What do we want? A new king! When do we want it? Now!"

"Y'know what," the voice says, exasperated, "let's just do the easiest one. Altogether, now…"

So as the crowd marches toward Elsinore's gates, they chant, "Laertes for king! Laertes for king! Laertes for king!" They punch the air and stomp their feet as they get louder and louder.

Tim focuses his eyes. *Aha.* There, leading the mob. In his perfectly starched suit, sporting long, flowing bronze hair, walking with all the confidence an Olive League school can buy.

Laertes—son of Polonius, brother to Ophelia. Recently bereaved, infinitely inflamed. The guy has always fancied himself a gentleman, but his temper is legendary. Tim once saw him bite through a leather riding-crop after getting a C on his astronomy final. Tim can only imagine how furious he is now that his father is gone.

Now I know where I am in the story. Laertes has returned from his schooling in France, driven to avenge his dad. Looks like he has picked up a few fans along the way too. Ophelia has gone mad with grief, but she hasn't drowned. Hamlet isn't back yet. Tim needs to get inside and wait for his brother to return—

"You there!" Laertes's voice booms through the air. The mob grinds to a halt in front of Tim, leaving a dozen or so yards of dead grass between them. Laertes scowls at Tim with a fiery glint in his gaze. "Prince Hamlet, you dog! You murderous baboon!"

Uh oh. My brother's face betrays me yet again. Tim begins to sputter. "N-No, Laertes, listen, i-it's Tim! I'm Tim!" Sweat beads his face—he definitely doesn't want to be on the receiving end of Laertes's rage.

Laertes spits. "Hamlet, you coward! Cowering behind your long-lost brother's name. After slaying my father and soiling my sister, you further insult me with your frailty. What a louse. What a worm!" He tilts back his head and laughs bitingly. The crowd takes this as their cue to join in.

"No, I'm not Hamlet!" Tim doesn't know what to do. Laertes never knew Tim well enough to distinguish him from his twin brother, so his voice and demeanor don't reveal his identity like they did for Gertrude and Osric.

He starts to panic and reconsiders diving into the icy moat. *How can I defuse this?* Laertes looks ready to kill...

Then it strikes Tim. He doesn't need to defuse this situation. In fact, he *shouldn't* try to mollify Laertes's anger. The script says that Laertes needs to plot Hamlet's murder with King Claudius, and that can't happen if Laertes is soothed and placid.

If Laertes thinks Tim is Hamlet, Tim might as well stoke the fire a little.

He puts on a loose, obnoxious grin. "How's it going, larva breath? Long time no see." He tries to relax his posture, roll his shoulders, and don his twin's confidence. "What's with the fan club?"

"I mean to dethrone Claudius." Laertes draws himself to his full height. "These fine folk agree with my musings. He has overseen the ruin of this state in a matter of weeks. He allowed my father to be struck down, and I shall do the same to him!"

The crowd begins to chant "Laertes for king" again, but it quickly dies out without proper direction.

Tim cackles. "Why would you do that?" He prods, provokes, and taunts. "Ah, little Larry. *I* killed Polonius!"

Laertes snorts. "You scoundrel! You unmitigated *ragamuffin!*" he cries out, rolling his R's in an extremely pretentious way. "With God as my witness, I shall make you pay for your poisoned tongue!"

"Well," Tim winds up for a comeback, "with Zeus, Odin, and Santa Claus on my side, I'd love to see you try!"

Laertes adjusts his flowing locks. "I am here to avenge my slain patriarch, not to quarrel with a yipping pup. 'Tis my destiny, my calling. Among the last words my father ever said to me were these: 'To thine own self be true.'"

"Hate to break it to ya," Tim interrupts the speech as rudely as he can, "but you're a jerk, so that was terrible advice. He should've said, 'Go find a nice person and take notes.'"

"That does it!" Laertes screeches. His face flushes and he grinds his teeth down to nubs. "I'll pluck your limbs one by one like a rooster's feathers!" He seethes for a moment before remembering all the eyes watching him. He scrapes together what dignity he has left, then calls to an unseen guard on top of the castle wall. "My good Dane, if you would kindly lower the drawbridge, this odious prince and I will cross Elsinore's threshold. Once we stand upon the royal grounds, I shall trounce and thrash his form from top to bottom, with all the ire of my ancestors!"

"Yeah, sounds good, fart face." Tim does his best impression of his brother's smarmy "I'm-better-than-you" smirk.

The drawbridge lowers, welcoming them into Elsinore with a nonverbal *thud*.

Tim gestures to the entrance. "After you, dear."

"I shall speak with Claudius," Laertes huffs as he adjusts his suit. "He shall know just what to do with you." He takes long, forceful strides and closes the dozen-yard gap between the two of them very quickly.

As he gets closer, Tim gets a good look at his face. Red, puffy eyelids. Deep wrinkles filled with shadows. A quivering jaw. He looks miserable, barely holding himself together. He treads across the bridge, Tim right on his heels.

Tim feels a hot lump in his stomach. Laertes has never been his best friend, not by a mile—but he just lost his father, and he is about to lose his sister, although he doesn't know it. Mocking and goading him like this feels monstrous.

I'll get the chance to apologize before we duel. Tim swallows his shame.

They step off the drawbridge and enter the castle grounds. The immaculate lawn, the towering topiaries, it's all the same as last time. Except now, so early in the morning, there are no shuffling servants or horseback soldiers.

Laertes stops and turns to Tim, who also shuffles to a halt. He lowers his voice, but Tim can hear the fury just behind the dam: "I shan't kill you today, prince. Ophelia's heart could not bear it. My devotion to her has saved your life." He begins to walk away. "You're welcome."

Tim is too chilled to think of a snarky retort. He just stands there as Laertes's supporters move past him, like they are a river and he is a boulder. Soon enough, he is alone on the grounds of Elsinore.

The breeze tickles the leaves of the topiaries, making the green lion and dragon shimmer. It's quiet.

Is this what it's like to be Hamlet? Antagonizing sad people? Starting unnecessary fights? Getting wrapped up in murder plots?

Tim forces his feet to move. He doesn't follow Laertes through the castle's front doors. Even though he has announced his presence to a few people, he still thinks it is best to be as anonymous as possible. There are many servants' entrances around back through which he can sneak.

Is Hamlet worth dying for?

That's an easy one. *No.*

He makes his way around the castle's stone wall. He passes gardens, orchards, stables, pens…This place is massive. He tries to remember a time from his childhood when he had explored these grounds.

Then why am I taking his place?

Tim's attempt to distract himself doesn't work. One's impending death tends to stick out prominently in one's mind.

As he walks, his shoes become heavier and heavier. The air becomes thicker. Thoughts swirl around his head, practically suffocating him.

Will it hurt, the poison?

I could beat Laertes. I know I could. What would happen if I won the fencing match?

What if I take Claudius out of the equation? He can't poison the wine if he's tied up in a broom closet.

Can Hamlet and I both just hightail it out of here? The script is just a pile of parchment, after all. It can't drag us into the ballroom and kill us.

Can it?

So many questions.

Before Tim can think of any more, he hears something. A bird trilling in the morning. Light, soft, and warm. No…Tim walks a bit more, and the sound comes into focus. Singing. No words, just abstract la-la-la's.

He rounds a corner and finds a beautiful pond. He remembers reading and writing here years ago, unfurling picnic blankets, thinking about the future while staring at the water's glassy surface. Wonderful, serene memories.

Beautiful azaleas and orchids dot the shoreline, along with moss, lily pads, and even a couple brown rabbits. Somehow, a beam of yellow sunshine illuminates the lush area. Like a spotlight. A scene is about to begin.

A large tree stands proudly next to the pond, and its thickest branch extends out over the water. Someone is sitting on that branch, making it sag like a frown.

It is Ophelia. She wears a white dress, and she has stuck a few flowers in her hair. She is the one who is singing.

Tim freezes and tries to remain hidden around the corner, but she has not seen him. Her hands are flying with expertise, weaving grass and flowers into some sort of hat.

"Tra la loo la…" Her voice is lovely, but distant. Airy. Empty.

She looks at her hands, but her eyes seem locked on a point a thousand miles away. Her face is saggy from a sleepless night, and chips of dried blood are under her fingernails.

She's mad with grief. He realizes how precariously she's perched over the water, how heavy her dress looks, and how crazed her eyes are. *This is it.*

He feels a tear dripping down his cheek. *No no no no.* He doesn't want this. How can this be happening?!

Should I get help? Try to stop her from drowning?

He is revolted at himself for even asking those questions. Of course he should stop his friend from dying! *What, I'm going to stand here and watch her drown, just because some script says she will? That's insane! She's real—flesh and blood, right in front of me. I have to help!*

And yet, he stays frozen.

Ophelia keeps singing, her fingers weaving the grass with surprising dexterity.

The branch creaks under her weight.

She doesn't notice. Or she ignores it. "La la la…"

This is the test. *Do I really believe this script is in control? Do I think I change this story?*

The branch snaps. Fate has not given him time to wax poetically about this decision. He has to choose right here right now. Intervene, or don't.

As Ophelia drops through the air, her dress plumes out like a swan's broken wing.

Tim runs away before he sees her hit the water. He cannot stand to watch something so horrifying.

But he hears it. *Splash.* The waves lap against the pond's shore. She keeps singing: "La la la." The air in her dress keeps her afloat. For a few moments. Then she begins to sink. Slowly. Slowly. "La la la…"

The singing stops. She is submerged.

He just runs. Around the castle, searching for a door so he can get inside and escape these terrible sounds.

Then nothing. She's gone.

And the silence is worse than any noise could ever be.

There—a small wooden door. A servants' entrance. He crashes inside and slams the door shut, as if that will suppress his thoughts.

You didn't even try to help.

No. No, I didn't. There's no point.

Tim is in the most remote corner of the castle. He wants to get to Hamlet's bedchamber in the residential wing. He starts walking.

There is a scream trapped inside him that he can't get out. It is lodged in his throat like a fist, and he knows it will be there for the rest of his life.

The shadows in Elsinore's hallways are long and dark this early in the day. So quiet, so still…The castle is like a museum dedicated to his last name.

He needs to get out of sight before the inhabitants begin their schedules—cooking, cleaning, hustling and bustling, all blissfully unaware of the body in the pond out back.

As he passes a hallway, he sees a figure lurking in the distance. He stiffens.

It is just a suit of armor, standing at attention in the hall. Looking right at him. The helmet's visor is pulled down, so Tim cannot see a face, but the girth, the posture, the air of authority…It is his father's ghost. No doubt. So why doesn't it move? Why won't it show its face this time?

Tim rubs his eyes and keeps moving. He doesn't have time for his dead dad's mind games.

Onward to Hamlet's chambers.

According to the script, someone will tell Queen Gertrude of Ophelia's death, and she will tell Laertes and the king. Next is Ophelia's funeral, and it is only a matter of time before the climactic sword fight. Only a matter of time before the bloody finale.

Before he knows it, he is striding past bedroom doors. *Time sure flies when you're running from existential guilt.*

He reaches Hamlet's room and enters, slowly clicking the door closed behind him. He rests a hand on the script in his coat pocket. Still there.

The plush easy chair beckons, and Tim surrenders happily. He settles in, and he wants nothing more than to close his eyes and drift off into sweet nothingness.

But his brain chatters away at breakneck speeds. When he blinks, he sees Ophelia falling from that tree, her white dress puffed out. Even if he could fall asleep, his dreams would undoubtedly be haunted by his father, Polonius, and Ophelia.

"Such madness…" he whispers to himself, if only to hear a human voice.

So. He believes in the script's authority. He doesn't want to, and he hates himself for it. But he clearly does. He didn't stop Ophelia from falling into the pond, he didn't jump in and help, he didn't even yell to alert the castle. Whether he likes it or not, his gut instinct leans toward the sentiment of *"The script said she's going to die. That means she's going to die, one way or another."*

This realization sits in his chest like a lump of coal. He tries to shift in the chair so he can breathe better, but this acrid fact refuses to ease up.

Fine. I'm held captive by this demonic play. So what am I going to do about it?

Once again, he wonders what his brother would do in this situation. He would be distraught over his lover's death, no doubt, but what about everyone else? He killed Polonius, and he has been hellbent on killing Claudius. He is the poster child for chaos and violence.

Would Hamlet volunteer himself for the gallows to ensure no one else would die?

Tim almost laughs at the notion. *No way.*

Hamlet would never help Tim. And that is exactly why Tim is going to help Hamlet.

"Fate has bound my hands," Tim says. "I can't strike it. So I'll kick it in the gonads instead."

Everyone here is just a pawn in a story. But Tim has knowledge. He knows how to play this game. And because of this, he has a choice.

The same amount of people will die. No one can change that. But Tim can make sure his brother will live. He can give up his autonomy today to ensure Hamlet will be able to make his own choices tomorrow.

Bong. A grandfather clock somewhere in the castle begins sounding. Tim sits up and stretches—his back is stiff and his eyes itch. Did he actually sleep for a while?

Three o'clock. Wow. Yep. He gets up to look for a bottle to wash out the post-slumber tang in his mouth. The room is a disastrous mess, so he isn't very hopeful he'll find a drink that hasn't expired a millennium ago.

He passes a mirror and catches a glimpse of himself. Dark hair pushed back. Sharp eyes. Lean form.

When the time comes, and he takes his brother's place in the final scene, will anyone notice? Could this plan be folly after all? A small voice in the back of his mind says, *I really hope so.*

He can see it now: He will enter the ballroom, dressed in Hamlet's fencing garb. He'll draw a foil, ready to duel to the death, fully prepared to sacrifice himself to save his brother. And then, someone will shout, "Hey, that's not Hamlet! That's good ole Tim!" He would feel good about himself for being willing to die for his brother—he would establish himself as his own man, independent from his family name, breaking the cycle of Hamlet selfishness—reality would diverge from the script, freeing him from its grip—and, as a cherry on top, he would get to live.

Win-win-win-win. That would be great.

He'd like to think that, at a glance, someone would be able to tell the difference between him and Hamlet. Osric had recognized him the other day as he had stormed out following Polonius's murder. Jolly old Osric—their aide and teacher when they were lads. But Osric doesn't play much of a role in the final scene. He wouldn't have a chance to recognize Tim.

Laertes wouldn't notice he is Tim and not the prince. Uncle Claudius definitely wouldn't.

That just leaves Gertrude. The queen, his mom. Gut instinct—*Would she know it's me in that duel, not my brother?*

Tim stares at the mirror for a moment longer. A perfect replica of himself stares back. When he blinks, it blinks. When he shakes his head, the mirror-man does the same.

No. She wouldn't.

He deflates.

He has trusted his gut throughout this entire misadventure. When to fight, and when to flee. Who to trust, and who to avoid. He had assumed it was some cosmic energy steering him in the right direction, helping him make the right decisions. But it was just the script, keeping him alive long enough for him to make it to Elsinore and die.

He reaches into his coat pocket and unsheathes the stack of pages. *The Tragedy of Hamlet, Prince of Denmark.* No author. No first name in the title. Doesn't specify which Hamlet.

He can't stand the sight of it anymore. He tosses it into the clutter of the bedroom. He chuckles darkly to himself.

Don't need it anymore. I've memorized all my lines. In the biz, they call that "off book."

"Eh, book off!" he says to the discarded script. And his laugh fills the empty room.

That play asks a great many questions. The character of Hamlet often philosophizes ad nauseam, probing the great mysteries of life at the drop of a hat. One minute he's going about his business, the next he's debating the morality of suicide. Talk about a tone shift. It's true to life, though. Tim's brother fancies himself a Renaissance man who can expertly wield every single art form, like a poker player holding a dozen cards in one hand.

But for all the questions it asks, the play never provides any answers. Perhaps that's the point. Life's enigmas are unknowable to mere flesh-bags.

As Tim stands in front of his brother's mirror, he recalls a few of the play's biggest questions.

During the opener of act three, Hamlet steps onstage and unveils a doozy:

"To be or not to be?"

Is it better to live or to die?

Yeah, no pressure. "Real parlor room conversation," his brother would sarcastically call it.

Which is nobler: to put up with life's rotten headaches and heartbreaks, or to take a shortcut and end them? Fall asleep, and never deal with another disappointment, sorrow, or struggle. It's no contest. Easy decision. All it would take is a flick of a knife or a mouthful of the right fungus.

These thoughts and analyses are from Hamlet's monologue. The way he presents his case, it sounds like he yearns for death. *Very accurate,* Tim thinks. *I've seen that look in my brother's eye before. It's not something easily forgotten.*

But, Hamlet argues, not many people choose the escape hatch. They continue through the mud and drudgery of existence. Why? Because we're terrified of what comes next. Religions and dogmas have tried for eons to explain what awaits us on the other side of the curtain, but the truth of the matter is that no one has ever come back and told us. And boy, if we put up with such suffering in this world, we must absolutely dread what lurks in the afterlife.

In the words of the play, "Thus conscience does make cowards of us all."

The fear of death turns us all into weaklings.

So…to be or not to be? Which is better? The play doesn't offer a definitive answer. Hamlet seems to lean toward the "not to be" option, yet he doesn't off himself. He would tell himself it's because he has a holy mission to avenge his father and off his uncle.

But Tim thinks it's because he's scared. He doesn't want to be trapped in a purgatory punishment, like his father. He doesn't know exactly what awaits him in the afterlife. And most of all, he's scared to make such an eternal choice. Hamlet has been indecisive his entire life—what if he drinks poison and immediately changes his mind? No, Hamlet could never make such a big decision, no matter how much he thinks he wants to. The ticket to the hereafter is one-way and nontransferable.

And here stands Tim, just as scared of death as the next guy. He doesn't know what comes next either—fire, darkness, sulfur? Death is one big question mark. But he is choosing to step into it anyway.

That's just one question the play poses. Another crops up later in the story, after Hamlet is banished to England. Tim imagines his brother standing on a dramatic hillside, delivering this speech with gusto.

"What is a man if his chief good and market of his time be but to sleep and feed?"

In a world of beasts, what is a man?

Over the course of this passionate monologue, Hamlet settles on a conclusion: The ideal human is a warrior. To be great, one must fight over nothing, if one's honor is threatened. A true man takes decisive, violent action—consequences be damned.

"Oh," the speech concludes, "from this time forth, my thoughts be bloody or be nothing worth!"

AKA, "From now on, I'm worthless if I'm not taking steps toward violence."

Tim has always hated violence. He fought Captain Travkin in self-defense and refused to even cut him, much less kill him. He worked with his friends to subdue Prospero. All the death surrounding Elsinore has made him sick.

According to Hamlet's speech, this makes Tim less than a man. Weak. Cowardly.

The thought that he'll have to slice Laertes with the poisoned blade and then kill Claudius weighs on him. He'll have to do these horrible things in order to save his brother.

And here he is...making a firm decision to embrace violence. Hamlet would be so proud.

So...what is a man? Tim takes a shaky breath. What, indeed.

Rapid footsteps in the hallway. Tim leaps off the chair, suddenly very nervous.

The bedroom door pops open and in strolls Prince Hamlet. Hair disheveled, clothes stained, hands caked in dirt. Going by the script, Hamlet has just come from Ophelia's funeral, where he antagonized Laertes and even jumped into her grave. That explains the grimy hands.

Hamlet sees his twin brother and grinds to a halt.

Tim offers a small smile and a nod.

Hamlet groans and moves to his mirror. "Honestly, Tim. Pick a side. Leave or don't." He leans toward his reflection and begins reining in his wild hair. "I've got bigger problems to quash right now."

"Let me guess," Tim says. "Pirates. Funeral. Fencing match."

Hamlet twitches once, then continues fixing his hair, refusing to look at his brother. "Eavesdropping is very rude, little brother."

"We're twins, Glenn."

In an instant, Hamlet's facade of apathy vanishes. He spins and charges at Tim, teeth flashing. "Don't you call me that! I'm the prince, and you're just an asterisk in our family history." He stiffens and pulls in his anger. He speaks again, this time cold and quiet: "Never forget who you are."

Hamlet's eyes are rigid, as impassive as the stone walls surrounding them.

A realization strikes Tim, and he almost staggers backward. After all these years, Tim has never fully trusted Hamlet...but Hamlet has trusted

Tim. He has relied on his twin brother, believing that he would return home someday.

But when Tim did come home, he ended up leaving again when Hamlet was in need. His darkest hour.

Tim has walked away one time too many. Hamlet will never fully trust him again.

These emotions threaten to overwhelm Tim, but he buries them quickly. He knows that he needs Hamlet to play along if they're going to switch places for the final duel. He needs to get Hamlet to open himself up to Tim one last time.

Get him to talk about himself. His favorite subject.

"Mom sent you off to England," he ventures slowly, like easing into a very hot bath. "How'd you manage to get back?"

"What do you care?" Hamlet snips.

"Call me curious."

Hamlet sets his jaw, but he clearly wants to share his latest escapade. He begins speaking in a short, clipped tone. "I was on a ship with Frederick and Christian, headed for England. While they were on deck taking an herbal break, I rummaged through their bags. Good thing, too—I found a message from Uncle Claudius, ordering my execution once we made port."

The story lines up with what Tim had read, minus one detail—the message was sealed, meaning that Rosencrantz and Guildenstern didn't know about the execution. They were merely instructed to hand over the closed envelope to the port authority once they landed.

But that doesn't matter to Hamlet. He is a hero in his own eyes, and anyone not on his side is a sworn enemy.

He continues, getting caught up in the story. "I knew I had to get off the ship as soon as I could. Luckily, at that very moment, I heard cannon fire. We were under attack! I rushed to the deck and saw a pirate ship looming next to ours. The captain stood behind the wheel. I could only make out his silhouette, but he sported a huge tri-pointed hat…"

Travkin?! Tim nearly bursts out laughing. *I can't believe it.*

Hamlet doesn't notice. He flails his arms and even provides sound effects as he describes the attack. The pirate vessel (which Tim knows to be the *Crimean Cavalier*) opened fire on them. He dodged the shrapnel and single-handedly fought off every thug that boarded. He did backflips and cracked witty one-liners too.

Tim knows his brother is an unreliable narrator, but he has accomplished his mission of getting Hamlet to open up, so he doesn't object.

"Finally," Hamlet says, breathless, "I was face-to-face with the captain. He had tombstones for teeth and a horrid hook instead of a hand!" (*Okay, that's not an exaggeration.*) "He sneered at me and said something bizarre. He said, 'I've been tracking you, prince. Time for a rematch.' Strange, right?"

Tim can barely contain himself.

"I was unarmed, otherwise I would have handily defeated him. I mean, I have two hands. It'd be easy. But I knew it was time to go. I evaded him, hopped in a rowboat, and made my way back to shore. As I bobbed away, though, I heard the captain yell, 'I'll get you someday, Hamlet!' He must've known me." Hamlet shrugs and basks in his completed tale.

Add that to the list: Hamlet wouldn't have escaped his banishment if Travkin hadn't been hunting me.

"Brother," Tim says, "I fought that captain in a bar in London. I tried to tell you. His name is Lidiya Travkin, the Red Wraith. He was looking for me! He thought you were me!"

Hamlet rolls his eyes. "Lydia's a girl's name, Tim."

"It's his name! He swore vengeance on me after I tricked him and made him look foolish."

"Now who's being dramatic?" Hamlet scoffs.

Tim pinches the bridge of his nose to keep his head from popping, then moves on. "So where are Rosencrantz and Guildenstern?" He knows from reading the play that these two wind up dead, but he isn't sure how.

A devilish smile plays across Hamlet's face. "Ah, yes. Those traitorous teats. Well, just before the pirates attacked, I had the brilliant idea to write a message of my own to replace the one they were carrying." He laughs once. "I bet they were shocked when they showed up at their own execution."

It takes a moment for Tim to absorb what his brother said. "You...You had Rosencrantz and Guildenstern killed?"

"Don't act so frail, clutching your pearls and fanning yourself," Hamlet growls. "It's survival. It was them or me!"

"Bloody hell!" Tim begins to pace frantically around the room, sputtering, stammering, and turning bright red. "They're our friends, Hamlet! Well, they *were* our friends. You killed Polonius and you've been itching to kill our uncle, but our *friends*? They were innocent! Morons, sure, but they've always tried to help you. They had no idea what was going on!"

Hamlet groans. "Then tell me, oh righteous crusader, what was I supposed to do?"

"You think about the situation for more than ten seconds and figure something out! Use your head—don't just jump to swatting people like flies." He shouldn't say what he's thinking…but he says it anyway: "You're just like Claudius."

All the air is sucked out of the room. Neither of them moves.

Tim went too far. Way too far. Hamlet's face is a piece of granite, etched in anger. He is like Elsinore's drawbridge, locked in the closed position for good. Tim is never getting back in.

"Listen…" Tim mutters, but it is no use. Hamlet's gaze could not be less murderous. "Believe it or not, Guv, I care about this family. That's why I came back."

Is that true? I don't even know anymore.

"Right." Hamlet turns to his mirror. It seems Tim doesn't even warrant a prickly comeback anymore.

"Fortinbras is on his way. Right now."

That gets Hamlet's attention. In the mirror's reflection, Tim sees a shadow of fear on the prince's face.

"I came to warn you all." Tim gulps. *Time to give the best performance of my life.* "He's out for blood. He means to rip us apart and parade our corpses down the street. He wants revenge for his father's death."

Hamlet ripples at that information.

Tim presses on. "Hamlet, I know you're to duel Laertes soon, but there isn't time. Fortinbras is on our doorstep."

Hamlet doesn't respond right away.

The distant grandfather clock strikes again. Four o'clock.

The prince says, without turning from the mirror, "I won't run from Laertes. Nor Claudius. If I refuse their challenge..." He finishes his sentence by grinding his teeth. "Not an option."

Tim expected this. "I'll do it, then. No one knows I'm here. I'll fight Laertes, pretending to be you. We each have our strengths." *The Fox and the Hippo.* "We both know I'm the better fencer. I'll beat Laertes easily and make you look like the belle of the ball. But while I do that..." He breathes. "You go out and talk with Fortinbras. You're the negotiator, the charmer, the face of Denmark. Even if people don't like you, they respect you. Go stop a war and save this nation."

Hamlet flattens his hair and finally turns from the mirror. His eyes are still cold and fiery at the same time, but his mouth is slightly curved. "Fine. I'll step up and save this family from ruin." Then he adds, pointedly, "I will be king, after all. I need to defend my throne."

Tim silently sighs. It worked. Hamlet will leave Elsinore, and Tim will take his place in the duel. The script will be appeased, and one Hamlet will survive.

His eyes dart across the floor, searching for the script he had discarded. He had thrown it among the clutter, but it isn't there anymore. Vanished. Gone from this world.

He smirks. *Of course.*

Hamlet interrupts his thoughts. "I'll make myself presentable," he gestures to his own stained clothes, "while you put on my fencing gear." He stabs a finger at his brother. "Don't embarrass me."

Tim doesn't care anymore. He continues smirking. "Whatever you say, Guv."

Hamlet puckers and balls up his fists. "You know what, Tim? You can call people 'Guv,' eat fish and chips, and spell words with an extra 'u' all the livelong day. No matter what, you're a Dane through and through. Like it or not."

"No, brother," Tim says. "I'm not a Dane. I'm not a prince. I'm not a Hamlet. I'm just me. I craft my own story. Like it or not."

With that, Tim takes a breath, filling his lungs for what feels like the first time in his entire life, and prepares for his final scene.

. . .

An eagle swirls lazily overhead. The air is still. There isn't a sound in all of Denmark, it seems.

Prince Hamlet stands on the dirt path just outside the woods. His clothes, which had gone through a pirate attack and a dive into Ophelia's grave, have been swapped out for his finest suit. Pearl buttons, velvet jacket, leather clogs…He wants to look every inch the diplomat. No, he *needs* to.

This is his chance to show them all. Gertrude, Claudius, Tim, everyone. Once he successfully deals with Fortinbras, no one will ever question his capability again. People will stop whispering as he walks by. Looking at him with pity in their eyes. Speaking to him as if one word will shatter him.

He's not crazy. He's not unbalanced. He can do this.

How long has it been? He checks the sundial strapped to his wrist and peers at the castle in the distance.

An hour has passed since he and Tim parted ways. Tim was dressed in Hamlet's fencing uniform. Hamlet had handed over his prized foil, said, "Don't bend it," and walked out of the bedchamber. Maybe he should have made sure Tim didn't chicken out of the duel.

According to Tim, Fortinbras is supposed to meet him here, where the path enters the woods. How, when, and why Tim set up this meeting, Hamlet has no idea.

"Tim…" He rubs the crick in his neck.

First, Tim left when they were fifteen years old, right after Hamlet had been named the future king—the most demanding, intensive title he could imagine. More than ever, he had needed an ally, a friend, a brother. And *pop*, Tim had run off in the middle of the night.

Then, Tim came back a few days ago. Out of nowhere. For no conceivable reason. Hamlet wanted to be happy to see his brother…but he couldn't get his hopes up too high.

And *then*, just when they were starting to get to where they were when they were kids, Tim hightailed it out of Elsinore again. Right when Hamlet was in the worst spot of his life.

How *dare* Tim show his face again! Waltzing into his bedchamber, talking about pirates, Fortinbras, and other drivel.

Well, now Hamlet will show him. He can do this. He can be king all on his own. Sure, let Tim wave his sword around and feel good about himself. Hamlet wears the crown—he'll be the one to stop this impending war.

Hamlet stomps his foot. "Where the hell is he?" Fortinbras is late. Is this a trap? Some sort of set-up, concocted between Tim and Norway?

Suddenly—

A scream pierces the silence. It's very distant, but it must be impossibly loud, for Hamlet to hear it from so far away.

The eagle hears it too. It stops swirling and plunges into the woods.

It came from the castle. Hamlet has lived in Elsinore his whole life—he knows the sound of voices reverberating off the cold stone walls.

What's going on?

He shuffles in place. Should he run back and see what's happening? Or should he stay and wait for Fortinbras? That Norwegian scum is behind the scream, no doubt. Maybe Hamlet can convince him to call off whatever attack is taking place.

Soft footsteps. Hamlet spins and faces the woods. A man walks along the path—he wears a ragged tunic and carries a dirty satchel, but Hamlet still recognizes his face. This is Erik Fortinbras, prince of Norway.

Hamlet sneers and squares his shoulders. Something is afoot, he can feel it, and Fortinbras is the mastermind. He opens his mouth to rip Fortinbras apart...but he stops himself.

Fortinbras's eyes are misty. His shoulders sag. He meets Hamlet's gaze and offers a sad smile. "Pleasure to meetcha, prince. But I wish we didn't have to, y'know?"

Hamlet is too stunned to speak. And what's worse, he doesn't know why he's stunned. Something is in the air. It feels like dread. Tangible dread.

The Norwegian lays the dirty satchel at Hamlet's feet. "Tim left a note for you inside the bag." He sounds like a man delivering news of a loved one's death. "He said it'll explain everything that just happened. Also, there's enough food, clothing, and money to get you safely out of Denmark." He takes a breath and wipes his eyes. "I want you to know, I'll make sure Tim is honored. We'll carry him out like he's one of our own."

An awkward moment passes. It seems Fortinbras is waiting for Hamlet to respond. Or maybe Fortinbras wants to say something more, but he can't conjure the words. Either way, the only sound is a crisp Danish breeze ruffling the dead grass.

Finally, Fortinbras continues walking along the path, passing Hamlet, who stands like a statue. What is his destination? Well, the path only leads to one place: Elsinore.

More footsteps. Dozens. Hundreds. Norwegian soldiers bleed out of the woods, all sporting blue uniforms. But their weapons are holstered. Their heads hang low. This isn't an invasion. It's a funeral procession.

Hamlet is surrounded by the marching soldiers, awash in a sea of blue. They all move at a steady pace, not charging, as if they know what is awaiting them inside the castle.

But what *is* in there? Hamlet has no idea.

He has no real choice. He picks up the satchel and slings it over his shoulder. He doesn't notice that his hands are trembling.

One step. Another. Each is a titanic effort.

Eventually, he enters the woods. The trees snuff out the sun, and their thick trunks hide the distant castle.

"Tim…" he whispers, but there's no one around to hear him.

Epilogue

Wow! What a sight! And what a smell! And what a feel! And a sound! Miranda hasn't tasted anything yet, but she is pretty sure London will wow her in that department too, when she gets around to it.

Her wild hair sticks out at every angle, snagging hats and bonnets from occasional passersby. She apologizes up and down—some laugh it off, others curse. Mainly the latter. Everything is so enhanced in the city. Structures are taller and wider, noises are louder, and personalities are amplified, be they good or bad.

She props her broken staff against her shoulder as she walks. It has been difficult to rein in her instincts to use her magic here, but she doesn't want to start a panic. Still, in such a strange place, it's comforting for her to hold it.

She remembers the day she got the staff, three long, long years ago. She remembers it perfectly, because it was also the day she overcame her father's control, released the captive men, and made some unforgettable friends. Eustace and Nicholas and Kent. And Tim. Good ole Tim.

Also, that was the day Caliban became her best friend. She smiles—it would be interesting to try to incorporate the sounds of the city into the next song they write.

Has it really been three years? It's funny—when Miranda thinks about her time on the island, three years feel like nothing. After all, that's where she's always lived. But when she thinks about how long it's been since she's seen Tim, it feels like an eternity.

A few weeks ago, she made a decision. A huge decision. She created a boat, used her magic to guide her to the mainland, and started exploring. As she had pushed away from the beach on which she'd grown up, Caliban had scoffed, "There's nothing but flesh-bags out there. I'll cover your chores for you, I guess. You're welcome."

Traveling on the open sea had been a dream. She could conjure water and food for herself. She didn't know quite where she was going, but she knew who she wanted to find.

She prances down a street, her bare feet sounding like flopping fishes against the cobblestones. Her soles are tough, though. People give her lack of footwear more glances than she loves, but it's no matter. She has made it to the city, after all these years!

It has taken a great deal of expert detective work, if Miranda can brag on herself for a moment. First, she had to find England. Then London. Then the Masterpiece Centre. And there it is, just down the street!

She starts walking faster without realizing it. What will Tim look like now? Will he have changed? Probably not—he seemed like a steady guy. Dependable. Then again, she only knew him for about a day, in extreme circumstances…But still! He was a good friend, and she considers herself to be an excellent judge of character.

She supposes she is taller and older too. Odd—she has never considered how she looks. There are no mirrors or boutiques on the island, but she sees six of each on this street alone.

Will Tim recognize her, after the passing of time?

Of course he will! They had such an adventure together. And…And they shared a connection. A special moment on the beach. At least, Miranda thought they did.

He has probably forgotten her. Made new friends. Had even bigger adventures.

Then again, how many other people does he know who live on a desert island? Yeah, she smiles. He'll remember her.

As she gets closer to the Masterpiece Centre, she feels a buzz of energy in the air. People are gathered around the ticketing booths, chattering and tittering like mongooses. They clutch playbills to their chests.

A huge sign looms over the front doors: "*A Tale of Argentina*." Under it is a hastily added notice: "*Sold out!*"

Again: Wow! Miranda feels her skin flush. She has written small tales for years, and now, here she is, seeking out one of the most successful storytellers in London!

There. A young man steps out of the theatre's entrance. Dark hair, sharp eyes. The pedestrians go bananas. A voice says, "It's him! Tim Hamlet!" Everyone begins shouting, patting his back, asking him to sign their playbills, trying to get as close to him as possible.

The crowd obscures his face, so she can't get a perfect look, but it must be Tim. She begins maneuvering her way through the crowd. Ducking under arms, sliding through open spaces, anything she has to do to see her friend.

The man laughs and grins and shakes hands.

Finally, Miranda is right in front of him.

Face to face.

The man sizes Miranda up and gulps. His smile disappears, and all the color drains from his face.

Miranda narrows her eyes. This man looks exactly like her friend…but it isn't him. "Who are you?"

About the Author

Luke Swanson was raised on a steady diet of stories. You can find him with a book constantly in his hand. He is the author of full-length fiction as well as a handful of published short stories. He lives with his wife in Oklahoma City.

Note from the Author

Word-of-mouth is crucial for any author to succeed. If you enjoyed *The Other Hamlet Brother*, please leave a review online—anywhere you are able. Even if it's just a sentence or two. It would make all the difference and would be very much appreciated.

Thanks!
Luke

Thank you so much for reading one of our **Humor** novels.

If you enjoyed our book, please check out our recommendation for your next great read!

Parrot Talk by David B. Seaburn

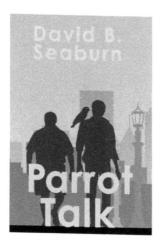

"...a story of abandonment, addiction, finding oneself—all mixed in with tear-jerking chapters next to laugh-out-loud chapters."

– Tiff & Rich

CPSIA information can be obtained
at www.ICGtesting.com
Printed in the USA
BVHW082002301020
592168BV00002B/9